Just a
Little Broken

A FAUSTIAN NOVEL

Le' Vian Dae

PAGE PUBLISHING, INC.
New York, NY

First originally published by Page Publishing, Inc. 2018

ISBN 978-1-64214-796-4 (Paperback)
ISBN 978-1-64544-325-4 (Hardcover)
ISBN 978-1-64214-795-7 (Digital)

Printed in the United States of America

CHAPTER ONE

"I Love You, Buttercup"

M orrigan Bloodchild walked up the cobblestoned stairs to the hospital in a snail's time. Her bootheels hitting the stone with every step a click, clack, click, clack! The noise further feeding into her delusions of hospitals. She couldn't stand them; with every inch of her body she couldn't stand them. The last thing she ever wanted in her life was to die in a hospital.

She opened the hospital doors and they felt heavy and burdened. As soon as she stepped inside, an unbearable stench hit her nose, till the point it caused her to cough and gag all at the same time. It smelled of urine, feces, straight bleach, and some other aimless supply what all she could figure it to be some type of nonbrand cleaning product that did *not* do the job. That smell alone made her want to flee that place and never to return, but there was someone more important waiting for her in one of those rooms.

She couldn't let any silly superstitious feeling or disgusting smell run her away from her promise. She poked her head outside to grab a quick breath of fresh air before continuing inside. As she went in she looked to her left and saw people sitting in the waiting room, some crying and some just sitting there with blank expressions on their faces. All with just these pale, blank emotionless faces sitting and waiting. Morrigan feared she, too, will soon become one of those nameless faces.

"Excuse me?" Morrigan spoke to the hospital attendant.

"Yes, ma'am, what can I help you with?" asked the attendant with a smile toward Morrigan. Her eyes spoke to her as to say, "Please, say nothing about the smell."

Morrigan's bottom jaw dropped suddenly as if in shock when she caught on to the lady's message, but quickly it closed as if not to let anything unwanted in.

"Oh, I'm sorry! But could you tell me which room Maye Bloodchild is in?" Morrigan responded, startled.

Morrigan managed to catch a quick look at the attendant's name tag and it read "Janice"; she couldn't really understand why it stuck in her mind. But she held a strange feeling she would see that name again, but in a way more wicked.

Janice went to her computer to find Morrigan's request.

"Here she is!" she looked up. Janice continued "She's in room 321."

"Thank you!" replied Morrigan as she walked away from the main lobby to the elevators.

She hit the elevator button going up; while standing there, so many things were going through her mind that she in no way was prepared to handle.

Ding rang the elevator bell, arriving. She welcomed the sound, because it interrupted her unhappy thoughts.

Morrigan rode it to the third floor and walked to room 321.

The smell changed drastically on this floor for the better.

Morrigan was grateful, because it helped her mood in a way that she needed to show she was unafraid even though she wasn't. When she got to the door her heart sank; she turned the doorknob and saw her mother, her aunt, and her grandmother. She saw her grandmother lying in the hospital bed, looking sad and terribly weary with her tired bones. She had no idea she was so sick. It was sickle cell anemia, and they caught it at the last minute.

Mrs. Maye Bloodchild was known for her pride, and it was long renowned that if she was sick, tired, or even slightly lacking the power to perform a task no one would know, she would keep that secret to herself unless she had no other choice otherwise.

"Where were you?" asked her aunt Stephanie sternly.

Before she could continue, Morrigan's mother, Raven, stepped forward in her daughter's defense.

"You know exactly what the hell she was doing, Stephanie! Don't play dumb, now I know you can act dumb, but you're not really that stupid!" Raven had a short temper and the mouth of a sailor when she needed it; she would simply put her self-respect on the shelf if it was just for the moment. But she sincerely respected her mother, so this was just mild compared to any other time. Morrigan couldn't take it anymore.

"Mom, you don't have to defend me in this nor do you have to." Maye could feel something was about to get started. Stephanie always had to have the stage, she thought.

"*Stop it!*" Maye screamed with as much strength she could stomach. Maye once had a voice that was strong and expressive, but now it was lowered and tamed in range.

"Shut the hell up, Stephanie!" Maye yelled to her daughter.

"Matter of fact, I want you out of this room," demanded Maye angrily.

"But!" Stephanie protested.

Before Maye could say anything else, Morrigan did for her.

"Just *get out!*" Morrigan hardly ever said anything to Stephanie, let alone in such a harsh tone, but today wasn't a good day and she was tired of her disrespect.

"Get out! You can see she's not feeling well and she's tired and you're starting shit! Okay? So just leave!" Morrigan didn't mean to come out with that word, at least not in front of her grandmother. Her face for a moment went into shame, but it subsided. Raven just looked at her sister and laughed; she felt sorry for her, but wouldn't pity her.

Stephanie looked at Maye with a questionable look on her face as to say, "Do you really want me to leave?" After Maye nodded yes, Stephanie walked out in a huff, she was mad that she was embarrassed, but that was all; she didn't really want to be there anyway.

Raven held her daughter for a moment, and then Morrigan knelt on Maye's side.

"Grandma, I'm sorry I wasn't here earlier." Morrigan pleaded she would have been there every day if she could, but she had to work to get something coming in.

"Oh, Buttercup." She stopped her. Buttercup was her little pet name for Morrigan; she called no other child by that name.

"You were working just like you were supposed to do, plus you never forgot me. You always stayed in touch. So I'm telling you now you did nothing wrong and don't let anyone tell you otherwise. Plus, you have made me so proud and I know this is just a taste of what you're going to accomplish."

"Thank you, Grandma," Morrigan responded in tears.

"Now I'm going to tell you something I don't want to, baby, but I must." When Maye said that, the air became tired and cold and everyone in the room picked up on it. Morrigan didn't want to hear what came next; she knew what it was, but couldn't stand to hear the words.

"No!" Morrigan interrupted. "Grandma, don't talk like that . . . please." But she was only grasping for straws.

"I'm tired baby," Maye continued. "I'm tired and I want to go home and be with my father," she said softly as she looked at her granddaughter. Raven sat down; she was a very strong woman and proud, but this was just too much for her to bear.

Morrigan cried and pleaded, "Grandma, Granny, please don't leave me. We need you . . . I need you . . . Just hold on a little longer." Morrigan felt guilty for saying those words, because she knew it was wrong and selfish.

"No, you don't, Buttercup. You're going to be just fine," Maye said reassuringly. "And I'll always be with you. I love you, Buttercup!"

"I love you too, Grandma." After saying those words Morrigan cried all the harder, because she knew that will be the last time she would ever hear those words from her.

"And I love you too, Raven, you did a very good job with this woman right here," she said as she faced Raven in a soft smile.

"Thank you, Granny!" said Raven, half choked in sobs. She went to her daughter and just held on to her as though she would lose her in that minute. Morrigan couldn't believe this was happening; to a degree she still had this invisible invulnerability cloak wrapped in her mind, as though her whole family will stay safe, always safe, and protected.

"Is everything taken care of, Raven?" asked Maye in a soft whisper of a voice.

"Yes, yes, everything," she answered as quickly as possible. She too knelt down beside her to whisper in her ear.

"And I'll take care of Buttercup."

After she heard that sentence, that promise and what it meant, she let go of all the pain, of all the sadness she once felt in that very moment. And then she passed away.

"Grandma, Grandma! No!" Morrigan cried and cried on her grandmother's motionless body. And screamed those words with such a striking intensity that they would never leave her mind, and that event would change her forever. She almost thought this was the end of her life; however, this was only the beginning for Morrigan, only the beginning of the fight for her life.

CHAPTER TWO

Summons

T he funeral came and went, and Morrigan went on aimlessly in limbo, trying to come to grips that she just went to her grandmother's funeral last week. While everything that she once held in firm belief started to shatter. She questioned everything now, and believed in nothing. Her blank expressions showed nothing, but the inner depression she felt in her soul. And that she too had become one of those blank, pale, emotionless faces sitting in the hospital waiting room, the very thing she feared.

All she truly had left was her mom, her best friends, and her music, not to mention her life, but she felt that those too were waning.

"Nothing lasts forever," thought Morrigan to herself.

Morrigan sat on the corner of Twenty-third Street contemplating whether she should go in the house now or later. It was now 2:00 p.m., and she just got out of class with about four hours to spend until her gig at the Shack of Horrors later.

"I wonder if Max feels like hanging out before showtime?" she thought to herself again.

Max is one of her closest friends. Hell, he's her best friend and the drummer in her band Mystic, and the one person besides her mom she could count on to give her good advice (even if she didn't want to hear it). Sitting on that stone was getting to her, because her ass was starting to hurt.

"Shit!" she rose when a spine-tingling pain went up her backside. She thought for a second or two on whether she should go home now. She knew she had to go home sooner or later to pick up her equipment for her show later, but she couldn't face what might be waiting on the door for her when she returned.

"Summons."

"I'm twenty-four years old, and I already have to worry about being evicted on my own." Just the thought disgusted her. She went into her purse to grab her cell phone for she could call Max, but before she could dial a number her phone rang.

"Damn!" she said. It was her mother, but she had no intention on talking to her, at least not now, so she waited for the ring to end. She decided to walk down to Twenty-fifth Street southeast where her apartment was to see what awaited her. She was walking so quickly, it was as if she was sprinting, but it was all her nerves; she dreaded to see what was there.

"Morrigan! Hey! Morrigan!" screamed Derek from across the street. Morrigan turned back as if in a state of shock.

"Now who the hell is that?" she said to herself. "Oh, hey, Derek!" she screamed back when she recognized him.

"I need a favor, please?" he screamed. Morrigan didn't really have time to chitchat; plus she had an idea what it is he wanted.

"Um . . . I'm sort of busy right now. I'll talk to you when I get back," she said as nicely as possible.

"Okay." He could tell she was on her way somewhere, because now she was practically running down the street, so he let her go. She rushed through the apartment building door, almost tripping on the stairs going up. She just wanted to get this over with as soon as possible. In a moment like this she would have begged God to "please bless it not to be a summons on the door," but she figured He wasn't listening. Morrigan was running with eyes half shut then quickly opened them.

"Whew . . . Oh! Thank you! Thank you." She didn't quite know who she was thanking, but she couldn't stop. She hasn't paid the rent in three months, not because she didn't want to, but because she couldn't. She didn't have the funds to pay, and she was trying her hardest to get it all up. She lost her job about a year ago, and that was taking care of the bulk of her bills. She knows it takes money to make money in the music business, so she didn't really count on instant gratification, but now would have been a really good time; luckily, she did have some money saved up, but that wasn't enough to save her place and keep her with money in the bank.

She almost forgot she was going to call Max, until he called her. Her phone rang loud in the small upstairs hallway, and the volume was only on three.

"Hey, Max! What's up?" she blurted out.

"Hey, Cookie M! Nothing much, just chilling. Ready for tonight?" he asked.

"As ready as I'll ever be!" Morrigan responded and that was the truth. This gig paid over one thousand bucks, and it was only split between two people, her and Max. So she had a bigger chance at paying off the overdue rent, well, at least part of it.

"Yeah, this is going to be a killer!" said Max over the phone while he was driving.

"Move the fuck out of my way, man! Shit, drive!" Max said to another driver taking his sweet time to move out of the lane. He didn't deal well with bad drivers, plus he had a short temper in the car. Morrigan overheard.

"Are you driving?" she asked flatly, but it was a question she already knew the answer to.

"Um . . . no?" said Max jokingly.

"Are you at least wearing your seat belt?" she asked to no reply. He knew Morrigan hated him driving without a seat belt and talking on his cell at the same time. Usually he kept it from her, but this time he slipped.

"Come on, dude! What the fuck did I tell you about that?" she said angrily.

"I'm sorry, Cookie M. But I was sort of in a rush." Cookie M was his pet name for her; he thought it added the right amount of sweetness to her rough exterior. Nothing looks-wise, he just thought she could be a little mean (plus she loved cookies!).

"You know what, dude? When you almost get yourself killed, don't blame me." She was just joking with him, but she had no idea how her words would haunt her later.

"Aww . . . Cookie M, that's not cool. Ha-ha," he laughed. "But yeah, this gig tonight is going to be awesome," he continued. "To think this could turn into a regular thing if all goes well tonight. This plus the 69 Clam, we could be set!" Max was excited not only for himself, but mainly for Morrigan. He knew the band, her music was her life, and that she deserved the shot, but he had no idea his words just a minute ago put a lump in her chest; now she was extremely nervous. She felt everything she had even more riding on this show being excellent.

"Uh, yeah . . . Yeah, that sounds great," she said vacantly.

"So? You want to get out of here for a couple of hours?" Max asked, trying to be upbeat. It was also part of his way to get her to open up. He knew she wasn't as cool as she said she was at her grandmother's funeral. He knew they were close and that she missed her very much. That was his best bet—distracting her.

"Yes! Of course! Let's get out of here!" Morrigan was almost out of breath. "Meet me on the corner of Twenty-third Street," she told him.

"Why?" he asked curiously. "Why can't I just meet you at your place?"

Morrigan was stumped, she didn't really have a reason, but then again maybe she did; she just didn't want to give it.

"Well, because . . . I mean, I'm leaving out now, so you might as well meet me there while I'm out." She quickly saved herself.

"Oh, well. Okay!" said Max a little off the way.

"I'll be there in ten!"

"Great! See ya there!" Morrigan responded. She started her way down the hall, then down the stairs. She was almost out of the building until something caught her eye out of the building window. She saw an elderly white man who looked to be in his early to middle seventies. And he was looking right at her, straight in her eyes through the window as if peering at her. It sent a chill up her spine when he smiled at her; it was slow and lingering almost, to scare her. With just the simplest thing, his cold, silver eyes that winked and teeth so gangly and black, it caused Morrigan to shudder.

She bowed her head for a second, but by the time she looked back up to see if he was still there, it was too late; he was gone.

She couldn't believe it; she ran out the door with pepper spray in hand just in case he was still there to try something. She busted out the door alert for him, waiting, with eyes darting back and forth, but it was nothing. He was nowhere in sight. All she could smell was mildew and sulfur. It was as strong as the rays of the sun or that stench in the hospital. But that was all she was left with . . . that and the strangest feeling that she had seen him before and will see him again . . . but where?

CHAPTER THREE

"Maybe It Was My Imagination?"

M ax didn't get a word from her. At least nothing of substance that would give him a slight idea as to how she was really feeling. She was so distant now; it left his thoughts conflicted as to how to help her, and he wanted to so much. "Maybe next time," he thought.

In the meantime, he dropped her off at the apartment's front stoop.

"I'll be back in thirty minutes. Think that'll give you enough time to get ready, because you can be so damn slow! Ha-ha." He tried to joke.

His joke went on deaf ears. "I think so, I just have to grab my gear, change clothes, and then I'm good," Morrigan spoke.

"Good! I'll be back, move, rock and roller!" Max yelled as he drove away.

She smiled as she watched him drive off. But as soon as she saw the front door window she got anxious; again her eyes darted back and forth looking for the old man, but hoping not to see him. When she didn't she took a relieved sigh, and started inside the building.

She dared not tell Max what she saw or thought she saw. "Maybe it was my imagination?" Morrigan tried to reassure herself.

She practically sprinted up the stairs to the second floor to her apartment. She was happy suddenly, cheerfully unlocking her door to get her guitar.

She usually did get that way before a show. She loved performing; communicating with the audience got her mind off things. For her, much like with many musicians, being on stage made everything right with the world, even when it wasn't.

Several hours had passed since Max picked her back up with her gear. They drove around to pick up the other two band members before heading to the Shack of Horrors for their first of hopefully a series of shows. Mystic (the band) basically consisted of Morrigan and Max, and whoever else Morrigan hired to take on another instrument during a live performance.

This time around it just happened to be Tim and Jasmine, two other struggling musicians Morrigan came upon a few years ago during the club circuit. Tim took masterful care of the bass, and Jasmine added her triple ten cents on rhythm guitar while accompanying Max's thunderous drum sounds, and Morrigan's cryptic song lyrics, siren calls, and wicked lead guitar. They were great musicians, and Morrigan felt lucky to have found them. Now the lineup was consistent with no ever-changing members, at least not now.

They arrived at the club in enough time to capture the performances of a few other acts, before Mystic was to perform. The bands were good too, but she wasn't worried. She was confident in herself and her band, and started looking around the club. She was looking at all the smiling faces and ecstatic expressions, overdosing on the hypnotic sounds that were surrounding them. It made her extremely excited too, made her forget if just for a moment the death of her grandmother last week, the summons that she felt was coming, and even that creepy ass elderly man that gave her goose bumps. All she could think about now was kicking ass onstage, and then right then the club owner announced in a voice like a mad scientist pumped up on his own potion, "My monstrous pets . . . Point your eyes up here and your tongue on pause as I introduce some newcomers to our deadly nest . . . *Mystic!*"

♪♫ The beast is the burden that makes your soul stray.
'Cause the beast is coldhearted, murdering babies.
I've let you, I've let you, I've let you down . . .
Don't cry as it burns you.
♫♪♫♪♫ *Rock guitar solo* ♪♫♪♫♪

Morrigan loved to work the crowd. It was like her drug; she got high on that, on all of it.

It was so irresistible.

With her caramel-brown skin, dark brown eyes, full face, and pouty lips, she was a looker, not that she dwelled on it. Of course, she was aware; she just had better issues to focus on than her good looks.

Her act was full of high-heel swaggering, mean riffs, tough looks, and quick licks.

She was always hard rocking; she made that a rule in her music, in her life. Don't let the platforms fool you; I'll kick your ass!

Her obsession with being a rock-and-roll, guitar-wielding vixen was different for a black girl born and raised in the ghetto of DC.

She always loved music, but rock and roll was her calling, and in the process sometimes it did make her feel like a bit of a misfit. Always misunderstood by others, but she used it to her advantage in her songwriting.

It didn't matter to her if she belonged; she had people to love her, but sometimes she just wanted to do her without being trampled for it. However, she did have a few kindred spirits, one being her best bud, Max. So in the end, it sort of balanced out.

It felt great to Morrigan to receive an amazing reaction from a different, larger venue.

Since majority of the time they performed at the 69 Clam, it was a great change of environment.

The audience was still in heat and cheering from her set, and that did do a lot to boost her confidence. Yes, even rock stars can get the blues . . . well, especially aspiring rock stars. She strutted off stage and Max followed in pursuit; he played the crazy rock drummer to par, but in reality, he was more grounded. They helped to keep each other grounded.

"Here's your pay for a job well done! Great show, you guys!" said the club owner as he handed Morrigan the cash.

"We'll talk tomorrow about the other shows right, Morrigan?" he continued.

"Yes, I'll be here. 11:00 a.m.," Morrigan responded, not trying to give away the desperation in her voice.

"Okay, great! You all enjoy yourselves," he said before he left them to a black glass-ridden bar table.

"Six for you," said Morrigan as she placed the money on the table at Max. "Thank you, ma'am"

"And six for me. You two been got yours, so don't look for anything else! Ha-ha," she jokingly said to Jasmine and Tim. She would usually always try to pay them in advance.

They all sat there for over several minutes, laughing, drinking, and cheering themselves on. The ambiance inside this place was great, and it felt so natural. They never wanted to let it go, especially Morrigan. She was enjoying herself, and Max noticed this; it made him happy until she just had to let her mind get the best of her.

She did that a lot lately, overthinking things or looking for the flaw in an obvious too-good-to-be-true experience. She focused on it so much, it got her back to thinking about that sinister old man she saw earlier. She couldn't quite put her finger on it, but she felt she had seen him before, with his dead silver eyes and gangly smile. But before, he looked more refined, even younger, at least is what she told herself. By now her series of smiles and happiness was replaced by troubled looks of confusion.

Max picked up on that, but before he could say anything, Tim asked, breaking the thought at the now small rounded table, "What are you planning on doing after this, Morrigan?"

"Oh, umm . . . just probably go home and chill . . . You know how it is," she responded. "I should study for finals, but I don't really feel like being bothered with it now."

"Yeah, I understand," said Tim. "Ah, she didn't want to do them anyway," interrupted Max.

His mind was distracted by his initial thoughts on Cookie M.

Before he could say anything else, out of the corner of his eye he saw a familiar face.

"Don't look now, Cookie M, but I think someone's looking for you." He egged her on.

Max tilted his head in the direction of three o'clock and gave a sly laugh.

"What?" She squinted her eyes in the direction he signaled and saw her ex-boyfriend Jack who was looking straight at her.

"Are you two talking again now?" asked Max curiously. He knew they broke up, but not if she informed him where they were playing tonight.

"Uh . . . nope, we haven't spoken since the breakup! Hasn't been a reason really," she yelled slightly over the loud music.

"Hmm . . ." He knew it would be a minute until they started back up. They loved doing that makeup-to-breakup shit, and not speak to each other in between.

Max thought it was stupid, but Cookie M never complained to him besides the regular relationship crap (as he did her), nor did Jack act like a jealous idiot, who felt like Morrigan shouldn't be with anyone else but him so he just stayed out of it. She made an awkward smile to Max before saying, "He's coming over here," with clenched teeth.

"He probably wants to take you to his hotel room and spank you . . . *Get it in*! Cookie M, ha-ha," said Max like the fool that he is sometimes. Tim and Jasmine stopped conversing instantly. All four of them looked at one another for a second before bursting out into smirks and silly guffaws like schoolkids who heard a goofy word. How times change.

Technically, Max wasn't that off. Morrigan was strange to say the least, so easily it would have been mutual spanking between the two later with Jack in handcuffs and Morrigan using the whip on him. She got off on that too.

Jack walked over to the table, confident in his dark blue jeans and worn-in leather jacket. Smiled at the band. It lasted a few seconds; he had a great smile. One of the things that attracted Morrigan to him were those fucking pearly whites!

He said, "Hi, Max, Jasmine, and Tim, how you guys doing?" They spoke in return.

"Hey Morrigan . . ." That one lingered, as he smiled showing those teeth, which seemed to shine all the brighter.

"How are you doing?" he asked.

"Hello to you too, Jack, I'm good, thanks for asking," she said as she looked him up and down, without giving too much away. An awkward silence followed before Jack interrupted by asking, "Can I speak to you in private, Morrigan?" He loved saying her first name completely, no changes, no shortcuts, 'cause he thought it was perfect the way it was.

"Well, it's a club, so how private can we get?" she asked sarcastically.

"How about we go outside then?" He put his hand out for her to grab, to which she does with no hesitation.

"Must be serious, " she mouthed to the band, which in return caused Max to mouth back, "'Cause you won't be back" before Jack whisked her out of the club. Max just shook his head and laughed; he knew his best friend. He knew she wouldn't have to ride back with him that night.

Jack and Morrigan stood outside of the club for a few minutes in silence, just looking at each other with eyes peeled as if to pick up the body language of each other. She stared at him in the soft dimmed lights outside in the cool darkness; it must've been midnight now.

He looked so handsome, she thought. He had a slender face, with brown hair that sat on his shoulders, and steel-blue crystal eyes that she sort of envied and went crazy for all at the same time. Jack was much older than Morrigan, white, and six feet one. He was divorced once with no kids, and in her eyes tall, dark, and mysterious.

Though she knew the truth, they shared a similar background, which is how they connected. Both were raised by single parents; both had it hard financially growing up living in crappy neighborhoods and wanted more.

He accomplished more, being the successful businessman that didn't lose sight of the simple things in life plus he loved rock and roll; while on the other hand she was still trying to make a name for herself. However, he respected her for this; she was a tough chick and he loved it, but in the process, they gave each other hell.

It wasn't a perfect relationship; *turbulent* is one of many good words to describe it, since they weren't easy people to love sometimes even to each other, but they made the most of it. Short story version, when they first met she wasn't the slightest bit impressed with him; she was tired of waiting and he was a bit rude, but she told him off and he couldn't get her out of his mind. Then through his connections he found out where Mystic was playing again to find her and pulled out all the stops (use your imagination on this one), and after a month of that it was a done deal.

Everybody thought it was weird for them to be together, especially her mom, some of his friends, and even Max. But in the long run they didn't care; it didn't matter to them, because despite their faults it was love there, but it was to be tested later way past normal boundaries.

"I know it's been awhile since we last spoke, and you might not believe this, but I wanted to know how you were holding up." Of course, he was referring to her grandmother's death. And even though she didn't tell him when the funeral took place or the fact that she even died, he made sure to pay his respects and support her. He heard through the grapevine.

"Oh, I'm so sorry for not telling you myself. I wasn't trying to be cruel. I just, I just wasn't really here through it all, and I honestly thank you, Jack, for coming, because you didn't have to. It wasn't like you really knew her."

"On the contrary, Morrigan, I did have to come. I couldn't have stayed away without being there with you." He meant every word, and continued, "I know we only met once, but I know she loved you dearly and was a very strong woman. She bluntly questioned my intentions with you, and I have total respect to her for that."

Morrigan was trying to hold back her tears, but it seemed like the harder she tried, the more they fell down her face.

"Oh, come on, sweetie, don't go crying on me now," he said as he took a cloth out of his jacket pocket to dry her tears. It wasn't working that much; by now she could practically wash her face with the liquid streaming from her eyes. She looked at him and smiled with bloodshot eyes.

"It's okay, sweetie, you'll get through it . . . You have me to help you, along with Max and, of course, your mom. You're not alone in this," he said, trying to reassure her.

"I know, I know." She sighed. "It's just so many things . . ." She raised her head back for a moment to look at the sky in all its glory with the stars shining bright. As corny as it was, she thought to herself how glorious it would be to be among those stars.

"I just don't understand how God can—"

"Don't say that!" Jack interrupted her.

"I can't try and pretend like I know how it all works out, but your grandmother believed and she wouldn't want you being mad and talking down like that. So *stop* it!" he continued, speaking in his rough tone, convincing and honest as best as he could try and get through to her.

She hated hearing that it made her so mad, she wanted to slap him. She snatched away from his grip, but she knew he was telling the truth. Maye was a firm believer, and Morrigan couldn't help now but feel like her grandmother would be disappointed in her.

However, she bounced back quickly, at least that's the ruse she tried to put up to Jack. She took a peek at him through her long dark brown hair that went past her shoulders. Smiled big, then walked seductively toward him like the vixen she was and said, "So how about it, baby? Forget about all the serious, boring talk and show me a good time. "

He saw right through it, but couldn't resist her tempting grace. Plus, he knew she was hurting and didn't want to talk about it now. So he looked at her, reading her face for a moment, then moved the hair that covered her right eye as if to get a better look at her in the moonlight.

She looked like the peekaboo girl Veronica Lake in just that minute past.

"Are you just flirting with me so I can shut up?" he asked jokingly.

"*Hah*!" She burst into laughter. "I think I'll have to kiss you to accomplish that."

He smiled then said, "Not if I kissed you first," before leaning in.

He kissed her with more fire than any of the young guys she might have shared a puppy love–inspired infatuation with. He kissed her like a true man, passionately, strong, but still sweet and gently. A few people traveling in and out of the club stopped for a few minutes to admire them. But they didn't notice; instead they kissed intensely in each other's embrace for several more minutes. They breathed each other before they let go.

Jack whispered into Morrigan's ear softly, "Let's get out of here . . . Your set's finished right?"

Just what she wanted to hear; she didn't want to go home.

"Yeah, yeah, I'm done . . . Let me just text Max I'm leaving." She whipped out her phone and sent the text to Max quickly. Who received it shortly after, looked at his phone, and smirked first before texting her, "Shit, you're still here!?! Thought you would've been gone . . . ☺ Lemme know in the morning how it went." After she received that, they were long gone into the night.

CHAPTER FOUR

It Ain't Like That

"Whips, chains, and vodka . . . and chocolate, don't forget chocolate, my sex away from you," Morrigan remarked to Jack jokingly, playfully slapping him. That's how a night began for them or ended.

"Chocolate is good, but why am I usually the one getting whipped in these situations. Doesn't seem very romantic darling," he responded with her unchaining him from the bedpost.

"Not necessarily, baby . . . We're an odd love, I suppose." He grabbed her quickly throwing her on the bed; laughing, she lay underneath him, arms spread, waiting to feel his presence inside her. He held back. "I love you, Morrigan," he told her softly, touching her lips with his thumb.

"Perhaps men are the ultimate teases," she remarked, not acknowledging his sentiment. He smirked then nuzzled her stomach before proceeding to bite and suck the skin, peering in her eyes while he played. She moaned, "Take off your boots."

"I'll obey." He whipped off her jeans to reveal the gray and blue lace crotchless panties she wore.

"Now wrap your legs around me," he told her; now she obeyed.

Last night was their abundant high, the thrill most people subconsciously strive for, but usually never obtain.

"Want me to drop you off at Max's?" spoke Jack, pulling his jeans back up his legs. The bed was a mess, sheets crumpled. He stared at her body as she redressed; the only thought that ran in his mind was exploring her curves again, but neither one of them had the time.

"Yeah, that's perfect! We have an appointment at the Shack of Horrors, and I can change clothes there," she replied as she buttoned her blouse.

"An appointment?" he asked.

"Yeah, I'm trying to expand the band again, it's basic stuff, you know, trying to perform and get gigs at different venues . . . Plus we still have personal ties to the 69 Clam which is good, keeps us afloat when times are rough," finished Morrigan.

"I'm familiar with the process, but that's really great! I truly hope you all get the deal, it would be a lot more exposure for you and the group," he said as he walked toward her.

"I can always help you know, that right?" he spoke as he kissed her neck slowly.

"Right," she replied flatly.

Morrigan wasn't really into that idea; receiving help always backfired at her. She just wanted to be able to depend on herself and not someone else.

"Can I see you again tonight?" he whispered in her ear with hopes high.

She turned from the mirror for a second and looked at him, trying to figure out whether his inquiry was candid; she could read him by now. She kissed him on the cheek and looked back into the mirror, brushing her hair, and simply said while biting her bottom lip, "Maybe."

"Who was she fooling?" he thought, for he knew that meant yes.

"Whenever you're finished with your business you can call me, if I don't call you first, that is," spoke Jack with a dashing smile. He dropped her off in front of Max's apartment complex. "And the number is still the same."

"Sure, I'll call you. Maybe," she said.

"All right, love you, sweets, be safe." He kissed her on the forehead before getting back into his car, waved her goodbye, then drove off.

"Such simple things," she thought to herself as she watched him drive away.

She arrived at Max's door slightly flushed, but it wasn't the first time. She knocked on his door with two shaves and a haircut. A minute later Max opened the door, cocky with arms stretched upward to the doorframe.

"Hey, buddy!" she said cheerfully, not wanting to let on to anything else, like she had to. "I need to change clothes," she told him before he could say anything sarcastic. When she brushed past him, she laid her purse down on his glass table and looked around his place intensively. He had a very nice home, different for the typical bachelor, because it actually had work put into it. However, some of that was courtesy of Morrigan's advice, of course.

She was looking for a huge black leather bag, containing everything from clothes, personals, and handcuffs, whatever she needed. She called it her stash to make it sound even remotely interesting, whether it was or not. She didn't see it out, and it must have finally dawned on him what she was looking for, because he then said, "Your stash is in the back," sarcastically.

"Could've said that shit before," she blurted while heading to his back closet.

"Shut up! It's not like you don't know where to look," he responded in a snarky tone.

"Whatever," she mumbled.

Even though he was pretty sure on what happened, he still loved questioning her about her and Jack's somewhat drawn-out love affair.

He started with an inconspicuous, "So . . .," or so he thought.

"You're a nosy little fuck, aren't you?" Morrigan said laughing, as she went to change clothes, then flopped on his couch to change boots. "Hotel showers are the best! Especially the ones with those high speeds, detachable showerheads, nice!" She was slightly rubbing it in.

"You know something, sis, sometimes you're a bitch."

"Ouch! But thank you, however flattery will get you nowhere!" she said smoothly.

"No, come on, Morrigan! It's the least you could do. Especially, since I'm not getting laid . . . True, it's not the most important thing, but I'm lonely," he finished jokingly in a silent whisper.

"Awe, poor baby, I'm sorry for being inconsiderate, I forgot you're recently new to the single life. And you haven't gotten laid nor would any decent chick blow you so . . . I understand," she finished sarcastically.

Three words he used, three little words he used to describe his emotions of her in that single moment, "I . . . hate . . . you."

"Oh shit! Such hostility and from a man I call my brother from another mother no less." She laughed it off.

"Exactly!" he said excitingly. "So why would you make me sound so diseased and wretched, I can't be that bad!" and he cracked it off with a series of blasts, you could laugh.

"Ha-ha-hah, you're not, bro," she said seriously. "Oh crap!" She remembered suddenly of their appointment.

"We should be moving. Are you wearing that?" she said in a somewhat condescending tone.

"What, you got something against my plaid yellow shirt and black jeans?" he said as he turned around, showing her his outfit, then fake grabbing his nipples and pretending to push up invisible breasts. "I'm sexy and I know it!"

"You're disgusting!" she smirked then threw him his leather jacket. "Let's get out of here and make this meeting. Hate to lose out because we were late," she said as she walked toward his front door, but before she could open it, Max called her, "Hey, Morrigan, here."

"What?" she turned around. He threw her his car keys.

"Don't want to drive?" she questioned as she caught them.

"Nope, thought you could while entertaining me with inappropriate stories of your love life," he finished rather flatly, but honestly.

"Tsk, jackass," as she gave him the old "rolls the eyes" look.

"And that's why you love me," then they rolled out the door.

"So is Blue Thunder still in the shop?" he asked her as she opened his car door. "Yeah, sadly, I want to get him out next week, but don't look like that'll happen with other bills and all."

"I'm sorry to hear that, sis, but if you want I can always get him out for you or at least help," he spoke candidly.

"Maybe," she said without putting much into it.

"I mean it, you know that, plus you wouldn't have to pay me back, you've done the same for me."

"That's okay, Max. Thank you. I appreciate the gesture, I really do, but I'll think of something. Plus, you know me," she finished stonily.

"Don't I though?" he said under his breath, before hopping in the passenger seat. Too much pride, he thought, got even worse after her grandmother died.

"It'll get better for the both of us with these two gigs, plus before we make it big, rock star–wise, I'm sure a good job will come through for you and hopefully a better one for me," he said, trying to cheer her up.

"Least someone is sure of that," she interrupted plainly. He sighed. "I know it might not seem like it, but things will get better, sis, you know that," he insisted as he brushed her hair back.

"Yea . . .," she responded half-heartedly. "Well, let's go."

Max was really worried about Morrigan, definitely more than usual. They shared a true bond, but even they weren't aware at how deep it really was.

He opened the dashboard looking for his smokes. "I thought you stopped smoking?" she asked after she saw him light one.

"Have you stopped drinking?" he asked. She looked away and kept her mouth shut.

"Ha-hah, thought so." Morrigan rolled her eyes.

"It's only occasionally. Loosen up! Let's listen to some tracks to shake us up!" He turned on the car radio. Alice in Chains's "It Ain't Like That" started.

"Hey! It's Alice in Chains and one of your favorite songs too!" He nudged her to get her to smile, while starting to drum the dashboard to the beat of the song.

It worked; she did start smiling, and they started singing the lyrics together in harmony. She felt great in that moment; they both did.

But right just then, before they went into the second verse, the stranger appeared in front of them walking across the street in the middle of traffic! Morrigan couldn't believe it; they locked eyes, his flashing gold to silver. He simply stared at her again, while smiling. His features weren't distorted this time, but he did look older, but mainly more tired, and paler in face. Her eyes followed him until he went out of her view around the corner of this random building. But she was still stuck on him, while having her foot on the gas; she sped up unintentionally.

"*Fuck!* Morrigan, snap out of it! Look at the road, *Morrigan!*" Max yelled at her freakishly as he placed his hand on her shoulder harshly. She jolted and rushed her foot on the brake in an instant. The car came to a burning screech, and with that she completely came to. She and Max looked outside and noticed she was two inches from hitting a mother and her baby.

"Oh my god . . .," Morrigan said softly. They didn't even try to regain composure before they both rushed out of the car to check on the mother and child.

"I'm so sorry!" Morrigan screamed. The mother had left her stroller in the middle of the crosswalk where the car was blatantly partially in the way of. She was still running to the sidewalk, while Morrigan chased after her and tried to grab her. Max went to get the stroller. Morrigan finally caught up to the mother, but she snatched away from her.

"Get the fuck away from us! Are you fucking high or something? You could have killed us, you crazy bitch, don't you realize that?" screamed the mother furiously.

"I know, I know, I'm so sorry . . . I didn't mean to, but I can't even explain it." Which she couldn't, hell, she couldn't even understand it.

"I wasn't paying attention, but I'm not high, I just . . . I don't know . . . I . . . Are you two hurt? Are you okay, I mean, physically?

Can I take you two to the hospital?" Morrigan pleaded, concerned. By this time Max got back with the lady's stroller.

"I'm so sorry, miss, are you both okay? Here's your stroller, uh . . . Do you need help?"

She took the stroller back unsteadily from him and looked at Morrigan, looked into her eyes, seemingly to read her emotions. She could unworldly tell Morrigan was genuine. "I'm okay, I think we're both okay, just a little shaken," she said before caressing her baby's face. "She didn't cry this whole time," the mother thought; she just couldn't understand it.

"Are you sure?" Morrigan insisted. "We could take you to the hospital for they can check you both out."

"Yeah," finished Max.

She believed it was an accident and became more sympathetic toward Morrigan than she would have imagined normally. She said nervously, "No, that's all right . . . No offense, but I don't think I want to ride in the same car with you." She tried to say with a smile, "Matter of fact, that's our bus coming now," and ran to the bus stop in time to catch it.

Morrigan and Max both stood there on the sidewalk and watched them get on the bus, sort of in shock. Car horns were honking and blazing incessantly as they ran back to the car. Max was dumbfounded; he just stared at Morrigan when they got in the car.

"What the fuck is going on with you?" he asked, desperately trying to keep from exploding.

"You wouldn't believe me, if I told you." She turned her head in the direction she had last seen the old man. "The fuck is going on?" she thought to herself.

However, she saw nothing but a building and an empty corner, and then quickly turned her head away, when she noticed Max following his eyes in the same direction. He looked at her in confusion; he didn't know what to think now. Was it still about her grandmother's passing, or even financial troubles? He couldn't get it; he started to push the issue, but didn't say anything else to her, at least not then. They just drove silently, and continued to the Shack of Horrors.

CHAPTER FIVE

It Was Close

M ax couldn't let it go; he felt her keeping tight-lipped had gone on long enough and he wanted some answers. She almost killed someone, a mother and child, and it was because she randomly trailed off mentally. He took out a cigarette, nervously lighting it. He took a few puffs.

"Morrigan, I love you . . . You know this, I love you more than a best friend, I love you as my sister and I need you to be honest with me, no more lame-ass excuses. I mean it!" he said sternly.

"What the hell is going on, sis? Is this all about Grandma passing? Or does it run deeper than this? Tell me."

"I can't really explain it, but . . ." She felt really obligated to tell him something, at least try to tell him the truth, but before she could continue to try and explain the situation, Kirk, the club owner, got their attention. "Hey, you two! Sorry for keeping you waiting, anyway if you two will come with me in the back we can get to business."

They all shook their heads in agreement and went toward his office.

The meeting went on for less than an hour; they went over the particulars, basics about performance times, schedule, pay, etc. Max and Morrigan didn't go into great detail about their obligations at the 69 Clam, and Kirk didn't ask.

They waited until they were out of sight and club view before speaking to each other. It wasn't until they reached the car that they broke into triumph.

"Yes! See I told you, sis, just got to be hopeful and have faith. Then it'll all work out!" He tried to encourage her. "Ha-ha, yeah I suppose," she responded happily, but with a sense of repetition. She heard Max, thanking God while she was contemplating whether she should call the storage facility to cancel her reservation. She felt it was a good thought, considering she still had a possible loop of time to get most of her rent paid. He observed her, trying to figure out whether she was okay to drive. "Want me to take over the reins?" he asked. "Um . . .," she paused hesitantly. "Yea! I can do it."

"All right," he hopefully finished.

After she started maneuvering the car out of the parking lot, she told him without any despair in her voice, "Let's celebrate! Let's go out tonight!" then her pretty eyes gleamed toward him in order to persuade him. "Uh . . . I don't know . . .," he answered reluctantly initially.

"Fuck that! I'm just joking, let's do it, let's celebrate!" he practically screamed out the window. Originally apprehensive by his initial response, his later words confirmed her elation. She started, "I'll call Tim and Jasmine when we get to my place." "*No!*" Max blurted out in disagreement.

"Let's break it to them at rehearsal." Which was in a few hours, so she agreed. He happily brought his plan to a close. "First we'll play nonchalant, and then hit them with it. In the meantime, we can stop off and get something to eat." She didn't know it at the time, but he was going to use this as the precise time to crack open the safe, the safe being her mouth. He glanced over to her for a moment; she looked calmer at least. She trumped his thoughts of her unaware, "So what do you want to eat?" giving him the opportunity to before deciding. "How about McDonald's?" he said without thinking. "What? Are you serious?" she exclaimed.

"No, we have to do this right." Then she thought about their financial situation. "Well, at least a bit better . . . How about Subway or 5ive Guys? Then we can head to Starbucks before rehearsal."

"5ive Guys!" he blurted excitingly. "I want big fucking burgers so packed with meat, cheese, and ketchup that I need a bib," he concluded jokingly.

"Shut up! Ha-ha." She laughed and cranked up the radio, so they continued on their way.

They arrived at her place after stopping to get food to chill and, unbeknownst to her, talk.

"Let me check the mailbox," she told him while he went to wait for her at her door.

"College bills, fuck . . . Car insurance, light bill, ugh . . . . Cell bill, all right, no good news," she mumbled to herself. "It could be worse," she mumbled again.

"It will be," whispered a mysterious voice. "Who was that?" she yelled when she jerked her head back to see the direction in which the voice came. But she saw no one, the building was always pretty vacant, but still she heard that voice, she thought. The voice was low, but deliberate and seemed to have surrounded her in a moment. However, she wasn't nervous; instead she shook it off readily and started upstairs. "What in the hell took you so long?" asked Max impatiently, still waiting. He was one year older than her, foolish and a bit goofy, but was an honest, loving jack-in-the-box. With his short black tousled hair, deep green eyes, and bright big smile, he could have easily fit the role of attractive front man or exotic lead guitarist, but when he laughed he could easily be described as the mad hatter, plus being in the front lines wasn't his style. Now he was a great guitarist, but he loved the drums and supporting Morrigan, but that also came with keeping her in order whenever she seemed in wrecking ball mode. She couldn't have asked for more in a best bud. "You have a spare key. Why didn't you just open the damn door? Idiot!" she questioned snarkily. "Because I didn't bring it, wench!" he snapped back promptly.

Those snappy, often biting comebacks were how they showed their love normally, but they hardly ever meant serious offense to each other unless it was something terrible. Luckily, it hardly ever got that bad.

She opened the door for they could go inside to relax and chow down. She had a great place, very befitting of a rocker bachelorette. It was a representation of her, dark and moody, with deep mystifying blues and purples surrounding, with a pot of lavender growing in her kitchen window. She loved herbs and many special symbols, which went along with her witch's heart, despite feeling as though she no longer believed in magic.

"As much as I love your place, it's sometimes a bit depressing . . . Let's get some light in here!" he finished justly. And he was right; there were only two natural brightly lit rooms in her home, the kitchen and bathroom, which she helped bring out as best her dark soul could. He opened her blinds and turned on her living room lights, which did much to brighten the place up considerably.

They had a good time in each other's company, which went on for about an hour; it was now 1:00 p.m. It was all fine until Max broke into an interrogation, least that's how Morrigan took it.

"Are you going to tell me what's going on, sis? I hope you didn't think I was going to just, I don't know, leave it alone . . . and be honest," he said as he sat back on her midnight blue lounge chair.

She sighed. "Oh, big bro, you sure want to know?" Without waiting for him to answer, she said, "Fine, I'll tell you." She turned the TV off as if to present her case more believably, while planning to make this as brief as possible and with enough truth to get him off her back for now.

"I've been having these weird dreams lately," she started.

"SMH . . . Hah, give me something better than that! So now you're having dreams, nightmares what?" He felt what she was starting to tell him was bullshit, and normally he would have been right. "I asked you to be honest!" he finished sternly.

"Max, I know this sound like shit, but it's the fucking truth! Why else do you think I didn't want to tell you anything? So just shut up and listen!" She continued, "They started shortly after Grandma died. I was already feeling depressed during the time she was sick and not being able to be around all the time, being broke, you know the deal." He shook his head in agreement.

"But it seemed to get worse after she . . . passed . . . After that I just started to doubt some things and have hatred towards everything that let me down. I can't really explain it anymore, but then the dreams started after the funeral."

He was disturbed, but oddly curious. He wanted to know exactly what she meant by hatred; he wondered what her hatred was toward, people, situations, or both. "What did you start hating exactly?" He feared to know the answer to his question. She said distantly, with a sense of aggression in her voice, "Believing . . . I hate that I wasted my time praying to a god or deity that may or may not exist . . . or simply doesn't heed my prayers."

"You don't mean that," he told her, at least he hoped she didn't. It was no surprise that Max was spiritually a believer. He didn't belong to a specific religion anymore; however, he was technically Jewish. Morrigan, on the other hand, believed in many things; she went from growing up Christian to becoming a Wiccan in her tweens to wanting to combine certain aspects from both practices. That idea stayed with her for years, but after a while it seemed nonexistent. Even though she still felt a calling to both paths, her faith all around was drowning now and it was going to take a major, almost catastrophic event or chain of events to turn things around.

He thought for a moment about what she just said, and about who he knew she still was. For the most part, he knew she was just lashing out. That was the conclusion; she was lashing out at whatever higher power that she felt had cursed her. In her mind, she felt it was better to believe in nothing and deny those similar impulses. Strong, but backsliding was her current situation both mentally and spiritually, but what was to become of her in the long run?

Despite the answers he came to, he didn't disregard her thoughts, but suddenly he grew more concerned of the dreams she mentioned. She usually always discussed her dreams with him, even if they were ridiculous misadventures into her imagination. And he couldn't explain it, but he felt it was more than nothing.

"Can you remember any details about your dreams?" he asked. She was disengaged, but started to tell him, "Well, I see me when I was younger, a little kid swinging on the swings, having fun . . . I know that little girl is me, because I . . ." Then she started thinking. "Old pictures . . . she resembles me, by appearance, similar clothes, anyway, I'm not alone. I see this guy approaching me and from his body form looks to be young like in his twenties maybe and he sits next to me on the swings. But I can't see his features."

"What do you mean you can't see his features?" Max questioned.

Now she started to get anxious. "I can't see his face, it's like distorted and a bit of a blur, and he talks to me but I can't make out what he says, however, his voice seems seductive. I know it sounds crazy, but that's what I remember, and he puts out his hand for me to grab . . . I can see his hands clear, but they're not . . ." But before she could continue her cell phone rang. "It's mom. I got to talk to her." Then she walked halfway to the back to answer the call. "Hello! Hey, Ma, I'm sorry, but I was busy trying to get some bills paid. But no, I wasn't trying to avoid you!" Lie.

While still trying to convince her mother, she now became muffled in the back to his ears. He couldn't help but feel as though she was heading down a dark path and thought about how much it would take to convince her to step back and get ahold of herself and keep tenacious. Just then his thoughts got the best of him and he was scared; he wasn't sure of what, but he had an intuition it would linger.

CHAPTER SIX

"Another Night of Debauchery?"

S tarted with an unfinished song during rehearsal—

I'd say your soul was bare, but not in your favor.
Turned inside out, bent you over.
You'll find out sooner or later, this world don't care for you.

"Stop! Stop, let's pause for a minute," Morrigan shouted over the crashing cymbals, stopping the band's rehearsal. She placed her ax in her guitar stand and turned around to face the band and met eyes with Max as she smiled at him slightly, but looked away beginning to speak.

"Jasmine, Tim . . . We have something to tell you, guys." They looked at her anxiously, and then started listening attentively as they expected the worst.

"Just lay it on us," spoke Tim thickly in his Brooklyn accent; he wanted it over with.

"All right." She sighed. The tension thickened in the small studio space, and she continued, "We've got the job." The two sat there frozen in their spot. "What? Wait?" was all they managed to choke out before smiling hysterically.

"Yeah, you poor assholes, we got it!" She shrieked. Max just laughed at his drums and chimed in with, "And we're going to go out tonight to celebrate!" There was so much laughter in the room that night and it spread throughout. Lib, the owner of the 69 Clam, picked up on the energy and poked his head inside the space he let them record and practice in, then spoke, "Lemme guess, got the new set of gigs?"

"*Yes!*" they all confirmed ecstatically.

"Congrats, kids," he finished, unsurprised at their success. Lib was fifty-eight, gray, and sturdy, the aging rocker till the end; he saw his fair share of drugs, groupies, and broken promises, but never got tired of seeing the new kids, the really hungry ones that would plow through the industry shit with or without the fame and fortune. Everyone called him Lib as it was short for Libbey. Morrigan commented on it once, saying, "He was one of only a few men that could make such an effeminate name as Libbey manly and tough." But he still preferred being called Lib, not that the kids as he called them cared. He saw real guts in Morrigan and Max, plus a bonding that could prove necessary in keeping them close through everything. So when Heckle and Jeckle first walked into his club at age fourteen begging for a place to play or at least practice, he eventually decided to take them under his wing, and they've been there ever since.

"Yeah, we totally did and we're celebrating," Morrigan answered proudly.

"Well, have fun tonight, but don't fuck it up . . . Morgue, can I speak to you?" he asked apprehensively. She looked up, if a bit startled. "Sure!"

Together they walked in the performance area toward the bar; she sat on one of the barstools, her studded jeans pinching the leather.

"You've been silent lately after the funeral, how's everything?" he asked in an uneasy tone.

"More than usual, hmm . . . What do you mean, Lib?" she asked foolishly.

"Cut the bullshit, Morgue!" he responded. Morgue was his nickname for her, not intentionally; it just got that way over time, when her outlook on life went from optimistic to dreadful. Plus it flowed with her name.

In the manner of a concerned mentor or teacher, he continued without changing his position, "Besides, we haven't talked in a while and Max brought it to my attention that maybe I should pry."

"Oh, he did, did he? Hah. Listen, Lib, I'm going to be honest. I have been contemplating some things and—" But before she could finish he interrupted her, assuming incorrectly what she might say. "You're not thinking about giving up, are you? Because . . ."

"No! That's not what I'm talking about, even though that thought has sneaked in my mind a few times," she said, trying to weasel out of this conversation quickly.

"It's just that I was feeling like shit lately, but I now know everything is going to be all right. I really do." She sealed it with an optimistic smile, but it was partially a lie. Other underlying issues were still bothering her. He thought she looked okay, not wrung through the dryer, so prying any more probably would do more harm than good, so he decided to let it subside unfortunately.

"All right, but you know I'm always here if you need me. Right?" he mentioned as he tapped her shoulder from across the bar table for confirmation.

"Yeah, of course, I know!" But inside she was thinking differently, "Someone always leaves, that's definite." And she couldn't have been more perceptive; people always leave whether by choice or force.

"This club is fucking awesome! Surprised we never visited before," exclaimed Max.

"That's because we rarely hang out at clubs, outside of work." She squished her face up in confusion; it felt weird to describe the band as work.

"Yeah, you're right," he said.

"We should do this more often though," she suggested as the default reaction. Max looked on into the crowd. "Yeah, whenever we have the cash to. Anyway, talk to Jack yet or should I say again?"

"Ooh, slick way to be subtle. He's supposed to be coming over tonight . . . Because he should go out of town tomorrow to settle the contract for, you really don't want to hear about that, do you?" she told him with a half smile.

"Yeah, no . . . So another night of debauchery?" he asked in his best cockney accent; it sort of failed on her, but she played along in an even more broken attempt.

"Don't be putting on airs! Of course, nothing less."

"Do you want another drink, before we get out of here?" he asked her, heading to the bar.

"Um . . . sure, vodka on the rocks," she answered.

"You got it, sis!"

The night started to wind down, and Morrigan was getting tired. She usually could go on all night, but she had to get busy early tomorrow.

"It's only 11:15 p.m., you sure you want to go home now?" Max said as he unrolled his windows. The breeze blew perfectly, cooling the inside of the car.

"Yeah, but mainly because I have class tomorrow morning at nine o'clock so you know . . .," she muttered.

He nodded understandably. She started to feel bad that she snatched him out of the bar so early.

"You could've stayed if you wanted to. I'm sorry I took you out so soon, I could've just got Jack to pick me up."

"It's nothing, come on, sis. Jasmine left us and I can easily go back to join Tim." She started thinking about what he said. "Easily?" she smirked under her breath. "What about gas?" She wanted to ask him about that, but didn't for the fear of sounding like a parent, a mom. *Blink, blink* made a little sound for the text message on his phone. His hand went to reach for it, but she stopped him in his tracks. "You better not!" and she reached into his jeans pocket for it.

"Yes, ma'am," he said. "Shut it, it's Tim. He's asking if you're coming back?" She looked at him for an answer with her head cocked to the side. "Hurry up, dude. Ha-ha."

"Text him back, 'yeah,' and here we are," he said when he pulled to the front of her apartment.

"Don't want me to go any further, do you?" he asked considerately.

She beamed a great smile. "No, I'm good. Thanks anyway, love. Oh!" she turned around back to the passenger window after stepping out. "Here, a very little something for gas" she said and handed him a ten-dollar bill. He looked at the money, then at her, and shook his head.

"Gas money, huh? Please, that's chump change!" he joked "But seriously, I don't mean that. Do me a favor though, babe, keep it. That ten dollars could go towards your own gas when you get Blue Thunder out." Then he winked his right eye; oh, how they shone so bright in the moonlight. "Please stop, sis," he asked her kindly, as kind as possible. She understood what he meant by that and winked back at him, then reached into the car to touch his face. "Did I ever tell you how sexy you are?" flirting with him casually. He stared at her, admiring her beauty. "All the time you tease, now get in the house!"

"Fine, be careful driving and call me when you get there." She loved and cared for him deeply; she held him close as there weren't too many people she felt that close to.

But before driving off he joked, "Yes, Mommy!" for he knew that burned her up, but in a smooth manner. She opened the building door with no problem; there were no spooky creeps stalking in the bushes at night, so she felt so relieved. The hallway was illuminated, but as usual there were a few dark corners and hiding places, but nothing too pausing.

However, when starting up the staircase she did get an eerie feeling that took her by surprise as there was nothing to drive her to that essence of fright. At least nothing physical that she saw of, but it was the typical feeling of someone watching her; it made her think of the old man, but again nothing besides suspicion gave that off, no smell, nothing unusual. As she climbed the stairs, walking felt heavy, almost as a burden to be given. Then footsteps, each a *tap, tap,* grew more menacing with each step; she couldn't seem to shake it. When she reached her floor, she peered over the staircase, wondering if she could at least catch a glimpse of someone. Not understanding why this was so important to her, she insisted, looking from side to side to each case of stairs to the very bottom.

"Nothing," she thought.

It caught her attention though there wasn't any sound, no one walking anymore.

"Hmm, maybe they went home?" she muttered softly in the vacant hallway as she started to her door.

She thought to herself how funny simple emotions could be when based on nothing; nothing but assumptions can change perceptions.

She continued walking, *tap, tap*. "Not again," she thought. Peeking over her shoulder once more, but again seeing nothing. "How freaked can you get?"

The few seconds it took to reach her door felt like a journey of days. She couldn't stand this anymore; she had a plan. Not necessary to catch the creep, but to give them a fright they weren't suspecting; it was just so amazing to her how calm she was inside. The footsteps ceased one last time.

"*Fuck! Hold!*" yelled a familiar voice in shock.

"What the? Jack? The fuck did you think you were doing? I could have fucking killed you!" Her voice was livid. "You're a fucking idiot!" she said with her switchblade still at his throat.

"You're telling me." He slowly motioned the blade away from his Adam's apple. "I suppose I didn't think that all the way through, huh." He was genuinely scared for a minute. "Stupid moment for a tough guy," he thought.

"I called myself trying to surprise you, looks like I did a pretty good job, almost too good a job." He managed out before leaning back on the wall. She scoffed, kicking her door, and one of the others unlocked. They both turned their heads in the direction of the clicks.

"Nosy ass," Morrigan mumbled. "It's nothing Mrs. Byrd!" The lock latched back on. Jack wrapped his arms around her waist, whispering in her ear, "Oops, I'm sorry, ha-ha." He was so childlike in that moment; it was disturbing, yet sort of cute. She rolled her eyes and nudged him off her. "I'm sure you are."

The door slammed sharply when she closed it from the inside. She took off her jacket and threw it over the chair. She sighed. "I know this isn't what you had in mind, hell, it's not what I had in mind, but I'm tired. I just want to sleep," she said almost sadly in a regrettable tone. Her disposition changed slowly, just to one sort of beat. "What's wrong, babe? You don't look too good, what's going on?" he asked, worried. She knew what was wrong; she thought she knew anyway. Maybe it was her own selfish self-loathing influencing her badly. "What should I say? What should I tell him?" she thought.

"Nothing really, I just have to get up for class early tomorrow, it starts at 9:00 a.m."

"Okay, what else is there?" he asked.

"Not tonight, sweets." She shook her head and let it hang on her right shoulder, greatly exposing her neck.

"Okay," he said as he took off his jacket, looking at her; he unbuttoned his shirt, heading toward her bedroom. Her eyes followed him curiously, the whole time wanting to follow him. Examining her place, he disappeared into her bedroom; she tilted her head to see if she could see him, but could not. It was so dark around her, despite the dim light appearing from the lamp in the corner beside her. She always preferred the darkness, for it offered solace, no judgment, so no scars shown to light. It was her comfort at times, if not too much. But now she was sensing some rejection, but from what exactly? The darkness itself, or the light within it she so desperately needed, but did not seek out? She doesn't know.

Jack appeared from out of the darkness to her, a tall figure in the night now wearing only his jeans. He then reached out, smiling, and kissed her lips slowly. "Let's talk," he said as he pulled her to the back. "Let's talk," she mimicked. "Sure."

"Morrigan . . . Morrigan . . . Baby, you have to wake up now or you'll be late for class," he whispered to her as he pinched her thigh. She pretended as though she couldn't hear or feel him, for this felt too relaxing like a dream almost to an end, unless she stayed asleep just a little while longer. But he insisted on being as annoying as possible with pinching, poking, and a surprise bite.

"Mmm, stop, sweets," she said softly.

He felt her whole body move under his as she turned over on her side.

"Don't you have class?" he asked.

"Mm, no . . .," she grumbled under her breath, wrapping her legs around him, gripping him tightly. "Sure, but wouldn't you rather repeat our encore?" she said softly, nibbling his neck. He moved into her, teasing, and returning her nibbles on her bare breast.

"But don't you have finals later this week!" he said suddenly, purposely disrupting his good job on her.

"Ugh, you can certainly ruin a lady's mood," she snapped before rising up from underneath him abruptly. "Now where's my bra?" she said, rummaging through the mess of sheets.

"Well, what about panties? Since you know you're missing those too," he said, chuckling. "Excuse me for actually caring about your expensive education."

She went to reach for her bra, which she spotted under his hip, but he pulled her firmly to him and their noses touched.

"I'll take you," he affirmed, staring deeply into her eyes. That took her aback slightly if just for a second, but enticed her all the same.

"If you think you can." She winked. "Seriously though, I need to take a shower, think you can straighten out this mess?" she finished while pointing at her bed. Still lying in the mess, he stretched out a bit, looked around him. "Uh . . . I'd rather not. However, I don't mind joining you in the shower." He smiled slickly. "So let's take a shower!"

She smirked in return, "I bet." She clicked her tongue and told him, "Come on."

He stopped her before they went into the shower, grabbing her arm tightly. "I hope we can work this out . . . finally."

She was more confused, then stunned; despite their differences in the past, she always thought it was something they could work out. Her confusion wasn't so much set in what he said, but how he said it; it was like it would be their last chance to work themselves out to keep together. Before he could say anything else, she placed one finger on his lips. "Shh . . . I believe you."

CHAPTER SEVEN

"I Just . . . I Just Can't"

M orrigan was walking down Twenty-fifth Street, going over the notes she wrote down from the project management class she left from. College, she can deal with; most of the classes in her major she could handle and understand. It's not that real life was too much, but it was fucking exhausting at times and boring. A few things swirled around in her head, not necessarily in constant order; she thought about checking the mailbox, being grateful for not being the project manager, and finishing a new song she was working on. She arrived at her mailbox in a series of sprints. However, when she inserted the small silver key in its lock her disposition changed completely, something to that of a nervous schoolgirl entering a zone forbidden.

"Maybe this isn't such a good idea," she thought silently. "But if I don't open it, could something worse happen?" That thought ran a little longer inside her mind.

Her first mind said to open it, and curiously it mentioned she could regret it if she didn't. Her mother always said, "Always follow your first mind, your second mind will steer you wrong every time." She turned the key slowly to unlock and face what waited for her in the narrow mail box; it was mainly junk mail, plenty of advertisements, notifications of sales, etc. Except for one single letter peeking from behind an air conditioner ad. *Superior Court of the District of Columbia*, it read in bold block letters on the upper right-hand corner of the envelope. She stared at it very straitlaced, reaching her hand past all the crap for it. Confirming any issues she initially had when observing the letter, everything was correct, her name, address, everything. Her head fell; it was no surprise to her that it was, so she grabbed the rest of the mail, and then started upstairs.

"I can't go through this again. I just . . . I just can't," she thought to herself repeatedly in a state of defeat and depression. She was walking around her place just repeating those simple words, "Not again, please not again," while shaking her head. This happened before, a few times before. She was thinking about those past times, when she was younger from being a kid to a teen. Some scenes were playing again in her head; now again she was watching her mother struggle and work her ass off, but seemingly to no letup, then to watching her clothes, her mother's clothes, her guitar, the beds, all their possessions being pulled out of their home onto the street. They had nowhere to go, no family to turn to, but then something good would happen. Trusting friends would pitch in and help, and things would get better for her mom and her, at least temporarily; she would get back on her feet, but it seemed to always be temporary.

"It's not what you know; it's who you know," her mom thought sometimes when she was turned down for a job, one that would make footing the rent so much easier. Raven, as dark as one of silk ebony and majestically strengthened, told her daughter that a few times and it was evident. Too bad they didn't know anyone. Morrigan hated those times with a passion, the constant moments her mom would second-guess herself or blame herself for not being able to keep the house, the apartment, not having the money to take care of this or that—those overall periods in her life she figured she was long away from. She despised it all, especially when her mom would blame herself; she knew it wasn't her fault, but the monotonous feelings of how we're going to do this, take care of that were extremely tiring. Finally, it seemed to them both that everything was getting better, stabilizing; her mom was blessed with a full-time job and things were staying better. But now it's happening again; this time it was only her and all on her.

"*Fucking pathetic!*" she screamed, throwing her course book across the room. It hit her living room wall, leaving a major dent, with a forest green scrap heading in a downward direction. She couldn't cry; she no longer had it in her, or so she thought. Morrigan slid down to the floor, still in a state of remembrance or dwelling of the past. This time, the scenes changed like an old multiplex theater, *click, click* as the picture became clearer in her mind; she saw her mom kneeling beside her bed, praying, reading her Bible, then it was on to the next room. This room was hers and she, too, was praying. Her room, unlike her mother's, which was open and beautifully decorated with golds and reds, was dark, very dark as the colors didn't shine through this time; instead they blended. Despite the aura, her younger self looked so hopeful. All this got her to thinking, yet again, but this time in a present time frame; she wanted so badly to call her mom and talk to her about everything, Grandma's passing, her situation now, and lastly to talk.

"What a failure I am, huh? Sorry, Mom," she said to herself, but that's too embarrassing; she couldn't manage it. How do you explain to your mother, who to you is one of the strongest women in the world, that in your adulthood you messed up? "It's like you didn't learn anything from me," she could hear her mom speaking to her in that, that dominant tone which was so disappointed. Maybe she would have said that, especially if she knew she was on the verge of giving up. Yeah, in that case she probably would have said those words. Mentally Morrigan wasn't present; her mind was so focused on things not even remotely encouraging. However, she briefly thought about what her mom and grandmother would tell her to do, to really focus on, pray, trust, and praise the Lord. Suddenly, she summoned up enough consciousness to say, "No . . . No, I won't," before it all bombarded on her and she fell into a deep sleep.

She didn't awake until the next day, way into the afternoon, still on the floor leaning against the chair, with yellow court papers in her hand. She tried to get her head together, rubbing the sleep out of her eyes. Staring at the papers for a minute, she finally rose from the floor and grabbed her cell phone and called the courthouse number on the back, then whatever housing resources listed on that same sheet of paper, along with any she could think of and asked those necessary questions. Even though she knew the answers, because she's called before, but maybe a different answer perhaps? No, nothing new. Deep down she knew what she needed to do. First, she went to her fridge, pouring a glass of vodka; she downed it. Then, she decided to call Max and ask him to meet her at the local park, so she could tell him mostly everything that was bothering her and what he probably needed to know; to her it was better her best friend first than her mother. But of course, he was pissed as well.

"Why wouldn't you tell me that shit sooner?" he screamed at the top of his lungs, almost stripping his vocal chords. "Seriously, Cookie M . . . You should have told me this."

Max was livid, but he was more disappointed than anything as he expressed it later in his tone. Her eyes followed him back and forth as he paced, fussing her out again. What could she say? He was telling the truth, so she kept her mouth shut and listened.

"You really piss me off with these keeping things to yourself, prideful bullshit!"

"I know . . ." She tried to intersect in his rant, but he cut her off at the start.

"No! You don't know! I don't think you do, Cookie M. I'm your best friend, drummer in your band, which is one of the most special things close to you, besides the people close to your heart. Of course, I like to think I'm one of those people." That brought a smile to her face; her lips curved upward and were apart just slightly for a half-croaked chuckle to be heard.

He grabbed her hands as he sat next to her. "You need to tell me what's going on, everything." Then he thought for a second. "Okay, I'll probably regret that one time or another, but still you're my sister, so I'll listen to you." They laughed in each other's arms with her head resting on his shoulder.

"You also need to talk to Mom, Libbey, too, and tell them what's up. They'll listen and support you," he mentioned one last time.

She knew it and agreed. "I should and I will . . . I just don't want her to be disappointed in me, you know?" she said with a heavy sigh, laying down her own disappointment.

"I know you don't, but you also know our mom. And she won't be disappointed in you, because this happened, but only because you haven't asked for help . . . Anyway, aren't you tired of the word *disappointment*?" He looked at her pleasantly; his voice spoke of his confidence in her ability to let her guard down, at least for the time being. Her eyes peering at him softly underneath her eyelashes answered his question.

"So what are you going to do?" he asked her as she rose from the park bench, stretching.

"I'm going to my mom's house, talk to you later." Then they temporarily parted ways for the day, until later.

CHAPTER EIGHT

Breaking the Silence

M orrigan stepped off the bus in Georgetown where her mother Raven lives. It was a nice neighborhood, better than most of the seedy places they were stuck in when she was younger. This afternoon the street was empty as she strolled down to her mother's red-brick home perfect for one person. Even though she had the key she always rang the doorbell a couple of times to give her mom warning her coming in.

"Hey, Mom, are you in here?" She looked around, puzzled by the area; it was so darkly laden. Raven always had her house brightly lit. Morrigan was surprised it wasn't; she was sure she would be home at this hour.

"Mom, aren't you in here?" The deafening silence startled her; she could have easily left and decided her mother wasn't home yet, but it couldn't have been. Her insides suddenly felt twisted, and she became nervously anxious to find her mom; despite how much she tried to dismiss it, her powers were still present. Her eyes darted as she tried to find the light switch, but they seemed to be hidden purposely. "Where in the hell is the damn light switch?"

She spotted her mom's keys on the kitchen table with help from the faint light coming in from outside, when then on the floor she made out a form; it was slightly stretched out and extremely still. It was a body.

48

Running to the body lying still on the floor, she hoped it wasn't her mother, but when she smelled her signature perfume, the fragrance Wicked, hope fell apart. The lights came on in an instant; the body *was* her mother lying there. Feeling her neck there was still a soft, faint pulse; if not searched for, it could've easily been missed.

"Mom? Mom! Wake up, damn it, please! Come on, you can't do this to me I need you." Crying hysterically, her voice became shot; she could think of nothing else but to awaken her mom in some possible way. She didn't even notice that the lights had come on by themselves or by someone hidden amid the scene. She could barely think straight; however, she knew she had to act fast. Rushing to the phone she dialed 911.

"Nine one one, what is your emergency?" the operator said monotonously.

"My mother is unconscious on her living room floor, I can't . . . I can't wake her! She won't wake up. She's breathing, but her pulse isn't strong! I need an ambulance at 410 Fifteen Street, NW, Washington, DC, please hurry ASAP!" Grabbing her mom in her arms, she was holding her tightly upright, just shaking and crying. Wanting this all to be over soon, she kept saying, "It'll be all right, Mom . . . It'll be all right, everything will be fine . . . I'll get us out of this!"

The hospital lights were like headlights, harshly shining in her face as she chased the nurse rolling her mother in the gurney down the hallway. She desperately needed Max to be there with her, consoling her through this, and as soon as she thought it, he came running toward her like clockwork.

"Cookie M! I got your voice mail, what happened?"

"I don't know . . . I just went there to talk to her and she was on the floor, unconscious."

"That doesn't make any sense. Your mom is completely healthy."

"I know . . .," Morrigan managed out. She was barely present now, trying to make sense of it all.

They sat in the waiting room, waiting for the doctor, waiting for answers. A few hours have passed and still nothing. She looked around once again to all the faces, the anonymous persons sitting around her. Max was the only face that stood out to her. Fearing the worst, she knew she was one of these faces and that this wouldn't be the last time she'll be forced here sitting, waiting.

The doctor came out with the expression on her face that she was just as confused by the event than the two of them.

"We're still running tests," she said to them, trying to think of viable results.

"So you have nothing?" Morrigan exclaimed as she threw a hospital pamphlet on the floor.

"She didn't say that," said Max, trying to cool her down. "Please, tell us you have something."

The expression on her face showed the opposite. "It's not diabetes or high blood pressure, it could be—"

"Don't bullshit me, Doc! You don't know what it is, do you?" Morrigan cut her off.

She sighed. "Morrigan, can I speak to you in private?" she asked her as if she was out of options.

"Whatever you can tell me, you can say in front of Max."

"Well, can I speak to you both in private?" She motioned them in a secluded room overlooking her mother asleep in the bed. "Honestly, I don't know what the issue is. We've spent the last two hours testing her against theories and nothing is pairing up well. You said not to bullshit you, Morrigan, so I'm not going to, your mother is as healthy as she can be. This is . . . outside of the medical field."

"Oh God," she thought, using the Lord's name in vain. "This will take faith." Something she was desperately in need of. Max touched her head, trying to console her; his inner apprehensive thoughts now came to light.

"Is she sleeping now?" Morrigan asked her.

"Technically, yes. She did wake up briefly while we were testing her. However, she was still out of it then went back to sleep. It's not a coma, I'm sure of it, so blessings for that, but I want to keep her here overnight till the rest of this week to keep watch on her. If anything changes, I'll be sure to let you know."

"Can we go in to see her?" Max asked.

"Not tonight . . . Get your sleep and come back tomorrow. I think that will be best, also she should be awake by then." The doctor left them in the room by themselves to ponder over what she told them. Max didn't know what to think to a degree, while she had a pretty good idea.

"It'll be all right, Cookie M," he said, breaking the silence.

"How do you know? I mean, how can you be for sure?" She didn't really expect him to answer this; she was just pissed off.

"I don't know! But I have faith that it will work out, better than wasting time in the alternative."

"Whatever, Max," she said dismissively.

"No, not whatever . . . Get out of that mess! Now is not the time for it." He was forceful with her, for he knew she could dwell in those feelings. He knew Raven wouldn't hear it, so neither would he. "Let's go home . . . We'll straighten out that other thing later," he finished, referring to the court papers when he saw them in her purse. She grabbed him quickly to hug him. "Thank you, buddy . . . for everything."

"I know . . . Come on, let's go." He hugged her back.

Her phone started to ring; the screen read to her, "Jack—(202) 397-7819." She pressed silent. He looked at her. "I'll talk to him tomorrow."

CHAPTER NINE

"Bouling Realty versus Morrigan Bloodchild!"

T hree days had passed since Raven was in the hospital and she still hadn't awakened yet. She told the doctor that she would be in later around visiting hours to check on her again. It worried Morrigan understandably more so than her potential eviction, which today was time for her court appearance. She and Max sat in the courtroom waiting for roll call, which went on for a while. She was just one of many people sitting on the hard benches, fighting to keep their home in the semicrowded area. Different shades of brown filled the area; it was so boring and depressing, she thought she would never have to deal with that crap again, but she wasn't so lucky this time around.

"Chill out, Cookie M . . . It'll be all right," said Max, trying to calm her down.

"Yeah, hopefully." She tried to contain her fear, but it was overwhelming. Her fear started to express itself as shaking through her leg. He grabbed her hand to resolve her. It barely worked; now she was trembling through him.

"Bouling Realty versus Morrigan Bloodchild!" announced the lady calling the court cases out. Morrigan almost jumped out her skin when she heard that, but managed to confirm her presence to the court.

"Morrigan Bloodchild! Come on, let's get out of here, dude. I want to look for this lawyer," she told him quickly. "But . . .," he questioned.

"But nothing . . . Let's go now," Morrigan responded sternly.

They went into the hallway to look for Mr. Emerson, the lawyer for the company. Max grabbed her arm to question her.

"What's the problem?" he asked.

"They can have it. I'm not going to fight it or contest it, I'm just going to pack up my shit and put it in storage," she answered abruptly. "I'm not going to fight or prolong the inevitable, man."

"But?" he tried at it again.

"Listen!" she interrupted him. "My unemployment is running low. I don't have time to keep at this anymore. I'd rather stay with my mom or try renting a room and save up money or something. I don't know. I just . . . I don't want to go through this anymore." He listened to his friend then asked an odd question.

"Do you have enough cash to get Blue Thunder out the shop?" She was puzzled at first because she didn't quite know what to make out of that random question.

"Uh . . . Um, yeah, and then some extra." Looking at him weirdly, she was trying to understand what her car had to do with her apartment. "Why?"

"Because you're going to use that cash to get your car out, to travel around, and be the natural-born rocker you are and stay with me in my place," he answered nicely.

"That's sweet, man, but I can't do that. I can't ask you to put me up until who knows when."

"But you're not even asking me! Nor am I asking you, I'm telling you. I know you, Cookie, and I love you, especially it's what best pals do, so don't make me tell you twice." He tried to crack a smile in it. "Come on, you know I don't like repeating myself."

That brought a tear to Morrigan's eye, her browns starting to fill up.

"Oh no," said Max. "Don't do that! No, come on! Don't do any of that crying stuff. You know we hate that sappy mess unless it's Disney movies." His voice was breaking up a little too, even though he was trying to remain manly.

"I know, but I can't help myself, dude. You love me? I love you too!" She gave him a big hug, and they started laughing loudly. They were quickly shushed by a security guard.

"Sorry, yeah, sorry," they both said quietly. She looked away from Max for a moment.

"Hey, that's him!" she told Max, motioning to him down the hall.

"Really? What a sloppy-looking guy." She hit his shoulder slightly to stop him.

"What? You know it's true, dudette, don't be shushing me."

"Ha-ha, oh man, I think we're bad people sometimes," she said, laughing.

"Ready, babe?" he asked her, grabbing her hand firmly to walk her down.

"Yep, I'm ready, luv. Let's do it," she answered; they walked down to Emerson's office to discuss the solution with him.

"Is forty-five days enough time for you?" he asked Morrigan promptly when they entered the office.

"Yeah, forty-five days is fine. Thirty would have been, too, but I'm not exchanging," she answered. The sit-down took about thirty-five minutes to work through, discussing most of Morrigan's options. She was glad it was almost over; now all she had to do was pack her stuff up.

"Where are we heading, my place or yours?" he asked her in his car, driving away from the courthouse parking lot.

"Mine. I want you to see what you got in store. Ha-ha." She referred to all the stuff in her apartment.

He scoffed. "I know exactly what you got in there! I remember perfectly." She plucked his ear. He glared at her and shook his head. She did it again.

"What is wrong with you?" he said, not actually expecting an answer. "Stop that!" With that she started laughing hysterically.

When he noticed how much she was enjoying that, he said, "You're going to make me regret this living arrangement thing, aren't you?"

"Ha-ha, no . . .," she answered in a cutesy way, while putting her fingers through his hair.

"Good! Bug your boyfriend." Instantly, her phone started ringing.

"You're a psychic, guess who?" she said, smirking.

"Speak of the devil," he responded.

"Don't say that!" she said sternly, giving him a seriously bent stare before answering her phone. He didn't catch her tone.

"Hello, my lovely!" spoke Jack happily over the phone. "How are you today?"

"Hey, baby!" she greeted him ecstatically. Max looked at her with one eyebrow up. She caught him swiftly.

"Don't judge me," she whispered to him, covering the mouthpiece. He smirked.

"I'm doing fine, Max says hi!"

"No, I didn't!" he corrected loudly.

"Shut up!" she argued. Jack chuckled. "Tell Max, I know."

"Forget about him, darling. So you sound pretty cheerful, what time is it over in London?" she asked.

"That's partially why I called you actually. Baby, I'll be back in two weeks. Thought we could make a date for the occasion."

"A date?" she answered nervously. Max turned to look at her.

"Yes, a date, it's something social. I take you on those to show how much I like you." She scoffed.

"You know what. It's just that I have something coming up and I don't know if."

"Is it gig related?" he asked.

"Uh . . ." Her voice trailed off. "Not completely . . ." She didn't know if in two weeks she'll be ready to face him. After all her economic situation greatly differed from his yet again. Morrigan always preferred to be stable when being in a relationship.

"Well, if not . . .," Jack started slowly.

"Never mind!" Morrigan interjected; she didn't want to worry him. "I'm sure everything will be fine. I'll see you in two weeks, lover."

"You sure, baby?" he questioned. "Because we could easily meet at one of your shows and—"

"Yes, Jack!" she said quickly.

"Okay, baby, see you soon. Love you," he said.

"Ditto!" She blew him a kiss over the phone before ending the call.

"Chick, this isn't *Ghost*! How you not going to tell the man you love him?" Max questioned her. She glared at him angrily.

"I said ditto, didn't I? How 'bout you mind your business?"

"I'm just saying . . . Ditto is not the same. Plus, it sounds a little selfish keeping that from him, knowing you do love him an' all." Max could really irritate the hell out of her sometimes, especially when he's right. She sighed and quietly said, "Just keep quiet and drive, Max," which he did for all about two minutes.

"So are you going to tell him?" he asked, referring to her moving in with him. That was undecided and bothersome.

"He wouldn't understand just yet."

"But you're not giving him another chance, plus you have to tell him eventually—"

"Shut up and drive," she interrupted him.

They arrived at her soon-to-be former home in no time.

"Let's get busy!" Max announced until he looked around and saw some things were already packed with more empty boxes scattered about, waiting to be filled.

"When did you do this?" he asked, slightly surprised.

"A while ago," she answered absently. Her mind was now focused on something else. She was looking for something, however she didn't know what. He noticed she was rummaging through a few boxes.

"It couldn't have been a while ago, because I was . . . What are you looking for?"

"Something . . ."

"That's really specific, Cookie M."

"Huh? Oh, ha-ha. Yeah, I guess not. I'm sorry, luv, it's just I'm not entirely sure what it is, least I can't remember. I guess I'll just know when I see it." Very determined, she noticed a box in the far right corner of her living room.

"Max, could you pass me that box over there, please? The one with the blue top."

"Sure, here you go!"

"Thanks!" She ruffled through it for a few seconds. "Hah! Here it is . . . my old amulet! See?" She showed it to him, a pentacle.

"Oh yeah! You used to wear these all the time until you stopped . . ." He stopped talking and stared at her. She just stared back intensely and frowned. Morrigan knew what he was going to say.

"Until you stopped believing," she mocked him. "Shut it!"

"Umm . . . well . . . Never mind!" He tried to dismiss it. "I didn't think you still kept these." He started whisking through the box himself to see all her old witchy items, ranging from a mini altar set, other magical tools, tarot decks, and candles, a few books for the solitary practitioner, as well as endless charms and amulets. Plus, a few Bibles too.

"Did you notice you packed *everything* in here?"

"What? I did?" She peeked. "Wow, I didn't notice I was so busy looking for this." She held up another necklace; it was an amethyst crystal quartz hanging from black string. Max was a little curious with her newly revived interest in this again.

"I'm giving this to Mom. I want her to wear it." She proceeded to take a similar necklace out, a shimmering black rosary and pentacle necklace, and placed both around her neck. "You want one?" she asked him.

"Nah, I still have mine. The previous ones you gave me."

"You do?" She was shocked. He looked at her and laughed.

"You don't remember anything sometimes, I swear. I still wear them too! Matter of fact . . ." He took a few out of his jacket pocket, a cross and Star of David. "See? Or sometimes I carry them around with me."

"No-brainer that *you* would carry jewelry in your pocket!" she joked.

"Chick, like you don't! Anyway, I think you should definitely give Mom that necklace," he said, reassuring her.

"Yeah, if I remember correctly amethyst has healing properties or protective ones," she mentioned.

"Either one is great!"

"True!"

They packed lots of boxes; mostly Morrigan's stuff was already packed. She received a call. It was her mother's doctor.

"Wait, Max! It's about Mom." He stopped hurriedly. "Hello! How's my mom, Doc? Is she okay?" she asked nervously.

"Yeah, how's Mom?" he yelled over the phone. He truly cared about them both. After all, Raven was practically his second mom. She helped raise him, took him in, so many years of friendship; they're family.

"Calm down, you two. Heh," said the doctor. "Your mom is fine. She just woke up, she asked about you two."

"Really?" asked Max. "Awesome!" Morrigan went to hug him.

"Can we see her now, Doc?" she asked.

"Not now," she responded. "We're still running a few tests."

"But you just said she was fine!" Morrigan added. "I assumed that all tests were ran."

"She is, but we just wanted to make sure before we released her."

She sighed. "Okay, I can understand that. So when can we see her?" she asked.

"Tomorrow morning, okay? She will be out of here and back home in a couple of days."

"All right. See you then." Morrigan confirmed and hung up on her. "We're heading there now, bro, come on!" she announced sternly.

"I knew it! Let's roll!" Max said in agreement.

"I can't believe I'm back in a freaking hospital!" she suddenly announced in an outburst. Max looked at her. "It's just . . . I'm sorry, bro."

"Its fine, sis. I'm sorry too. Just be patient, it'll be fine. Least Mom is coming out soon." They held hands briefly.

"Yeah, you're right." Morrigan started to sing, her voice strained with heartache.

♪♫ *Cards are strewn across the table. And I woke up with regrets.*
I've slept by picture frames of my wanted past.
I've slept underneath crosses made of tin.
The heart reflects. ♪♫

"That's a beautiful song, sis. You sound wonderful too, as usual . . . When did you write it?" Max asked sincerely. Most times she would tell him when she was working on a new song, but he had no idea of this one.

"Yesterday sort of, it came out of nowhere." Then she thought. "Well, maybe not out of nowhere, it's not even finished. I'm sitting on it, thinking."

"Thinking about what? That sounds awesome so far! You should continue to work on it. If you need any help, you know I'm always here." She gave him a sweet smile.

"Thank you, bro, I appreciate you. Know that!"

"Think nothing of it, sis."

The doctor walked out toward them. "I see you two like early starts. You two can see her tonight. Don't stay in this lobby all day though, come back later."

Max sighed. "So whatcha want to do?"

"Let's get something to eat and go to the Clam."

"Sounds good, maybe we can finish that song?"

"Max, no! Let's work on our set list for the House of Horrors."

"Dude, it's the Shack of Horrors," he corrected her.

"I know, I know, I'm terrible . . . haha," she joked.

"Yes, you are! Haha."

♪♫ *I had a friend, a good girl. Did everything that was asked of her.*
She fell in love, was way too young,
And then her groom was nothing but naught! ♪♫

"That sounds good, bro. I was thinking we could add that to the list."

"I'm with that, and 'Fuchsia,'" he added. "We should let Jasmine and Tim in on the loop now too."

"Cool with me! Think we should move a couple of my boxes to your place tonight after we see Mom?" she asked.

"That was kind of random, but would be good. Have less to do in one day, y' know?" He agreed.

"Yeah, that's the point because I rented a storage unit and I'm putting most of my stuff in that. I don't want to crowd your place too much, y' know? Plus, as you know I have a lot of stuff."

"Clothes and shoes, especially," he interrupted jokingly.

"*Ha!* Yeah," she chuckled in response while stretching her right arm. It was kind of sore from rehearsal. "Also, I changed my mind, I, we should take off 'Fatale' and add 'They Live' instead."

"Wait . . . What? I thought we had decided on 'Fatale,' it's a good song, it's solid." He tried to no avail to convince her.

"Yeah, well, I fell out of love with it. 'They Live' works better for this set. It's a powerful punk song. Anyhow, Morrigan has spoken." She hit his drums, mimicking a judge's gavel going down.

"Well, shouldn't we at least vote on it?" he tried again.

"No, it's not even a competition. It's an edgier song that breaks some rules."

"That's true, Cookie M, very true."

"But if you like it that much," she interrupted. "We can play that too just for you."

"Really?" he asked eagerly.

"No! Of course, not! But I love that look on your face," she answered, not changing her expression. He sat there a little stuck in his feelings.

"You are a wicked she-wolf. Listen, sis, I know 'They Live' is a better song. I just thought we could do 'Fatale,' too, maybe? I'm not sure on it either, I guess. Plus, I thought the bridge on 'They Live' still needed some work."

"Already fixed it!" she said proudly.

"Ah hell, really? Awesome! Let me see, well, hear it." She played it for him. Afterward, she told him, "I don't want you thinking I don't value your input, luv. It's just when I'm sure on—" He cut her off.

"I know, sis, when your mind is set and sure on something, it's unwavering, much like the song. After all, the song is everything you said it'll be. It's going to be fucking amazing to play on stage, dudette!" he said excitedly.

"Rock and roll, man!" Then they hit knuckles. He added, "Also, I guess I didn't want you thinking 'Fatale' is a bad song because it's not."

"Aww, isn't that sweet, bro, didn't want to hurt my feelings?" She pinched his cheeks. He snatched away slightly.

"Ah, fuck you! Blistering bridge too."

"Ooh, don't be so crass, brother . . . And thanks!"

Libbey was walking past their rehearsal space in the basement. Listening to them deliberate and practice. "Every time I look at you two, you make me prouder and prouder," he said speaking of his admiration of their friendship. "You two are powerful, especially together. I've been thinking about something more so now I'm not sure as to why, but I want you two to promise me, you'll keep it together. Not necessarily musically because it doesn't have to always be like that, you guys just should stay together. Stay close . . . Promise me."

Both were puzzled as to what brought that on from Libbey.

"Are you getting soft on us in your old age, Libb?" Morrigan chimed in.

"Yeah, Libbey," Max started in. "You know we're closer than everything. What's up?"

"I'm serious you two, promise me." They looked at each other kind of nervously. Morrigan couldn't help but think something was about to go wrong. However, she wouldn't dare say it aloud for fear that it could.

"We promise, Libb." They nodded in agreement.

"Good!" Libbey responded. "Now, Morgue, how's your mom?"

"She's supposed to be well, she's up now," she replied.

"That's great!" he said happily.

"Matter of fact, what time is it?" she asked.

"Seven PM," Max answered.

"Oh, shoot! We got to get out of here, visiting hours you know?" she said while rushing to her purse.

"Well, tell her I hope she stays well and gets back to raising hell soon!" Libbey joked. He grabbed Morrigan to give her a hug.

"Stop!" She laughed, lightly tapping him on the shoulder. She gave him a kiss on the cheek.

"You know Mom can always raise a good hell." Max squeezed in.

"We're outta here, see you later!" she said while walking out the door.

"All right, later you two," he replied.

"Love you, Lib," said Max.

"How are you feeling, sis?" asked Max suddenly.

They were walking in the hallway of the hospital to Raven's room.

"I don't know, man, all right, I guess," she replied solemnly, which quickly turned to annoyance.

"What a time to ask me that, dude!"

"I'm sorry, I'm just concerned, jerk!" he responded by lightly bumping her.

"Are you going to tell her anything?" he asked.

"Not now!" she said. "Come on, bro."

"I'm just saying you should tell her something soon," he responded. "I'm trying to help." She sighed.

"I will, bro. I promise," she said. "Just not now."

"Good! We're here. Room 318 . . . Let's go in," he urged her. When they went inside, her mom was already fussing over a movie on TV.

"Come on, Ma, with all that!" she said. "You know how those Lifetime movies are."

"Ruby! Max! My kids," Raven exclaimed. Max laughed.

"Ruby." He picked with her name for Morrigan.

"Shut up! You don't use that name," Morrigan groaned.

"Come here, give me a hug," Raven commanded. Morrigan sat down beside her on the bed.

"How are you two doing?" she asked happily. "I've been knocked for a bit. Missed some things."

"Oh, we're fine, Ma!" Morrigan replied. "You haven't missed much."

"Speak for yourself, sis," Max said. "I've been feeling abused and unappreciated." Morrigan glared at him. He laughed when he caught her glare.

"Just joking!"

"Never mind us, Ma, how are you doing?" she asked her mom.

"I'm doing well, much better than before. Doc said I'm going to be out of here in a day!" she answered.

"That's great!" they both exclaimed. "Absolutely!" Max finished.

"Yeah, she said it was stress related, Mom?" Morrigan asked.

"Supposedly," Raven replied. "She's not sure what brought it on though."

"Could it have been random or something ignited a past stress?" Max asked.

"That's what she said, but don't really know. However, I'm fine now. Thank God!" she replied. Max smiled.

"Yeah," Morrigan said. "Mom!" she started excitedly. "I've been thinking about a lot of things and without getting into a whole story I want you to wear this," she finished before taking out the necklace.

"It's beautiful, Morrigan!" she said, holding the necklace. "Thank you, sweetie!"

"You are welcome, Mom. I just thought it could possibly help you in some way or multiple ways." She chuckled. Max smiled looking at them, thinking about his own mom who had passed away years earlier from breast cancer.

"I love you, Mom," she said. "I love you too, Ruby."

"And I *love* you two too! Come on in here, group hug!" Max announced, comically running toward them with his arms outstretched. They all joined for the hug; it was sweet and meaningful. Morrigan gave Max a kiss on his forehead.

"Wow, a forehead kiss. Big deal," he joked sarcastically.

"Oh, shut up! You're lucky I gave you that," she said.

"I suppose I am." He slapped her thigh playfully.

"You're a boob man." She laughed. "What?"

"Boob!" She picked. They exchanged friendly barbs and hits for over a few minutes.

"You two are a trip!" Raven observed.

"Ooh, ooh! Mom, we got a set of shows starting in a week at a new club," she announced.

"Gosh, really?" she exclaimed. "That's amazing to hear!"

"Yeah! It's at the Shack of Horrors. It's this cool new venue over there by U Street." Max explained. "We already had a show there. They seem to really take to us!"

"Performed your asses off, huh?" she asked.

"Heck yeah, Mom!" he responded.

"Yeah, we wrote a bunch of new songs for it too," Morrigan chimed in. "To join older songs, of course, and the occasional cover song or two," she finished proudly.

"Yes, we're set, Mom," he confirmed.

"Congratulations, you two . . . I'm going to be front row!" she announced. "Now get out of here, it's getting late!"

"Mom, it's okay. It's only"—he stopped to check his watch—"nine thirty PM."

"Exactly! It's late and only getting later. Go home, I'm fine. Don't worry," she finished.

"Okay, Ma, we're leaving. I'll call you when we get home," said Morrigan. "Bro, you know it's senseless to argue with my mom. It can kill you." She laughed it off. "Anyway, he's staying over my place tonight."

"I am?" he asked.

"Yes, you are," she answered. "Ma's right, it's getting late. I'd rather we be together."

"Aww." He placed his head on her shoulder. "I knew you cared." She slapped his head.

"Come on, babe," she said. "Good night, Ma, love you!" she yelled.

"Yeah, good night, Mom!" he yelled, struggling through a head-lock Morrigan randomly put him in.

"Good night!" she yelled back. "Be good and be careful and don't forget to call me!"

"We won't!" they responded in unison.

"You want to drive, Cookie M?" he asked her, standing on the driver's side in the hospital's parking lot. She was standing on the passenger's side looking for her lip gloss.

"Uhh . . .," she stammered. Looking up, straight ahead behind a car behind him, she caught a glimpse of a man. She almost missed it until she realized who she saw or thought she saw. She shot her head back up immediately, staring past Max, but the man was gone again.

"As usual," she thought to herself. Max caught her and spun around.

"You see something or something?" he asked nervously in a goofy voice.

"Ha!" she laughed; he almost reminded her of a movie she once saw starring Mickey Rooney. "Uhh . . ." She shook her head trying to dismiss it. "Yeah, one of your ex-girlfriends!" she mocked him. He turned around slowly, glaring at her. Still grinning, she glanced to the side to see if she could catch another glimpse of that old stranger.

"Screw you, M," he said angrily. "You should be careful considering you were almost one of my many exes," he said feeling vindicated.

"Don't you wish?" she responded, rolling her eyes. "Give me the keys first." He threw them to her over the roof. She caught them; walking over to him, she kissed him softly on the lips. He stared at her surprisingly as it caught him off guard. She moved her eyebrows up and down quickly and smiled at him.

"You're just mad because I made you my bitch," she said slyly.

"Oh shit!" he blurted. "You're cold."

"I know," she replied. "Get in the car!" Placing the key in the lock, she shot a look back, hoping not to see anything creepy. The wind blew softly through her hair, giving her a sense of peace. She saw nothing, got in the car, and drove off.

"Let's stop off at the carryout and get something to eat," he mentioned when they were near her house.

"I got food in the house," she stated.

"I'm buying," he said straight.

"Can't argue with that," she responded, making a U-turn.

"Thanks, man." She thanked him walking into her place.

"No problem!" he said. "So what's the sleeping arrangement?" he asked.

"We can both sleep in my bed. I'll give you a taste of what you're missing," she partially joked.

"Oooh, really? And what would Jack say to that invitation?" he played along.

"What he doesn't know won't hurt him . . ." She paused. "I'm just fucking with you! Seriously though, we can share my bed."

"Cool." He agreed. They talked the rest of the night about packing and went to sleep.

"Good night, luv," she said.

"Good night, sis."

A week had passed since visiting her mom in the hospital. Enough had changed. Raven was released shortly after and back home resting, doing well. Morrigan finally got her car Blue Thunder out of the shop, and Mystic was preparing for their gigs. However, today Morrigan and Max were officially moving out of her apartment.

"Now we *have* to get the rest of this stuff out today!" Morrigan announced to Max while grabbing a box to put on the U-Haul truck. "Because we only have another day before our shows start."

"I know, sis. I know," he responded. "We'll have everything out today. It's not that much stuff left anyway."

"I just want us to be prepared. And not dragging down 'cause of this mess," she finished.

"You have an all-day rehearsal planned tomorrow, don't you?" he asked suspiciously, standing on the truck's step, narrowing his eyes at her. Her eyes shifted down.

"Maybe . . ."

"Morrigan!" he screamed, voice tinged with aggravation.

"Okay, maybe just a few hours?" she mentioned, trying to convince him.

"Dudette, we're prepared!" he stated.

"I know, I know . . . That's not really the only thing I wanted to do . . ." She tried easing into for she knew this wasn't going to go smoothly. "Do you think?"

"No!" he commanded. He just *knew* what she wanted to do.

"You don't even know what it is," she said.

"Yeah, I do! Yeah, I do! And it's a no! A hell no!" he yelled angrily.

"What is it?" she asked, sticking her lips out, hoping he wouldn't guess correctly.

"You want to record and you want me to ask Gaston if we could borrow the studio for a few hours to do so," he finished with contempt.

"Damn!" She shrunk. "That was pretty spot on." He sighed.

"It's just two songs. He might let us." She tried again.

"No, dude, he's a jerk! Only an asshole can have a name of Gaston! I hate him, hell, you hate him! Besides, I'm on the cleaning crew, even though he tries to treat me like his personal assistant," he argued.

"One up from slave!" she joked, trying to lighten the mood. He just gave her an unpleasant look.

"I'm sorry, sis. You know I love you and this band, but no way!"

"Remember that time I asked Stephanie for money concerning band equipment that you begged and sulked for me to ask? I said 'fuck no,' too, but eventually I thought 'okay, fine, I'll make the plunge, maybe it'll be different this time.' Nope! She still doesn't let me live it down and you know I paid the bitch back!" she finished frustratingly.

"Fuck, dude." He sighed, agreeing grudgingly. "You're right, I'll ask. Thanks for the guilt trip!"

"You're welcome, but listen, bro, I'll even ask with you." Then she thought. "No, I'm the one who wants this, so I'll ask."

"You know that dude has a mad crush on you, right?" He reminded her.

"I was trying to dismiss that part." She sighed.

"I appreciate what you want to do, but I can ask. All he can say is yes or no," he told her.

"Deal." She confirmed, walking back inside the building. Placing a box on the truck, he started to jump off until he noticed a familiar car approaching. It was silver with slightly tinted windows on a BMW. He knew exactly who it was. Startled, he almost lost his footing, jumping off.

"Uhh . . . Morrigan!" he yelled to her nervously. "I think you should come out here now!" She didn't hear him.

"Morrigan, sis!" he yelled again. "Come out here, now!"

The person began to park in front of the U-Haul truck; that's when Morrigan came walking out carrying a box, fussing at him.

"I'm coming, pest! What is it you're rushing me for so much?" Her eyes narrowed on the handsome gent who stepped out from the driver's side and stared directly at her.

"Oh . . .," was all she could manage.

"Yeah . . .," eased out Max. "I tried to tell you," he whispered.

The older gentleman walked over to them.

"Hey, Max," he said, still focused on her.

"Hiya, Jack," Max responded.

"What's going on here, Morrigan?" he asked her.

"I think now it's pretty obvious," she said sarcastically.

"Oof . . . Now that's not making the situation better," Max murmured quietly.

"*Shut up, Max!*" she screamed at him.

"Shutting up! Grabbing more boxes." He went into the building.

"Don't tell him to shut up, he's right," Jack stated.

"What in the hell are you doing here so early?" she asked him angrily. "And without calling!"

"I called myself trying to surprise you!" he argued back. "Imagine I'm the one who gets the surprise! My girlfriend moving out of her apartment without telling me! What a way to break it off!" Morrigan dropped the box she was carrying.

"You think I'm breaking up with you?" she asked, shocked.

"What would you think?" he said.

"Wait . . . We're back together?" she asked.

"Of course, we are! You aren't breaking up with me again?" he asked, wanting to confirm.

"No, I'm not. Considering I didn't really think we were in a relationship again," she admitted. He gave her a look. "I'm sorry, babe, I wasn't really thinking about us," she finished, sighing. "This is my fault." She sat down on the step.

"Come sit beside me, babe," she said nicely, putting her hand out. He sat down, grabbing her hand.

"Tell me what's going on?" he said.

She explained everything to him what she could. It was a kind of cathartic event. She noticed something too; he listened.

"Can I come out now?" Max asked. He was eavesdropping the entire time in the hallway with a box in his arms.

"Tsk! Dude, come on out here!" she yelled at him.

"I just need to put this box on the truck, didn't want to interrupt," he said as he flew to the truck. She looked at him and shook her head.

"That's your brother," Jack stated. She giggled. He longingly looked at her.

"Why didn't you tell me any of this before?" he asked, unprepared for what she was about to say.

"To be fair, she didn't tell me at first either!" Max yelled from the trunk, listening. She growled.

"Because I wasn't sure if I could trust you," she answered honestly. "I mean, can you seriously ask me that with a straight face and not have an idea as to why you wouldn't be the first person I would disclose my financial problems to?" she asked.

"Wow, Morrigan." He sighed. "That was a few years ago." He referred to a past event that broke them up before.

"Yeah, well, I wasn't sure if I could trust you again, honestly, I'm still not." He looked at her painfully; she could tell he was hurt.

"I'm sorry, Jack," she said.

"So am I . . . I'm here now and want to prove to you that what happened and how I acted years ago is in the past. I was wrong and inconsiderate and I've changed, I'm sorry, Morrigan," he said sincerely.

"That's what they all say," she said.

"Well, I'm not all honey. Believe me," he stated. She smiled softly. "How about I help you two move the rest of your stuff? After all I have a date planned for us today."

"Sure." She accepted.

"Absolutely!" Max yelled from the sidewalk. "With you we could definitely breeze through the rest of this!"

"He has ears like a cat or rodent . . . I love him so I'll compare him to a cat instead," she said affectionately. Jack laughed.

"Just to make sure, we are together-together, in-a-relationship together?" he asked her again.

"Yes, babe!" she answered.

"I just want to make sure we're on the same page this time." He chuckled.

"Awesome!" Max yelled again. They all laughed.

"So let me get the rest of this stuff!" Jack said. "I am going to miss this place, baby," he told her before going inside the apartment.

"Me too." She admitted solemnly.

All three moved various boxes on the truck designated for the storage and to their cars for what was meant for Max's. It took hardly any time together. After everything was done they all stood outside Max's apartment complex.

"Think you can get used to picking and dropping me off here?" she asked Jack.

"Of course, I can get used to anything with you," he responded happily.

"Jack? Before you guys go, can I ask you something?" Max asked.

"Sure! What is it?" he responded.

"Over here." He motioned to the side. "You stay there!" he commanded Morrigan. They whispered for a few minutes, leaving her on the outs, wondering.

"Now they're laughing!" she thought to herself. "What the hell?"

"Okay, baby, time to go," Jack said, walking toward her. "She won't be back tonight, Max, hope you don't mind."

"I don't, just continue to treat her right," he answered. "Be safe, you two!"

"Good night, Max," she said. As she and Jack got in the car she asked him, "What did you two discuss back there?"

"Oh, you'll find out soon," was all he said as he smiled, and for whatever reason she let that be as she enjoyed the ride peacefully.

CHAPTER TEN

Four Months Later

"**T**his place is perfect man!" Morrigan excitedly exclaimed to Max.

"For us, then other artists over time . . . It's going to be great, bro!"

"It really is," he agreed. "Put the studio here and maybe a lounge area here. Or something," he thought aloud.

"*Yes!* Once we secure this loan, all's good. I have lots of ideas for the studio. Just to make the most of this place," she finished.

"I know you do, sis . . . I'm proud of you."

"You'll be here, alongside, right?" she asked him.

"That's sweet, but management is not my thing," he said. "But I'll always support you."

"Surely, that's why you're going to be my engineer. Thanks, my man!" she reaffirmed him.

"So when's that meeting at the bank again?"

"Tuesday. We sign the papers Tuesday!" she reminded him.

"Great!" he exclaimed.

"Well, I got to get back to work, babe. See you tonight at home?"

"Yeppers," he agreed.

Morrigan went to work as a sales associate at a clothing store and secretary at a law firm, both part-time positions. Ideas were finally working for her, while things were starting to get a little harder for Max.

"I need to see you in my office, Max," spoke Gaston promptly.

'Yes, sir?" Max wondered what the hell he could want now.

"I partially wanted to let you know that you're doing an excellent job here. Expert cleaning in fact, true attention to detail, really great," he started.

"But?" He figured on a catch lurking.

"Straight to the point, always admired that about you." Max sighed annoyingly.

"But I've heard that you've been trying to start your own recording studio."

"Can't say I agree with that. Which birdie spread that rumor?" Max asked.

"No one specifically, just something I've heard around. Is it true?" Gaston questioned. Max smiled and looked him in his eyes.

"Can't say so," he answered.

"No, huh? Well, maybe it isn't you per se, probably your sister." Max didn't say anything to deny or confirm.

"Okay, you're dismissed, Max." Max went to walk out of the office door.

"I'm glad to know because that's competition for me. I would hate to fire you over something like that," said Gaston smugly.

"That's interesting you would have that authority, sir, because I don't work for you. Thanks for the warning though," he finished sarcastically.

"How is Morrigan by the way?" he asked. Max turned around quickly, peering him up and down.

"She's perfect! Thanks for asking! Matter of fact, I'll tell her you said hi," he announced cheerfully, which caught Gaston by surprise, his mouth dropping instantly. Max closed the door with laughter in his wake.

"Hey, dude!" Morrigan greeted Max when she got home.

"Hey, sis. How's life?" he asked her coolly.

"You know what, bro? Life is good, really good . . . How was work?" she in return asked him.

"Work was work," he answered glumly.

"Meaning?" she asked him, begging for an answer.

"Interesting," he answered.

"Put down the pen, Max," she demanded. "What's the deal? Did Gaston say something to you?"

"He threatened to fire me if I continued to pursue this label with you in no uncertain terms, like I said, interesting," he said, still writing.

"What?" she exploded. "He has no right! However, how in the hell did he find out?"

"That's the same thing I'm wondering about," he spoke to her calmly. "That he didn't let on, but I'm not worried about him, sis."

"He has no authority to fire you," she continued.

"I know," he confirmed, still writing.

"What are you writing, bro?" she finally asked, wondering why he was so calm.

"Just filing a report," he answered.

"You're telling on his ass, aren't you?" she guessed correctly.

"No, it's routine paperwork," he lied.

"Your ass! I know the deal!" she said. He laughed. She grabbed his hand and clutched it.

"I'm not going to let anything happen to you, bro," she told him firmly.

"I know . . . Neither will I," he supported.

"Sorry, miss, we no longer have that size in stock at this location. Would you like for me to check a different one?" Morrigan spoke pleasantly to a customer when a fellow employee approached.

"Girl!" said Kiki.

"What's up?" Morrigan replied.

"I don't know what's going on, but management wants to see us all at lunch, or before lunch, something like that," she told her.

"Downtown Fourteenth Street has it, would you like for me to have them hold it for you?" she responded to the customer. "Okay. Ooh, sounds serious . . . What do you think it's about?"

"I'm not sure, but it's been buzzing only new players are going to be called forth. So best of luck, M." They clutched pinkies.

"You know it. See you then, dudette," Morrigan replied. Lunchtime seemed to come quickly after that. Everyone was directed to the conference room.

"I guess now is the moment of truth, huh?" she asked Kiki.

"Listen up, everyone!" announced one of the store managers. "We're not going to need you all for the next three months. Business is slowing down, and we've decided to stick with our veteran employees. This is a seasonal position after all. However, the newest ones that have showed great strengths will be kept on file for future callbacks," he finished. Everyone looked at one another confusingly.

"Seasonal?" Morrigan questioned out loud. "I think I can safely speak for everyone when I say we all applied for these positions under the guise that they were permanent part-time positions, not seasonal."

"That's right!" Kiki confirmed. "On our paperwork, seasonal isn't listed. I know I didn't apply for that."

"Well, it doesn't mean you all no longer work here. After the next three months, we'll call you back for what is available," responded the store manager. "Um, after next week your schedule, just ignore it." Everyone was floored.

"Well, I guess we have part of next week to work together," Kiki told her.

"I'm going to fight it," Morrigan said suddenly. "It's not like we don't have a case."

"Are you sure?' Kiki was hesitant to make waves. "They did say they will keep us on file."

"Do you really believe that, Kiki? Seriously, do you really believe that after the way they informed us?" Morrigan questioned her. "It just breathes of shadiness."

"Maybe we should let it go . . . It's only three months," she suggested.

"You do you, I know what I'm going to do though." She chuck-led. "Anyway, my band has a show tonight. Wanna check us out?" she asked her.

"That was random! Of course!" Kiki laughed.

"Well, I like to move on to happier events," Morrigan told her. "Great! So I'll see you tonight?"

"Yep!" she said.

"Later, babes," Morrigan said as she went back to work.

"Later."

"Cheers, my disturbed little pets!" Morrigan greeted her band in her usual manner. All of them were backstage of the Shack of Horrors awaiting their set.

"You got anything to tell us?" Jasmine asked her.

"About what?" Morrigan didn't have a clue what she was refer-ring to.

"About the studio and the loan," Tim interjected. Jasmine gave him an annoyed look.

"Sorry," he told her.

"Max!" Morrigan yelled at him.

"I know I wasn't supposed to say anything to them until we were really sure, but we're band members. I mean, what's the harm?" he stated.

"There's no harm." She sighed. "It's just that nothing is final-ized. I didn't want to get anyone's hopes up. Yes, we do sign the papers tomorrow, but?"

"No, no buts!" Tim interrupted excitedly. "There you go! Tomorrow!" She looked at him.

"Sorry," he said sheepishly.

"Don't apologize. You're optimistic, that's good!' she told him happily. "I used to be that way too." They laughed. "Just remember all that onstage tonight and tomorrow," she told them. They cheered.

"Mystic on in three!" announced the owner, Kirk. As they were about to go onstage, Morrigan held back Max while Jazz and Tim went on.

"What's up, sis?" he questioned her grip.

"I'm sorry, I don't know why in the hell I decided to tell you this now, before . . .," she stammered. "Me, Kiki, some of the others are going to be out of work at the store for the next three months, that's what they told us at lunch today." He looked at her dumbfounded. Jasmine and Tim started beckoning them to come onstage.

"We'll talk about it later," he said.

"Yeah," she agreed.

"Hello, boils and ghouls!" she greeted the crowd ecstatically. "Did we have you waiting long?" The audience cheered.

"Well, that's what you need. Get over it!" she teased them, winking back at Max; he winked back.

"This is a new tune. It goes a little bit like this." She sang.

♪♫ *Hey, street cat! What's up, street cat?*
Really don't belong on my block, dingbat! ♪♫

Mystic played with such an ethereal intensity, the audience was open to everything they threw at them. That night, the universe was perfectly connected in her eyes. When she closed them she only saw cosmic dreams.

"Today's Tuesday, boi!" Morrigan exclaimed to her brother. "Tuesday . . . Thor's day."

"Dudette, you know that's Thursday," he corrected her.

"Right, right, I know that," she confirmed.

"I know you do," he said.

"I guess I'm just really excited," she said.

"I know that too," he said with a calm response.

"Tiw's day, August the twenty-fifth," she continued anxiously.

"Dudette! Please! That's enough," he yelled.

"Sorry, dude, I'm sorry!" she apologized.

"If I didn't know any better, sis, I'd say you were nervous," he mentioned to her. She scoffed.

"I'm not nervous," she told him.

"Yeah, you are." He picked on her in a singsongy voice then poked her arm.

"Don't touch me!" she said, annoyed. He laughed.

"Libbey, tell Cookie M it's okay to be nervous sometimes," he asked Libbey.

"Sign the papers today?" Libbey asked.

"Yep, and she nervous."

"I'm not nervous! I'm just"—she paused—"anxious. But also, very excited. This is a big deal," she stated.

"It is a big deal!" Libbey told her. "And it's natural to be a little, especially over, an exciting thing that's important to you." He comforted her. "Stop teasing her, Max!"

"What? Man . . ."

"Thanks, Lib." They hugged.

"So what time is your appointment?" he asked.

"In a few hours, but . . . Oh, I forgot to tell you, Max, we have to stop by the Horrors first. Kirk wants to see us," she told him.

"Why?" he asked.

"He didn't say, just to come in before one o'clock," she answered.

"Guess, you two better get a move on, then?" said Lib. She checked her watch.

"Yeah, I guess we should. Come on, Max! Thanks again, Lib! See you later!" she told him.

"What do you think he wants?" Max asked her.

"I don't know. Gets curiouser and curiouser," she told him. "He did sound differently over the phone. Hopefully, it's all good, man!" She wrapped her arm around him.

"Yeah, Cookie M," he said.

They arrived at the club shortly before 12:30 p.m.; it wasn't open yet, but Kirk, the owner, let them in.

"I didn't have a chance to bring my other bandmates," she started. "They're working."

"It's okay, I really need to speak to you two. You can relay the message to them. Come in my office." He motioned.

"This must be serious?" she asked outright.

"Morgue?" Max tapped her.

"Just hit us with it, Kirk," she stated, completely ignoring Max.

"Please, come in my office," he asked them sheepishly. She scoffed.

"Okay, we're in your office," she stated, irritated.

"I don't know how to say this," Kirk started shamefully.

"Then just say it," she told him.

"I have to let Mystic out of your contract." Her heart dropped.

"Great! Anything else?" she bounced back sarcastically. Max looked at Kirk in disbelief.

"I'm going to buy you out of it." He tried to remedy.

"Okay, where's the money?" she asked sternly. "Check, I'm assuming."

"Why are you letting us out in the first place?" Max asked.

"He's asked a good question. Kirk? We've had no problems with performances, no fights with other bands, general traffic, so can you answer his question honestly?" she asked him, her tone becoming more aggressive.

"It's complicated. I'm sorry, I really like you guys and your group, but I'm working on an overpacked roster. I can't anymore. It's a fine, a whole bunch of shit. I'm really sorry," he finished.

"Great, so when do we get the check?" she asked bluntly.

"Tsk, Morrigan, really?" Max chastised her, trying to be diplomatic.

"Whatever!" She dismissed him.

"It's right here," Kirk answered, giving her the check.

"You're not the only band I had to let go," he mentioned.

"Really?" they asked in unison.

"Yes." His voice changed suddenly, almost robotic in tone.

It was a quick drone; even his eyes spaced off as if he was in a trance. Morrigan didn't catch on, but Max did.

"Um, Kirk?" he stammered.

"Huh? Oh yeah, you can still perform here sometimes, just not as a contract yet," he stated.

"Are you all right, Kirk?" Max asked, concerned.

"He's fine!" she added impatiently. "Thanks, Kirk, this adds up. We gotta go. Come on, bro, we have somewhere to be." She left quickly.

"See you, Max," Kirk said solemnly.

"Maybe . . . Later," he responded before stepping out.

"Cookie M!" he yelled toward her in the parking lot.

"Big deal, dude, we got papers to sign!" she said excitedly.

"What changed?" he asked her surprisingly. "I thought you were upset?"

"Well, I was. Still am kind of. However, I don't want that to ruin our day. I want us to be right in our mind, positive!" she told him surely.

"Whoa, okay great! Um, did you notice anything weird back then about Kirk?" he asked.

"No. Why? Should I have?" she answered honestly.

"Uh . . . Tsk . . . No, I don't think so. Forget it. He was probably feeling guilty for being a putz." He dismissed his thoughts.

"A punk ass putz, my brother!" she jokingly corrected him.

"*Hah!*" He laughed. "Yeah, let's get on!"

They arrived at the SBA office fifteen minutes before schedule. It wasn't long before they were called into the office of the SBA manager.

"Sit down, please, you two," she told them nicely.

"Thank you," they said in unison.

"Ready to sign those papers?" she asked them.

"Yes, absolutely!" Morrigan answered eagerly. She couldn't believe this moment was actually happening.

"Could you give me the file for the Bloodchild account?" she asked a new employee who caught Morrigan's eye. Randomly, she felt something disingenuous about her. It brought upon a lump in her stomach.

"I might have to use the restroom," she whispered to Max.

"What now?" he said quickly.

"Yeah, I—" Before she could finish, her file was brought in.

"Okay, you two, here are the papers . . ." Her voice trailed off as though she was puzzled by something in the file. "Huh. That's odd," the loan manager stammered.

"What's odd?" Morrigan questioned, her stomach firmly in knots.

"Yeah, is there a problem?" Max asked concerned.

"I'm sure it's a mistake, but it says here that you've been denied because of lack of funds," she said.

"What?" Both jumped from their seats.

"We were called and told everything was likely to be approved. That we could come in to sign the promissory notes and everything," Morrigan stated sternly.

"You are amongst the panel, now you're telling us there's a problem?" Her voice heightened.

"Apparently, there was a last-minute flag in the report and it came in. We can't fund anyone because our limit is drawn. Um . . . Plus, it shows poor credit score because of student loans," she responded.

"But that's ridiculous! She makes payments on those," Max disputed.

"Exactly!" Morrigan agreed.

"I know, I know! We went over this before. I saw the paperwork myself. There was no problem. I just don't understand it." She admitted her confusion. "There should have been no problem, but . . ."

"So what happens now?" Max asked her.

"You can apply again. It'll take another six months. Or I could—" Morrigan interrupted her.

"Another six months? That's ridiculous! All my information, our information is right there. And now it's a poor credit score," she argued.

"But in those six months we will, should have the funds." The loan manager tried to reason with her.

"Supposedly," she corrected her in her uncertainty.

Max grabbed her by her arms; looked daringly into her eyes and asked, "Cookie M, what do you want to do? We could fight it." Then she thought about her retail job ending. "Or we could try again?" he finished. She thought about everything, everything yet again bombarding her hopes and dreams, so close to be crushed. It was too much.

"Fuck it!" she told him. "What's the point? Let's go, man. Bye, miss." Then she rushed outside, leaving him in the office. She was crushed mentally, spiritually, and felt herself about to snap in front of everyone around. She couldn't take any more embarrassment; however, she saw the new employee again and she sort of winked at her, but Morrigan was so upset, she didn't even realize the oddness of the gesture.

"I'm truly sorry, mister."

"Yeah, we've been hearing that a lot lately." He cut her off. He sighed.

"I'm sorry too," he thought to himself.

"Mr. Damento—" she tried to say, before he interrupted her again.

"Is there any way you can consider this further?" he asked desperately.

"I was planning on it," she answered him with an understanding smile.

"Great!" he was honestly hopeful.

"I'll be sure to call you when I find something. Here's my card." She gave him her contact information.

"Thank you, Ms. K. I really appreciate it. Have a good rest of the day."

"Go check on your best friend," she told him before he left to find Morrigan. "Tell her it'll look up."

"I'll try," he muttered.

He found Morrigan by Blue Thunder, sitting on the hood.

"Give me strength," He whispered again.

"I'm sorry I got you wrapped up in this shit, bro," she told him when she saw him approaching.

"Dudette, it's not shit. I've always supported your dreams, especially since they include me," he joked. "What are brothers for?"

"It's fucked up, dude! Least in the past we got a year or two of peace, you know, some freedom! Now I can't even get a solid six months free!" Morrigan exploded.

He listened to her frustrations while thinking of a way to possibly better the situation. It was a stretch, for he knew it wasn't going to go over well with her; however, he figured it was worth a chance.

"Desperate times call for desperate measures," he thought to himself.

"Well, maybe you can ask Jack for the money or some of it?" he asked nervously, stammering for a second. Her face twisted up. "Here it comes," he thought.

"Are you fucking out of your mind?" she exploded again; this time her anger directed toward him. "I can't do that. I *won't* ask him again! It's out of the question! I can't even believe you asked that or considered it!" she argued.

"But he seems different than before. I think he's changed." He tried to convince her. She looked at him in disbelief. She felt her own best friend was turning on her.

"Plus, he came through with recording our demo. And that's showing a lot of promise, getting rave reviews!" he pleaded.

"So the fuck what?" she ripped. "Big damn deal! Money is part of the reason shit was ruined between us before, and *you know* this! I'm not dependent on anyone. I pay for my own shit!"

"I know that and I agree with you, but it's not dependence. Forget about the shit he did back then, well, don't forget necessarily . . . This is to at least secure it!" He tried desperately to convince her.

"No! It's not happening, plus if I did, what about our other expenses? We still got the monthly rent to worry about," she told him.

"Fuck the rent!" he said.

"No! Been there, done that! I'm *not* going back. Let me give you real talk, brother, we're only working part-time. I only have the one now."

"But the check and what we have saved—" She interrupted him.

"Half of that goes to Jazz and Tim. That other goes on remolding the studio, there's hardly equipment, remember? Then utilities, car notes, whatever the fuck else!"

"But Jazz and . . .," he stammered.

"Get real, Max, I don't care what they said. It's unrealistic. I was being unrealistic about all of this."

"You sound like you're giving up," he told her.

"I don't want to set myself, you, or anyone else up for failure," she finished, disheartened.

"You're not babe, the EP . . . When one door closes, another one op—" he attempted.

"No, brother, please stop with that." She sighed. "I just can't with that right now, man. No door opens bullshit because guess what? Sometimes the doors don't open, they just don't . . . at least not for me." She paused to gather her thoughts. "I got to clear my head."

"Okay, so where are you going?" he asked.

"I don't know, probably the Clam," she answered.

"Then I'll come too," he said.

"No, Max! Just stay away from me. Let me wallow in my self-pity, okay? I want to be left alone," she insisted.

"At the Clam?" he said.

"Who's there now?" she yelled aggravated.

"But . . .," he started.

"I'll call you later," she told him before hopping into Blue Thunder. Morrigan arrived at the 69 Clam when Libbey was starting to close.

"Hey, kiddo! So how'd it go?" he asked ecstatically. She sighed.

"It didn't . . . Need any help?" she asked, skipping the subject.

"As long as I've been doing this? Morgue . . . I get it, code for moving on. What was the reason?" he asked.

"Lib, I just need to," she started.

"I get it . . . I'm sorry. How about you do the bar?" he asked, skipping the subject.

"How about I do it all?" she asked.

"What? No. I'm not going to ask you to do that."

"I've done it before. Have you already counted the register?" she asked him.

"Yes. How about we jam tonight? Old times. You can sleep upstairs," he suggested, trying to open her up.

"Good. I'll clean up. You get out of here and go home, Lib," she told him. "I don't want to bring you down."

"You're not! You don't have to finish here, Morgue. I can." He tried to tell her to stop, to rest.

"Yes, I do. Really, it's no problem, Libbey. I plan on chilling here awhile, so I'll make sure everything is done."

"Will you at least?" he mentioned in a concerned tone. She must have read his mind.

"Yes, I will call Max when I'm leaving. I told him I would anyway," she said, reassuring him.

"Okay, call me too when you officially close up for tonight and when you get home."

"Yeah, yeah . . . You sound like my mom." She chuckled half-heartedly. He felt for her.

"I'll be fine, Libbey, don't worry about me." By now she was ready for him to leave.

"I'm not your father, but I do worry about you, both of you." She patted his back as he made his way out the front door entrance.

"I love you," he stated to her before he got into his car. She watched him get in and drive away; she waved and smiled.

"I love you too, Libbey," she whispered. Her smile quickly faded. Something felt foreboding as she turned around and stared into the empty club space. The stage area was dark with chairs scattered across, while the bar was dimly lit. It vaguely reminded her of an episode of *Celebrity Ghost Stories* or various other television series based on the supernatural. She walked across the room toward the light switch and turned them all on to start cleaning everything. Having finished cleaning a few hours later, she sat down at the bar to try focusing on songwriting. When she looked outside faintly, she saw it was nighttime; almost pitch-black the darkness was except for a few streetlamps. She felt comfortable enough to hum an original tune and sing the lyrics she'd written down.

♪♫ *You'll find out sooner or later, this world don't care for you.* ♪♫

"Well, now I think that's a bit unfair," spoke an older man's voice; his voice, a stranger to her ears, startled her. She instantly dropped her pen and peeked out the crack of her eye in the direction she heard the voice to see the stranger sitting in one of the chairs she previously set up on the table. She knew Libbey kept a gun behind the bar counter; after all he taught her how to shoot, but somehow, she knew it wouldn't do her any good in this situation. Turning around slowly on the stool, she poured herself a stiff drink, sipped it, and asked calmly, "Who or what the fuck are you, old man?" staring him directly in his eyes, which were initially a golden brown, nothing menacing. Until in a blink his eyes became an intoxicating silver, brightening the more he smiled; laughing, he seemed very pleased.

"You're good . . . This is going to be fun," he said.

"I have yet to be amused," she said, unimpressed. "Who?" She caught herself before taking another sip. "What are you?" she asked again.

"It's funny, most people in this situation would reach for the gun behind the counter, start screaming, freaking out, not you, Morrigan," he finished.

"I figured you knew my name, it's only natural. I'm not going to ask the same question again," she finished sternly.

"I'm just an old man," he said softly.

"Old, perhaps but not a man. I've been in here for hours, no trace of you. I didn't even hear you move that chair. I wasn't that engrossed in my songwriting. Plus, I've seen you at the oddest times, tonight being no exception. I'm figuring you're just appearing. You've been watching me," she told him.

"I have," said the stranger, confirming her suspicions.

"So what do you want?" She figured he had to want something from her. His appearance softened.

"I want to help you, Morrigan," he told her as though he cared.

"Is that right? You want to help me. Why?" she asked in disbelief, slightly irritated.

"Because I see so much potential and passion in you. I've also saw your hurt, seen you crying inside, of course, since you hate crying on the outside," he said comically. That did kind of impress her. "Sometimes the world doesn't care, but you deserve opportunities to pursue your dreams and live! Not just exist on this miserable planet. The Divine cares. He wants the best for you and wants to show you just how much. So does your grandma." His words penetrated her soul; as unsure as she was about everything, she felt hope that he was telling the truth about God, that she wasn't lost or unlooked. However, something left her feeling uneasy.

"No, I . . ." She tried to dismiss him.

"He knows you don't believe . . . That's why he sent me to give you a message, some gifts," he said. She went to grab her guitar off the counter; he noticed.

"You really love that guitar, don't you?" he asked, startling her slightly.

"Uh . . . yeah, especially the person who bought her for me," she hesitantly answered.

"Libbey, right?" he guessed correctly. "He's a father figure."

"Yes . . . and my grandma pitched in some too," she answered softly yet nervously before playing a riff to fit the song she was writing; this was distracting her from the conversation that she wanted no more to be a part of.

"He's right, it is a beautiful song," he said to her while listening to her play. It made her think.

"I knew I saw you there that night at the hospital," she mentioned to him; he nodded his head in agreement. She continued playing while now keeping her eyes on him. Then suddenly there was a golden flash across his eyes that turned to silver.

"Oh, shit!" she exclaimed after her lower three strings broke suddenly. "Oh, I'm sorry for the language," she apologized when she caught herself.

"It's okay," he said understandably.

"That was odd. Damn! That hasn't happened in a while, least not so many at once," she thought.

"I'll restring it," he told her. "For you won't have to use yours."

"No, that's okay. Thanks anyway."

"Come on, it's one of my gifts to you," he said. Uncertainty plagued her mind, but ultimately, she figured what's the harm?

"You have guitar strings in that black bag of yours?" she smirked.

"Yes, actually I do. And I think you will like them." He crouched down to pull out a shiny pack of royal blue guitar strings.

"Hah!" she let out loudly, almost by accident. "Cute."

"You love them though, right?" he asked then smiled. She had to admit.

"Yeah, I do," she answered, happily pouring herself another drink. She watched him for what seemed like an hour. The way he made the process seem a process she knew all too well just restringing her guitar was now so alluring. She blamed it because of the circumstances, plus the alcohol. Immediately after placing her glass down, he announced he was finished.

"Done! You like them?"

"Uh, yeah, it's really cool! It's just my color and style! Thank you!" She went to place her baby back in its case when he stopped her.

"Wait, no, come on, you have to try it out first. Make sure it fits your sound, and you've got a hell of a sound, kid," he told her.

She thought for a minute, held her guitar in her hands, studied the strings, and brushed her fingers across them; a soft ringing occurred that seemed like magic. She didn't see anything troubling in his eyes to deter her, so she agreed.

"Okay, I'll play a lick." She strapped her ax on and started playing beautifully. It was intoxicating, the more ferociously she played, as her energy built up until suddenly she saw blood. A slight stinging from her middle and ring fingers followed, distressing her.

"Ouch!" she exclaimed surprisingly, pricked by an E. She sucked her fingers, then noticed that her blood was doing something irregular; it was trailing on the fret board purposefully, warping into strange symbols. The stranger chuckled; not saying a word he stood up slowly, took her guitar from her, placing it in its case. It was so easy; she couldn't move in any capacity, just frozen, until an extreme sharp pain shot up her left arm, causing guttural screams to escape her mouth. The pain became worse as some sort of aura took hold as the stranger disappeared in the shadows of the club space almost as easily as he appeared; she started crying. Morrigan fell to her knees as the skin on her arm boiled and blistered from an invisible fire. Slashes attacked her arm as her skin split; it felt as though she was being ripped apart as the torment spread. She couldn't see anything of what was happening, just extremely bright, almost blinding colorful sparks that surrounded her. She briefly thought to scream for help but figured it was useless. Eventually, her whole body went numb while trying to make it to her feet; she collapsed spot on the floor.

CHAPTER ELEVEN

"There's No Blister"

"Hey, Lib! Is Morrigan with you?" Max called him early the next morning, worried that she didn't return home last night.

"Huh? What?" he stammered out of bed, trying to catch his bearings.

"What do you mean is she with me? She didn't come home last night?" he asked, scared.

"No! And I'm worried . . . I called her cell several times and she never picked up."

"I'm sorry, Max. I haven't spoken or seen her since . . ." He thought. "Last night!"

"She didn't call you?" Max yelled over the mouthpiece.

"No! I figured she crashed. I didn't think to . . . You don't think she's still at . . ."

"The Clam!" they both shouted in unison.

"We have to try, Lib. I have a really bad feeling here."

"I'll meet you there in an hour. Try not to worry so much, Max. Calm down," he told him. "She's fine!"

"All right, I'll see you," Max said before hanging up.

They arrived at the 69 Clam exactly at nine o'clock in the morning; it was locked tight.

"Is everything the same, Lib?" Max asked him.

"Seems that way." He looked around before unlocking the front door, which could be locked from inside or out. Max stepped in first, flicking on the lights, not sure what to expect.

"Morrigan!" they both yelled as they ran to her sprawled out on the floor near the bar, slumped on her left side. She didn't awaken. Libbey ran behind the bar for water and a towel, yet noticed everything was in perfect condition. Nothing was out of place. Max kept hollering out her name before finally slapping her, which also didn't work.

"Here!" Libbey suggested. "Try the water!" Max splashed some in her face, still nothing. He really started to freak out.

"Cookie M!" he screamed while shaking her violently until her head hit the floor with a hard thud.

"Ouch! Fuck! Damn it!" she screamed when the jolt woke her.

"Stop it, Max! Are you trying to kill her?" Libbey questioned him worriedly. He used the towel to pat her head gently and dry her face.

"Well, she wasn't waking up. I'm sorry . . . Least it worked," he stated. He continued Libbey's efforts, brushing back her soaked hair.

"I'm so sorry, Cookie M. Are you all right? I didn't mean to hurt you, but you weren't waking up! I was terrified, I . . ." He looked at her; she was extremely startled, shaking even. Then his eyes caught attention to her arm. It was covered in various designs, a large snake being the central piece, vivid colors, and seemingly ancient scripts culminating in a massive sleeve tattoo starting from her wrist, and then he hurriedly pushed her shirtsleeve back and pulled her forward to see it rested on her shoulder blade. It shocked him to his core and scared the shit out of him more than what he was already.

"Cookie M, what have you done?" he asked her, concerned. Libbey also looked. However, he was speechless; he just slumped in a chair. She looked at Max a minute, and then noticed her fresh mutilation. Touching her arm, it stung for a moment until it got used to the flesh of her fingertips. It was her arm, but it no longer felt as hers. She felt sick.

"I don't know, sweets." She stared at him. "I don't know."

"What do you mean you don't know? You have a large fucking tattoo on your arm and you don't know!" Max screamed at her again.

"You're so melodramatic at times, Max," she told him indifferently, unlike herself. Both caught on to her tone. "It does state reason to be concerned, Morgue," said Libbey.

"I mean . . . I'm sorry. I think I know. I just can't remember it all that well," she started nervously.

"The fuck? That's the same as you don't know! I just can't believe this!" While he went on another one of his tirades directed toward her, she drifted deep into thought, staring at her guitar case on the bar table. Thinking about the strangeness of last night, as odd as it was, she knew it happened.

"Max, Libbey," she said abruptly. "There's no denying . . ." She tried to manage over Max.

"Max, shut the fuck up!" Libbey commanded. "She's trying to speak." Max stopped immediately. "Continue, Morrigan," he said.

"Thank you, Libbey. There's no denying what took place last night," she started. "The question is . . . will you two believe me?" she wondered. "Try us," Libbey said sternly. Before she told her recollection of last night, she wondered if her guitar looked the same. She ran to it and flung open the case and studied it. Everything was the same, except a few things. "I knew it. I knew it," she repeated to herself. "It happened."

"What, sis?" he asked, hearing her.

The inlays on the fret board were completely different. In place of white pearl dots were red inklings of veins or vines running up and down the neck with tear shapes and other symbols she couldn't understand. Plus, the strings were blue. A few tears slipped from her eyes. The second confirmation made her realize that everything happened the way in which she remembered it, as if the new markings on her arm weren't enough. She turned around to face them slowly, ready to relay her tale.

After she finished she took her guitar out and began to play; it calmed her despite the underlying haunt. She paused her playing briefly to look at them, reading their afflicted expressions.

"Do you two believe my tale of woe?" she chuckled. Libbey and Max stared at each other, thinking.

"Yeah, actually we do." Libbey broke the silence. "I didn't buy your Stratocaster designed in that way," he confirmed.

"Thank you, Libbey. You too, bro?" she asked.

"Yes," he answered softly.

"Why?" she asked.

"Your ax never looked that way before, plus I trust you," he answered.

Libbey walked up to her, grabbing her newly tattooed arm. "Plus, this . . . whatever this is . . . is completely healed! I can tell it's the real deal, not that it couldn't be faked to some extent, but there's no reason for you to go through all this. I've never known you to know professional makeup artists!"

"There's no blister?' Max asked.

"Not the one . . . No peeling, no scabs, or bleeding, nothing to indicate it was done recently. As if it's been there all along," he told him.

"And it hasn't," Max said.

"I know tattoos. Shit, I used to do them for a living. I can't believe I'm saying this, but this is something supernatural," Lib stated.

"This is too much!" Max ejected.

Morrigan laughed. "You're telling me . . . I think I might need to tell you guys about something else, it's this reoccurring dream I've been having," she mentioned nonchalantly.

"The one where you're on the playground?" Max asked.

"Yeah," she confirmed.

"Playground?" Libbey questioned.

"I keep having this dream where I'm a kid on the swings and this young dude approaches me and he's asking me this weird question," she told him.

"What's the question?" Lib asked.

"That's the thing . . . I can't hear it fully, only bits and pieces, but it's something about singing."

"Singing?" asked Max, confused. His phone started ringing.

"Don't answer that!" Libbey told him.

92

"He's handsome," she said softly.

"I wasn't, Lib. Wait . . . What do you mean handsome? So you can finally see him?" he asked curiously.

"Answer it, it's Kirk," she told him unexpectedly. He looked at his phone. "It is him, how did you . . ." He answered. Lib looked at her, wanting to question her knowledge of who called but dismissed it; instead he asked her, "What does he look like? Is it the man who you told us was here?"

"No," she answered. "This man is much younger, like maybe his middle, late twenties. The stranger from last night was much older, older than you, Lib."

"*Umm* . . . Cookie M?" Max interrupted. "Kirk has something important to ask you, it concerns the rest of the band too."

"Give it to me." She grabbed the phone from him before stepping into a corner, whispering and mumbling.

"What's that about?" Libbey asked him.

"I don't know, he wouldn't tell me, but how fucking weird is that, she knew exactly who was calling?" he stated. Before Libbey could respond they overheard her talking.

"I'll have to talk to my band . . . Yeah, I'll get back to you after. Okay, I will, thanks again. Bye." She hung up. "That was a kind of unforgettable phone call."

"How so?" Max asked.

"He called to tell me he knows this guy who is a tour promoter, whose supervisor put him in charge to organize this US concert tour for three or four months. The band he originally had in the lineup had to drop out, and he asked Kirk if he knew of any bands or solos who would be interested, and Kirk told him about us," she stated.

"Really? That's amazing!" Max exclaimed excitedly.

"Yes! He gave him our demo and got the callback today!" she said.

"Did he say why the other band declined?" Libbey asked her.

"Only that two members had something that came up that conflicted and they wouldn't go forward without them," she answered. "Anyway, he called him today confirming that we, Mystic, can have that opening slot if we want it!" she squealed.

"So what did you say, Morgue?" Lib asked.

"Hell yeah, we'll do it!" Max answered. "Sorry, continue, sis." She chuckled. "I told him I'll think about it and that I have to talk to my bandmates."

"What's to think about?" Max ejected.

"Again . . . Hell yes, we'll do it! Jasmine and Tim will agree, if not we'll just be a duo or two-person band like the White Stripes." He convinced her.

"Yeah, man!" she agreed.

"Wait," Max thought a moment. "What's the catch?"

"Not a huge one . . . But we must consider joining his label, well, supervisor's label after the tour lets up. This thing is for unknown bands mostly," she answered.

"What?" he asked.

"Before you frown, buddy, Kirk put in place a contract stating that we're not bound into having to sign to his label, that this tour is not a promise, just a consideration depending on how well they treat us, of course, and that he can't kick us off unless we're major fuckups who ruin it for everybody. Also, he can't sue us afterwards, like for the proceeds or merchandise, if he didn't like us. Very in-depth, I asked a lot of questions. We can see the paperwork before we sign on the dotted line. I see it as sort of a win-win. We publicize the heck out of him, his brand, and ourselves, while he pays for us. At the same time, we're showcasing our music and our talent. Libbey, what do you think?" she asked him. "Honestly, tell us."

He thought about it briefly; however, he was more concerned with what had transpired much earlier. "I think it sounds like a great deal for you, honestly, too good to be true, but worth finding out about. It's more exposure for you guys, I think you should go for it! I got your backs," he expressed sincerely.

"Woohoo!" they cheered.

"Stamp of approval from the Libmeister!" She goofed around.

"Really?" Max asked.

"Yeah, why not?" They chuckled.

"How long do we have to think about it?" he asked her.

"A couple of weeks," she answered.

"What's your first mind say, Cookie M?" he asked her.

"That we do it! But take at least a few days before we tell him that." They did a hand gesture in agreement.

"I'm really proud of you two," Libbey stated. "But haven't we forgotten about something?" They looked on in confusion. "What?"

"Are you fucking kidding me? The mysterious ink on your arm, Morgue!" he announced.

"Oh right, well, it's nothing I can do about it now. Plus, it looks really vicious!" she answered vacantly.

"Yeah, dudette, makes you look tough! It's cool!" followed Max in equal expression. Libbey just shook his head in disbelief and rolled his eyes. "Kids . . . Well, I guess you have a point. Keep your eyes open."

"Plus, maybe it's a good thing, Lib. Look, we got a tour," she told him convincingly. "Don't worry so much."

"Yeah, hopefully," he told her. Inside he was apprehensive about the whole situation. "We'll see," he thought to himself.

"Hey, hey, Lib . . . Come on." She walked around him, hugging him from behind, placing her head on his left shoulder. "You got to trust me. Are you going to miss us while we're gone?" she asked him sweetly.

"Of course, I'm going to miss you two cashews. You're my, y'all are like . . . my kids," he admitted reluctantly.

"Very specific nut . . . I'm more like a pistachio though," she joked. "Look, bro, he's going to miss us!"

"Oh, Dad, we're going to miss you too!" Max went to bear-hug him.

"Get off me, both of youse!" he yelled; she laughed at him, mocking him. "So are you going to help us pack for our first official tour?" she asked him excitedly.

"No," he said flatly. They looked at him all wide-eyed and disappointed. "Of course, I am! Although, I'd rather help you figure that out," he answered honestly.

"Woohoo!" they cheered, after slightly booing. "We got to stop by the storage. Most of our equipment is there, especially mine" she mentioned. "I also have to stop by my mom's house in a few days to tell her the obvious awesome news."

"How do you think she's going to handle it?" Libbey asked.

"It'll be different for her, me being gone for over a month, but she's strong, as you guys know. She'll handle it fine." She was unsure; her mother, Raven, is very blunt.

"What about the tattoo?" Max asked.

"I'm going to have to hide it until . . ." She trailed off. "Y' know how she feels about people being heavily tattooed. Not that I care about that," she finished.

"As we can tell," Libbey stated while referring to her many other tattoos.

"Shut up, Lib!" she fussed. "I just don't feel like explaining the obviously warped truth."

"Understandably," Max chimed in. "Good thing it's nearly September."

"You ain't lying, brother, you aren't lying." There was an awkward silence amid them, the three as a triangle, reminiscent of a Mexican standoff.

"Well." Libbey broke the stillness. "When are you packing?"

"We have time for that. I'll let you know. Want to tell Jasmine and Tim now?" she asked Max.

"Yes, milady!" he answered.

"Well, you heard the man, Lib! We got to hit, probably the end of the week though, cool?" she told him.

"Great! Now get the hell out of here for I can straighten this place up!" he joked with them.

"Whaa? Okay, Lib, we'll see you soon," she told him while grabbing her gear and jacket. Libbey looked to his right and saw on the table where Morrigan told them that the stranger sat was a glass of scotch. He couldn't remember whether it was there before; he wanted to ask them, but they were pulling off. Holding the drink in his hand, he stood there, looking at them out the window. "Lord, help us," was all he whispered.

CHAPTER TWELVE

A Few Days Later

"Okay, guys, act like you know how to behave in my mum's house," she told her friends sternly, speaking primarily to Jasmine and Tim. Max stood there immune to the whole situation.

"Hey, we're not idiots, Morrigan. We know how to act," said Tim, slightly offended.

"Yeah, especially your mom will kill us," Jasmine mentioned.

"Exactly! That's the point. Come on," she told them. All four started walking up the street, when Max motioned the other two behind Morrigan. "She's just nervous, you guys. Sometimes Mom can be a bit overbearing," he explained to them.

"Shut up, Max!" she snapped. "I don't need you talking about me behind my back to them like I can't handle my mom." She sighed. "He is right though. I'm nervous . . . I get this way sometimes when I talk to her, she's just so much sometimes," she explained. By this time, they had stopped walking; she continued to explain, "I love my mum, but sometimes . . . she can be unbearable. Quick to jump the gun!"

"Sounds like we've all been there," mentioned Jasmine.

"Wow, says the one who was in her own place at seventeen thanks to her parents," Morrigan snappily reminded her. "Sorry."

"I had to get there somewhere! They drove me to it!" Jasmine stated. "No offense taken, girl."

"Yeah, poor little rich girl," Morrigan joked; they all shared a laugh.

"I just don't want the time before we leave to end in an argument," she mentioned.

"Way to focus on the negative, Moor," Tim stated.

"You know, that's the same thing I said," Max agreed. She gave him an annoyed look.

"Okay! You're right! Pleasant thoughts, and good vibes, darlings." She tapped the temples of her head.

"You're such a hippie!" Jasmine told her while wrapping her arm around her. Morrigan responded by placing her hand over her mouth from behind and pulling her back. "You know I love you, right?" she told Jazz, kissing her left cheek. "Love you too," she responded. "We got you!"

"Yeah, I got you guys too." And Morrigan meant it. "Now let's roll." They all felt confident within themselves, while in that instant she rose more confidently, wearing some of her best witchy rock-and-roll garb, which consisted of a long bell-sleeved light fabric lace dress in navy blue, dangling around her neck one of her signature colorful cosmic and crescent moon necklaces, and her black platform boots clicking on the cobblestoned streets beneath her inspired her to sing softly. She knocked on her mother's door.

"Hey, Ma!" she greeted Raven. "Hey, Ruby!" They greeted each other cheerfully. "Hey, Mom!" Max spoke. She spied behind him familiar faces. "This must be serious. I see you brought the whole gang with you," she told her daughter. "Come on in."

"Yeah, Mum, it shows unity." She chuckled. "But this is serious. Sit down, please."

"Just tell me," Raven insisted.

"We're going on a three-month concert tour in the US in a week and a half," she told her confidently. She looked shocked, reading her daughter's facial expressions, she couldn't tell whether she was joking or not.

"What?" was all she could ask.

"We've already agreed. Signed the papers and everything, they're taking care of the bulk of it. All we need to do is pack. The bus will pick us up the end of next week. We're pretty much set," she finished.

"Papers . . . You mean contracts?" her mother asked her. "Yes," she said.

"I bet you didn't even have enough sense to have them professionally looked at," she told her condescendingly. "Or either one of you for that matter. You all signed, correct?" She directed her viper toward them all.

"You know what, Ma, I did! We did have the contracts checked out by lawyers. I actually do know some people. You're not the only one anymore. I'm not completely useless," Morrigan argued.

"And?" Raven asked sternly.

"And . . . it all checks out well and legit. Even Kirk signed and we all have copies. Done," she finished.

"By the way, I never said you were useless," Raven mentioned to her.

"Not this time," she corrected her.

"Well, I'm sorry if I did. I don't mean to sound upset. I kind of wish you would have discussed with me first before signing off. Three months, huh?" she stated disappointedly.

"Sorry, Ma, but after some thought we decided to jump on it. This is good for us, great exposure . . . I don't know, I thought you'd be happy," she said indifferently.

"I am! I genuinely am for you, the band!" She snickered softly. "I always knew it would happen. I just wish, as I said before, I would have been informed when you first found out. Plus, I'm a little worried. You all are going to be gone for three whole months! That is determined, right?" she asked.

"Yes, Mom," Max confirmed. She looked at her brother lovingly.

"Ma, the main reason why I didn't tell you and told Max not to is because I wanted to be prepared first before I, we, came to you with this. I love you, Mom, so please, come on, cheer up. Smile, smile!" She laughed.

"I love you too, Ruby, all of you. Okay, I get it. I understand, I'm proud of you. It's thrilling, isn't it?" she asked them excitedly.

"Yes, it is, Ms. Bloodchild. We can't wait!" Tim blurted out.

"So, Mum, we could use your organizational expertise for packing, think you can help us out?" she asked her.

"I bet!" She looked at all their eager faces, sort of wanting to crush them. "Sure, I'll help you."

"Whew! Awesome! Thanks, Ma." They were all relieved, for they knew things would be packed accordingly, at least during the beginning. Raven was no joke when it came to cleaning and organizing. Morrigan always felt she did it for fun.

"Hey! How about we have a going-away tour party or something?" Jasmine suggested to everyone.

"No, Jazz," Morrigan answered flatly, sort of cringing at the offer.

"Why not, girl? It's a cause for celebration! Plus, your mom is like our band mom. We could have it here, she'll cook, and we'll buy everything and help set up. I mean, if it's okay with you, Ms. Bloodchild?" she asked sheepishly.

"I think it's an awesome idea, Jazzy!" Raven announced in agreement. "But you all are going to help cook too." Morrigan rolled her eyes.

"Come on, Cookie M, don't be a downer. It's a cool idea!" Max tried to convince her.

"We have to rehearse," she told them.

"You have to rehearse 24-7?" Raven asked sarcastically; she gave her mom an annoyed look.

"Yeah, come on, sis! We could have it this weekend and still prepare, pack, and rehearse," he told her convincingly. Tim nodded in agreement. She thought briefly. "Sure, let's do it!" she agreed ecstatically. "We can get some stuff today."

"Great!" Everyone was ready in more ways than one.

"Ugh," Morrigan groaned. Her newly tattooed arm was bothering her slightly, an inside pain she dismissed, and no one noticed at the time.

"Come on! Mom, you want to ride with us?" she asked her mother.

"Yes, let's go," Raven responded. They all drove to the store, preparing for the weekend and the joy to behold. While driving back, Morrigan passed an elementary school still in order, one she used to attend. Next to it was an abandoned building, and glancing at it she felt a sense of familiarity; however, she can't recall what stood there before that condemned structure.

"Mom, what was that building before they shut it down?" she asked.

"An adult school for low-income and at-risk adults. Why?" she wondered on her sudden interest.

"Nothing . . . Thanks." She dismissed it.

The scene changed to a slightly blurred playground, a rather bright day with children playing; however, it zoomed in clearly on a little girl on the swings laughing, her hair in pigtails. Until suddenly, a tall man in a deep black suit with black cherry embroidery on his blazer approached her; he sat in the empty swing next to her and opened out his hand toward her.

"Hi, Morrigan, you have such a wonderful voice for one so young." His voice is pleasant, alluring. "Do you want some candy? You can have this and so many treats, if you come with me and sing for me and my friends." She's slightly tempted and looked what shows in his hand were candies of various sizes and colors that pleased her, but it morphed into a disgusting mixture of snakes and bugs. "Take this!" he commanded distortedly, blood red swallowing his eyes.

"No! I don't want anything from you!" Morrigan screamed out from a nightmare. Jack shook her until she woke up. "Huh? What?" she questioned in sweats.

"Babe, what's up with you? You've been waking up like this often lately. Freddy Krueger after you or something?" he joked with her. She chuckled at him.

"No . . . Not him anyway, but some . . ." She caught his expression of confusion, which changed her mind of explaining it to him. "It's nothing, just some weird ass bad dreams."

"Sure, you're right," he responded sarcastically. "And what's with that tattoo?"

"I told you, it's fake. To toughen up my image some more," she lied, and then took a cigarette out of his fresh box.

"Doesn't look fake." He rubbed it roughly.

"Stop!" she told him annoyingly.

"Since when do you smoke? You don't even like it when I do it, occasionally," he questioned her.

"Remember, my image," she said, taking a partial puff, but it wasn't in her. "You're right," she said before putting it out and searching in her purse for something.

"I never saw anything wrong with your image. You're a tattooed badass anyway!" He grabbed and kissed her passionately. "Didn't know you needed a sleeve to prove that," he said.

"You're right, I'm bullshitting you. I just want to try something new without the permanence," she told him, still lying. "Even though it is permanent," she thought to herself. She couldn't wash it off with anything.

"I guess I can understand that," he said. "Except, why the large snake, it's kind of cool though black with iridescent scales. What's these other markings?" He fingered the snake, trailing it; it started to make her feel uncomfortable. She pulled back.

"I don't know! It's something of a rainbow boa," she told him, like she had a choice in the design. As much as she hated to admit to herself, she loved the tattoo to a large extent, just not how it came about.

"Epicrates cenchria!" he stated the snake's binomial name matter-of-factly, which both impressed yet provoked her. "How the hell do you know that?" she fussed.

"I just do." He kissed her on her forehead, getting out of bed.

"Of course, you do," she told herself.

"Just like you know its common name," he said, smiling.

"I don't want to talk about snakes anymore or tattoos," she announced.

"What?" He pretended to be surprised. "Not you, no talk of tats," he joked with her.

"Yes, me, instead I want to invite you to Mystic's going-away tour party as Jazz describes it." She invited him. "It's this weekend. At my mum's."

"I'd love to, but you know your mom hates me," he reminded her.

"Whose fault is that?" she asked knowingly.

"Yeah . . . Babe, I don't know." He hesitated.

"I'll talk to her, well, prepare her, but you got to make that right," she told him firmly.

"I know, baby, I'll do that. I'll be there, but can we go together?" he asked sheepishly.

"Still scared of my mum?" she asked him jokingly.

"Of course!" he admitted. "Why wouldn't I be? I have another idea too, how about I take some time off, ride out to those cities with you?" he asked sincerely.

"How much time?" she asked, feeling him out.

"Three months," he answered.

"You wanna tour with the band?" she asked him.

"I want to see Mystic on tour! I'm sure my company won't be driven into the ground if I take a few months off," he told her.

"I can't let you do that," she said seriously.

"You're not letting me do anything. I want to do this for you, for us! Please?" he pleaded sweetly.

"You sure the advertising world won't miss you?" she asked him.

"Please, you've seen my office. They'll probably be thrilled I'll be gone for a few months." He reassured her.

"Nobody to get on their ass?" she joked.

"Amongst other things. Hey, but maybe I could take on the tour as a client? So we both could be working, I wouldn't just be your groupie." He laughed, asking her. "I could send stuff out from the road, and my office can handle it back here. Are they working with a company or is it DIY?" he asked her, not realizing the contention revolving his question. She clamped up.

"I don't know about that. I mean, I don't know." He caught her hesitation.

"Hey, I wouldn't be dealing directly with you, well, it wouldn't be like before. I mean that. I'll be dealing with the label. Uh, you can think about it. I won't make a move unless you say so," he said.

"Okay, yeah!" She smiled happily. "I'm excited about that!" she blurted out. "All of it!"

"Yeah?" he asked her. "Yes," she confirmed. "Excited enough to want to do this?" he asked, kissing her as she lay back.

"Maybe," she said, pinching him.

"Cute," he said, reciprocating by pinching her butt.

"Ouch." They laughed, before becoming entwined with each other again.

CHAPTER THIRTEEN

The Weekend

"**O**h, my god, this is so fucking great!" Tim exclaimed. Raven glared at him.

"Oops, sorry, Ms. Bloodchild," he apologized, feeling bashful. "Mm-hmm," she murmured.

"Where's Morrigan?" she asked. "It's odd the front woman not being at her own band's party."

"Uh, yeah, she'll be here soon," Max stammered, knowing she would be arriving with Jack. Raven caught that tone. "Max," she said.

"Huh?" He faltered.

"What do you know about Morrigan?" she asked him.

"Nothing," he said quickly.

"Max . . ." Her doorbell rang; it was them.

"Saved by the bell," he thought to himself. She went to answer, but Max ran in front of her. Morrigan and him had it planned that way. "I got it, Mom."

"Mm-hmm," she murmured before heading to the kitchen.

"Where's Mom?" Morrigan asked him.

"She just went to the kitchen, sis. I saved your ass and mine for at least temporarily," he told her. "Hey, Jack."

"Hey, Max." They spoke to each other.

"Thanks, bro. I'm going to go talk to her," she stated. Then Jack thought. "No, I'll handle it myself," he said. "I'll still come with," she told him as they headed into the kitchen. Before they could, Max grabbed her by the arm. "You might want to talk to Jazz again, before we leave," he said, motioning his eyes to her in a corner drinking out of a flask. Morrigan saw her and sighed. "Party has just begun," she stated. "I'll talk to her tonight."

"Okay, sis. Thanks." Then he let her go.

"Hey, Ma! Whatcha doing in here?" she asked pleasantly.

"Besides checking on the food?" Raven answered before turning around to look at her. However, her eyes signaled on Jack standing nervously in the kitchen near the door.

"Hello, Ms. Bloodchild," he greeted with his tongue slightly getting caught in his throat.

"You're a little old to be calling me Ms. Bloodchild, aren't you, Jack?" she asked him sarcastically. "Especially, after fucking my daughter."

"Mom!" Morrigan interrupted her. She glared at her daughter.

"Over," she continued with her statement, "when she's young enough to be your daughter."

"Mother dear, Jack actually wants to talk with you about what transpired between us those years ago. We've already discussed the issue, and he thought it was about time you two did as well," she told her mother.

"Well, why hasn't he said something to me?" Raven asked. Jack started to speak, but Morrigan interrupted him, placing her hand on his chest.

"He wants to. He's going to, but can you imagine why I haven't allowed him yet?" she asked her the obvious. "Anyway, Mum, just bear with me for a moment. I'm acting as the mediator, I'm not staying for the main conversation between you two. I'm just starting it off if you will. Now, can you two respect each other?" she asked them both.

"Of course," they both agreed. "Now, will you please hear him out, Ma?" she pleaded with her.

"Are you two back together?" Raven asked them.

"Yes, we are," they answered in unison.

"Okay. Morrigan, get out of here. Let us talk," she told her.

"Behave, you two," she warned them before walking out, taking a Dr. Pepper with her.

"It smells so delicious in here," Jack announced suddenly, referring to the aroma that filled the house.

"That's the shrimp and pesto basil Alfredo sauce, along with this seasoned chicken breast. I'm going to mix it all together just the way she likes it," she told him.

"I know. One of her favorite dishes, with fettuccini noodles?" he mentioned.

"Mm-hmm . . . So, Jack, what must you tell me?" she asked him impatiently.

"I want to apologize to you, Raven, about the past," he stated.

"Is it the past?" she asked him. "Is it truly in the past?" She looked directly into his eyes.

"I believe so," he told her sincerely. "Admittedly, I hesitated when Morrigan invited me to this, not because I didn't want to go and support her before she left, but because I was afraid to face you."

"You were right to be afraid." She chuckled. "However, if you come right, you have nothing to be afraid of. Least you're honest," she mentioned.

"Believe it or not, I do love your daughter, Raven. I love Morrigan. I regret the course of action I took in the past. And I'm not making excuses for myself, but she's so strong and independent," he stated.

"Don't forget stubborn. She gets all that from me," she admitted while sitting on a stool. "Have a seat, Jack," she told him. "Want a soda or something?" she asked him.

"No. No, thank you. I'm fine for now," he answered. "Listen, Raven, I wasn't used to a woman like her, so determined, so sure of herself, especially not in a young woman. She caught me completely by surprise, and it enticed me, but I admit I was also intimidated by her. I guess I wanted, or at least I thought I wanted, someone I could control or mold."

"Not anymore though, huh?" she asked him suddenly.

"Absolutely not! I was an idiot then. When I realized I didn't have someone like that . . ."

"Someone weaker? Hmm, more submissive?" she asked him, smirking. He shamefully paused, studying her expression.

"Yes," he answered lowly. "I foolishly thought I could make her be that type of person, woman," he said honestly. Raven laughed for a minute, then sighed. She had this all figured out before.

"Oh, you did, didn't you?" she asked indifferently.

"Yeah, but I know all too well now, nobody tells Morrigan what to do," he finished.

"I could have told you that," she said getting back up to check on the food, stirring the meat into the sauce. "Sure you don't want anything to drink?" she asked him again.

"Umm . . . Maybe a coke?" he questioned, sort of surprised by her insistence.

"No Coke drinkers here," she told him. "Try something else, something stronger. You know, Jack, I figured the first half of your relationship out when she first told me she was seeing you, not initially I may add, she took her time, kept you from me because she knew I would be against it, completely. See, I'm a mother, I'm supposed to know these things. You as an older man can hopefully appreciate this wisdom, initially you see these pretty young things and they're so wild and free, it's rejuvenating. But sooner or later that complexity kicks in. Either they want a little more security from you or you from them, then you're scared. Question is, are you willing to give more when it's needed then leave them be? My daughter is a free spirit, she always has been, along with being strong-willed. Sometimes, I think it backfires." She sighed, admitting something precious to him. "I've been guilty of that sometimes myself. Are you listening to me, Jack?" she asked him sincerely.

"Yes, I am. I am truly sorry for all the pain I caused your daughter and you. I think she still feels distrustful towards me," he shamefully admitted.

"Of course, she does!" she exclaimed. "Even I am, well . . . I was." She stood up, walked over to him, then leaned on the table. "You fucked up, royally. It'll take some time, but eventually I think she will fully forgive you. I'm impressed with you, so I'm going to give you a few more tokens of advice, this is your second act, and you two are going to be tested, especially you this time around. Don't ruin it. Also, continue to love her but leave her wild." She gave him a heartfelt chuckle, then tapped him on the shoulder. "Now go on out there and tell them the food is ready."

"Okay, Raven, thank you." He thanked her sincerely.

"Sure, now go on and make sure they get seated," she ordered him kindly.

"Yes, ma'am," he agreed before heading out. She shook her head softly, "Men," she said to herself.

Everyone was enjoying themselves while waiting to dine; over the exuberant atmosphere sporadic beats played. He spotted Morrigan over in a corner snatching something out of Jasmine's hand. He wanted to approach her, but Max stepped up in front of him.

"She's handling a situation," he told him seriously. "So how did it go?" he asked him.

"Better than I imagined. It was definitely worth it," he answered.

"Hey, Libbey! Jack's here!" he announced suddenly, scurrying off into the kitchen to help, along with not wanting to be present to that event.

"Food's done!" Jack announced, glaring at Max hurrying away.

"Jack," Libbey greeted him coldly, yet shaking his hand.

"Lib," he replied. Their reception was a cold one, opposite of the warmth surrounding them.

"Why are you here, Jack?" he asked him.

"Morrigan invited me," he answered. "I'm sure you know that already."

"Oh, I do! I know why you're here, but I'm curious as to why you're *really* here. What's your intentions with Morgue, Jack? Let's be honest, you two have been down this line several times before, is there a finish or an endless parade of hurdles?" he asked him. "Do you even know?"

"Interesting analogy, Libbey," he observed. "Do you really want an explanation, or are you perfectly content in playing the father figure routine?" He started to tap his chest with his fingertips, then turned to face him. "I care deeply about Morrigan, and I do love her, contrary to popular belief. I acknowledge I screwed up immensely, but I'm dedicated to being a better man to her than I was in the past." He tried to convince him.

"Father routine? Says the one who tried to set her up!" Libbey's voice flared, his body tensed up. That's all well and good, but—" Jack interrupted him.

"I made a very stupid mistake, a terrible mistake, and I'm trying to make it right!" he stated.

"Congratulations, Jack. I hope you can accomplish that, because despite how she may put on she really cares for you, about you. So here's a bit of fatherly advice, it sounds typical but why mess with perfection? If you break her heart again, or fuck up in any way . . . Believe me when I say this, if Raven hasn't already gotten to you first, I'll kill you," he stated, grabbing his shoulders firmly.

"I know, Lib," he said. "Can't say I'll blame you," he admitted.

"Good. Enjoy the party." He patted his back and walked toward Raven.

"So you survived times two? Awesome!" Max said, suddenly appearing alongside him.

"That was kind of screwy, Max. I thought we were buddies?" he jokingly asked him.

"We are buddies, but she's my sister and I'm shorter than you." He sipped his soda. Jack smirked. "Understandable. What's going on with her and Jasmine?" he asked him.

"Long story," Max answered.

"If you fucking try to grab this drink from out of my hand again, I'll beat the shit out of you," Morrigan threatened through clenched teeth, not wanting to disturb everyone. "Then there'll be a brawl in my mum's house, because you're a good little fighter too, but I like to win *any means necessary.*" She put the flask in her back pocket.

"Dinner's ready, girl." She tried distracting her.

"That can wait . . . This is important, Max asked me to talk to you, and I'm glad he did. I can't believe I didn't say this shit sooner," she told her angrily. "Now I'm not going to give you an intervention because I believe people only quit because they want to change for themselves and not before. And I also think people should have at least one vice, hence why I haven't said anything about the drinking . . . After all, I gave you this freaking flask. But that shit you're putting into your arms has got to stop, immediately! What are you going for, being another Billie Holiday?" she told her straight. "It's becoming a habit, and the thing I noticed with habits is it gets worse when shit gets serious."

"You can really be a bitch sometimes, Morrigan," she told her.

"That's the point, luv. Tsk, listen, dudette," she said, grabbing her head, bringing her face closer to hers. "I love you, and the band loves and cares about you, we just want you to be healthy. Can you understand that?" she pleaded with her, staring into her eyes.

"Yes, Morgue. I'm sorry, I'm going to stop. I promise, I'm going to get my shit together," she promised her repeatedly.

"Yeah?" Morrigan asked.

"I promise," Jasmine stated.

"I'm not going to have to kick you out of the band?" she asked her. Jasmine laughed lowly, sniffling through tears.

"No . . . I mean it," she reassured her.

"Okay, let's get some food in our bellies!" They hugged each other; with their arms still slightly wrapped around each other they walked toward the dinner table, all plates fixed and full of portions. Jack and Max pulled a chair out for them both.

"Everything all right?" Jack asked her.

"Yes, just a little girlfriend discussion," she told him.

"Really? Should I be worried?" he jokingly asked her.

"Oh, shut up." She laughed, slapping his arm.

From Kirk to Tim, to Libbey, to Jasmine they all sat down to eat, drink, and otherwise enjoy one another's company. Some told jokes, some questioned their feelings on the upcoming tour, while others expressed their general excitement with everything that was happening. Morrigan looked to each smiling, beaming face and couldn't help but fall for the optimistic scene; she had complete faith because at that moment they're a family and nothing was going to break them apart. None of them realized or even thought for a second this would be the last time all of them would be together, for a lot can happen in three months.

CHAPTER FOURTEEN

Seven Days Later

"Everything checked off the gear list, Max?" Morrigan asked him nervously. She was getting on his last damn nerve, pacing back and forth like an expectant father in a waiting room.

"Yes, Cookie M."

"The backup gear list too?" she asked him.

"Yes, Cookie M," he answered.

"What about our personal stuff, clothes, shoes, accessories?" she asked.

"Yes, Cookie M?" he answered monotonously. She sat still for a minute.

"Jazz still clean?" she asked.

"Oh my gosh! Yes, Morrigan!" he snapped. "They even called they'll be on their way here shortly. Thank you for talking to her by the way," he mentioned.

"No problem," she said before sitting down. Raven snickered to herself about their interaction.

"Ruby, everything is going to be fine." She tried to reassure her.

"Yeah, I know. It's just three months is a long time. I want to make sure we have everything," she mentioned.

"Whatever we forgot, if we did, we'll purchase on the road, okay, M? But I'm pretty sure we have everything we need. Except you girls are different, so I don't know," he said before sitting back down. She scoffed at his remark.

"Jerk," she mumbled.

"Just stating the obvious," he said. Raven decided to step in.

"Have you spoken to Jack yet?" she asked her.

"Yeah, about an hour ago. He's not coming here. He's going to meet us at the pickup location. He was still at the office, making sure they have everything set up between his firm and the label so that when we're gone he doesn't have to worry about anything when he sends out his information for the pieces," she finished.

"Well, see? Something you can relax about," Raven told her.

"Yes," Max said. "I'm certain this is going to be much different than our regular band van tours, but more awesome! Come on, sis!"

"I'm ready for it! Don't let this ridiculous outpouring of emotion mistake you, I'm game for this, we have everything we need almost handed to us, finally we've been given a break, everything else is on us. If we can't hack it during this tour, that means we really don't belong after all, which I know is bullshit! So we have nothing to worry about!" she promised ecstatically.

"That's what I like to hear, dudette!" he exclaimed. "We got this!"

"Yes, you all do. Don't ever doubt it, especially not yourselves, especially not now when you need each other more than ever. You're going to be on the road for a long three months, it might not seem like it, but believe it, it's going to be an extreme test with different people, different influences, temptation around every corner. You cannot forget what brought you together and put you on this path. Hold on to each other, and stay close to the cross, you're going to need it," Raven exclaimed to her children.

"Wow, bro, she sounds exactly like Libbey!" she announced.

"Yeah, she does," he agreed. They shared a heartfelt laugh before the doorbell rang; it was Jasmine and Tim, along with Libbey who was going to give them all a ride to the bus terminal.

"Hello, happy family!" Libbey greeted them all as they entered the home. "Are you all packed up and ready to go? I know these two are," he said, referring to Jazz and Tim.

"Yes, Mum helped us immensely . . . as usual," Morrigan stated.

"Yeah, they're ready. You guys got here in the nick of time, I thought my daughter was going to blow her top," she joked. Morrigan scoffed.

"I wasn't *that* bad," she stated.

"Uh, yeah, you kind of were," Max chimed in.

"Whose side are you on?" she asked him sarcastically.

"Okay, time to roll, bus leaves at twelve, better get a move on," Libbey announced. "By the way, where's Prince Charming?" he asked Morrigan.

"He's going to meet us there," she answered him.

"Mm-hmm, sure," he murmured, unconvinced.

"He is!" she sighed. "Give him a chance," she asked him.

"Maybe," he said.

"Yes, Lib give him a chance." Raven told him for her daughter's sake. "Well, a second chance."

"Damn, Rave, he got you too?" he asked shockingly.

"Yes and no . . . He might be legit this time, at least for Morrigan, think about it," she whispered to him. He thought silently, pondering her suggestion.

"Okay . . .," he said.

"Anyway, are you going to watch over my kids, our kids?" she asked him seriously. Morrigan sighed again.

"Ma, he can't hold our hands all the time. He taught us everything he knows over the years. The rest is on us," she told her.

"Yes, that's true," he agreed. "But I'll still keep tabs on them," he whispered to Raven. They giggled to themselves.

"Also, what's up with that tattoo, Morrigan?" Raven asked her as they headed out the door. The three persons aware of the secret surrounding it traded glances. "What, you thought I wouldn't notice? I'm your mom after all," she stated.

"It's a . . . It's a fake!" Libbey answered quickly. "She went to one of my old tattooist buddies he does makeup for Hollywood pictures now. You know how the kids are, they like to try new things without the permanent consequences of their actions," he joked.

"Oh!" she exclaimed, suddenly peering at Max, who sort of froze in his tracks. "I'm surprised you didn't get one, Max."

"Uh, no . . . Not me, I thought about it, but I don't need a lot of ink to know I don't want it," he said nervously. "Stupid," he thought to himself.

"Uh-huh? Well, if it's fake, right, Ruby? You have enough, you sure don't need a sleeve," she stated.

"Mom . . . You can never have enough tattoos, get real," she joked it off, before mouthing the words, "Thank You," to Libbey.

"Yeah, be a fool like everyone else then," she rudely stated.

"Ouch," Libbey remarked.

"I don't mean that!" Raven pleaded. "I'm sorry, you know how I feel about it. I have a few of my own, so forget I said anything."

"Yeah, yeah," Libbey said, before peering at a silent Morrigan, seemingly unaffected by her remarks. They finished packing the gear and suitcases in the truck and proceeded to drive.

"Bye, bye, house. We'll be rock stars when we see you again!" Morrigan exclaimed as she looked out the window. Jasmine cheered in agreement.

"Yeah, epic rock and rollers!" Tim exclaimed in agreement, joined by Max.

"And . . . there it starts." Libbey shook his head but smiled. Raven looked at him and laughed.

"They're good kids," she told him.

"No doubt . . . But still kids, in adult bodies," he mentioned.

"They'll be fine," she said.

"I hope." He worried.

"Hey . . . Us meddling kids are right in here, y' know," Tim stated, slightly offended.

"Old folks are granted permission to talk about you like you aren't there. Especially the owner of this vehicle, and unofficial band manager. So stump it." He laughed. Morrigan's phone rang. Blondie's "Hanging on the Telephone" played. She answered; it was Jack.

"Hey, babe, where are you guys? I've been here an hour waiting," he teased. "Also, Kirk is here." Kirk yelled over the phone. "And . . . I see some really cool surprises here for the band. Might want to speed it up." He amusedly laughed. "I can't wait to see you."

"Me too, sweets." She glanced at Libbey in the rearview mirror; he caught her stare and scoffed. He still wasn't impressed.

"We'll be there soon," she told him. "Keep your shirt on."

"I'll try," he replied, then they hung up, continuing on their journey.

"We have our own tour bus! How insane is that?" Max exclaimed after they finished packing everything in the storage compartment. He proceeded to jump on the bus, exploring the sleeping options before realizing it was a better dream in his head. "How in the hell are we going to sleep in these things?" he asked, referring to the tight berths tucked into the mainframe.

The bus was cramped with five sleeping berths, a small lounge area among it somewhere, something resembling a bathroom behind the berths, and finally an actual bedroom reserved way in the back; however tiny as it appeared, it was overall decent. Libbey laughed at Max's demystifying shock, partially reliving his own long-ago touring days.

"What did you expect, Max? A spacious living area with ample room for rehearsal, screwing, and whatever else your little rock-and-roll heart desires?" he playfully teased him. "Sorry, kid, they're nothing like that. Morgue, doll, brace yourself," he warned her. All of them got on exploring the interior.

"Least it smells good," Libbey and Jack remarked in unison, surprising them.

"You toured?" Libbey asked him, partially intrigued.

"Briefly. I was in a rock band in my day," he admitted to him. "We had a small following, enough to put us on the road for a while so I am aware of the bus myth," he finished.

"Wow! You didn't tell me that, Morgue," he mentioned.

"You never listened," she told him, rolling her eyes.

"Not bad, you understand the lifestyle," he said, shaking his hand. "So you're going to be with them on the road? The whole three months?" he questioned him. "You ready for all that entails?" He was curious to know if he could handle the pressure.

"Yes, I'm going to be working, too, so I won't be hounding her. Just supporting her. I'm really proud and excited for her, for the band," Jack stated surely. Libbey pulled him in closer this time outside of the bus. Morrigan and Max stared at them out the window.

"Wonder what he's saying to him?" he asked her.

"Most likely giving him the talk, you know Libbey, bro," she told him. While it irritated her occasionally, she understood his hostility toward him. She didn't want to admit it, but she still harbored some herself.

"Are you really prepared for this lifestyle, Jack? Being with a musician on the road, I mean, this is just the beginning. Have you really chewed down to the bone about this?" he asked, firstly trying to scare and test him, secondly trying to help him.

"I've talked to myself about it, I'm ready. I'm just going to take it one day at a time," he said unconvincingly.

"Mm-hmm. Okay, what if she sleeps with someone during it? What are you going to do? How are you going to handle it?" he asked concerned. "Going to jump ship?"

"I trust Morrigan," he told him convincingly.

"I know you do, she's trustworthy, but what *if?*" he asked him again.

"I'll cross that bridge *if* I get to it." Slightly irritated, he questioned his sudden interest in their relationship. "What do you care, Lib? Just a week ago, you threatened me for even being with her and now what? You're trying to school me in rocky road relationships 101? Pardon the pun," he argued.

"Listen, Jack, I'm not that much older than you so man-to-man." He sighed. "I'm worried about her, the band too, but mainly Morrigan. I'm not going to be there 24-7, but you partially are. I can trust Max is going to do his part, but I'll appreciate it if you truly care about her to do your part and look after her," he pleaded.

"Of course! I'll do everything in my power, but where is some of this coming from? Is there something else going on I need to know about?" he asked, seriously freaked by his insertion.

"No! No, just watch, fight, and pray." He realized his tone; trying to reassure him, he told him good luck. "I'm sure everything will be fine, just be careful . . . Good luck, Jack."

"Thanks, Libbey."

"Hey! What are you two whispering out here amongst the trees and engines?" Morrigan asked them as she and the rest of them got off the bus.

"Oh, nothing, sweets," Jack responded. "Libbey was just giving me the father talk."

"Yeah, that's Dad all right." She humored. "Thanks for getting him in check, Pops."

"It's what I'm here for," he stated. "You guys like your mobile home?" he asked the other two.

"We'll manage," Jasmine told him. "So I guess the main bedroom goes to the front woman?" she asked, referring to the back bedroom.

"Of course! I'm going to need my beauty sleep," Morrigan joked. "But we can share sometimes," She told her.

"Actually, you three might have to fight over it sometimes," Jack said, referring to Max, Jasmine, and Tim. "I'm going to be traveling in that gorgeous beaut," he mentioned, pointing to his darkly colored RV in a short distance; it was relatively the size of the tour bus, just better laden inside.

"If you want, my darling, you can ride with me when you get tired of sharing the tour bus life," he offered, hoping she'll accept.

"Oh, how will I start my touring diary if I do?" she joked, hugging him gently. "Thanks, babe."

"He came prepared," Raven stated. "I'm liking you more again already." They laughed.

"That's just temporary, everyone," Kirk chimed in. "If all goes well, they'll supply the bands with better, more spacious buses."

"Don't hold your breath," Libbey whispered.

"I'm going to be riding with you all the whole time, sometimes on your bus, but mostly separate," Kirk continued to explain. "Since I'm acting as your de facto road manager, being paid by the label, of course, don't freak!" he joked. "Anyway, continue to come to me with any concern. Also, in case you all didn't know, I'll be in great touch with Libbey too. Two club owners/managers sticking it out together. So . . . I think that's everything! Time to get on the road, we have to get to the hotel by two thirty. Rehearsal by five thirty, and your first show by eight PM sharp. Well, Mystic will promptly be on by nine o'clock. Yeah, I think that's it," he finished excitedly.

"So soon?" Jasmine asked, a tinge of anxiety in her voice. "I just thought we'd have a day to chill, I guess."

"No more chilling, darling, welcome to road life," Kirk said.

"You all right, Jazz?" Morrigan asked concerned. "You ready?"

"Yes! Absolutely!" she answered chirpily.

"Good! Because we got this!" Morrigan stated confidently, motioning them all in for a group hug. "I believe in us, there's no turning back now. So let's look at this moment and leave whatever negative thought behind and focus on the coolness of now. Good vibes, everybody!"

"Hippie!" Jasmine lovingly teased her. Morrigan grabbed her mouth again.

"Hippie-punk," she funnily corrected her.

"You guys need to head out now," Libbey reminded them.

"Wait, Ruby, don't forget to call me when you get there and keep me up-to-date with everything. Okay?" Raven reminded her.

"Of course, Ma! Don't worry, we won't," she said, also referring to Max.

"They can't call you every second, Rave. They have to work." Libbey picked with her.

"I don't want them to every second, just . . . You know what to do, have fun, best of love, and get out of here, you should go. Don't want you to get held up. I'm going to miss you," she finished, hugging her daughter. They shared their goodbyes, hugs, and waves, sending them off proudly. Raven and Libbey looked at each other in the wake of a brief sadness. Analyzing the situation Raven spoke, "They're officially all grown-up."

"Yeah, you did well, Mama Bear," Libbey commended her.

"I know!" she beamed a great smile.

"Want to get something to eat?" he asked her.

"Yes! And drink!" she exclaimed.

"Let's cool these emotions off," he agreed, as he started his car.

"You cool?" Jack asked Morrigan.

"Yes," she answered. "So you sure you can make it with us?" she asked him.

"Yes! Listen, I'm here for you. No matter what!" he responded deeply, grabbing her hands.

"Um, that's good to know, really. But I meant following us to the hotel," she told him.

"Oh. Yeah, yes, I have the directions and everything. It's handled," he confirmed, showing her the paperwork.

"Great. Don't want you getting lost," she said.

"Oh, never that," he said as he kissed her on the lips.

"Come on, lovers, let's move this show on the road!" Max yelled at them from the bus.

"Got to go, babe! Later," she told him as she ran toward the bus opening. She quickly got on, giving Max a kiss on the cheek, then stared out.

"Let's rock the shit out of them! Woohoo!" Morrigan exclaimed before shutting the door.

Kirk introduced them to the driver; his name was Jerry, a sort of burly dude, who knew Libbey a bit from the day. "It's my duty to get you all there safely and surely, so hang tight!" he told them.

"Awesome! Thanks Jerry," she thanked him. "So how'd you know Libbey?"

"Long story, but mainly from gigging and venues. I'm also a guitar tech and part-time roadie," he answered.

"One of the best in the biz!" Kirk commented. "He could be yours if you want? Got to ask him that though. Couldn't have better."

"You bullshit, Kirk." Jerry laughed.

"Really?" she wondered, looking back and forth between them. "If you don't mind the extra load from an up-and-coming 'possibly annoying but totally grateful' band?" she asked him.

"You're sweet. Sure! I mean it, I'll be at your rehearsal," he said seriously.

"Yay!" she said ecstatically. "Hey, Kirk, when are we going to meet the other bands?" she asked.

"If not at the hotel, definitely at sound check," he answered. "We'll introduce you before the performances."

"Cool," she thought.

"I wonder what they're like?" Jasmine asked, thinking of their personalities.

"Who cares? We're here for us, not them," Morrigan said plainly.

"Are you always so sure?" Tim asked, disbelieving.

"No, but as long as they're respectful towards us, I'll respect them too," she answered honestly.

"I can agree with that," said Max. "Hey, did the tour bus come equipped with this decor?" he asked Kirk, curious of how perfectly it matched Morrigan's moody, hippie style. Among the wooden vinyl, the bus had a royal blue plush carpet, with similarly colored couches of eggplant-colored paisley print etched on them; however the lighting could be adjusted. The bedroom was similar, dark blues with various lavender shades, and black accents filled the space as the bedding.

"You've noticed that, huh?" he answered. "I thought that it matched Morrigan's taste well, I wanted something to make you guys comfortable."

"Well, you'll need more black, if you're including me," Jasmine mentioned.

"Yeah." Morrigan scoffed. "Like that's happening. Thank you, Kirk. I appreciate you looking out."

"No problem," he said. She took out her acoustic guitar and started playing a song.

"That's pretty cool. What's the name of that?" Kirk complimented.

"'Lavender and Teal,'" she answered. "It's unfinished though, can't get the words just right, but the music is finished." It was a dreamy, ethereal tune perfectly played acoustically. That made Kirk a little nervous to hear.

"Uh . . . Y'all do have plenty of finished songs, right?" he asked anxiously.

"Of course, Kirk! Chill out, we're perfectly prepared," she assured him.

"Yeah, I trust you. Okay, we're getting close to the hotel now. Look alive, people!" he announced. They pulled up to a Courtyard Marriott somewhere in Maryland. It was a slightly busy area filled with chain hotels and various office buildings, still in the urban area.

"I'll be right back, I'm going to check us in and get the keys," Kirk announced stepping off the bus.

"Thank you, Jerry, you got us here safely," Morrigan told him.

"I told you, now let's get you guys unloaded," he said.

"Shouldn't we wait for Kirk?" she asked him.

"No, he's a professional. Everything is taken care of," he told her confidently. Kirk stepped out a few seconds with a few key cards, and paper receipts.

"Let's get you guys inside!" Kirk exclaimed. Jerry looked at her. "Told you." She smiled. Jack came stepping up a few minutes later with a few bags of his own. "I got to do our room. I'll be right back, babe," he told her.

"Our room?" she questioned. "Never mind," she said.

"All right, the band is sharing two rooms, two double queen rooms. Cool?" Kirk told them.

"Absolutely!" Max agreed. "Even though Cookie M probably won't be with us that much."

"Whatever, dude!" she remarked. He laughed.

"My gear is coming with me," Morrigan said seriously. "All of you need to take your gear with you," she ordered the band.

"All right, Mom," Jasmine sniped.

"She's right," Kirk agreed. "Take it from me, you don't want to have your gear stolen before a show or period if you can help it." They met Jack inside in the lobby.

"A key for you two." He gave to Morrigan and Jasmine. "And you two." He gave to Max and Tim. "So it's two o'clock, we're making good time. Get acquainted with this place, we're going to be here for about a week. I'll see you all back down here at four forty-five for rehearsal at five thirty with your gear. I'm in room 717, same floor, so buzz me if you need me," he finished, heading to the elevator.

"I'm in room 732," Jack whispered to her from behind. "If you want to stop by and hang out after practice." He flirted.

"Perhaps, later," she told him, kissing his cheek. "Let's go, you guys!" she told them. He helped them in their rooms, rolling amps and suitcases.

"Seems silly taking all this stuff upstairs, when we have to take it back down later," Max complained.

"Don't start, Max. Like we're going to have to do all week. How about this, you leave your stuff on the bus? It should still be there this evening," Morrigan reasoned with him.

"Hopefully, some wannabe rocker kid doesn't spy your shit." Jack supported.

"Um." He looked to Jasmine and Tim, who looked equally unsure at him. "You're right, I'll let my stuff stay up here." They smirked.

"These are nice rooms! Much better than that bus, but I'm not complaining." He tipped his head to Morrigan. She playfully slapped it.

"Ouch! Sis," he said. Each room had a conjoining door that connected it. The rooms were nicely spacious, with gray exterior and two colorful geometric-shaped paintings adorning a wall near the chair. Each room was identical to the other, white bedding, nothing fancy, clean, a basic television, coffee maker. The bathrooms had the usual amenities, hair dryer, iron and ironing board, small bars and bottles of soap and shampoo.

"I'm going to need a shower before the show tonight," Jasmine said, flopping on her bed near the door.

"I'm going to need one, too, we probably can drop by here after rehearsal," Morrigan stated. "You guys want to go over the songs we're going to rehearse and play tonight?" she asked them.

"We can do that at rehearsal," Jasmine said. "I want to explore this place some more. You game, Tim?"

"Absolutely." He grabbed her hand, lifting her off the bed.

"We should have something planned, for we won't have to get there and start thinking of something to play. That wastes time," she mentioned.

"Oh, come on, Morgue. Like you don't have two lists, one for rehearsal and show. I saw you scribbling in your notepad," Jasmine teased playfully.

"She does," Max supported.

"Okay, so when we get there don't complain, 'cause I ain't hearing it," she told them straight.

"Whatever," they said before walking out. Morrigan rushed after them. "You guys got your key cards, right?" she asked them.

"Yeah, we got them," they said without looking.

"Are you sure?" she asked. They searched in their pockets briefly.

"See?" They showed her.

"All right, peace!" She let them go, fanning them away. "What kind of room did you get, sweets?"

"One king and sofa bed," he answered, sitting on her bed.

"Ooh, nice. How about a celebratory fuck?" she asked him, grabbing his face, kissing him passionately.

"You're a dirty little twist, you know that?" he responded equally as filthy, picking her up in his arms.

"You love it," she told him.

"You guys are disgusting!" Max remarked. "Get out of here! Now!" he commanded.

"You heard him, sweets!" Jack said, proceeding to take her out the room.

"Oh, you know where my green journal is?" She struggled, trying to talk to Max. "That's where the song lists are. Just go over the songs for me, please," she playfully screamed as Jack tried to drag her. "Okay?" she yelled.

"I got you, sister!" he yelled back, shutting the door. "Kids," he thought to himself.

They undressed each other quickly, throwing whatever loose clothing on the floor, until they were just down to their underwear. His hand followed along her inner thigh, his fingers teasing her until he swiftly took off her panties, a blood orange lace with hot pink bows on each side. She lay there across the bed innocently enough, exposed, awaiting him, then suddenly she sat up on her knees.

"Stand up," she told him, removing the last article of his clothing, his boxers. He jokingly tripped, making her giggle. She went to her purse to grab a condom, which she placed on his tumescent penis, placing the tip between her lips to roll it down.

"Okay, now turn me over," she ordered him softly, indicating she wanted him from behind.

"Whatever you say, darling." He got on his knees to grab her waist, lifting her hips to angle with him. He entered her slowly; with each inch going deeper, she moaned softly. He pumped her slowly. "Harder . . . Harder," she begged and he served. "Oh, fuck!" She groaned with each solid force. Slowly beginning to lose her time, she glanced at the clock. It was four twenty.

"Oh, shit! Get up, Jack!" she yelled. He declined, driving her harder. She moaned passionately.

"Let me up, Jack!" She pushed him off with medium force; he fell to the side. "Shit!" he exclaimed, as she flew into the shower.

"Sorry, babe, if you want to join me, you better do it now!" she announced to him over running water. He ran to meet her.

"I was so close," he admitted to her, jumping inside, pulling her close to him.

"I know, babe, but—" he interrupted her. "I know. I get it."

"We can kill two birds with one stone. You better finish now," she suggested. He wasted no time, lifting her by her thighs, getting inside of her. His sudden force slightly slammed her against the porcelain tile. "Aah!" she uttered harshly, wrapping her legs and arms tightly around him.

"Did I hurt you?" he asked sincerely.

"No, no," she uttered in gasps.

"Good," he moaned. They finished in unison, with enough time to get dressed and meet everyone downstairs; the only problem was Max is the only one in the lobby.

"Where's the rest of them?" Morrigan asked, referring to Tim and Jasmine.

"Don't know," Max said.

"It's only four forty. They still have time," Kirk mentioned, looking at his watch.

"All right," Morrigan said, sitting down. Jack joined her.

"So what were you two doing?" Max knowingly teased them. They glared at him. He giggled. "Sorry, I asked." It was four fifty-six.

"You know, we probably could've finished how we originally planned," Jack whispered in her ear.

"Ha-ha," she sarcastically remarked. Max overheard him, and chuckled.

"Fucking text them, Max!" she ordered. As he was about to, she saw them walking toward them without their gear.

"Never mind. The fuck was you guys doing?" she asked them argumentatively when they approached.

"We were in another band's room next door," Tim answered, laughing.

"Did you know you can connect to the other hotel from the second floor?" Jasmine asked excitedly.

"Yeah, I know, I saw the sign," Morrigan confirmed flatly.

"What's going on?" she asked her.

"You two are late," she said tensely. Tim looked at his watch, it was five o'clock.

"It's only five," he said immaturely.

"Yeah, Morgue. No biggie!" Jasmine mentioned.

"You're fifteen minutes late. And you don't have your fucking gear!" Morrigan argued.

"Oh, sorry. I guess we forgot," Jasmine apologized frivolously.

"You guess you forgot?" she asked sarcastically.

"Cookie, M," Max said, trying to calm her down. She dismissed him.

"So that's probably going to take you another five minutes or so to get, right?" she asked them, sighing. Everyone listened.

"Are we expected by five thirty, Kirk?" she asked him seriously.

"Um, yeah," he uttered nervously. "But I'm sure we'll get there by that time, I'll just call them and say we might be a little late. No problem!" He scurried off to make the call. She looked at them furiously.

"Sorry, Mor—" they stuttered.

"Just get your shit and come on!" she agitatedly interrupted them. They walked briskly toward the elevators.

"Well, that's telling them." Jack tried joking, managing a stifled chuckle. She glared at him. His head dropped; he could tell she wasn't feeling it.

"I'm sure it won't happen again, M." Max tried to convince her.

"Don't defend them, Max," she told him.

"I'm not defending them! I'm pissed they're working on twenty minutes my damn self, but let's just move forward for the rehearsal. We can talk to them later," he told her.

"It's a damn shame, dude! Our first day on tour, first rehearsal, and they're already fucking up! We have a show tonight!" she argued.

"Don't worry, they won't fuck up that," he told her. "They're just excited."

"I'm excited, too, but I still got my ass down here with five minutes to spare with a set list," she explained. "You were down here, before me."

"By only a few minutes," he said.

"You're making excuses," she told him.

"Listen, you're right. Okay, you're right. I agree with you," he tried telling her.

"You know what, I'll be fine," she admitted, slightly tensed.

"Chalk it up as youthful exuberance, Morrigan," Jack explained to her calmly.

"Thank you, Jack," Max said. "Here they come." He noticed, pointing at them.

"Gang all together!" Kirk remarked, coming to join them.

"In a manner of speaking," Morrigan grumbled. Max tapped her.

"Ready? Let's get this equipment on here," Kirk said, as they traveled out to the bus. It took them about thirty minutes to get to the spot.

"How long's our set?" Morrigan asked Kirk.

"Forty-five minutes, luv," Max answered.

"Great! I have ten songs marked down, some of our best, I think. We may or may not perform all ten, depending on how the rehearsal goes. However, I do want us to start with 'Finger,' it's short, loud, and fast, it'll make a statement. Show them what we're about. Then we can finish with a longer track, like 'Mr. Tyler Brown,' or something. Max?" she finished.

"I looked over it, I think it's solid, also I took the liberty of circling the definite eight we should do," he said.

"It works. I love it," Tim said.

"I don't want to do 'Finger,'" Jasmine suddenly stated, looking over the list.

"Like I could give two fucks," Morrigan told her meanly.

"I was just joking," she responded lowly. Morrigan scoffed, strapping on her guitar.

"Not the time, Jazz," Even Tim warned. "Come on, let's play," he muttered.

"Oww!" Morrigan vocalized, before hitting into a rapid-fire punk riff. They all met her when she sang the first word, and it was magical.

Overall, it was a good rehearsal, not as dynamic as Morrigan originally envisioned, but it rocked. They worked out some kinks, dropped "Mr. Tyler Brown," played around with various interaction techniques (despite her slight irritation from earlier), and felt thoroughly prepared for the show that night. Cheers broke out for them as they finished up.

"Thank you, thank you . . . I would like to thank my awesome bandmates for helping to support my vision," Morrigan joked.

"Aww, she still loves us, Tim," Jasmine remarked, running to hug her.

"I'll always love you two fools. I just didn't like you too much earlier. You know how I get when I'm ready for business if I see you slacking, I'm going to snap," she told them, returning the hug.

"Yeah, I know. You had all right to snap, we were in the wrong, and I'm sorry," she apologized.

"I'm sorry too, seriously," spoke Tim.

"Just don't do that again. I might not be able to hold her off next time!" Max jokingly warned.

"Oh, get bent, Max," she told him.

"If that's the rehearsal, you guys are going to give them hell tonight!" Jack honestly complimented them.

"He's right, that rocked!" Jerry agreed. "I'm seriously impressed and honored to be a part of your road crew."

"Wow!" Jasmine exclaimed, feeling awesome.

"You shouldn't tell us stuff like that, it can get to our heads," Morrigan jokingly insisted.

"Come on, let's get you guys ready for tonight! We still have time, let's get y'all back to the hotel," Kirk explained excitedly.

"Whew! Awesome!" Morrigan jumped offstage wearing a beat black wide-legged jumper paired with a yellow-green short-sleeved shirt, and placed her guitar in its case and into Jack's hand.

"She's putting you to work in more ways than one, huh?" Kirk noticed, messing with him.

"Yeah, I can't complain," he answered, helping to carry her gear.

"Mystic, we're out!" she announced, then they headed to the bus.

"Dudette, is the back straight?" Morrigan asked Jasmine as she prinked over herself in the mirror for thirty more minutes. She was wearing gray skinny jeans with black ankle boots, her blouse a lace violet color paired with a black under bust corset that had a slight floral pattern of similar colors.

"Dude, you asked me that already!" Jasmine exclaimed wearing a long-sleeved white lace dress that came to her knees, slightly irritated. "Yes, the bow is straight. You look fantastic! Now, come on we should get out there for this sound check, you of all people should understand. Also, I want to introduce you to the band we met. I think the drummer's pretty cute."

"All right, I'm looking hot, you look hot, we're sexpots!" Morrigan told her.

"Always!" she agreed. They walked out into the concert space in enough time to see one of the accompanying bands finish their sound check.

"Wow, you guys are freaking awesome!" Morrigan complimented them. "I can't wait to see you guys perform tonight!"

"Same here. I love your style, it's like punk blues, folk metal! That's fucking cool!" said William, the front man of Danger Prone, a pop punk band from California.

"I guess I don't need to introduce you all," Jasmine remarked.

"No, you still can," William said, eyeing Morrigan.

"She's our front woman as you know, her name is Morrigan," she told him, before whispering, "She has a boyfriend," while tilting her head back.

"Damn," he mumbled under his breath when he noticed Jack in the background.

"Anyway, that's the cutie drummer," she whispered to Morrigan, pointing him out. "His name is Rick."

"Not bad, a blondie, he's a doll. Kind of dreamy," she responded.

"I thought so too." Rick was your long-haired type, charming and seemingly, but something was behind that sweetness. "You know how I feel about dating musicians though, as hypocritical as that sounds . . ."

"It's valid," Morrigan finished her sentence. "It's mainly the person to look at for themselves, but it doesn't help almost all of them act the same."

"Men suck!" Jasmine remarked, thinking about her past relationships. She tended to date jerks, drug addicted, interested only in one thing, jerks; however, no guy she dated got her hooked. Jasmine was no angel; she started drinking when she was thirteen on account that she was a trust fund baby with parents that shouldn't have had children; they were unconcerned with watching and properly raising a child. Over time, her alcoholism went up to some recreational drug use in the six different bands that she was in; however, all that simmered down when she met Morrigan and Max to join Mystic until recently. They felt like a family to her more than one she ever knew.

"What do you think, M?" she asked her, wanting to know her thoughts on him.

"Introduce me to him," she said.

"Hey, Rick! Come over here," she called him over to them.

"This is Morrigan, she's my sister, band sister, sister-sister." They laughed, sharing their hellos and handshakes.

"You excited about tonight?" he asked her.

"Yes, is this your first tour?" she asked, noticing his slight nervousness.

"First actual funded one, it feels good for someone to take you seriously for once, y' know?" he mentioned, something Morrigan felt all too well.

"You're preaching to the choir, man," she told him, patting his shoulder.

"Do you know who the third group is?" he asked.

"No, I haven't even met them yet," she answered.

"Neither have we," he said, referring to his band. "I don't even think they're here yet. First show starts at eight, what time do you all go on?"

"Nine," she answered.

"We go on before you, at eight o'clock," he told her. "They must be pretty special, don't have to show up for sound check."

"Or the opening acts . . . They must be a popular band." She pointed out.

"You're right, I guess we'll see at ten PM."

"Yep . . . Hey, Max! Come meet Danger Prone." She introduced them to each other. "Is that a Scooby Doo reference?" she asked them, laughing.

"How'd you guess?" William chuckled. "My sister inadvertently inspired it, she's a lot like Daphne."

"Red hair and all," Rick mentioned.

"Danger Prone! Are you guys ready? Your manager asked me to prep you guys," Kirk mentioned before glancing over Mystic.

"We've been ready!" William laughed, throwing his arms up. "Is it time for us to go on?"

"Not yet, we have to move to the upper-level concert area. That's where you all are performing."

"Kirk, who's the other band?" Morrigan asked.

"You all will see at ten," he vaguely answered. "Be patient."

"Curiouser and curiouser," Morrigan remarked, while they all headed upstairs.

"We're Danger Prone, go get a bone, doggies!" William yelled into his mic before blazing into their set.

"Wow, isn't their set fun?" Tim exclaimed over the music and cheers. Danger Prone had the crowd moving, semi-moshing with their upbeat, spastic music and kooky lyrics.

"Absolutely! He's definitely a good drummer," she said, turning to Jasmine. "Take your time with him, gurl, don't hurt him too bad," she warned her.

"Always." Giggled the girls.

"Is Mystic ready to take control of this show?" Jack asked, appearing behind Morrigan.

"Ooh, baby . . . You spoil me. There's another group after us, sweets," she humbly mentioned.

"And?" he said, kissing her cheek. "They're only going to be thinking about you guys."

"Shh," she shushed him, pecking him on the lips.

"All right, all right, thank you guys so much for the love! We are Danger Prone!" William exclaimed to the crowd. "Now, it's not in my job description, but I want to introduce this next band to you, beautiful ones. We saw them during sound check tonight, and they're incredible. We believe you're going to love them too. Put together a huge round of applause for Mystic!" He bounced off the stage. It caught them all a little off guard, realizing it was their turn.

"What are you waiting for, goddess? Make them scream in ecstasy," Jack cajoled her, kissing her neck. "Make them want more. Come on, you guys!" Kirk was waving at them to come up. They made their way to the stage slowly, each one walking on the stage in a predetermined act. First Max, with his drumsticks in hand, sat at his kit, then Jasmine went to the side mic, picked up her guitar, thirdly Tim, with his bass in tow, until lastly Morrigan stepped up to the center microphone, strapping on her guitar, a shimmering metallic blue; she shined underneath the multicolored lights. She looked out toward the audience and spotted her mom and Libbey, standing next to Jack. Naturally, gleaming she waved to them, then she started to speak.

"Hello, my freaky darlings . . . Thanks for the blood warm welcome!" she greeted the audience in her usual eccentric manner. "Wasn't that the sweetest thing he said! You guys, it was a great set, they really rocked it, so give it up for Danger Prone one more time for us! Thank you! Now, y'all ready to hear some more rock and roll?" she screamed enthusiastically. "Lemme here you, are you ready? Let's go!"

"Finger" starts playing.
♪♫ Oww! Now, do you understand? I don't want you in my bed. I don't need, no, never need another hole in my head. I'm putting my foot down, no, I'll never come around, keep pressing your finger on my nerves, you're bound to lose it. ♪♫

They played an intense four songs ranging from punk feminist realness to ethereal storytelling. During a brief interlude, Morrigan thought it was the perfect time for introductions.

"While we transition into the next half of our set, I want to introduce you to my bandmates. One of the best drummers I know and best brother, too, give it up for Max! To my left, show your love for my sister Jazz, keeping me in harmony, and to my right, my brother, bassist Tim helping to shower us in rhythm. And me, well, I'm Morrigan. I also want to do a shout-out to some important people in the crowd, my mom, and our mentor. I didn't think they would make it out tonight. So that's awesome! And another one of my good friends." She waved to them again, smiling. "I love you guys. Okay, enough with the sappy stuff, let's continue with the show. You guys ready?" She glanced back.

"We're ready!" they announced, going into a blissful song until eventually ending their set on an absolute high note. The audience was enraptured with their performance, still expressing joy while Jasmine finished the last notes of the song as the others slowly walked off. Morrigan blew kisses to the audience, before running offstage to greet her family.

"I didn't think you all were going to make it! Thanks so much for coming!" She enthusiastically hugged them.

"Of course, we came, we had to!" Raven told her. "We wanted to keep a surprise though."

"Yeah, better than you nervously awaiting us to show up," Libbey added.

"Did you know?" she asked Jack. He shook his head slowly.

"Yeah," he admitted. "But I was sworn to secrecy!"

"I'm so glad you two are here!" Max exclaimed, showing up.

"Absolutely!" Jasmine agreed, while Tim thanked them too.

"I'm thrilled we didn't miss it, Mystic was magnificent!" Raven energetically said. "Libbey, you taught them well."

"I just gave them pointers. They did the rest. I'm seriously proud of you all," he said.

"I knew you'd reign, my goddess," Jack complimented her. "I love you." She smiled at him happily. Thirty minutes had passed before the main act started to appear on stage; cloaked in darkness they could see four distant figures setting instruments up, testing them until eventually a familiar woman's voice spoke into the microphone.

"Hello, we're Spin Dreary, maybe you'll remember this, it's 'Tears in Wonderland.'" Everybody lost their composure, but none more than Morrigan and Max.

"Oh, shit, Max!" Morrigan spun around so fast, she could have given herself whiplash. "Spin Dreary, we're opening for Spin Dreary? This is insane!" She grabbed Max's hand so quickly; she pulled him toward her, he didn't even notice.

"Hell yes! This is freaking perfect, sis!" he replied. Spin Dreary was an alternative rock band that achieved international fame with their second album, *Thinking Fast and Slow*, before breaking up shortly after the tour ended for their third album. They were known for being hard to categorize to a genre and were one of Mystic's biggest inspirations. They were out of the spotlight for years, and when their fourth album never came through, people figured 1994 was the last year of Spin Dreary. Almost everyone started head banging massively.

"Who's Spin Dreary?" Raven asked. She almost wasn't heard.

"Who's Spin Dreary?" She studied her mom's face. "Never mind, only one of the greatest bands in our generation. It's been ten years since their last album, we thought they will never reform!" Jack looked on in disbelief, before stifling an "Oh, wow." She caught on to his reaction.

"Oh, wow . . . what?" she questioned him.

"Nothing," he answered quickly.

"Something," she responded. "'Oh, wow' means something."

"It's really nothing, babe," he said, taking his eyes off her, staring at the stage. She followed his eyes, toward the lead singer and guitarist, Mizzy Lynch.

"Did you date Mizzy or something?" she asked him humorously. He didn't respond.

"*Wait!*" she screamed in excitement. "You really dated Mizzy Lynch from Spin Dreary?"

"You said it, not I," he replied, looking at her seriously.

"Whoa," she managed, stunned.

"That's so cool!" Mystic announced collectively, which completely shocked him.

"What?" he asked confusingly.

"I'm sorry, Jack, apparently, we didn't raise them that well," Libbey joked with him. Morrigan tapped him to hush.

"How come you never told me that?" she asked him, grinning.

"Because it doesn't make a difference. It was a long time ago," he said, trying to explain.

"I don't care about that, of course, it was . . . This is when dating an older man can turn awkward," she remarked. "I honestly don't care about the before, unless you still have feelings for her."

"No, I don't. It wasn't even serious, we dated for the duration of our tour together. When that ended, we ended. I just never thought I'll see her again," he finished.

"Still . . . I can't believe you didn't tell me, you 'casually' dated one of my heroes during your gigging years. You have to introduce me, us!" she insisted, acknowledging the band as well.

"Totally!" Jasmine agreed.

"I don't know, she might not even remember me. Or she might and doesn't want to see me again," he replied indifferently.

"Tsk, babe." She scoffed at him. "Why would it, Jack? I thought you said it wasn't serious."

"Uh-oh," Libbey remarked.

"It wasn't!" he insisted.

"We'll find out," Jasmine said suddenly, grabbing her arm.

"Forget it, let's go to the front! Woohoo!" Morrigan yelled, running to the stage front.

"This is awesome!" Max yelled to them ecstatically.

"You know they got the band name from this song, right?" Morrigan told them.

"We know!" Tim yelled.

"Right. Sorry," she replied. They couldn't believe their luck, opening shows for their favorite band, their favorite band coming back, and the shocking coolness surrounding them. They never wanted that time to end; it was too surreal.

"Least go over there and say hi," Morrigan whispered to Jack back at the hotel's conference room. The show had ended righteously, with the accompanying bands celebrating at an after-party of sorts provided by their hosts, with their heroes Spin Dreary.

"You just want to go over there so you can play fangirl with one of my exes," he told her uncomfortably.

"Fine. I'll introduce myself," she told him confidently.

"You won't need to, girl," Jasmine stated. "I see her coming over here, right now. Look!" she squealed. Mizzy Lynch was making her way toward them; the whole group was there staring at her in amazement, with Jack the only one slightly looking away. Mizzy was blonde, slim, and totally upbeat, beaming as she strutted over toward them with a beer in her left hand. She was pretty short though, only five feet two, making her two inches shorter than Morrigan, who suddenly felt giant, one of the rare moments in her life of constantly having to step on her tiptoes to reach the top shelf of anything. Being taller than one of her idols was oddly gratifying.

"Jack? Is that you?" she said, placing her right hand on his left shoulder as a bid to turn him around.

"Miz?" he exclaimed as though he didn't see her coming.

"It is you! How are you?" She hugged him briefly; he returned it.

"I'm absolutely perfect! I'm surprised to see you here, performing no less," he said.

"Yeah . . . Everybody got over their shit with each other and decided to give the fourth album another go at completing. Plus, we had our families and decided we're mature for better now," she explained to him.

"You married?" he asked her.

"Divorced. But I'm a mom now of one," she said.

"Oh, I'm sorry to hear that," he apologized. "The divorce part, not the mom part." She laughed.

"I know . . . It's . . . We were just in different places in our lives, but it was amicable, especially for our son's sake," she explained.

"That's positive." There was a brief silence, prompting Jack to introduce them. "Miz, this is my girlfriend, Morrigan, front woman of—"

"*Mystic!*" she interrupted him.

"It's finally great to put a face to a name, and you're Max, right?" she asked him correctly.

"Yes, we are!" Max stated happily.

"And they're Jasmine and Tim," Jack finished, surprised. "How'd you . . ." Morrigan squealed, slightly shocking him.

"Mizzy knows our name," Max squeaked out alongside her. He had the hugest crush on her for years; she still looked amazing, even better in person. Morrigan squealed excitedly again, this time with Jasmine.

"I'm sorry, she loves you. They love you, and of course, the band . . .," Jack told her. She giggled.

"It's great, I love them too," she responded honestly, still beaming.

"How do you know us?" Morrigan exclaimed.

"I'm sorry, where is my mind sometimes? Our producer who's helping us do our long-awaited fourth album talks about you guys all the time. Especially you, Morrigan, it's kind of weird. I can see why Mystic is amazing! We watched your set backstage, well, on the monitors since our manager wanted to keep shit private for our first show in ten years, blah, blah, or we would have totally been in the audience. You two really had people moving," she told them to their shocking delight.

"Damn, it's really been ten years?" Jack acknowledged.

"Yeah . . . ?" she realized.

"Then we haven't seen each other in about fifteen years or so," he mentioned. She thought.

"Wow! Yeah, about fifteen!" she exclaimed.

"Excuse me . . .," Morrigan interrupted them, counting down the missed years. "But who's your producer?"

"Oh, I'm sorry, right! I can't believe I didn't say that. He said he works with you, Max. He's back there somewhere. His name is . . . Gaston!" she announced to their shocking disgust. Their mouths opened.

"Gaston?" they collectively shrieked, frozen in horror. Mizzy was slightly taken aback by their reaction.

"I . . . just walked into something, didn't I?" she asked.

"You have no idea," Tim said suddenly.

"Oh no! I thought we escaped him back in DC," Morrigan told Max, ruggedly upset.

"Babe, I don't get it, what's going on?" Jack asked her.

"Nothing! It's not important," she lied.

"Your two reactions say otherwise." He pointed out. "Come on, what aren't you telling me?"

"Like I said, it's not important," she said again, staring over in Gaston's direction.

"Well, it is kind of important, Cookie M. We probably should tell," Max whispered to her. She sighed, not wanting to give it more attention than it deserved.

"Proceed," she told him.

"It's interesting that he would tell you we work together," Max said, facing Mizzy. "Because any other time I'm his flunky . . . I don't even work for him," he complained.

"Max," Jack remarked, wanting him to get to the point.

"Okay, long story short, he has this obsessive crush on Morrigan," he explained. "He asked her out on a few dates, she always turns him down gently, but that doesn't stop him from trying to do things to me to get back at her. It's creepy."

"What?" Jack asked.

"Actually, I can believe that," Mizzy agreed suddenly. "It even made me uncomfortable the degree in which he mentioned you, it was weird . . . to say the least," she told them.

"Why didn't you tell me this sooner?" he asked Morrigan.

"Because it wasn't important at the time," she said again.

"Oh, damn it, Morrrigan!" he exclaimed. "Attacking Max to upset you, you don't see that as important?"

"I didn't say that. Plenty of times I jumped on his ass, but I realized that's probably what he wanted," she argued. "Plus, you and I were on the outs . . . again. It just didn't seem like something I should have ran back to tell the ex," she explained.

"Regardless . . . you should have told me!" he insisted.

"I'm going to go. You guys stay," she told them. "I'm not feeling it anymore. It was great to meet you, Mizzy!"

"Is he headed over here?" Jasmine noticed.

"Quick, get out of here. I'll stall him," Mizzy said. "Hey, call me, Morrigan, we're going to be on this tour together, might as well get to know each other. Plus, we have the same guy in common. That's always fun, right?" she joked.

"Thanks, Mizzy," Jack remarked.

"Oh, hush!" she told him.

"Okay, cool. Thanks." She started to walk out of the room, Jack followed her. "Stay here, talk. I'll be fine."

"No, I want to be with you," he told her meaningfully; he warmed her.

"Okay," she said, smiling, letting him hug her waist.

A few hours later after the party ended, the rest of the gang made it back to their hotel rooms where they were surprised to see Morrigan playing her blue-black acoustic-electric Ibanez quietly on her bed, scribbling down notes on paper with Jack nowhere in sight.

"What the hell are you doing in here tonight?" Max asked jokingly, entering the room. "I thought you and Jack would be tonsils deep into each other." He chuckled.

"Hardy, har, har." She laughed sarcastically. "Jackie boy is sleeping alone tonight. I thought it'll be fun if we had a band experience together in our rooms."

"Nice," he responded.

"He's mad at me now because of that . . .," she remarked.

"You used and abused him, sis?" Jasmine asked casually.

"You know me well," she answered; they dabbed knuckles.

"You see how terrible women can be, man?" Max asked Tim.

"Yes, I do," he responded lightheartedly. Morrigan lay back on the pillows she put up against the wall, eyeing them.

"So you guys ready for this?" she asked them honestly.

"Well, like you said, we kind of have no choice. Got to show we belong," Tim mentioned to her, trimming his beard, his skin the color of oak, smooth, with no visible marks or blemishes. "Are you ready with this, front woman?" he asked her smirking.

"I'm a little anxious," she admitted.

"You got this, Morrigan. After all, you got us this far," he told her.

"We got us this far. I just maybe pulled you guys by the reins a couple of times," she explained.

"Tim's right," Jasmine agreed. "You saved my life, Morrigan," she mentioned, referring to when they first met.

"She does have expert leadership qualities," Max quipped. Morrigan yawned.

"Oh shit," she said, cleaning off her bed.

"Someone's tired," Max commented.

"Someone's exhausted," she corrected him, yawning again.

"All that sex," Jasmine quipped. Morrigan snickered, rolling her eyes.

"Let's make a circle, you guys," she said seriously.

"Ah, come on, I'm tired, Morrigan. Can we do it tomorrow before our show?" Tim asked.

"Too bad, we're going to do it now too. Come on, let's do my witchy woo-woo shit," she told them. "Let's join hands." They stood in a circle, holding hands, looking toward one another. She used to do this in the past; she would say a few encouraging words then they meditated, thinking positively on what was to come. They assumed she was getting back in the habit; they were mistaken.

"Dearly beloved, we are gathered here today . . . to get through this thing called life," she started.

"Come on, Cookie M!" Max whined, breaking the circle.

"Okay, I'm sorry! All right, seriously. Get back in the fucking circle! I didn't tell you to break it," she fussed with him. "Seriously, my mum raised a good point earlier, we got a lot coming, a lot of time for things to try and break us. We're going to make it through it unscathed, all right?" She looked at them. "And if we do get scarred, we're going to illuminate those fuckers proudly? All right, this is our time!" she encouraged them.

"*Yes!*" they agreed, practically cheering.

"I love you all, very much. No matter what happens, know that, hold on to it," she pleaded.

"We love you too," Max responded, speaking for them.

"Yes, we do," Jasmine said agreeing with him.

"Now, let's hit the sack. We got another big day tomorrow," she told them, turning on the radio to ease them all into sleep.

CHAPTER FIFTEEN

"Last Month Was a Blur"

"Whoo!" Jack, Kirk, Jerry, and the rest of them cheered as Mystic finished their set in Long Island, New York.

"Thank you, my fellow bloodsuckers . . . We love you too." Morrigan briskly walked off set, almost silently afterward, walking to kiss Jack, wrapping her arms around him.

"You were awesome, as usual . . . Never change," he told her. "What I do to deserve you?"

"Just what you're doing now," she answered. "Great job, you guys," she said, looking back.

"Amazing! I'm proud to say y'all sets honestly get tighter and tighter each time you play," Kirk complimented them.

"We're still raw, though, right?" Tim asked.

"Of course, perfect balance. You guys ready for Boston?" he asked them.

"Yes, honestly we are!" Max said excitedly; he and Tim did their signature handshake.

"Aren't we, Cookie M?"

"Mm-hmm," she murmured.

"Good, 'cause we're heading there tonight. It's going to take us about ten hours, so let's finish it up." He snapped his fingers, starting to discuss with Jerry about the upcoming journey.

"It's almost unbelievable. Last month was almost a blur, now we're already into our second week this . . . second month. Wow." Tim acknowledged.

"Whoa . . . He's right. We're almost in winter, you know what that means." Morrigan noticed.

"Got any cool witchy rituals set up for us, doll?" Jasmine asked her.

"No, Jazz. You know, I don't do that anymore," she said, sighing.

"You don't do anything anymore," she remarked lowly.

"What the fuck does that mean, Jazz?" she snapped. "Oof." Her arm suddenly started to feel heated.

"Nothing, just nothing. Forget I said anything," she told her.

"I do that anyway, as if I need you to tell me." She scoffed. "Let's go, sweets." They walked out to his RV, leaving them inside.

"Max." Jasmine grabbed him sharply by the arm. "Have you noticed something weird with Morrigan lately?" she asked him.

"No," he answered.

"You don't think she's been a bit snappish this past week?" she asked.

"What do you mean?" he asked, dumbfounded.

"Cut the shit, Max!" she exclaimed. "You're her brother, if anyone's going to know something is wrong, you will."

"I really don't know what you're getting at."

"Then maybe you haven't been paying attention," she responded, walking away from him. Max stood there silently, thinking of what she meant; he couldn't place it . . . yet.

"Maybe, you were a little harsh to Jasmine just now," Jack mentioned to her as they got in his vehicle. "She was only asking you were you going to start doing your rituals again, is all."

"What are you going on about?" she asked agitatedly.

"I mean, you used to do that before a show and sometimes after, you stopped last week." She rubbed her tattooed arm.

"You know I don't believe in any of that anymore."

"Yeah, I know that but—"

"Just drop it, Jack, okay?" she asked him nicely.

"Consider it dropped," he said, driving to the hotel to rest. The rest of the drive was awkwardly silent; they went into their shared hotel room.

"I'm going to ride with the band," she told him suddenly.

"Okay," he said lowly, sitting down on the bed, taking off his shoes.

"I want us to get as much practice in as we can before we get to Boston."

"You'll also have plenty of rehearsal stops along the way. Y' know Kirk misses nothing," he reminded her. She didn't say anything at first; instead she stared out the window, tapping the glass.

"I know . . . I just need to distract myself and not with you."

"Ouch," he remarked. She rolled her eyes, flipping back her hair.

"I didn't mean it like that," she said softly as not to hurt his feelings.

"I know. I'm messing with you. However, you have to be careful with me. I'm a sensitive type," he told her, laughing.

"Yeah."

"Come here, please," he asked softly. She walked to him slowly, sitting on his lap. He brushed back her hair.

"I've been talking to Mizzy lately," he told her.

"Random," she said.

"Yeah, I was wondering why you haven't gotten back to her about writing a few songs together? I think you two could write some great tracks." He tried to reassure her.

"I don't want to deal with—" He interrupted.

"I'm not talking about him, it'll just be you and her. I don't get it, you were so excited about it when we mentioned it to you. It appears you've went off the grid lately. She really wants to write with you."

"How about you write songs with her," she said sarcastically, rising up from him. The phone in their room rang; it was Kirk telling them what time to get ready.

"Time's changed, we're leaving tomorrow morning, six o'clock," she told him, hanging up the phone. "Seems as though we now have some more time together," she moaned softly.

"Are you sure that's what you want?" he asked her.

"Of course. You're starting to act as weird as Jasmine," she said.

"We could probably say the same thing about you," he honestly remarked. She made a deep breath.

"I'm going to talk to Max, I'll be back," she said, putting her boots back on, grabbing her guitar and jacket.

"Baby, I'm sorry, I didn't mean anything by that," he apologized, reaching out to her. She slightly snatched away from his grasp.

"It's not that. I just need to talk to him. I'll be back."

"Please, don't take all night," he begged her.

"I won't."

"I love you!"

"Mm-hmm," she murmured, walking out the door, closing it. He sighed when he heard it shut.

"Good going, Jack," he thought to himself.

"Where are you coming from, darling?" she asked Max as she saw him just getting to his room.

"Nowhere," he answered, smirking.

"Loving young women into a stupor again, my darling brother?" she teased him.

"Don't you have an older mister-mister to demonically fuck?" he quipped.

"Oof! Damn! That's a good one, brother! You're getting better at those," she congratulated him. He bowed to her.

"I call it as I see it. Plus, Jack seems a little worn out sometimes. Haven't been taking it easy on him, have you lately?"

"Why, has he said anything?" she joked back. "Let's sneak off to a show, jam, or something?"

"Now?" he asked her.

"Yeah, I just want to hang out with you. Unless, you're too exhausted. I don't want to wear you out too."

"Never, my dear. Sure, Jack and you don't have anything planned?"

"Well, we do. He's missing me now, but we have all night. Kirk says to be ready by six, that's when we're taking off," she told him.

"Ooh, yes! Extra sleep time," he exclaimed.

"You goof! Get your sticks," she told him.

"All right, let's roll," he said stepping in for a quick minute, meeting her back out in the hall. They joined arms, walking to the elevator.

"*Damn!* Ugh!" he yelled, tripping on the stairs leading up to the stage.

"You klutz," she whispered to him shaking her head, dragging him onstage.

"I'm sorry, I'm not a cat in the dark like you," he responded, lifting himself up.

"You're right, you're a blind bat."

"Hey, bats aren't blind," he corrected her.

"Hmm . . . True. Now, shut up and help me find a light."

"You can see so well, right? Well, *will* a switch to you," he sarcastically remarked.

"Never mind, prima donna, I've found the switch." She hit it; the lights, though dim, brightened the lofty theater.

"Awesome!" she said to herself, examining the area.

"This is pretty great," he agreed, grabbing a couple of wooden chairs.

"Hey, remember when we used to do this back in the day?" she asked him.

"How could I not? This is how we met Libbey. I'll never forget the look on his face when we finally told him it was your idea, not mine, to break into his club!"

"No, he wasn't too thrilled about that. Mostly blown though."

"Yeah, I think that's when he realized how badass you actually are."

"Yeah . . . He didn't quite know how to take us after that."

"Who would?" Max responded. They laughed and played, reminiscing about their antics in the past and their late-night dreams.

"What luck a drum kit is still set up for us?" he asked her. "Huh, truly reminds me of the good old times." He finished playing a familiar beat.

"I've always loved that song," she commented.

"Yeah, I know. I know you, sister." He smiled at her; she smiled back, but suddenly by his gaze she felt guilty.

"Brother, I've got to ask you something," Morrigan said solemnly, slightly looking up from tuning.

"That sounds serious," he responded lightly, his smile slowly fading.

"It is."

"Well, shoot, sis."

"Have you noticed anything weird about me lately?" she asked him.

"Besides that, thing?" he said, pointing to her arm. She chuckled.

"Yes, aside from this. My attitude." He fell silent, his eyes looking away from her. She could sense his hesitation, which insulted her.

"Tell me the truth, bro. I count on you to be honest with me, so be honest," she told him.

"I've dismissed it, but Jazz brought it to my attention earlier today. Honestly, sis, you have been sort of reclusive lately." He paused. "Sometimes even aggravated, like we're not in this together."

"Thank you . . . for telling me." She sighed softly.

"Not to mention, you were a little rough with Jasmine today. What was that about?"

"Jack said something similar. I don't . . ."

"What's going on?" he asked.

"I don't remember some things after, but I don't think it's . . . I hope it's . . ." She thought, wanting to explain. "Listen, I'm sorry if I've come off a bit nasty lately. I'll try to act better, I promise," she apologized.

"I believe you, Cookie M," he said, hugging her by the shoulders. "Now let's get you back to Jack."

"Yeah, he has called me a couple of times," she said, putting her phone back in her pocket. "You tired?" she asked him sweetly.

"Yeah, I want to sleep," he responded. "Are you guys okay?"

"Aww, you care . . . Yeah, we're perfectly fine. Let's get you back to bed." She kissed his forehead.

"Of, course I care," he told her. "Duh!"

They arose to leave the dark theater; it was cold but still inviting, until suddenly they both heard a noise in the background.

"What was that?" he asked, holding her arm. She looked back toward the stage; thinking she saw a figure, she looked harder, but saw nothing.

"Forget about it, it's nothing, let's go. We didn't break shit so they can't blame us." They cracked up laughing, heading outside the window.

"Good night, dude," she told him when they got back to their rooms.

"See you in the morning, sis." He went inside. Assuming Jack was asleep, she snuck inside as not to wake him; the room was pitch-dark with an exception from the clock light highlighting the time.

"Twelve thirty isn't bad," he said yawning, arising to turn on the light, somewhat shocking her.

"I thought you were sleeping?" she asked him.

"I was waiting for you."

"With your eyes closed?"

"Yep, I'm more alert that way," he answered her.

"Really?" she asked, sitting beside him. "Care to prove that?"

"Oh, absolutely. That's if you're talking to me again?"

"I never stopped . . . Babe, I'm sorry about earlier. I thought about what you said, and I needed to talk to my main man about that."

"I thought I was your main man?" he jokingly whined.

"Always after him," she smirked.

"Was it a good talk?"

"Yes, it was. I certainly needed it. Also, I'm going to call Mizzy. I promise!"

"Good. But let's discuss that tomorrow. I want to prove to you how well rested I am."

"Oh." Grabbing each other, covering themselves in kisses, they rolled around in the bed until the next morning.

"Well, look who decided to join us," Tim joked when he saw her getting on their bus.

"Cute," she remarked. "Got everything?"

"Everything."

"Good. We're off! Come on, Jerry, take us on!" she commanded.

"So what do we owe to this pleasure?"

"Listen . . . Okay, I sincerely want to apologize to all of you as a band. It's been brought to my attention that I've been distant and irritable lately and I'm sorry about that . . . a little bit." She giggled.

"All's forgiven," Jasmine stated.

"Sweet, but that didn't answer my question," Tim remarked.

"Moving on, dude, like I haven't rolled with y'all lately. Now let's work out this new song, I think it's missing something."

"I'm just shocked to see you on here and not with some tall dude chasing after you," he finished. She shook her head in agreement.

"Maybe I should go back to being on your asses more, is that what you're saying?" she teased him.

"No . . . No, that's okay," he stammered.

"No, you're right! I've spent too much time away from you guys. I should—"

"I was just joking," Tim admitted nervously.

"Oh . . . Are you sure?" she asked sarcastically. "Because I was just thinking . . ."

"No! It's great, I'm appreciative of the break you've been giving us. Honestly," he persuaded her.

"Oh . . . Then maybe we should get practicing."

"Yeah, I couldn't agree more." Max laughed at them, as they started on the road.

"What's this song called?" he asked.

"I got nothing, I'm hoping after we finish it maybe a title will jump out at me or one of you."

"All right, show us what you got so far." She brought out her journal, most of it written to its capacity. She turned to one page; half was blank, with several lines crossed out almost to extinction.

"This is how it goes . . . Just bear with me." She had her guitar in her hands, tuned it a little, then played for them.

♪♫ *Tell me what to say. Tell me what you've got for me.*
I've heard heaven's a skip away.
Ooh, your backyard's fired, oh, always my mind. ♪♫

Tim came up with a riff almost instantaneously, while Max continued the beat she provided, but Jasmine kept listening. Morrigan stopped.

"That's it. That's all I got. I'm having trouble, there's this disconnect," she told them.

"Try rearranging it, the second to the third line," Jasmine suggested, replaying the riff.

"Okay . . . Let's do it together." They sang the lyrics together, harmonizing, correcting the order, which in turn inspired them.

"Whew! That's good," Max said. "It's giving me chills."

"Hey, I got some lyrics too." Jasmine shared with them. Morrigan passed her, her journal and asked her to write them down. Jasmine did, passing it back to her.

"Try that," she told her. They repeated the process.

"I love that, Jazz! Your lyrics fit perfectly," she told her. They spent the next thirty minutes finishing the lyrics. Morrigan brought out her cassette recorder and they played into it. All was going well until Morrigan suddenly stopped.

"Jerry! Jerry! Stop, stop! Stop the bus now!" she yelled suddenly. All of them were still working on the song when she kept calling out to Jerry to stop driving and park.

"Stop, stop, please stop right now! Park over here. I have to go in that record store! Please," she begged him.

"Kirk isn't going to be happy about us breaking schedule," he admitted to her.

"He'll get over it, just park right here, please, I need to go in there right quick," she insisted.

"Morrigan, what's going on?" Max asked her, concerned.

"Yeah, let us in on it," Tim said, but she had already rushed off the bus into the shop across the street.

"I better go see what's going on with my weird ass sister," he joked, stepping off. He followed her into the shop where she was in the back shuffling through records, until she lifted something out, saying, "*Yes!*" He ran to her.

"Sis, what's the deal? You came all the way out here, interrupted our excellent songwriting session to buy a new record?" he asked, catching up with her at the cash register.

"And a record player," she told him excitedly. "Just get back on the bus, I'll show you what for on the bus," she said ecstatically. "Tell them all to hang tight, it's going to be great!" she insisted happily.

"Are you sure?"

"Dude, where else I'm going?"

"Fine. We're waiting." He walked outside, where Jack was standing too.

"What going on with her?" he asked him.

"I don't know, I just know she bought a vinyl and record player and said, quote, 'It's going to be great!' unquote." He mocked her until suddenly she appeared right behind him with a big brown paper bag.

"Not a bad impression," she told him.

"Damn! You move like a cat," he told her.

"Hey, babe," she greeted Jack.

"Hey . . . Everything okay?"

"Everything's fine, band stuff." She kissed his cheek. "See you later." He shrugged his shoulders.

"Okay, I'm following you guys." He got back into his RV.

"Come on, Max! Let's go!" She pushed him back onto the bus. "Sorry about that, Jerry, now you can continue on schedule. Onward bound!"

"Dudette, what's up?" Jasmine asked her. "I thought you wanted to finish this song?"

"I do and we will, but I just had to check that place. It's weird to explain, but I've been thinking about this song lately and how it'll be so perfect to play at the concert the end of this month. I knew the record would be in there, I knew it! Plug that in, please, bro." She took out the purple vinyl, slightly covering it with her body.

"Check this out! I know you guys remember this band." "Just One Happy Day" by the Nymphs was played.

"Fuck yes! Inger Lorre!" Max exclaimed.

"Inger Lorre!" Tim repeated affectionately.

"Patron saint of fucked-over musicians," Morrigan stated.

"She was a fucking goddess! Too bad she kind of dropped off the face of the earth," Max mentioned.

"Yeah, the Nymphs could have been huge. I forgot all about this album!" Jasmine stated.

"Okay, we have to do 'Sad and Damned,' simple as that!" She snapped her finger to emphasize it. "We have to learn it in time. We only got two weeks. This is our homework, kiddos."

"She's so cute, she sounds like Libbey," Max joked.

"I'm serious! That song is perfect for us to perform!" she insisted, though they weren't sold.

"Since when we start doing covers again?" Tim asked her lightheartedly.

"Since I said so," she responded argumentatively.

"I was just joking, Morrigan," he replied softly.

"Stop joking. That's your problem, you joke all the damn time," she argued. Her left arm singed slightly, so she stretched out her arms. The band fell awkwardly quiet; they all looked at one another.

"Um, do you want to finish working on our song?" Jasmine asked her.

"Uh . . . No, you guys can take a break. I'm going to go in the back, try to figure out 'Sad and Damned.' I'll get back to y'all. We can finish it later, I promise." She tidied the paperwork that they were writing their song on and placed it neatly back in her pad. "It'll be right here for us later," she told them nicely, before heading into the back bedroom with the Nymphs record, her guitar, and another writing pad, closing the door.

"Dr. Jekyll and Mrs. Fucking Hyde," Tim remarked. Jasmine shushed him.

"Don't shush me. I'll make all the noise I want to . . . if she doesn't hear me," he whispered, laughing.

"Come on, you guys, let's finish this song," Max told them.

"Without Morrigan?" Jasmine asked.

"Yes, she laid down the foundation, we can finish the rest," he answered. "We'll surprise her."

"All right," Tim said. They finished the song shortly after, when eventually she emerged.

"Hello, darlings!" She flopped down, next to Jasmine. "What'd I miss?"

"Not much, you got out here in time, we've just arrived to a pit stop."

"Awesome! I'm starving."

"Me too. Come on, girl!"

"Oh, Max, here." Morrigan passed him her notes on "Sad and Damned."

"Oh, awesome! You did all this back there?" he asked.

"Yep! The rest we got to do together, uh, of course. I probably fucked up on a few parts though, so don't be too impressed." She humbly disagreed. He scoffed.

"Pish-tosh, dudette! You did damn good, as usual."

"Pish-tosh?" she questioned.

"Whatever, let's get something to eat."

"I'm game for that!" Tim announced.

Several hours later, several pit and practice spots down the line, they finally arrived in Boston, Massachusetts.

CHAPTER SIXTEEN

"Let the Magic Say It All"

"So are we all going to lunch or what?" Max asked the band after rehearsal; everyone agreed except Morrigan.

"I'm going to have to take a rain check on that, Jack and I got a date," she answered.

"Oh?" he remarked surprisingly. "Haven't heard you say 'date' in a while."

"Yes, it's our way of making time for each other on the road."

"Don't you two make plenty of that already?" he asked.

"I'm not talking to you anymore." They laughed.

"So where is he?" Tim asked her. She thought.

"I don't know. He was supposed to be here about ten, twenty minutes ago, he did have something to send to the office . . . the pictures from our photo shoot!"

"Awesome!" they exclaimed.

"Still . . . He's late . . . He was supposed to be here. I don't know what's going on," she said seriously, checking her phone. "He hasn't called." She called him; it went straight to voice mail.

"Hey, babe, it's me, you're not here. Are we still on? Call me back."

"Want to hang out with us until you get in contact with him?" Max asked her.

"No . . . Um, I'm going to try and find him. It's not like him not to contact me, so uh, he must be somewhere in here. I guess. I'll be all right, go get something to eat! Thanks though, babe," she answered.

"All right, sis, see you later."

"Yeah, doll. Be good," Jasmine told her.

"Why? That's no fun!" she joked. She walked among the various rooms down the hall. The recording studio was a large one, opulent in style, almost resembling a small theater in proportion. She wasn't sure what she wanted to do, look for him or go exploring, but waiting for him was not in the program.

"I wonder what's the story behind some of these rooms? Or more of the equipment?" she thought to herself. The studio was well-known for only using vintage equipment and gear; many pieces (including the rooms they inhabited) came with their own little backstory, and while some were trivial, others were notoriously infamous, just the place Morrigan wanted to be when they recorded their debut EP next week. Before she could go into one of the rooms, Jerry had spotted her.

"Morrigan!" he called out to her. "Morrigan!"

"Err . . . Hey, Jerry!"

"What are you still doing here? I just saw the band leaving."

"Nothing really, waiting for Jack, is all."

"Oh."

"You haven't seen him, have you? I've been waiting awhile," she asked him.

"No, I'm sorry, I haven't. He shouldn't be too far behind though."

"Okay, thanks anyway."

"No problem." He continued walking down the hall.

"You said you were looking for Jack?" Gaston asked, coming out of the room she was slated to go in. Her blood ran cold.

"Yes . . .," she answered slowly.

"I've seen him about thirty minutes ago."

"Oh, yeah?"

"Yeah, he said he was on his way to meet Mizzy for something. He was rushing, it seemed important," he told her. She darted her eyes up and down, with her hands in her back pockets; she didn't say a word.

"You look really good, Morrigan. Amazing in fact," he complimented her, which in turn disgusted her. "Did you two have anything planned?" he asked nosily.

"Where did you happen to see him?" she asked abruptly.

"Upstairs . . . He was headed in the direction of the conference room," he answered.

"Thank you." She walked off briskly, then turned around telling him. "I know." Then she continued upstairs. He smirked, seemingly pleased with himself.

She arrived upstairs where the space opened wider; farther down the hall revealed a closed conference room door that read "Occupied, meeting in session." She checked her phone to see if he called back and left a message. He did neither. For a moment, she thought to herself to see if she should call his number again or knock on the door. She decided on the latter, before entering.

"Excuse me," she stated, seeing both Mizzy and Jack inside.

"Morrigan!" Mizzy exclaimed excitedly. "Come in! We were just messing around on some songs. Come join us, we need you!" She laughed happily.

"Oh yeah? Hey, Miz!" Mizzy was sitting at the piano keys, while Jack was standing near her beside the base, writing on some papers.

"Hi, baby!" he greeted her, grabbing her by the waist with one hand to kiss her on the cheek. She pulled back subtly.

"Hello, darling. I thought we were supposed to meet for lunch?" she asked him.

"We were?" he asked before thinking. "We were!" He remembered.

"I'm not keeping him from you, am I?" Mizzy asked, concerned. Morrigan shook her head slowly as no before looking at him.

"I was going to call you, but I didn't want to disturb your rehearsal." He stupidly made up, quickly remembering they had a date planned. Morrigan glared at him angrily, tapping her left foot. She hardly blinked, not taking her eyes from him.

"How about you show her what we've been working on, Jack?" Mizzy suggested to him, feeling extremely awkward.

"Right! Great idea, Miz!" he exclaimed, hurriedly grabbing the sheet for the song they were writing. He gave it to her, and she glanced over it, quickly discarding it.

"It's good," she said half-heartedly, passing it back to him vigorously.

"It's nothing," Mizzy said.

"No, I mean it. It's really good," Morrigan said. She was right; the lyrics were great, but she wasn't enthused enough to admit it. "I didn't even know you still wrote songs," she told him.

"I didn't either," he said nervously.

"It was random . . . We didn't even think we were going to sit down and write. I might have dared him a bit," she confessed, trying to excuse him.

"It's no problem," she told her, glaring at him again. He mouthed the words "I'm sorry" to her.

"I'm going to go, I hope we can get together soon, Morrigan," Mizzy told her, rising up to leave.

"How about now?" Morrigan asked suddenly. "How about we go to lunch? I can show you some lyrics I wrote down the other day. After all, I owe you."

"What about Jack and y—" she started to ask.

"Oh, what about him?" Morrigan interrupted her. "He snoozes, he loses. He'll be okay by himself," she answered her.

"I will? I'm right here, you know?" he asked.

"Yeah," Morrigan said, smiling, glancing over at him. She winked; his expression changed.

"Really? It's no problem?" she asked, looking at both.

"Apparently not," Jack stated sharply, stepping away to gather their papers.

"I can't believe we're finally getting together to write," Mizzy stated, surprised.

"I know, I'm truly excited. I have to warn you though. I'm so going to get my fangirl on!" she confessed happily. They were almost out the door when Jack called out tensely.

157

"Morrigan, can we get together before your show tonight?"

"Sure, whatever," she said, then they left him alone.

"I cannot believe I'm with my idol, Mizzy Lynch! Having lunch and finally writing songs!" she exclaimed ecstatically.

"Please, Morrigan, stop talking about me like that, to that extent. I'm honestly just as appreciative that I was able to touch someone with my partial journal entries." They shared a quick laugh.

"You're extremely talented, so watch out and listen close, you'll be having this conversation with your ultimate fan too one day," she told her honestly.

"You think so?"

"I *know* so! Just keep writing, loving, and playing. I believe in you. You have a lot of people close to you that trust and believe in you," she assured her.

"Thank you so much, Miz. You have no idea how much that means to me! Sorry, fangirling again. I'll try and put a sock in it."

"Please do!" They laughed again.

"Just continue to be yourself."

"Thanks, I will."

"Also, I'm sorry if I ruined something that you and Jack had planned earlier. We didn't intend on our session being that long, he did tell me he was meeting you later, we must have lost track of time," she apologized to her.

"Think nothing of it, Miz, it's not like it was your fault."

"Well, he's a good guy. I haven't seen him in years, but he's still sincere. I'm sure you know him better than I do now, so I don't need to tell you this." She convinced her.

"No, you don't. Thanks anyway." She looked at her watch. "It's about time we start heading back."

"Are you always this punctual?" Mizzy asked her.

"Nope! But I try to be." They giggled.

"You're better at keeping on time with your shows than I was years ago, so are you excited about the big Halloween bash?"

"*Yes!* Almost as much as I am about us recording our EP next week! All Hallows' is one of my favorite holidays," Morrigan exclaimed.

"What's your other favorite?"

"Christmas!"

"I second that." She laughed. "Have anything special planned for the bash?"

"Nothing I can disclose with you. Sorry, Miz."

"I understand. We're still pondering ideas. All set with your EP? I mean, what tracks you want to lay down?"

"Yes and no. We're still deciding on whether we want to add on a few songs."

"Piece of advice?"

"Absolutely!"

"Just stick with the ones you're most confident with . . . and play the heck out of those until you know them backwards. Those you record."

"Thanks."

"No problem! And if you need any help just call me."

"I appreciate that." She thanked her.

"Now let's make our show." They arrived at the venue in enough time to prepare their respective bands at sound check, which is where Jack approached her.

"I think we need to talk, babe," he suggested.

"You've always had the best timing," she told him. "I'm not sure if you noticed, but we're trying to finish our sound check for tonight."

"I know that, I'm not trying to disturb you, but—" She cut him off.

"Where have I heard that before?" she asked him sarcastically.

"Baby, I'm sorry. It was an honest mistake. I didn't even know my phone had cut off until you arrived. I had all intention on making our date. I wouldn't stand you up, you know this," he pleaded, while she shook her head understandably, not actually believing him.

"Y' know, sweets, you would've known if your phone was still on if you would've picked it up to call me. Hmm . . . Guess that songwriting session was pretty important, huh?" Her arm heated up slightly; she barely noticed. He sighed.

"You know it wasn't like that. It was an accident! Listen, I'm truly sorry!" he apologized.

"Whatever, sweets. I really don't have the time. Can we do this later?" She dismissed him nonchalantly.

"Whatever you want." He walked off.

"Great!" she exclaimed, walking back onstage.

"Everything all right?" Max asked her.

"Peaches and cream," she told him half-heartedly. "Let's finish!" she ordered them.

"Right," he said. Then they finished their set.

Danger Prone had finished their set, and it was a few minutes before Mystic was due on when Jack spotted her getting a drink; he snatched it out of her hand.

"What the hell are you doing?" she snapped.

"What the hell are you doing?" he asked her back. "You're about to take the stage, since when do you drink before?"

"Firstly, it's just a wine cooler, and I was only taking a little sip. Secondly, it's none of your damn business," she argued.

"I'm just looking out for you, babe. Can we talk?" he asked her again. She scoffed.

"You didn't get any better timing from earlier, I see. To remind you I'm due onstage now."

"Later then? Please? I promise I'll get better timing," he joked.

"Sure. And don't beg, it's not attractive." She brushed him off with her hand before heading onstage. "Don't drink my beer!" she warned him from the stage. He immediately took a swig, smiled, then took a step back.

"You bastard!" she joked, shaking her head. "Tsk, men," she thought.

"Let the show begin!" she yelled to the audience.

"One, two, three, four!" Max counted off, rocketing them into their set.

♪♫ *Ooh, baby, baby, let the magic say it all.*
Ooh, hey, sexy lady, catch me off the ball, let us shake it all off! ♪♫

"Come here, darling!" She pointed out one of the ladies dancing in the audience to come onstage. "Come on, it's all right. Dance your pretty self onstage with me. You're not too shy, are you?"

"Uh, no, no . . ." The young brunette hesitated. She was excited, yet nervous now.

"What's your name?"

"Lexi."

"You know the lyrics, Lexi?" Morrigan asked her flirtatiously.

"A . . . a little," she whispered.

"Speak up, it's fine."

"A little!" she admitted loudly.

"That's okay, I'll teach them to you if you dance with me?"

"Of course!" the young girl agreed excitedly.

"Great, let's dance!" They danced in a cutesy way onstage together, touching each other on their waistlines slightly. Morrigan grabbed Lexi by the hand and brought her to the microphone.

"Listen to me," she told her, before singing a few lyrics. "Your turn." Lexi nervously sang after her, and shook her head into her hands, feeling embarrassed.

"Oh no, no, none of that!" Morrigan exclaimed, grabbing her by the wrists, pulling her hands from her face. "You did such a great job with me, that deserves a kiss." She proceeded to kiss her on the cheek. "How about two?" Then she ran her fingers through her hair, and planted a small peck on her lips.

"Oh my gosh!" Lexi mouthed happily. Morrigan helped her offstage. "Thank you!" Lexi yelled to her.

"Have a good night, doll!" she yelled back. That small kiss sent most of the audience into a frenzy; they didn't know what to expect now while Mystic kept playing confidently, knowing she just set it off. Everyone was fine with the act, except Jack who suddenly felt a little out of place. They wrapped up their set shortly after when Morrigan slapped Max's butt when they were walking offstage, something he was used to, that Jack also caught.

"Hi ya, darling," she greeted Jack backstage, grabbing him roughly to kiss him passionately, which he happily obliged.

"Not a bad makeup. Still mad at me?" he asked; she shrugged it off.

"Making up is always best," she responded. After catching Spin Dreary's set, a nearby magazine reporter caught up with them to ask her about the kiss.

"What do you want, bottom-feeder?" She shrugged him with equal prejudice.

"I'm sure fans want to know about that kiss."

"What kiss?" she asked humorously.

"That kiss onstage." He dug his grave.

"Oh, well, I kissed three people onstage, including a few of my band members. Be more specific," she told him sharply. He stammered. She smirked; as she turned to walk away, he tried to approach her again to which Jack stepped in.

"You might want to drop it? I'll change that, drop it," he warned sternly to which captured Morrigan's attention. She turned back around and said, "It's okay, sweets," and put her hand on his chest to step back. "I'll amend a Lana Turner quote, 'I liked the boys and girls, and the boys and girls liked me.' Now, bye-bye." She waved at him and pulled Jack by the shirt collar to follow her. Tim bowed to her, overhearing the whole thing.

"They just don't know you like we do," he said.

"Just the way I like it," she remarked, accepting a drink from Max.

"Y'all hanging out with us tonight?" he asked her. She looked at Jack, who shook his head no.

"Rain check, bro," she told him; he raised his bottle to her, which she clinked. "Good night." They exchanged, leaving.

"What was up with that kiss?" Jack asked her randomly after their nightly ritual, lying beside her in bed. His response equally surprised her and pissed her off.

"Ah fuck! Not you too." She sighed.

"I'm not bugging out over it or anything, I'm just wondering why, you usually never do *that* onstage with your fans," he mentioned.

"It was barely even a kiss, a small peck on the lips! Shit! It lasted what? A second?" she remarked agitatedly, falling back against the headboard.

"Yeah, maybe to you." He hesitated. "I know I didn't show it earlier, but I guess I was a little put off by it," he admitted. She snapped her neck at him in shock and anger. "I don't want to start a fight! Okay, Morrigan? I'm serious, I don't. I don't want to fight with you. But could you please not do that again?" he pleaded.

"So you're telling me what to do again?" Her arm singed slightly.

"What? No! I'm asking you. I'm telling to you as someone in a relationship with you, that I don't want you to do that again!" He tried to reason with her.

"You are trying to tell me what to do again." She accused him.

"Don't start that shit, Morrigan! Please, do not start that shit again." He begged her, while she rolled her eyes and scratched her arm to try to relieve the burning sensation. He calmed down, looking at her, worrisome.

"I'm sorry, but I'm asking you as your lover, please don't make out with your fans. I'm terribly jealous." He tried relieving the tension, stroking her hair. She didn't move; she just scratched and rubbed, staring into the room. Until suddenly she spoke.

"Sure," she answered him slowly. He sighed in relief.

"Thank you." He kissed her forehead.

"Sure," she repeated monotonously, turning her side light off and lying down. "Good night."

"Good night, baby. I love you," he said. She didn't return his affection; instead she stared at the wall in silence until she fell asleep.

A few hours later when she proved to be in a deep sleep, he got up to get a drink of water; when he returned he proceeded to wrap his arm around her, until he felt fiery pain burn his fingers.

"Shit!" he exclaimed, instantly snatching his hand back to examine it. He turns on the light and hurriedly felt her tattooed arm again, but this time it was cool to the touch. Completely normal.

"What the hell?" he thought to himself anxiously, still feeling all over her arm. He hoped he was imagining it, but he couldn't shake his apprehensive thoughts that something negative revolved around that tattoo.

"Oh, Morrigan," he said aloud softly, holding her tightly close to him.

CHAPTER SEVENTEEN

Pulling His Pants Back On

T he next morning the interaction between them was awkward and quiet. He deeply wanted to put the night before behind them, but he could tell she was still upset.

"Do you still want me present at your recording session next week?" he asked her over breakfast. "Despite the big jerk I can be sometimes?" She giggled, trying to bounce back.

"Of course, I do," she answered him lowly, smiling softly.

"You still love me?" he asked. She walked over to him and kissed him his lips.

"Yeah," she answered.

"Great! That's all I need," he said honestly. She smiled gently. "I love it when you smile."

"Yeah, yeah . . . So what do you want to do today, before my show tonight? You are going to show up, right?" she joked.

"Of course! Have I ever missed your shows?" he asked her.

"Well," she started.

"Don't answer that. You might remember something I hoped to forget."

"I wasn't going to say anything."

"Okay, sweetheart."

"So what do you want to do?" she asked him again.

"Now don't start that again!" He messed with her. It made her laugh heartily.

"Hey, how about we do that?" she asked eagerly.

"Do what?" he wondered.

"Watch movies!" she suggested. "With room service!"

"That sounds perfect to me!"

"Good. Now come here," she ordered him flirtatiously.

"Gladly." He lay down beside her, and she wrapped her arms around him. He dared not ask her if she felt anything hot last night; instead he kept it to himself. All day they watched their favorite films, talked, and enjoyed the service of being waited on. It went by fast, until the alarm rang and someone knocked on their door.

"It's Max," she said, still getting ready.

"How do you know?" he asked her.

"Sis, hurry up! Time for sound check!" he yelled from the hallway.

"It's our sister-brother connection," she told him, putting on her finishing touches to open the door; Jack beat her to it.

"How you doing, Max?"

"I'm well, Jack, thanks for asking. I see you kept my sister in all day." She flashed him a rough glance. "I'm just messing with you. Seriously, are you two ready to go?" he asked.

"Yes, we are," Jack answered.

"Good. Kirk is climbing our asses, he wants us to make a good impression tonight. He must know the owner or something."

"Just put on a killer show, like you guys usually do," Jack suggested.

"Especially like last night!" Max mentioned absentmindedly. Both glared at him.

"I'm going to stop talking," he said aloud.

"Good idea," they remarked in unison.

"Sis, you go on ahead. I want to chat with Jack," he mentioned as they walked up the hallway.

"Okay, I need to check on Jazz anyway, keep it civil, you two," she told them, running up to meet her.

"So, Jack, you going to be at this sound checking?"

"What?" He looked at him weirdly.

"I'm not saying you have to be at every one, but you didn't show up."

"I know, Max. I'm going to be there. Yesterday, was an accident." He tried to explain.

"I'm not trying to beat you up or anything, but you know where I'm coming from . . . right? Man-to-man," he asked him.

"Yeah, I understand," he answered.

"Then we're cool. Also, are you all right with last night? I wasn't trying to bring up harsh feelings just now," Max asked, referring to earlier. "I caught y'all glares."

"Oh." He chuckled. "Yeah, everything is fine. It didn't really bother me," he lied.

"Great. I don't really know what got into her, but I'm sure she didn't mean anything hurtful by it."

"Ah, that's showbiz. I've been there. Just wanting to put on a good show, is all," he said, trying to convince himself more than Max.

"Awesome. Let's catch up with the girls, man," he suggested, as they walked faster.

"Break a leg," Jack told her as they were about to go on.

"I'm a musician, not an actress. Thanks." They kissed each other lovingly, just as Danger Prone was walking backstage; Morrigan saw Rick slip Jasmine something in her hand that she readily accepted.

"What is it?" she asked, approaching her sternly.

"What is what?" Jasmine questioned her.

"You know exactly what the fuck I'm talking about, Jazz." She rushed through her pockets, and pulled out what she hid. It was a miniscule purple Ziploc bag, inside a white powdery substance.

"Cool," she said sarcastically. "Seriously, Jazz, you're starting to be more trouble than you're worth," she remarked.

"What? It's not that much," she tried explaining.

"Shut up, Jazz! Give him this shit back. Better yet, I'll give it back." She stormed backstage, and threw the substance back at Rick, which he caught.

"This is yours! Keep it!" she ordered him harshly. "No offense, William, but I think you need to check your boy! I don't want him peddling that to my bandmates."

"What the hell?" William asked shockingly, staring at Rick. "I thought you said you quit that, man!" he argued.

"I did, kind of . . . But man, she was willing."

"Shut the fuck up! You're not supposed to be doing that shit anymore! Are you trying to ruin this for us? What in the hell is wrong with you?" Morrigan stomped off, overhearing them fuss, trying to lower their voices.

"Why did you do that, Morrigan?" she yelled at her. "God! You're such a bitch at times!" she argued, crying. Morrigan looked at her confusingly, then slapped her.

"Maybe you didn't hear me before, but if you don't straighten up, you're out! No more back and forth, no more pleasing, you'll just be gone. So you have a choice, are you in or are you out?" She looked at the stage, then backstage at Rick, then back at Morrigan.

"Jazz, I'll take her up on her offer," Tim suggested. "Come up here, we need you."

"Jasmine." Max nodded for her to come onstage.

"Sorry," she apologized lowly to her, stepping onstage.

"Morrigan, is everything all right?" Kirk stepped to her anxiously.

"Kirk, don't get your panties in a bunch. It's handled. Can I go onstage or what?" she answered sharply.

"Don't let me stand in your way, madam."

"Good boy." He tipped his head to her.

"Have fun," he wished her.

"Yeah, we're just a bucket of laughs." She strutted to the microphone. "Hello, honey pies and sugar cookies, sorry we kept you waiting. Or am I? Maybe that's all a part of the show? In any case, we're Ends Ville, we're worth the wait. Let's rock it, kiddies!"

They blazed through forty minutes of their set. It's all going great; the crowd was loving them until she considered the audience. She might never have admitted it, but a small part of her performance was to impress Jack; instead this time she saw him and Mizzy in deep conversation. Smiling and laughing, moving in closer to each other, not even paying attention to her, to their show. She was livid.

"Stop the song, my pets! Cut it out!" she yelled, stopping their song midway. "This is starting to bore me, babies, and if I'm bored that means I'm not giving you darlings our best! I promised you the best, isn't that right, Max?" Everybody stopped dancing, talking, whatever, and looked straight to the stage, including Jack and Mizzy.

"You did, luv," he agreed from his drum set, confused.

"For this song, I'm going to need my best mate up here, grooving with me. Tim's an excellent drummer, too, take his place." Tim walked over to her and asked, "What song are we doing?"

She called them all over and whispered in their ears the song. Tim gave Jasmine his bass to play, he took Max's sticks, and Max picked up Jasmine's guitar and took their newest positions.

"You losers should know this song by now, came out a few years ago, by a freakalicious band called the Yeah Yeah Yeahs," Morrigan announced in the mic, holding her guitar tightly before she sang.

♪♫ *Cold light, hot night, be my heater, be my lover . . .* ♪♫

She and Max started playing seductively toward each other, as though they were feeding off each other sexually. During one of the song's instrumental breaks, she stepped to him, kissing him passionately. Max initially hesitated but gave in to her advances, kissing her back. Jack took notice of that, but it didn't end there. Gaston was also in the audience; during the performance he smirked at Jack.

As the song got heavier, so did they, dancing on each other. Morrigan played a guitar lick swiftly, then grabbed the microphone, continually singing the verses, and grabbed the back of Max's neck from behind her, pulling him in. He kissed her neck. After the song ended she reciprocated; they kissed each other heavily, wrapping their arms around each other. Morrigan giggled as they both playfully ran offstage.

"I believe that was exciting enough for everyone involved. Hope you all enjoyed the show! I know we did," Jasmine spoke into the microphone. "Oh shit," she thought to herself as she saw Jack storm backstage to confront Morrigan. He grabbed her forcefully.

"What the hell was that? Do you want to be with him? Or is it something I'm missing?" he asked her angrily.

"No way, he's my brother. It's just for show. I thought it could brighten things up. Least you paid attention to that," she answered nonchalantly.

"Jack . . ." Max tried interfering.

"I'm not fucking talking to you," he said rudely.

"Don't talk to him like that," she said firmly.

"Since when do you resort to cheap tricks?" he asked her.

"Love that band!" she exclaimed.

"Don't fuck with me, Morrigan," he said angrily, which tested her.

"So serious, darling . . . . It was only a joke." She reached to caress his face.

"I'm not laughing."

"You're not kidding." She scoffed callously. "This is boring me, too, go write some more songs, I'll see you later tonight." She brushed him off. He caught what she implied.

"Write some more songs? Is that what this is about? Babe, nothing is going on between me and Mizzy." He tried to convince her.

"Well, you seemed really interested in your conversation with her earlier." She peered over to Mizzy.

"You know what, Morrigan. Don't bother."

"Don't bother with what?"

"Seeing me later tonight. I think you need to stay in your own room for a while. Because I'm not playing this game with you."

"Unbelievable," she remarked in disbelief.

"Well, believe it, babe," he said sadly, walking away from her.

"Morrigan, I have a few minutes before we go on, I need you to know nothing is going to happen between us. I care for him, but that's as far as it goes. I respect he's in a relationship with you."

"For now!" She laughed unemotionally. "Thanks, Miz, but I don't need your reassurance."

"Okay, well, maybe you should be careful of how much of yourself you give the audience." She tried to advise her.

"Don't really need that advice either, thanks anyway." She dismissed her, hearing the audience call out Spin Dreary.

"They're calling for you, Miz. Don't you keep them waiting too long." Mizzy hugged her randomly; she didn't hug her back.

"Call me," she told her meaningfully, then went onstage, greeting the audience.

"Great show! You had me a little worried, but . . ."

"Save it, Kirk," she told him flatly. "I'm out of here," she announced.

"You don't want to stay for the show, M?" Jasmine asked her.

"Nah, I'll see you ladies and fellas later. Have fun, but not too much fun." She winked at her.

"Of course." She chuckled lightly.

"Cookie M."

"Stay here, Max. I'll see you later." She walked out of the club to the parking lot, where Jack's RV was nowhere in sight. She called him but he didn't answer, so she got a cab and went to a nearby bar.

Later that night, she made her way back to the hotel. Before heading upstairs, she checked her phone again; the only new call was from Max, so she called Jack again, this time leaving a voice mail apologizing for her behavior earlier. She waited thirty minutes in the lobby. Nothing. She greeted the receptionist, asking if he's in. She informed her gently that he's not accepting any new messages until the next morning, so she left a sweet message for him, then headed upstairs to Max's room.

"Damn, Cookie M! I was about to go out looking for you," he told her worriedly, as he opened the door. She straggled in; he could tell she had been drinking.

"Take this." He gave her an aspirin with a glass of water. "I guess you haven't talked to him."

"No, he's pissed at me. I can't blame him, I'm a fuckup," she admitted.

"You wear it well."

"You're sweet."

"Y' know, sis, if you wanted to make him jealous, you could have told me, so I could talk you out of it." She laughed.

"I'm sorry, man, I shouldn't have set you up like that onstage," she apologized.

"It's okay, it's not like I wasn't into it," he admitted to her. "I got what I dreamt out of it."

"How so?" She sat up eagerly.

"I guess I always thought about . . . what we've could have been. But that's a stupid, crazy thought."

"Maybe not." She reached over to kiss him, but he backed up.

"Sis, what are you doing?" he asked her nervously.

"I've thought it sometimes too, that's probably what came out onstage." She unbuttoned her blouse, trying to seduce him. "We could find out tonight."

"What about Jack?" he asked, before letting her kiss him.

Deeper their kisses became as they fell to the floor; heavier the feeling got between them. Their friendliness dissipated as she took off his shirt; he unzipped her pants.

"Make love to me," she whispered softly in his ear, as he planted himself between her bare thighs; their skin touched. His jeans to his knees, sucking her neck, her hands in his hair, he lifted her up slightly to enter her; she could almost feel him inside her, but he stopped, pulling back completely.

"We don't want to do this. We can't." He rushed up to his feet, pulling his pants back on. She sat on the floor, staring at him in disbelief.

"You love Jack, you love me too, and I love you but not like this." Her eyes wide, mouth gaping open, she started crying.

"Don't do this, Cookie M . . . Please, don't do this. We're not meant to be together. You love Jack and he loves you, I don't want to ruin that. If we were to do this, I'm afraid it wouldn't be real. You'd hate it yourself if we reduced ourselves to a soap opera." He helped her up; she straightened herself.

"You should take the bed. I'll sleep out here," he told her, holding her.

"No. Um, I shouldn't stay in here. I'm going to go back to my room," she managed through sobs.

"I don't want you to be alone. You can stay here! You should." He tried to convince her, as she went to the door.

"No! I shouldn't be here, Max. I'm sorry. I'll be all right, I just need to sleep it off."

"But—" She hugged him, before he could say anything else.

"I love you," she told him emotionally.

"I know, but . . .," he stammered.

"Just . . ." She hushed him. "Sleep well, bro." He watched her until she disappeared, starting to follow her. Something told him to stay inside; initially wanting to ignore the strong feeling, he decided to heed it and closed his door.

Morrigan went back to her room, but didn't stay long; instead she checked the hotel phone for new messages. Still no response from him. Max called though to make sure she made it in; she hesitated but answered. The duration only lasted a minute or two until they awkwardly hung up. She took a few minutes to primp herself up, then went downstairs to the hotel's bar. There she's over a few drinks in, calling Jack again; she wanted to leave another voice mail but decided against it. Another few drinks later, she checked her phone, nothing. Finally, she discarded it in her purse.

"Another one, please," she told the bartender.

"I hate seeing a pretty lady drinking alone," Gaston remarked, after approaching slowly.

"That's original," she remarked, rolling her eyes. "Who says I want company?"

"No one, but I do hate seeing you upset." She chuckled lightly.

"Who says I'm upset?"

"Well, for starters you're drinking harder than I am. Secondly, I sense tears being held back."

"How perceptive." She noted. "Do I look that bad?"

"Never. Nice body armor by the way." He complimented her new art. She groaned slightly; it was bothering her.

"You okay?"

"Everybody's been asking me that lately. I'm fine, it's just hot in here."

"It is warm in here, or it could be us drinking," he suggested.

"Possibly . . . I haven't seen you lurking lately," she mentioned, skipping the subject.

"Oh, I've been trying to stay away, give you space, I know you don't like me much. Plus, you're in a relationship again."

"Now you respect that?" she asked him sarcastically.

"Well, honestly, I've never disrespected that, you being with someone. I stayed away then too."

"You're right! It's when I'm single I get the stalker effect. Or my brother gets the brunt of it afterwards." She chuckled.

"That's not fair. I suppose Max told you."

"Your sneaky, devious plays?" She laughed, then sighed. "Absolutely!"

"Well, I'm sorry about that. I guess I got a little high-strung."

"Oh? Apologize to him."

"I have," he admitted. "He dismissed me."

"Understandable." She noted. His facial expression explained he understood.

"Great show earlier. Was all those portions planned?"

"Cute."

"I mean it. It really was a great show! I think I overheard Kirk discussing another tour with Spin's manager." She sighed at his compliments, unimpressed.

"Not my finest moment," she admitted to him. "Maybe the music just moved me too far off the edge?"

"Hey! No. We all have moments in this industry, it wasn't all that bad anyway. You can use that type of press to help Mystic. Sometimes the downfall is you might have to keep it up." She glared at him. "Sometimes!" he told her. "You guys are new, still forging your path, so nothing is written in stone to regret. No regrets." He lifted his glass; she clinked it.

"Okay?" he asked her. She studied his face, his eyes; he was an attractive man. Dark brown hair, blue eyes with green specks, nicely structured jawline, yeah, he was handsome. Something she never noticed before, or declined to realize.

"Do you want to fuck?" she asked him suddenly, extremely direct. So much so he was initially stumped, which entertained her.

"Wow, he's speechless. For the first." She playfully slapped him, sipping her drink.

"Yes, I do," he answered honestly.

"This is against my nature, but . . . lead the way," she confirmed.

Off to his room, the atmosphere was still; they were the only ones roaming these empty halls.

"Wait." She stepped in front of his door, blocking their entrance. She kissed his cheek, whispering in his ear, "I have to make sure of something first."

"What?" he asked vacantly, kissing her.

"Let's get a few things straight. This is a onetime event, never to be repeated. Also, this stays between us. No one is to know what happens here tonight. You got me?" she asked, lifting his chin subtly to fully view his face. He paused before answering.

"Deal."

"Life or death?" she asked him randomly.

"Death," he answered. She smirked, grabbing his key card; she pulled him inside as the door opened, where they disappeared into darkness. What followed was a slam.

"Tick, ooh tock, tick, ooh tock," she sang to herself softly, while he slept. Sex with him was devoid of emotion, something that she strived on—feelings. Much different than with Jack, who was thoughtful and tender, most times anyway. Not Gaston though, so she went through the motions of it rather unconsciously, as though she had no control. Despite the nothingness of it, the lack of intimacy, he still made her cum, she still orgasmed, bodies in motion. All she had to use to get her through was the heat erupting inside her; she clung on to it desperately. She drifted to sleep shortly after their first ordeal. Surreal dreams flooded the doorway; she dreamt of the wrong things, whether sex with Max would've been more emotional, if so possibly even better than when she's with Jack?

Gaston moved under the sheets, slowly and deliberately, touching her back; she flinched. He repulsed her, yet enticed her poorer judgment, so she didn't fight the perversion any longer; instead she broke one of her rules temporarily. She welcomed it.

It was one o'clock in the afternoon. She woke up weak, drained from being with him practically all day; he was conked out beside her, his back turned. Straggling, she didn't even fully dress herself; however, she grabbed every trace that she was ever there. Swaying slightly, she nearly fell out the doorway, then suddenly without explanation she ran, ran down the hall to the elevator, till she arrived at her room. She threw her stuff on the floor, ran in the bathroom, ran her bathwater, then vomited in the toilet.

"Feeling dirty is . . . should be overrated," she thought to herself, soaking in her misery. She didn't mean that; she felt sick pondering over everything that transpired the night before to now. The worst part was she couldn't even pretend it didn't happen, so she sat there singing "I'm Only Happy When It Rains."

As she was stepping out of the tub, there was a knock on the door, alarming her.

"Who is it?" she called out, drying herself. The knock continued unanswered. She was hesitant to look out the peephole.

"Who is . . ." She peered through, then flung open the door.

"Jack?" He had a bouquet of flowers.

"Morrigan, I'm sorry I overreacted yesterday. And for not calling back, I had time to think . . ."

She overtook him, pulling him in close, hugging him, and apologizing.

"I'm sorry too, I . . . I didn't . . . I wasn't thinking. I'm . . .," she managed, half choked with sobs.

"It's okay, I'm over it now, babe." Tears were streaming down her face; he couldn't quite understand why.

"Let's sit down," he told her. "Stop crying . . . What happened?"

"Nothing, I wasn't sure if you were coming back or not?" she admitted to him without saying much else.

"Of course, I was coming back. You might not enjoy this, but I can't be without you," he admitted. She laughed.

"Sure, you're right," she said.

"I am . . . Did I hear we have a couple of days' vacation, starting now?" he asked, referring to one of her voice mails.

"Yes, we do. Wait . . . That's not the only reason you came back is it?" she asked him jokingly.

"No!" he answered honestly. She laughed at him again.

"I'm just kidding. Hey, I've got an idea. How about we spend it together? Just the two of us, no leaving this room or yours, no inter-ruptions, well, except room service, but that's okay," she suggested to him. He thought; she said, "Tsk."

"Come on, you know you want to." She nudged him.

"*Yes!*" he screamed, hugging her to lie her down. He kissed her lips, eventually leading himself downward, a gasp escaped her.

"Wait . . . Not here." She stopped him. "Where's your room?"

"Tenth floor," he answered.

"Good. Let's go."

They spent their two days harmoniously together uninter-rupted, that is until Monday.

"I almost forgot to tell you, when I ran into Kirk Saturday . . . Yeah, Saturday morning he told me the executives are coming in tonight."

"The suits." She acknowledged.

"Yes, the suits. They want to see the bands, meet you all afterwards."

"I guess it's coming close to that time. I'm not staying after the show for it."

"It's not like you're compelled to join their ranks. It's just a meet and greet. You don't have to do anything you don't want to do. Not that you ever. I really should listen to your mom more," he thought aloud.

"What?"

"Nothing. Go! It'll be fine, I'll be there to help you maneuver through . . . if you need me, that is."

"Just because I like your pretty face," she told him. "You can escort me."

"As if I wasn't already invited?" He laughed, as she walked over to the patio window, sat down, and drifted away from him.

He figured something was on her mind; he couldn't tell what that was though. Facing him sideways, her expression was stoic; steadily she rocked her chair, considering nothing, maybe the sky, if so, hope? Too bad she didn't see it; the only thing she could see was that their days of absolute bliss were over. Her mood did improve over the course of the day, as they prepared for their shows and performed. It was the ending that practically snuck upon her.

Jack was a whiz at it though, maneuvering through executives, something she humbly admitted to him before being whisked away by Max for a private chat.

"Cookie M, where were you the past couple of days?" Max asked, wondering. "I tried calling you, it always went straight to voice mail."

"Jack came back the next morning," she answered. "I was with him the whole time." He looked at her, with bright eyes that slightly dimmed.

"You guys made up? That's . . . great!" he stammered over himself. He wasn't sure how to feel after that.

"Try not to sound so excited, brother," she said, looking at him dispassionately. "Your mind is made up, isn't it?"

"Yes. I don't want to regret us. Anyway, let's not talk about that anymore," he answered, glancing over at Jack talking to one of the label executives.

"No, let's!" She led him in the opposite direction to the bar. "I didn't tell him, babe."

"Are you sure that's a good idea?" he asked her, concerned.

"Is honesty always the best policy?" she asked.

"We know better," he told her.

"Just so you know, I don't regret it, not us," she admitted. "Not that . . . anything y' know."

"Dudette, of course, you can't. I'm spectacular." She scoffed, rolling her eyes, laughing. Then she stopped; sensing negativity, she scanned the area.

"What's wrong, sis?" he asked, noticing her sudden behavior.

"Jack, right? I should formally introduce myself, I'm—"

"Gaston." Jack acknowledged. "Your name travels."

"Hopefully positively."

"That's to be determined."

"I guess I had that coming. You two being together, I suppose she told you some unsavory things about me." Jack shrugged, not letting on to anything.

"I really do respect Morrigan, she has a cool style, an explosive drive. She can never stop. But you know all about that."

"She's a powerhouse, hard worker. I'm extremely proud of her," Jack admitted, glaring at him.

"Yeah, of course. I agree with all that, but that's not what I meant exactly. There's a side of her, you know it well that I personally never thought I'd get to experience." He cryptically noted to Jack about their night together.

"Please enlighten me, man." Jack confronted him subtly.

"I promised her I wouldn't, but if you must know."

"I think you should get over there," Max told her, pointing in their direction, before realizing she was already near them.

Right before Gaston could reveal any damning evidence of their secret tryst, she grabbed his face firmly; her grip across his jaw extremely tight, she pushed him forward a few steps away from Jack.

"Are you senile? Or just fucking stupid? Say another word and I'll snap your neck where you stand. That I'll gladly explain to him." Loosening her grip, she smirked.

"Let's go, sweets, I'm tired." She clutched his arm, leading him out. Gaston looked on in embarrassment and anger. Max walked past him, chuckling under his breath. Realizing how foolish he looked, he soon left also.

"What was that about?" Jack asked her at the car.

"Nothing. He's just jealous," she said, staring him anxiously in his eyes. "You know this."

"You sure?" He asked.

"It's nothing, come on, let's go," she answered sternly, getting in.

"Okay," he said, following her inside.

They quietly arrived back at their hotel; she initiated sex that he accepted, except this time it was colder. He felt something strange about her, not completely unknown to him because she was distant. It reminded him of the times when they weren't getting along too good, yet the chemistry between them if just physically was still strong, so they would take their relationship to a strictly sexual one. And while they both enjoyed it, it wasn't intimately familiar; eventually they either parted ways or gave them another serious effort.

Earlier was still bothering him. Holding her face, he asked before she climaxes.

"Did you sleep with him?" She paused with shock initially, trying to determine how he figured out, and how much information Gaston revealed.

"Yes," she answered lowly. He sighed deeply.

"Okay, I can . . . I can deal with that. I hate it, I'm not going to lie . . . Not like you did," he told her disappointedly.

"But I didn't lie, it was one time . . . It was nothing! I couldn't tell you, when you came back. I didn't want to ruin us. He means nothing to me!" Caressing his face, she reached to kiss him but he pulled back.

"Can't you say you're sorry?" he asked her desperately.

"I did! I did!" She trembled.

"Morrigan, I forgive you, I do."

"I am sorry!" She tried to convince him. "*I am!*" She reached for him, while he got out of bed.

"Who are you?" he asked, standing.

"I thought I knew, but . . ." He shuts the bathroom door behind him. "I don't know anymore," she said softly.

The next day, they climbed the walls in a state of mourning, as he prepared to leave the very next day. He didn't tell her outright, but she could tell it's coming; by now she knew him, what he'd do.

"I love you, Morrigan, and I want you . . . always. But I can't stay . . . I intended to, I need some time though," he told her tenderly.

"Don't go," she begged him. "Please? I lo—" she said, hugging him. He caressed the back of her head.

"Now I know what Libbey was talking about, your mom too. I have to leave you wild." He kissed her forehead gently. "I'll see you soon," he said, getting into his van.

"You sure?" she asked, her voice cracking, a few tears streaming down her face. He wiped them.

"Yes," he answered honestly, proceeding to drive away. She held her composure until he's out of sight. Shortly afterward, she walked into Mystic's rehearsal; everyone's talking and laughing yet noticed she's distressed.

Jasmine and Tim dared not ask, so Max spoke up, "Okay, I'll bite. I'm the brother after all, what's wrong with you? Where's Jack?"

"Well, Jack just . . . left." Her expression changed instantly. "I don't think he wants to be bothered with me anymore after he found out I . . . fucked Gaston," she answered bluntly.

"Wait . . . What?" Max exclaimed, dumbfounded by her admission.

"What the fuck?" Tim mouthed silently.

"I think she just said Jack left because she fucked Gaston, but I could be wrong," Jasmine blurted out.

"No, I did say that," Morrigan admitted.

"I don't think you've ever said anything more shocking out of your mouth until now," Max stated.

"I haven't . . . I can't explain it, duh, but I can't blame it on alcohol either." She then took out the flask she gave Jasmine that she still had but refilled and sipped from it. "I'm fucking up," she stated.

"'Heart of glass' Gaston," Jasmine stated in disbelief.

"I know," she said, pointing to her in agreement.

"And I thought . . . least a little that you two full-blown making out onstage was weird," Jasmine stated.

"Yeah, who would've thought," Max blurted out suspiciously, scratching the back of his head. Morrigan glared at him, smirking.

"Yeah, that's not suspicious at all," Tim remarked.

"Well, did he say anything before he left?" Max asked.

"Not much," she lied.

"Did you apologize?" he asked.

"Duh, Max," she said, strapping on her guitar. "After the fact but yes, I did." She sighed. "Listen, I don't want to talk about this now, so let's play." She started to play a riff.

"What are you going to do?" Max asked, dismissing her.

"What the fuck can I do, Max? Better yet, tell me what to do!" she snapped at him. "I fucked up! There's nothing I can do, except give him some space! I think I would want that if the roles were reversed. Now I don't want to discuss this shit now, it's not important to this." She pointed, signaling the band, their music. "Let's do this fucking song," she finished.

"What the hell was that?" she exploded at them after they finished the one song.

"I could be wrong, but I thought it was 'Murders in Rue Morgue,'" Tim joked to a few chuckles.

"Tim, shut the fuck up! That shit was weak. I could barely hear your lame ass bass. What the hell was you doing back here, huh, writing stand-up? Just admit it, you seem to put more effort into that anyway."

"I know something's jumped up your ass lately, Morrigan, but you don't have to be such a bitch about it!" Tim remarked.

"Hey, hey, all right, we're a band, let's stop the hostilities," Max said, attempting to defuse the situation.

"Oh, come on, Max! Stop bullshitting! You feel the same way too," Tim exploded. Max stammered.

"No, Max. It's okay, let him talk. Let him get this shit out," Morrigan insisted. "I'm such a bitch right, T? Right? Then why the fuck are you still here? You really don't have to deal with my bull, you can just slack off!" Morrigan argued.

"So what are you trying to tell me? You don't want me . . ." Tim paused.

"I'm saying if you're that unhappy with my attitude you don't have to put up with it, therefore you don't have to be in this band any longer," Morrigan explained. "Shit!" she exclaimed, flicking her arm. It heated.

"Okay, Morrigan, that's enough! I'm serious, that's it, separate corners!" Max yelled. They all looked at him confusingly.

"All right, Dad!" Jasmine remarked jokingly.

"Shut up! Jazz," Max snapped. "Sorry."

"Do you really mean that, Morrigan?" Tim asked.

"Ye—" Morrigan started to answer.

"No! She doesn't!" Max replied.

"Well . . ." Morrigan tried again.

"Shut it! You back there." He pointed to her. "You sit and chill." He pointed to Tim. "You . . . Stop that recorder." He directed Jasmine. "We need to talk . . . Now!" He demanded Morrigan, walking her out the room.

Tim sat next to Jasmine, rather perplexed. She looked at him.

"She doesn't mean any of that, Timmy. You know she loves us." She tried comforting him.

"I know . . . But sometimes . . . Lately, she's been too different. And what's up with that damn tattoo?"

"She has a lot riding on this, it's just getting to her. I don't know. Max isn't giving up any details either."

"Like we don't!" He thought. "I guess you're right though, she does. Hmm, maybe I wasn't putting my all into rehearsal?"

"Dude, are you kidding me? We were fucking awesome! That song is great! She's just hurting over Jack. Anyway, don't sweat it. If Max is around, we're safe, our Morrigan we love will always be there," Jasmine stated.

"Yeah, I sure hope so," Tim said.

"Me too," Jasmine said to herself. "I wonder what daddy-o Max is laying into her right now?"

"Dude . . . Bad choice of words. I can't even process the whole Gaston thing," he remarked. "Do you think something odd happened between them?"

"Yeah, that was weird wording. Let's not mention that anymore. I don't know, but I don't want to find out if it had," she told him.

"Maybe we should play matchmaker?" Tim mentioned.

"What?" Jasmine said confusingly.

"I mean with her and Jack, dude."

"Let's . . . clean this place up before they get back." Jasmine averted.

"Yeah," he agreed.

"Bro. I didn't mean it," Morrigan admitted nonchalantly.

"No, we're going to ta—! Huh?"

"I didn't mean it. I'm over it though. I guess Tim is right," she said, thinking. "Wow, Timmy is right on something," she admitted.

"We all have our moments sometimes," Max told her. "Seriously, you're not cracking up on us, are you?"

"I'm trying to keep it together," she said softly.

"Try harder, the bash is up, grrl. Don't need you fucking shit up almost at the finish line," He said, laughing. She smirked.

"Look at you, making an executive decision. I thought you didn't want to be in charge."

"Well, I'm in charge when you're off the rails." He gave her a hug.

"Good boy, come on, let's see if I still have a band left." They walked inside to a calmer scene.

CHAPTER EIGHTEEN

All Hallows' Bash
Splits the Tide

" Y ou see Jazz?" Timmy asked Morrigan.

"No. Not since this morning. It's okay, we still have time. The show isn't until a few hours," she answered. Tim looked around nervously, hands deep in his pockets, tapping his foot.

"Is there something you need to tell me, Timmy?" she asked.

"Huh?" he said vacantly.

"Timmy, don't bullshit me." She grabbed his shoulder, pulling him closer to her. "What's up?"

"Listen, don't be mad."

"What?" She raised her voice.

"Just listen! Jazz asked me to promise not to say nothing, but I got a bad feeling."

"Spit it out, Tim."

"I saw her a little while ago, she looked kind of high. She said she was going to meet Rick," he admitted.

"Fuck! You should have fucking told me earlier," she argued.

"I know, I know . . . I'm sorry."

"Let me call her." She dialed her number; it rang for a few seconds before going to voice mail. Morrigan tried that a few more times. "She's not answering." Max walked in smoothly, with a lady on his arm.

"Hey, smooth operator!" Morrigan called out to him, attracting his attention.

"Oh, bandmates! This is . . ." He started to introduce his date, trying to show off.

"Yeah, that's great. I'm sure you're great, gal. Have you seen Jazz?" she asked him.

"Jazz? No. What's wrong?" he answered, concerned.

"Hopefully, nothing. This idiot here promised her he wouldn't tell us that she was meeting Rick," she answered, pissed.

"Dude!" Max scolded him.

"I'm sorry!" he apologized.

"Just shut up, Timmy. She's not answering her phone. Do you guys know Rick's room number?" she asked; they all look at Tim. He noticed.

"I have no idea! She wouldn't tell me."

"Wow, that's intelligent," Max remarked.

"I got to go find her," Morrigan said, phone in hand.

"Hey, um, I know I'm not in this, but I couldn't help over-hear," mystery girl mentioned. "But are you talking about Rick from Danger Prone?" she asked them.

"Yeah!" they all answered hurriedly.

"He's my ex." Max took his arm from around her slowly. "He's in 224. Probably high as fuck now," she mentioned annoyingly.

"Did you see him earlier today?" Max asked her.

"Unfortunately, I was trying to avoid him. Your friend Jazz? Pretty goth-like girl?"

"Yes. That's her," they answered in unison.

"You might want to hurry. I saw her stumble in there earlier."

"Oh, come the fuck on!" Morrigan exclaimed angrily. "Fucking ridiculous!" She stomped off in a rush toward the elevators. Max and Tim rushed behind her.

"You two stay here, I'll handle this." She blew out air inten-sively. She grabbed her tattooed arm, rubbing her wrist in a circular motion.

"What if something goes down?" Max asked. She double pressed the elevator up button again.

"Well, useless," she said, referring to Tim. "Should stay here."

"I can still help in case." The elevator dinged, its doors opening. They all stepped on.

They arrived on the second floor, walking to 224. Morrigan knocked loudly and impatiently.

"Who is it?" a drugged-out voice asked from the other side of the door.

"Open up!" she yelled, knocking harder.

"All right, all right. Just give me a minute." Rick opened the door after a few minutes, shirtless. They heard another door inside slam shut. Rick's eyes were bloodshot; he rubbed his eyes when the light from the hallway shined on him. He leaned over, using the frame to support him; he examined them.

"Oh hey, what brings you guys here?" he asked sluggishly.

Morrigan pushed past him, inside the dark room. Max and Timmy followed suit. The hotel room was dark with only a sole lamp on that's covered by a dark green scarf. It smelled like bodies and heat. She looked around for Jasmine; turning a corner she noticed underneath the closed door that the bathroom light was on. She pointed to it slyly.

"Hey! You could've just asked!" he said, closing the door.

"Shut up, Rick," Max told him, turning on the lights.

"You come in my space, taking over. What's your problem? What do you want?" Rick argued.

"I said, shut up, Rick!" he yelled, throwing things around, trying to make room to walk. Tim traveled behind silently, yet surely.

"What's all this shit, man?" Max asked, referring to various drug paraphernalia scattered throughout the room.

"Coping mechanisms," Rick responded casually.

"Coping mechanisms?" Max laughed. "What you need coping with?"

"William fired me," he answered lowly.

"I wonder why?" Tim broke his silence.

"So you decide to cope with the very thing he fired you for?" Max said. "Makes sense."

Tim chuckled under his breath.

"I wouldn't expect you to understand," Rick replied.

Morrigan knocked on the bathroom door. She heard stifling sounds behind it. She tapped again.

"Jazzy, are you in there? Jazz?" she asked softly.

"Morrigan?" Jasmine said slowly, her head low. "Please, don't come in here," she begged her, sitting in the bathtub, pushing the syringe in idly. Morrigan slowly opened the door, then peered in; seeing her shoot up set her in a rage. She scoffed.

"You're pathetic," she remarked. Jasmine's eyes darted sharply on her in shock. She's still slightly out of it. Morrigan grabbed her roughly by the arm, practically lifting her out of the tub. She shook her a little, resembling a rag doll.

"You're so weak! You were always weak, little dudette in distress," she insulted her.

"Please, you're hurting me, Morrigan! I can stop!" She pleaded.

"Who the fuck is you kidding? You're not even worth cleaning up." She pushed her back down with the needle still in her arm; it jostled.

Morrigan looked at her disgustingly, in her underwear. She turned her back on her.

"Morrigan, please! Help!" she begged.

"I can't save you again! You're not worth it." She walked out past everyone.

"Where's Jazz?" Max asked her, leaving out. "What is it?"

"She's fucked up in there. You two deal with her. I'm out! I've got a show to prepare for, so do you two so make it quick."

"But . . .," he stammered. Morrigan left, heading to the elevators.

"Morrigan!" they called out to her; she ignored them, stepping onto the elevator. They walked back inside to try and clean up Jasmine.

A few hours passed. Kirk waited for them at the club. Morrigan was already there, checking over their gear and set list. She went backstage, sitting down to wait for their set. She enjoyed the snacks. Kirk followed her.

"Feeling like a real rocker now?" He tried to converse.

"I guess," she answered.

"Where's Jack? I haven't seen him in a few," Kirk asked her.

"In his skin, I assume," she answered rudely.

"Well, where's the rest of them?" he asked.

Her left hand suddenly moved deliberately; fingers bending, she spoke, "The other two are coming." Her hand calmed, resting.

"Two?" he asked, before Max and Tim stepped in with Jasmine behind. Morrigan saw her enter out of her peripheral vision. She turned around, resting her chin on her right hand, looking up to her, laughing. Kirk, sensing the tension, got out of there fast.

"See you're all here. Great! Have a great show!" he wished them, leaving. Morrigan sat back in her chair, staring at the three of them.

"So who's going to say it?" she asked happily, a confrontational guise hiding in her voice.

"We've cleaned her up, Morgue," Tim accepted.

"As much as you can a harrowing junkie." She smiled, her left fingers tapping on the chair arm.

"That's enough, Cookie M. She's trying," Max stated. She steadily looked up to him, questionably.

"I never imagined you for an enabler, Max . . . or a fool," she told him. "This is a joke."

"He's right, Morrigan," Jasmine told her, stepping in her way. "I am."

"How many times have I heard that?" Morrigan asked, circling her like a vulture, swirling her finger around her neck. "Poor little rich girl," she whispered, only for her ears. She grabbed her from behind, her arms covering her chest.

"Give up the ghost, we won't blame you." She giggled, kissed her cheek then walked to the side of the stage to catch some of the show. Jasmine still felt her fading grasp; she cried, running to the restroom, her purse in tow. Tim ran after her. Max chased after Morrigan.

"What did you say to her?" he asked angrily.

"Just gave her a wake-up call," she responded coldly, not taking her eyes off Danger Prone.

"You need to cut that shit, dude!" he responded sternly.

"Go comfort the crybaby," she said, now facing him.

"That's fucked up, Morrigan," he told her, walking away. But Tim ran out to them.

"Jasmine's locked herself in the bathroom. She won't let me in and she's stopped talking to me," he said worriedly. Morrigan didn't budge.

"Come on!" Max nudged her. She rolled her eyes, reluctantly following them. Tim and Max banged on the door, trying to coax Jasmine to open it, while Morrigan stood in the background, annoyed.

"Two strapping young men, break the door down!" she yelled.

"Mystic is on in five!" announced a manager, immediately after they break through.

"Tell them we'll be out there soon. Go, Tim!" She grabbed his shirt, urging him out. She and Max stepped in to see Jasmine unresponsive, lying on the floor against the toilet. With the cord still tied tightly around her arm and the drug-induced needle sticking out, she suffered a seizure, with foam covering her mouth. Max knelt to her, checking her pulse.

"Well, aren't we a rock-and-roll cliché?" Morrigan remarked coldly.

"Morrigan, she's dead!" Max yelled, his voice frantic.

"You a doctor now?" she remarked callously.

"What the fuck is wrong with you?" he argued, his face distorted, a product of his confusion. She walked away, to the front where Tim was talking to a manager. She got a nearby guard's attention.

"Are you all ready?" the manager asked her.

"Yeah. My rhythm guitarist is dead though, she killed herself. It's just the three of us now."

"Jazz is dead?" Tim reacted, dumbfounded by the news.

"She overdosed!" Max looked at her in disbelief.

"Overdose, suicide, same diff," Morrigan replied coldly.

"What's wrong with you, sis?"

"Should I tell them you're cancelling?" the manager asked her.

"No, we'll just be a few minutes," she answered. Tim looked at her confoundedly.

"You can't be serious? What the hell has happened to you? You used to care about us. You knew it wasn't just about the music." Max confronted her.

"Yeah, Morrigan, I don't think I can play tonight," Tim said emotionally.

"Get your ass onstage!" she commanded him. He hesitated.

"Now!" she yelled, pointing. He begrudgingly agreed, looking at Max.

Max went to further approach her, as they walked back into the room with emergency services. She slammed him against the dressing room wall with almost supernatural strength. She was never a pushover, but the way she grabbed him seemed deliberate, almost to injure him. However, she held back.

"Back off, Max, I don't want to hurt you, brother, so back the fuck off," she said slowly, with her right arm on his neck.

"How dare you talk to me like that? To me," he asked *sadly*. He considered her eyes and saw nothing.

"I'm sorry, Maxie." She hadn't called him that since they were kids.

"But something's changed," he finished her sentence.

"You have no idea, brother," she agreed. She backed away from him and started clenching her left fist and groaning. Her arm was burning immensely.

"Are you okay, sis?" he asked cautiously.

"I'll be all right, but I need your ass on those drums tonight. I'll take care of Jasmine. I promise," she reasoned. He reluctantly agreed, stepping away from her. He peered back once to her, then back to the bathroom where he saw Jazz's motionless leg. Tears started to stream down his face, as he ran to the stage. She watched them pull out Jasmine's corpse. She and the medical examiner exchanged information, then she stepped onstage to the audience's applause. She fanned at them to stop, before speaking.

"I've always wanted to play this song because I thought it was really cool. Plus, it's so fucking relatable . . . But tonight it has a whole other meaning. This is for . . ." She peered to her left, staring at Jasmine's guitar, a '79 black Telecaster. She looked back to Max, before taking off her guitar and picking up Jazz's. "This is for my sister, Jazz. Our sister . . . I'm sorry, rich grrl."

She began to play the haunting opening riff, with Max, then Timmy joined in when she wailed the lyrics.

> ♪♫ *Sitting in my room, waiting for the sun*
> *I hope it comes, I hope it comes!*
> *I'm sad, I'm damned, I need someplace . . .* ♪♫

Throughout the song, she thought of Jasmine and her playing together, laughing, just screwing around. During the bridge, she imagined her onstage with them again; now with tears running down her face, she began spinning around from the microphone as Jazz disappeared. She continued the song to the end, as it faded to black.

> ♪♫ *I'm damned, I'm damned, and I'm so, so sad.* ♪♫

CHAPTER NINETEEN

"She Blitzed the Whole Night"

Morrigan sat in the funeral parlor, staring off into the distance. Max and Tim stood by her, waiting for the mortician's return. As the mortician arrived back to the desk to inform them, Morrigan saw a familiar face departing from a parked car in front of the business.

"I'm sorry I'm late. Had a little trouble finding the place," Jack spoke consistently.

"Jack?" Morrigan stammered, surprised at his arrival. "What are you doing here?" She glanced at Max, who in return winked at her.

"Per your orders everything will be taken care of for Jasmine by the ninth. I'm sorry again for your loss. All information regarding delivery is in this packet. Could you look over it, please, to make sure everything is accurate and sign and initial?" she asked Morrigan.

"Oh, of course." Morrigan unwrapped from Jack's embrace. She walked to the desk, read, and signed paperwork. Appreciation was traded between them, and Morrigan met the group to leave.

"I guess that's the last of it," Morrigan told them. "Shall we?"

"So how long are you going to be in town?" she asked Jack.

"As long as you need me," he answered. She smiled; he brushed her hair back.

"Are you two following us? We're just going back to Mom's house, Cookie M," Max said.

"Do you want to?" Jack asked her.

"Um, no. Can we just go driving? I don't really want to go back home just yet," she answered.

"Of course, I know just the spot," Jack said.

"Thanks, sweets. I'll call you guys later. Love you, bro." She kissed Max on the cheek. "And you too." She hugged Timmy.

"Love you, sis."

"Yeah, see you later, Morrigan." Everyone got in their respective cars and drove away, with Jack driving Morrigan to this secluded lake area.

"I almost forgot about this place," she admitted.

"Honestly, I almost did too," he told her. "I thought about it a lot shortly after I left the tour. I missed it, being with you," he admitted to her.

"I guess it's never any fun alone, is it?" she asked.

"Nope." He smiled, sitting on the picnic table.

"Is the cabin still back there?" She pointed to the far right.

"Yep. It's cleaned up and stocked with food," he answered her.

"Really?"

"Yeah . . . Admittedly, I came back here to cry recently." She laughed, before catching herself.

"Oh, baby, I'm sorry. I truly am sorry."

"I know," he said softly.

"Join me by the water?" she asked.

"Sure thing." He stood, walking with her to the lakeside. They stood together silently for a few minutes before Morrigan broke down.

"I've got a real witchy ceremony planned for her! Something she always wanted . . .," Morrigan barely managed.

"That's real nice," Jack answered, rubbing her shoulder.

"Something told me not to, but I figured maybe for her funeral they'll be different. Can you believe her parents didn't even offer to . . . ? Didn't even want to come!" He pulled her into his chest, where she sobbed.

"They don't even care that she's dead! Their only child! And they could give a fuck less!"

"Shh, it's okay, shh, forget them! They're not important. You don't need them, whatever else you need I'm here." He comforted her.

"I was so terrible to her before . . .," she managed through sobs.

"Don't . . . Listen, maybe we should go inside?" he asked her. She shook her head lowly.

"Okay, come on." They walk to the cabin-style home; it's comfortable inside with so much life.

Jack sat her down on the sofa, giving her a box of tissue that she practically attacked, while he went in the kitchen. He came back out with two cups of hot chocolate with marshmallows on top.

"Here, you need the sugar." He chuckled, passing her, her cup. She chuckled half-heartedly.

"Thanks, sweets." She sniffled, blowing her nose. "Max called you, didn't he?"

"Yes."

"I guess he figured I need you. Maybe I do." She smiled reluctantly, yet softly. Jack remained silent to her admittance.

"You're probably wondering why it wasn't me that called?"

"I was, but I figured you must have your reasons. No matter how much I may disagree with them."

"Try to understand, Jack. I was embarrassed and I thought what a reason to come to you after what I did."

"I don't care about that," he said.

"But I do! I've been terrible to those closest to me. I was such a bitch to Jazz, right before . . ." He rose, sitting down beside her.

"She begged me to help her, but I just turned my back on her. I didn't want to help anymore. I was tired of helping a lost cause. I treated her like shit, just like her parents, and I left her, but I love her, I miss her, and now she'll never know how much I truly loved her!" she babbled, tears streaming down her face.

"No, don't say that. I believe she knows! She knows how much you love her." Jack tried to reassure her.

"No! Can't you see I'm wicked? I did it, I killed her. I drove her over the edge and killed her!" Morrigan continued.

"Hey!" Jack yelled, snapping her back to reality. "You did not kill her!"

"But I let it happen! Sweets, you don't understand. Halloween was almost like when we first met her. It was Max and me, he dragged me to this show, and I bitched the whole way there about not wanting to go because I had finals and needed to study, but, man, he would not hear it. It was again just the two of us, doing our White Stripes thing and we saw this band play." She smirked, relaying her story. "I can't even remember the name of the band, but they weren't that great, I mean, they were decent, I guess. Anyway, I think Max was dating the drummer's sister or something, that's how he got the tickets. Their guitarist was awesome! She blitzed the whole night, and I remember thinking after a few songs we had to have her! Our eyes met several times throughout the show, and hers were so full of life. But as soon as the show was over, she disappeared backstage. I saw her eyes again before she left, then they were so lost and lonely. I asked them about her and they couldn't tell me shit. Her own band didn't know anything about her. So I talked to Max about stealing her away from them, and we waited several minutes before I thought, 'I don't think she's coming back out.'

"I felt weird, so I went back there to find her and saw their dressing room, went inside, but I didn't see her. Until I noticed the restroom door closed. I knocked and heard a stifling sound. I introduced myself, she didn't respond at first, until I asked her name, then she answered. Then she asked me not to come in. I could tell she was crying, I know the feeling, the sound of sadness too well. I told her, 'I couldn't do that, and that I loved her playing.' I went in slowly, and saw her on the floor, halfway in a state of awareness. She was about to take another hit, until I snatched it away from her, destroyed the drugs. She fucking hated me, cussed at me, tried to stop me, then I slapped her. I said, 'You don't have to do this. You still have a chance.' She sank to the floor and cried, I joined her down there, holding her tightly. Max eventually realized I was gone for a while, he went back and saw us on a dirty backstage restroom floor, talking it out like a couple of childhood gal pals, mascara running, lipstick smudged. Anyway, we took her to a rehab and stayed with her for the night, and I remember telling her before we left the next day that we want you to join us, faults and all. She hesitated but we managed to convince her, and she managed to convince us that it'll be all right . . . And it was for a long time, until . . .," Morrigan finished, lying back, exhausted.

"Can you believe you and I met shortly before that night? Good people came into my life during that time," she said.

Jack listened to everything she told him. He silently imagined how it all looked before he decided to speak.

"I'm sorry, baby, you're going to hate what I have to say, but I need to tell you this." His voice was solid and still, still comforting. He continued.

"Jazz was heading down a path of self-destruction with or without your assistance or enabling. You need to realize she was damaged way before you all met and while you kept her as far from the edge as you could, there was nothing more you or Max could do. Unfortunately, there was a sadness in her you couldn't fix, only she could. Now I believe she loved you and the band, and I even believe she tried, but she couldn't defeat her demons anymore. Jazz knew you loved her, and I'm sure she wouldn't want you blaming yourself for her death."

"You're wrong, sweets, I don't dislike what you had to say. I respect it and you. I'm trying to say thank you." She grabbed his face in her hands, moving closer to kiss him. He pulled back a little to speak.

"Do you think we'll ever get our crap together one day?" he asked her humorously.

"I don't think so . . . Now kiss me," she demanded, smirking; he complied.

"Maybe we should take this to the bedroom?" he suggested.

"Isn't this a sofa bed?" she asked. "And haven't we slept in crazier places?"

"Those are both good points," he answered, standing up abruptly, opening his shirt, then he thought, saying, "Wait, maybe we shouldn't do this. You are in an emotional state, and I'm fine with just caressing and cuddling." She scoffed, unzipping and pulling down his jeans to his knees.

"I've never known you to be such a sap." She egged him sternly. "Take off your clothes."

"Hey, I'm not a sap. I just ca— ah, fuck, that feels good." He acknowledged when he felt his member go into her mouth. She pleased him for a few minutes before stopping.

"Now assume the position," she commanded him.

"You got it, goddess." He took off his shirt, got on top, undressing her.

CHAPTER TWENTY

Suddenly Was Ragged and Worn

J ack awoke the next morning expecting to feel Morrigan in his arms, but alas she was nowhere inside to be found. She didn't even leave a note. He thought to himself briefly on where she went. Either her mom or Libbey's, then he looked at the time. He called Max, who answered.

"Is she with you?" Jack asked.

"Yes, we just got in."

"Are you all at Libbey's?"

"How did you know?" he wondered.

"Max!" he exclaimed.

"Yes, dude. We're here," Max answered.

"Good, keep her there. I'm on my way." Jack hung up, getting dressed.

"I'm disappointed in you, Morgue. You got your poor brother running around here making calls for you to your mom, to me. Like you can't talk to us, or tell us whatever. You've been raised better than that," Libbey reprimanded her.

"I know, I know . . . I'm sorry, Lib. I couldn't call you guys, I couldn't face anyone. I'm not in my right mind. Hell, he even informed Jack. Ugh, ah!" She slammed her tattooed arm on the bar top.

"Morgue?" Libbey asked, concerned.

"I'm fine!" Her voice suddenly was ragged and worn. "I mean, I'm fine." Her voice turned calmer and natural. She fanned herself. Libbey observed her.

"Maybe Raven was right, you aren't equipped for this." He acknowledged aloud.

"You know what, fuck you, Libbey! Fucking listening to my mom, huh? Like she ever believed I could do this anyway, or better yet you, you're not even in the business anymore! So why should I listen to a has-been anyway?" she snapped.

"Who in the hell do you think you're talking to, kid? I helped raised you." She scoffed.

"Whatever. I need a drink."

"Good luck getting one from me," Libbey stated.

"I can get one myself."

"You're not coming behind this bar until you calm down." Morrigan took it as a challenge, stepping up. Max, who overheard everything, jumped in, placing a glass of soda in front of her. He put his hand on Libbey's shoulder as to calm him.

"This isn't a drink," she stated rudely, sipping the liquid.

"But you drinking it though," Max said firmly. She sighed, rubbing her arm. Libbey could have sworn he saw steam arise from her tattoo in that moment.

"I'm sorry, Lib. She's going through some things." Max tried to defuse the situation.

"Yeah, I see." He noticed, backing off. By the time she finished her drink, Morrigan too apologized.

"I'm honestly sorry, Lib, I don't know what got into me that fast. I'm sorry, I love you." She got off the stool to go and hug him, but stopped at the flap.

"Can I come through?" she asked him sweetly. He chuckled.

"Of course, come on back here." He lifted the bar flap. She hugged him tightly.

"It's okay, kid." He felt up and down her tattooed arm, but it was cool to the touch. "I love you too."

"All's right in the rock world again," Max remarked.

"Not quite, she still needs a spanking," Libbey remarked.

"Hey!" Morrigan exclaimed, breaking back, slapping his shoulder playfully. They laughed.

"What in the hell are you doing here?" she asked Jack argumentatively when she saw him approaching. Then she looked at Max. "Brother, you're turning into a little snitch."

"Wait a minute, he already knew you were here. I just . . . confirmed," he stated before walking away.

"Be nice," Libbey warned her. "Go handle your business." He went to the back.

"Don't be mad at Max. I knew you would be here," Jack admitted. "How did you get here?"

"I caught a cab. You were conked out, didn't even realized I showered or the horn honking."

"Sneaky little thing, you are," he remarked.

"You weren't supposed to come here," she told him.

"Last night, you said you needed me," he reminded her. "Well, it was a maybe in there somewhere."

"I lied. I just said that to . . . fuck you," she stated, out of options.

"You're lying now for sure."

"You should leave, Jack. Just leave me alone."

"Oh, let me guess. Is this the part when you try to push me away for fear of hurting me again?"

"Can't say I didn't try . . . Sweets, I really am damaged goods. So . . ."

"You're our damaged goods though, at the risk of having this sound like a polygamist relationship." She chuckled.

"A smile. I'm not going anywhere, babe, least no time soon. Come here." He pulled her to him, wrapping their arms around each other.

"Trust me," he whispered in her ears. She dug her face in his chest, scared, on the verge of tears.

"Damn! I can't do this!" She jerked away from him. "It's not in me . . . to be . . .," she stammered briefly. "To be dependent," she admitted frustratingly to him.

"Morrigan, what's the deal? You get sweet for a second then it's like you get a weird realization. A wrong one, may I add, because it's not dependence. Everyone needs to trust someone," he responded. "And I'm here crazy about you in all your seductive quirkiness. Isn't that enough?" he asked simply.

"Yes." She sighed. "Last chance, sure you don't want to run?" she humorously asked.

"Do I get a waiting period?" he jokingly remarked. "Come here." They walked toward the bar; she slightly leaned on him in his arms. Almost falling he caught her.

"Thanks, doll," she said.

"No problem. So what about the tour? Is it over?" he asked.

"No. I mean, I think the show should go on. Not right away, because it'll feel too weird. We're thinking about resuming after Jazz's funeral. I can't perform now," she told him.

"And I don't think you should," he stated.

"Me neither," Libbey agreed.

"Don't take this as offensive, but . . . word on the street is you're going to hold auditions for a new member?" Jack asked.

"Absolutely not! I talked it over with Timmy and Max, and we've decided to keep it with the three of us. I will feel extremely uncomfortable replacing Jazz with some new player, who doesn't know the story behind the songs or . . . No. Mystic is now a trio. I stand by that," Morrigan replied sharply.

"Morgue, I stand by your choice," Libbey announced.

"I second that." Jack raised his glass.

"However, err caution . . . Management may not like that decision," he warned her. He and Jack traded glances.

"Too fucking bad," she stated, popping a handful of pistachios in her mouth. Her eyes immediately met with Max, who's silently drying mugs to the side.

"One day at a time, baby," Jack said, rubbing her back.

"Yep . . .," Morrigan dazedly responded.

CHAPTER TWENTY-ONE

"Best Blood"

"**S**is, I've got to admit. You've planned an excellent service for Jazz," Max commended her.

"Thanks, brother."

"Yep . . . Part witches' orgy, part GG Allin."

"Dude, shut up!" She playfully beat his back.

"All right, I quit! I quit!" He grabbed her wrists. Her laughs stifled as she held back tears.

"I know, Cookie M. I know. I'm going to miss her too." He held her briefly, but she pushed him away slightly to gather herself.

"I'll be all right, thanks, brother," she told him, smoothing her clothes out.

"How about you talk to her?" Max suggested.

"Good idea. I'll be back." Morrigan walked through the intimate group of people in their outdoor celebration of life after death. It was a small service with only close friends and other band members, eating and drinking, some cool tunes played in the background. Rick was not in attendance. Out of the group a few people left small tokens appreciated by Jasmine in her casket. The occasion was lively and casual, moody and spirited, what Jasmine always wanted.

"Hey, Mum. Thanks for coming." Raven hugged her daughter as she reached the casket.

"Of course, I'm going to miss her too. It was just last month." She sighed.

"I'm sorry, sweetie." She hugged Morrigan again. "She looks wonderful, you did good by her."

"Yeah . . . I tried," Morrigan stated.

"I'll give you time to . . . I'll be over here," Raven told her, walking over to Libbey, Max, Jack, and Timmy.

"Hey, Jazzy Grrl." Morrigan chuckled half-heartedly. "Haven't heard that in a while, huh?" She looked at her and studied some of the contents surrounding her.

"Looks like people left you some cool merch, dudette." She picked up a CD. "That was sweet of Mizzy, she had the rest of the band sign your CDs that we practically wore out when we found how mutually obsessed we were over them! I made good with her by the way. Jack, too, as you see. Performing that song with her was sick! I just never imagined I'd sing it in your memo— ah shit . . . I'm going to miss bitchin' and playing with you, man. I was such a dick and I'm sorry for that, but I love you always. Best blood." Morrigan leaned in and kissed her cheek and forehead.

"And at the risk of sounding like a total sap right now, which I know you would hate, I'm going to stop. I'll talk your ear off another time. Also, I remember how much you loved these cuff links, so, my lil skull sista, I'm giving you one." She took off her left diamond-encrusted skull cuff link and stuck it in Jasmine's jacket pocket. "Just in case you need to hock it." She laughed.

"How do you think she's handling it?" Max asked Jack.

"I think she's got it okay. As much as she can. Anyway, that's what we're here for so she won't go it alone," he said.

"Yeah, you're right. Now, what's this shit?" Max observed, seeing several paparazzi rushing through to Morrigan.

"Security is on its way!" Raven yelled to them both as they ran to Morrigan.

Lights flashed in Morrigan's eyes, as all the questions and attention startled her.

"Was it drugs, Morrigan? How long was Jasmine using? Is it true she got Rick on it? Will you be hiring someone to replace her soon?"

Her arm and attitude flared as she closed Jasmine's casket to try and keep them from taking any more pictures.

"Seriously? You vultures, she's right here! Damn! You fuckers have no respect for anything!"

As Morrigan leaned slightly on it protecting her, one of the cameramen tried lifting the coffin top back up; she snapped. She grabbed him by his collar, pulling him to her and powerfully pushing him on the ground. Max and Jack arrived in time, with Max stepping on the thrown guy's chest.

"Stay down!" he told him. Jack wrapped his arm around Morrigan, trying to lead her out.

"Get the fuck out of here! Take your shit and get out, she's not answering your prying bullshit questions! Morrigan, let's go," he yelled at them.

"Oh, it's the boyfriend! How did the kiss with Max make you feel? Or seeing your ex Mizzy?" one of the lead reporters asked.

"Don't make me punch you in the face, man," Jack answered sternly. "Okay? Now, get your shit and get out. Here's your ride." He pointed to security, as he whisked her away from the scene. He put her in the limo, trying to close the door, but she stopped him.

"No, I have to go back and make sure Jazz is okay," she stated.

"Your mother and I, and Libbey will handle that, you stay in here," he told her.

"But . . ."

"No! Max watch Morrigan!" he insisted when Max came running, getting in beside her. Jack ran back to the scene. Morrigan and Max watched out the window as the paparazzi were escorted away. It was so chaotic, they were wishing it was a nightmare they could sleep off, no such luck. Tim arrived at the limo shortly afterward to tell them the coast was clear.

"Come on out, they're going to put the last bit of dirt on . . .," he managed to speak.

"Thanks, Timmy." She thanked him. "Let's do it together." All three remaining members of Mystic walked over to their fallen bandmate's final resting days of her physical form. They each took turns spreading the dirt, mostly as a symbolic gesture of saying goodbye.

"We're all going to miss you, sister," Timmy stated, placing a sunflower on top.

"Eloquently put, brother," Max complimented him. Morrigan looked to them both.

"I love you, guys. Let's go." The whole family entered the limo; they're the last to leave the grave site, heading to Raven's home, with the knowledge they stayed together.

"Wake up, kiddies." Morrigan tapped the noses of Max and Timmy the next morning.

"I'm heading to the studio, you guys wanna come?" she asked.

"Are you sure that's a good idea?" Raven asked, startling her.

"Fuck! Sorry, Mum! Don't sneak up on me like that. I should work. Play! Or I'm gonna lose my mind." She peered at her band brothers. "You two dolls coming or what?"

"Yeah, we're coming, Cookie M," Max answered, hitting Timmy.

"What the hell are you hitting me for, man?"

"Just get up, you bastard! Is Jack taking us?"

"No, I'm driving!" she answered.

"Blue Thunder is here?" Timmy excitedly asked.

"Yeah, I kept him parked here at Mum's since we were . . . gone." She paused. "Jack is still here though." She confirmed.

"Full house, huh?" he remarked.

"Timmy, honey, you ain't lying! Everybody just decided to stay. I guess everyone feels I'm incredibly fragile and going to crack without their monitoring." She laughed hysterically. Max and Timmy stared at her. "I'm just fucking with you, guys."

"Morrigan," Raven uttered.

"Sorry, Mum. Well, I got to get ready, so I'll meet you two down here later."

"Bet," they agreed.

They drove up to the studio, a small one-level building on Ventura Avenue, when Morrigan observed the studio from her driver's side window.

"Something feels off in there," she warned, her left fingers deliberately tapping the steering wheel.

"How so?" Max asked from the passenger side.

"I don't know but I'll step in first," she told them. "Y'all staying in the car or lobby?"

"Lobby," Max answered. "Car," Timmy said. They looked back at each other.

"You guys wanna play rock, paper, scissors for it?" she sarcastically remarked.

"We're waiting in the lobby!" Max responded, dragging Timmy's ear toward the door. The three of them crossed the small-scale parking lot, entering through the main lobby area.

"Good morning, which studio is open?" she asked the front desk receptionist, her left fingers tapping again.

"Studio C," they answered in unison.

"Thanks, man!" She started to jog down the hallway.

"Oh, Morrigan! I'm sorry about Jasmine." She turned back.

"Thanks, Dex." She steadily walked to the door of Studio C.

Initially, when she entered the room is pitch-black and quiet. She clenched her left fist, her tattooed arm singed. She flipped a light switch to the recording studio booth; it's empty, but the light gently illuminated the background behind her.

"Your beau is a real knight. See for yourself," Gaston remarked from the shadows at the mixing station behind her. He threw a recent magazine toward her, showing her in shades huddled in Jack's arm as he tried to block the paparazzi from her at Jasmine's funeral. "Look how strong he is, protecting you."

"You're a warped little narcissist. I don't need protection. However, he is pretty cute, isn't he?" She admired the cover, before tossing it back in his face. She smirked. "You're probably the one that sent them there, aren't you?" She questioned.

"I'm not that cruel," he responded.

"I beg to differ." She chortled at her own response. "Why are you even here? You're not our producer."

"You spoke too soon, darling, because I am now. Saddest thing about your first one, he died too," he callously remarked. Morrigan's tattooed left hand started to contort against her thigh, the fingers bending and tapping methodically.

"Perhaps, you'll be next, babe," she told him coldly, not batting an eye. She chuckled, then winked.

"I'll just . . . get my band in here. What do you say, we lay a few tracks down? See how you do?" She challenged him.

"I'm ready if you are," he said.

"That's what I like to hear." She smiled before leaving out with the disgust instantly arriving on her face.

"What happened in there?" Max surprised her.

"I thought I told you guys to wait in the lobby!" she exclaimed, seeing both Max and Timmy right outside the door.

"No, technically you gave us the choice," he responded.

"No one likes a smart-ass, my dear brother," she said to Timmy's guffaws. "Shh! Damn, Timmy. Follow me." She grabbed them over the shoulders, pulling them to the nearest corner hall away from the door, where they encountered Mizzy.

"Holy shit!" Morrigan exclaimed. "I guess I'm not the only one hitting the studio early today."

"Only the best musicians do," Mizzy jokingly remarked. "I'm actually about to get lunch. You guys want to join me? By the way, I have something important to tell you, Morrigan."

"Tell me when we get outside," she insisted. They followed her in the Blue Thunder to a diner thirty minutes away. The four of them sat at a booth inside when a waitress passed them menus to look over.

"I need a drink," Morrigan declared.

"Are you recovering, Morrigan?" Mizzy asked. Mystic looked at one another briefly.

"Somewhat. How'd you guess?" Morrigan answered.

"It takes one to know one, I think," Mizzy announced.

"Wow!" they stammered in shock. "Excuse me, can I get a beer?" Morrigan called out.

"Dudette!" Max hit her.

"Oh, stop it! Hell, you might need one too after I lay this information on you."

"That reminds me," Mizzy began.

"Wait, until I get my drink first, please. Thank you." She thanked the waitress. "Hit us with it, Miz."

"It's about your producer."

"Lemme guess, he's dead, and Gaston is taking on us too. Did I miss anything?" Morrigan stated.

"Yes, but there's more. Gaston is in with the owner of the record company. This tour is part of a larger project, find the next big thing or some bullshit," she informed them.

"Why am I not surprised?" Max reacted. "Gaston always wanted to get in on that market. Plus, he's in the pocket with a few labels."

"No such thing as a free lunch, huh?" Morrigan mentioned. "How'd you find out, Miz?"

"They included us in a meeting over the state of the tour now that Jasmine died. And since Mystic indefinitely left they're trying to pull rank in any way possible."

"What are the terms?" Morrigan asked her.

"There's to be more meetings, between each of the newer bands individually, primarily it's focused on Mystic on whether you return to the tour, if not, join the label. You have to choose one. They would have the meetings after the tour regardless."

"They can't force us into this, that's why we signed the contracts!" Timmy anxiously stated.

"That can be void if we record an album in conjunction with the tour . . . Our EP isn't finished, remember?" she reminded him. "And since we're out of a producer . . ." She sighed. "How did Phil die anyway?" she asked Mizzy.

"Massive heart attack. The day after Jasmine."

She sighed. "Fuck! When it rains, it pours, since our producer was one supplied by the label. If we don't produce our own they can put another of theirs in charge and our project will officially be part of the label too. It's their way of trying to own us," Morrigan finished.

"All that was in the contract?" Timmy asked in disbelief.

"Timmy, stay asleep," Max told him, pushing his face away.

"Gaston isn't wasting his time. He was already in the studio when I went there. He informed me of Phil. Of his newest role."

"What are you going to do, Morrigan?" Mizzy asked.

"We're going to return to the tour and get a new producer first thing before we play another show. Least to distract them until I straighten this out, because they're not getting our shit." She paused, thinking. "I have to call Libbey, he'll know of someone. Matter-of-fact"—she rifles through her purse, taking out her cell phone—"low battery. Damn!" She slammed the phone on the table. "Any of y'all have your cells on you?" They all checked, coming up empty.

"Sorry, I left mine at the studio," Mizzy answered.

"Anybody got a few quarters?"

"I do!" Timmy handed her.

"Great! I'll be back." She flew outside to the nearest pay phone. They viewed her on the corner, speaking. She rushed back in.

"Well" Max asked.

"It's arranged," Morrigan answered. "We need to get back to the studio."

Arriving back, the gang entered the double doors when Gaston greeted them.

"I thought we were going to record?" he asked.

"We are, with Jerry," she told him confidently as Jerry entered readily behind them.

"Let's hit it."

Gaston begged to challenge it, but his cell phone urgently rang in which he answered.

"Yes?" he answered. The rest of the band walked off to enter the recording studio, while Morrigan lingered on to listen.

Gaston gave off vague answers, and tried as she might she could not hear who was on the other end of the conversation. There were no mumbles, no stifling voice heard; such an unnerving silence, it stressed her. She turned her back when he hung up the phone; she began to walk away.

"Morrigan," Gaston called out to her. She stopped, slightly turning her head.

"I really hope we can work this out for your sake, and the band." She looked, studying him.

"Work out what exactly? And for what?" she asked in return. "What are you up to?"

"Not me," he answered.

"Not you. Then who, Gaston?" She approached him slowly. "There's someone." She thought maybe the stranger. "Who do you really work for?"

They stared at each other, standing face-to-face.

"How's Jack doing?" he asked suddenly, ignoring her questions.

She scoffed, hurriedly walking away from the space.

CHAPTER TWENTY-TWO

"They Will Know When We Show Up"

"Why haven't you all been working?" Gaston yelled into the phone, waking Morrigan in a jolt from her hangover the night before.

"Okay, one, tone down that volume in your voice, because I don't know who you talking to. Two, you know damn well we've been in the studio, so don't come to me with that bullshit," she corrected him.

"That's not your job! Your duty is to fulfill this tour, not record some fucking EP or finish your album, you can do that when you sign," he continued.

"Fuck you, Gast! First, you are not our manager! I don't need to discuss this shit with you! Anyway, where's Kirk?"

"He's not higher in chain than I am. None of the other managers are. Not after that shit with Danger Prone and let's not forget Mystic. I'm officially overseeing all the bands, so we'll be seeing a lot of each other, doll, no more fiascos. But I'm partial to carnal impulses," he confessed.

"Oh, great! Life just loves me!" she quipped, before slamming the receiver down. She thought before picking it back up, dialing. A male voice answered the other line.

"Guess who just gave me the wake-up call I regret wasn't a nightmare?" she said.

"Heart of glass!" Max correctly blurted. Morrigan sighed.

"We might have to get back to the tour, Maxie. Sooner than anticipated. Gaston and the rest keeps fucking, calling me incessantly. And I can't keep ignoring them."

"I understand, sis. We'll talk about it at rehearsal, okay? See you later, but I have to go."

"Yeah, dude, but what are you doing?" she asked.

"I have another call, Cookie M. I will see you later, all right?" he said, rushed.

"Well, okay." She hung it up, still lying in bed. She scratched her tattoo, thinking of the phone call with Gaston, deliberating whether to leave out or not.

"Fuck it." She sighed, throwing off her comforter, ready to start the day.

Morrigan walked coolly into the dank rehearsal space, taking a few sips from Jazz's flask that she kept; there Max and Tim anticipated her reaction when she set her eyes instantly on the new girl in her path. Her greeting was less than warming.

"Who the fuck is this bitch?" Morrigan questioned as rudely as her expression suggested. She eyed her up and down, viewing her as an outsider, intruding.

"Morgue!" Tim chastised her, slapping her arm. He sat on a drum stool.

"Don't," she replied. Max was seated on a circular sectional gray couch set in the middle of the room with a mock stage at the back. Their gear and equipment surrounded the couch, ready to play.

Nonchalantly, he pointed at the new girl in her trendy bohemian-gothic fashion. "Chastity, Morrigan. Morrigan, Chastity. The label sent her over." Casually, he rose, walking to Morrigan.

"Really?" She placed her guitar case down beside her. "They sent someone?" She analyzed the moment, referring to the numerous phone calls and messages she has received but promptly disregarded from management.

"Send her back." Morrigan began to turn to face Max, when Chastity effervescently introduced herself.

"Hi! I'm Chastity. As Max so graciously acknowledged." She extended her hand out to Morrigan. "The label just sent me over as an impromptu tryout, which I thought was sudden, but they said they tried contacting you." Morrigan declined to shake, staring at her, unimpressed. Chastity pulled her hand in awkwardly. "Anyway, here I am!" She closed with an uncomfortable giggle.

"Well, la di da, it's Sandra Dee," Morrigan quipped.

"Cookie M, that's rude," Max casually remarked. She scoffed, rolling her eyes.

"I love your tattoo, Morrigan! It's so . . . creative!" Chastity suddenly complimented. Morrigan's arm steamed, then her fingers tapped against her thigh incessantly as if applying Morse code; Chastity noticed. Morrigan heard a voice whisper so clearly in her left ear, speaking to her, she reacted subtly.

"Interesting," Morgue whispered trancelike.

"What's interesting?" Chastity interrupted.

"Formalities!" Morrigan announced. "You extended your hand to me, I guess the least I could do is reciprocate." She extended her hand, they shook, but then Morrigan moved to her wrist, gripping it tightly; however, Chastity did not waver. Both gave a strong handshake, sharing a heat between them, as though two embers rubbed together.

"Tell me, Charm School." Morrigan gracefully invaded her space. "You got any ink on this soft skin?" She softly swiped her index finger across Chastity's throat to her black chiffon blouse, gently pulling her collar, trying to expose her chest when her fingertips singed at the slightest touch. Chastity quickly pulled herself back.

"No," she sternly asserted. "Afraid not. It's one of those ideals embedded in my brain from my 'moral' upbringing. My body is a temple."

"While mine is a canvas," Morrigan, smirking, admitted, admiring her reaction. "Well, enough chitchat." She checked her watch.

"You're here, got time to run through a few songs? You do know our songs, right?"

"Um, no!" she mistakenly answered, taken aback. "I mean, of course, I know your songs. It's just not today. Today, I wanted to introduce myself and get a feel of the group. I heard of . . ."

"Jazz," Morrigan answered.

"Yes. I'm sorry," Chastity apologized.

"That's the lifestyle," Morrigan stated, shrugging her shoulders. "Oof." Max sighed.

"Yeah, well, again I felt weird about dropping in on you all so soon. Of course, the label expects more, but I think respectful timing is everything. How's Wednesday? We could jam?" she asked.

Morrigan peered at her mates.

"Oh, yeah, Wednesday's fine, three PM?" Max and Tim suggested.

"The jury has spoken," Morrigan remarked. "Be here at three."

"I will! See you all then, thanks. I got to go now," she agreed.

"Your mom picking you up?" Tim bantered. Chastity grinned.

"Eh, no. Do I seem that . . . conservative?" she asked.

"Nah, just messing with you. It's what we do," Tim answered. She chuckled, turning to leave.

"Hey! Charm School, we'll get you out of those clothes yet." Morrigan winked, smirking. Chastity blushed, then departed, slightly losing her balance toward the entrance.

"Thanks, Morgue. Scare her away," Tim remarked, slapping her arm.

"You act as though she's staying, dude?" Morrigan questioned him. He seized up. "Do not forget, our objective is still the same," she told him, gripping his shoulder sternly but not enough to cause injury.

"I haven't forgotten, Morrigan," he answered softly yet surely.

"Good boy," she stated gladly.

"Well?" Max coyly asked, now seated at his drum kit, tightening the cymbals.

"She's hot," Morrigan blatantly stated.

"Really, Morgue, is that all you noticed?" Tim jokingly asked. She and Max instantly made eye contact.

"She's one of them," she answered. Max nodded.

"One of who?" Tim clueless, wondered.

"Suits, Tim," she answered.

"Corporate suits," Max further confirmed.

"She's probably one of their daughters," he mentioned to soothe Tim.

"Oh, yeah, an insider!" He seemingly caught on.

"Yes, their insider," Morrigan agreed, rather impressed with his deduction.

"I'll get to know her better," she suddenly mentioned.

"And how do you plan to do that?" Tim asked in disbelief, stopping his tuning.

"Come on, as long as you've known me. I have my ways," she confidently admitted.

"Yeah, I know your ways. But isn't Jack coming back soon?" He randomly inserted.

"How am I supposed to know?" she quickly asked.

"Aren't you two back together? I assumed." They looked at him in silence. "He probably doesn't trust you yet. Give it time," he finished, unaware.

"Since when do you care?" she agitatedly asked. Max looked at him, wearing an expression that said, "I told you not to bring it up."

"I, I don't!" he stammered. "Well, I do, but you're grown! Let's just rehearse," he suggested, wanting to skip the subject. Max shook his head, smiling.

"By the way, Mom called before you got here. Wanting to speak with you," Max mentioned.

"Oh yeah? She say what she wants?" she casually asked.

"No, just that she needed to speak with you," he answered.

"I'll call her back," she said nonchalantly, turning the knobs on her amp.

"Really?" he insisted. She sighed a sigh of irritancy.

"Is there something more, Max?"

"I mean you've barely talked to Mum since all this. And when someone mentions her, your response isn't the most pleasant," he mentioned.

"What do you mean, we were just at her house?" she told him.

"Yeah, for a couple of days, after Jazz's funeral, you've been in a hotel for a week!" he reminded her.

"So what? Okay, so yeah, it's long intervals of no contact, but she knows I love her. It's been a long month."

"You weren't that talkative when this started," he mentioned lowly. She scoffed impatiently.

"Listen, sis, I'm just saying. When you can't, you're going to miss it," he warned her.

She sat silently, her head hanging low; the air was stagnant.

"Are we still rehearsing?" Tim nervously asked, breaking the mood.

"Oh, that reminds me," Max stated. "What have we decided on the tour?"

"They will know when we show up," she vaguely answered.

CHAPTER TWENTY-THREE

"Spellbinding Mix of Sex, Danger, and Sneaky Tricks"

66 **A** lmost time for Mystic to go onstage. You guys ready?" Kirk announced to the band backstage at a new venue. "How are you all feeling?"

♪♫ *Numb my soul, damn, I'm cold.* ♪♫

No one answered, while Morrigan strummed her guitar, focusing on a new song.

"Don't everybody jump up at once," Kirk said sarcastically. Max checked the audience from behind the curtain.

"Full house," he stated somewhat nervously, itching for a smoke. "Wow, I can see Libbey and Jack from here," he happily told her, expecting a reaction. Morrigan, unmoved, continued singing in a hypnotizing vocal register, playing, and writing lyrics.

"Not bad for a semi-surprise welcome back, is it Max?" Kirk responded. Max smiles agreeably. "Believe it or not, I've missed you all. I'm glad you decided to come back."

Morrigan set her guitar down on her lap, lay back, and sighed, staring at him.

"I didn't take you as the sentimental type, Kirk." She suddenly broke her silence, taking a sip from Jazz's flask.

"I hope that's iced tea," Kirk remarked.

"Now where's the fun in that?" She chortled. "But for the sake of your health, think of it as tea."

"Whatever you say, Madam Morrigan." He partially bowed.

"Oh, come off it!" she told him, standing.

"It's time," the owner announced. Mystic gathered their instruments.

"All right, kick ass! Hold no prisoners!" Kirk stirred them up. She placed the back of her hand on his chest. "Cool it, Kirk."

"You're right, you're right, little too much. Still, have a kick ass show, lady." He winked.

"Thanks."

"Let's hear it for a new favorite, a spellbinding mix of sex, danger, and sneaky tricks. Help me give them a raucously hot welcome! *Mystic!*" the owner screamed into the mic. Tim stepped out first, followed by Max, and lastly Morrigan. She stepped to the microphone, adjusting it slightly, then a roadie placed her guitar over her.

"Hey, how is everybody doing tonight?" she spoke to a roaring crowd. "I want to apologize on behalf of the band for being away for a while, as you know we suffered a terrible loss."

The crowd drowned out her speech momentarily with emotionally charged indistinct words.

"Thank you, I know. Thank you all so much for your support. This is probably sounding cliché, but by no means is it insincere. We couldn't have survived without your support and respect. Now Jazz wouldn't want the show to stop, or us leaking over her too much, just enough though." She giggled. "So without further ado, we're going to keep this as punk rock as possible for you . . . *Hit it!*" Max began with a smashing beat with Tim when Morrigan entered with a spastic riff. The first song went well without a hitch until disaster struck during the second.

"Oh, shit!" Tim muttered when two of his strings broke midsong. Morrigan, overhearing, turned midway to see what was happening, but saw a roadie coming out with a new bass. She continued singing, and they played the rest of the song successfully.

Then, during "Rue Morgue," Max accidentally busted his snare, but they kept playing without missing a beat. Until, Morrigan's microphone began to static while she's singing and an insane amount of feedback came through, the audience groaned. Tim's amp randomly blew out, despite all their equipment being tested fine.

The mic sparked angrily; she knocked it to the floor. Yet, she began her solo when she saw the stranger in the audience, laughing to her disbelief, eyes of piercing silver. Ignoring him by continuing to play, he winked, then her high A and lower B strings instantly popped, nearly scratching her eyes; she slapped them away, but one scarred her left cheek.

"Oh fuck," she whispered to herself. Jack and Libbey looked on helplessly with the rest of the audience. Embarrassed, she looked at them before turning away. She briefly stared at Max and Tim begging for an answer, but they had none to give. She contemplated running offstage before doing just that with her guitar. Everyone's mouth dropped in stunned silence and disbelief. When only a few minutes later, Morrigan appeared back onstage, instead this time carrying an acoustic guitar and bass, which she handed to Tim.

"Can you still work it?" she asked Max.

"You know me, sis, it's nothing I can't give a good beating," he told her confidently.

"Don't I know it?" she said, reaching over to him, grabbing the back of his head, kissing his forehead.

"We're doing 'Little Bird Blue,'" she told him, as they prepared. By now a technician set another mic and stand up, which she surely approached.

"That was some weird shit, wasn't it?" she remarked. The crowd agreed in unison. "Maybe, that's a sign we should slow it down for you, dudes and dudettes, huh? Yeah. I was going to keep this a surprise until we had an official release date, but this next song is from our recently finished upcoming debut EP," she announced to everyone. Gaston, who's standing backstage, looked on in uncomfortable amazement, while Mizzy, Jack, and Libbey clapped and congratulated with the audience. "We're still working out a title for it, but the name of this new song is 'Little Bird Blue.' This was the last song Jazz and I wrote together," she finished, before playing a soft rock progression. The audience quieted down, listening attentively as she sang.

♪♫ *Tell me what to say. Tell me what you've got for me.* ♪♫

Their performance was met with huge applause, even by Chastity who was hanging in the audience. Mystic joined hands, taking their bows, but it was not to be enjoyed.

"Aah," Morrigan painfully groaned, crouching over slightly. "Ouch!" Max exclaimed, snatching his hand away from hers when he felt fiery heat. Jack, realizing, started to make his way to the stage, when Chastity yelled, "*Above! Watch out!*"

Everyone looked up, noticing one of the overhead lights swinging wildly. Morrigan pulled her bandmates back, so they all swung back out of impact when the light suddenly crashed down exactly where they were standing, abruptly ending their set. Jack ran onstage to Morrigan's aid, with others following suit.

"You guys all right?" she asked.

"Uh, yeah, I think. Weird, huh?" Tim remarked, rubbing his leg. A small piece of frame etched itself inside partially.

"Dude, you're going to need help. Jack, help him up."

"Yeah, no problem. Careful, man," he responded, easing Tim up. She and Max sat still for a few moments, admittedly too scared to move.

"Holy shit. I never thought I'd be happier I gave up smoking," he managed through deep breaths. "I can barely breathe."

She too breathed heavily, partially examining the skirmish crowd, until her eyes set on a figure at the far back, leaning on the frame of an exit doorway. The stranger smirked amusingly before disappearing.

"Come on, bro. Let's get out of here!" She jolted up, pulling him up eagerly. They ran out, meeting the others out front with medical attention.

"Is Timmy going to be okay?" Mizzy asked Morrigan later that night at the hotel restaurant.

"Yeah, turns out a foreign entity entered his body during our fantastic show," she answered sarcastically. Max blurted out an ironic sound. She slapped the back of his head in response.

"Did I miss something?" she asked curiously.

"Nah," Morrigan responded. "We should be able to pick him up from the hospital tomorrow."

"It's that serious?"

"Not really, she just wanted them to watch him overnight," Max answered.

"Can't say I don't care, right?" She modestly tried to dismiss. "I'm sorry, Spin Dreary didn't get to play their set," she apologized to Mizzy.

"The life we live, you take the hits. I'd like to make a toast. To an awesomely dangerous rock-and-roll show!" She raised her glass; they clinked.

"Oh, man," Morrigan awkwardly murmured.

"Don't sweat it, you rocked in a difficult situation," she told her.

"She's right," Libbey agreed. "Most would've ran, but you turned it around, so feel proud and keep it moving."

"We really set the bar didn't we, sis?" Max chimed in.

"You're not kidding." She spied Chastity alone at the bar, drinking. Jack suddenly cleared his throat obnoxiously loud, prompting Libbey to excuse himself.

"Come on, y'all, let's see if we can scam this place out of some free samples," he suggested.

"Uh, yeah," Mizzy, realizing, responded.

"I'm fine for now."

"Get up, Max!" Libbey commanded impatiently. Max pouted, begrudgingly leaving Jack and Morrigan alone at the table.

"Smooth," Morrigan remarked.

"Yes, I have quite the exit strategy," he admitted.

"Isn't that normally directed towards yourself?"

"It can go both ways," he told her. "I've missed you."

"I was wondering when you were going to say that," she said.

222

"You could've said it too!"

"I've missed you," she admitted.

"Oh, now you say it!" He laughed.

She placed her hand on his cheek lovingly; she smiled.

"I can't believe you made it tonight!" she exclaimed.

"Of course! I wouldn't miss your official return performance, not this one."

"I wasn't sure, after . . . I mean, I wouldn't blame you if. I don't blame you. Lately, however, you've been missing in action," she mentioned lowly.

"I needed some time," he began.

"I understand," she interrupted.

"Anyway, we should talk about us," he insisted.

"I agree."

"Let's go," he said. They stood to leave when she looked back over to Chastity, feeling compelled to go to her.

"Hold that thought, babe. I need to speak to someone, thank someone." Her arms were around his waist.

"But I thought we were going to spend the night together." He frowned.

"We are! It's important though." He glanced at Chastity.

"Okay."

"Oh, don't pout. I'll call you when I'm coming up," she confirmed. He sighed.

"Yeah, okay. I love you." He kissed her cheek; she kissed his lips.

"Be good," he told her. She winked.

"Mind if I join you?" She subtly approached Chastity from behind, sitting next to her.

"Of course not! Please! You want a drink? Bartender?" She got his attention. "I'll take another and she will have?"

"Margarita, please," she answered. "What's a good girl like you drinking in these wee hours? Bad things can happen, y' know," Morrigan teased her.

"Who says I'm always a good girl?" The bartender arrived with their drinks.

"Touché." She raised her glass. "Anyway, I came here to thank you for saving my life and my brothers. Good looking out, or up!"

"I like how you refer to them as your brothers. I'm thrilled to have noticed, honestly, it's a miracle," Chastity stated. Morrigan grew impatient.

"You actually believe in those?"

"And you don't?" It went unanswered. Chastity, feeling uncomfortable, sought to fill the air. "Admittedly, it's my Catholic upbringing speaking."

"I clocked you," Morrigan stated happily.

"Yeah, you clocked me," she admitted reluctantly, glancing at her. "Okay, I have to say it, you were awesome tonight! Beautiful and magnificent, it was transforming! I think you're gorgeous anyway, but your performance, whew! I'm sorry, I'm gushing," she complimented, covering her mouth.

"I . . . don't know what to say, thanks." Chastity giggled.

"Seriously, though." Morrigan took a sip. "What did you really think?"

"I loved it, you're a professional. Despite the mishaps, you improvised, made it intimate. It rocked, you rocked!" That caused Morrigan to think.

"Y' know, you gave a wickedly good audition. I was sincerely impressed with your performance, which brings me to another reason why I want to talk to you." She paused. "How would you like to join Mystic?" she asked.

"No way! Seriously?" She freaked.

"Seriously. How else can I properly repay the person who saved my life and my band?" She took another sip. Chastity squealed excitedly.

"I would love to!" And without thinking, she kissed Morrigan. However, Morrigan, keeping her eyes peeled, didn't remove her hands from the stem of her glass. Suddenly, Chastity opened her eyes, stopping to speak.

"I love this song!" she exclaimed, pointing up to the song playing over the speakers.

"She turns me on, don't get me wrong. I'm only dancing," Morrigan sings softly, mesmerizing her. Chastity placed her hand on her thigh.

Morrigan straddled her on the bed, slowly leading her tongue up the front of her neck, to her full rose-pink-tinted lips. Their tongues exploring, until Morrigan pulled back, towering the blushing femme. Chastity undid Morrigan's belt and unzipped her jeans. One by one, from the bottom to midway, Morrigan unbuttoned Chastity's silk blouse. She crouched, blowing her belly button seductively, then lightly peppering her stomach with kisses. She then placed both hands on her breasts, squeezing them gently, before violently ripping open her blouse. Chastity gasped, realizing her chest tattoo was now exposed. Morrigan pressed her left hand hard on it, testing her theory.

"*Shit!*" she exclaimed as it scalded. Chastity screamed. Morrigan covered her mouth, gripping her cheeks tightly. Chastity quietly began to sob.

"I knew it was something off with you." She flicked out her blade from her jean pocket. "I just couldn't place my finger on it. Until now that is." She chuckled. "Who sent you?" She slowly uncovered her mouth.

"The label. My mom is an executive," she answered hesitantly.

"Why?"

"To watch you . . . Make sure their plans go accordingly."

"What plans are those?"

"I don't know!" Chastity denied. Morrigan started to choke her.

"To sign!" she admitted. "To sign on their label, I don't know anything more than that. Anything else they said, if I got close to report what I see. This clearly wasn't part of the scheme, to get this close."

"Makes sense, the tat is kind of a giveaway. Who did this to you?" She pointed the tip of her blade to her chest.

"One of my mom's friends, some blonde woman. My mom thought it was time I prove my worth," she said convincingly.

"Your mom let this happen?"

"After my dad died, she fell into a dark depression. I didn't realize until late how dark it was," Chastity admitted tearfully. "I couldn't disappoint her again."

Morrigan sighed. "Unbelievable." She flopped down beside her. Chastity lifted slowly.

"I'm sorry, Morrigan. But I ended up really liking you." She placed her hand on her back, underneath her shirt. "You were electrifying tonight! Onstage and off," she complimented. Morrigan chuckled. "We didn't seal the deal yet." She grabbed her by the back of her head, kissing her deeply. Her left hand wrapped around her neck; she pushed her aggressively.

"If I find out you're lying to me, I'll kill you," she threatened.

"I believe you," Chastity whispered in response.

"Good." They continued kissing passionately when Morrigan unfastened her bra. Chastity removed her shirt. Morrigan cupped Chastity's breast, sucking her erect nipple, with her right thumb caressing the other. They undressed fully, surrendering themselves to each other; a moist touch erupted between their thighs as the night climaxed. A night of freed forbidden desires.

The next day, Morrigan, wearing a multicolored kimono, blue shorts, and blood-orange bra, opened the door for Max. It's a silent entrance based on verbal cues of years growing up together. He followed her onto the terrace where it was sunny and breezy, with a hint that winter was coming.

"Fancy digs," he remarked upon entering the terrace.

"Well, 'they're' footing the bill, might as well enjoy it," she responded.

"Fair enough."

"Sit with me, Max," she told him, sitting on a stone cushioned bench under an oak tree.

"This a serious talk?" he remarkably asked.

"Yes, unfortunately," she said.

"You fucked her," he straightforwardly stated.

"Of course, I did!" Initially taken aback she raised her arms in the air admittedly.

"Are you sure that was the wisest decision?"

"No. But it was certainly the boldest one. Enough so to have them think they're in," she stated.

"I take it you're letting her join, superficially."

She cocked her head to the side, a knowing expression riddled on her face.

"What do you think? Especially, I don't trust her."

"Yet, you slept with her? Don't you see the dilemma? I mean, the blatant contradiction," he remarked. She sighed.

"It was a mind trick, Max darling."

"Let's hope you're not the one who falls victim to it." He expressed concern.

"I'm trying my best here, Max. The attitude, the drinking, voices, and poor choices," she stated.

"Hey, you rhymed," he said half-heartedly.

"Cute." She lowly chuckled. "Listen, babe, we briefly discussed it after the funeral. The first since this all happened. And I foolishly thought if it goes unsaid, then all will be well," she confessed.

"We've both been guilty of that," he agreed.

"Clearly, something is wrong." She raised her tattooed arm to show him; her kimono sleeve loosely fell to her elbow. "Sometimes it honestly burns, an undeniably burning sensation isolated to this area." He stared at her partially in disbelief, partially in realization.

"How bad is it?" he asked.

"Nothing, I guess overly extreme, I can fan it cool, mostly it lasts a few seconds then soothes on its own," she answered.

"We have to get to the bottom of this, sis." He reached to hug her, she hesitated. "One way or another, there's got to be answers somewhere."

"I agree. And I think I know where I can find some. I promise you, bro. I will figure this out."

"Not without me, we're in this together," he promised. She sat back, checking out the scenery.

"How'd you know?" she asked him.

"Know what?"

"That I was with Chastity last night."

"Jack called me, looking for you," he answered.

"Keeping tabs on me now?" She scoffed offendedly.

"He said you were supposed to meet him," he corrected her.

"Two of you best friends, huh?" She remarked.

"Jealous?" She rolled her eyes to his insinuation.

"Honestly, maybe we should start. Listen, sis, you can do what you want, but everything has consequences," he sharply finished.

CHAPTER TWENTY-FOUR

"Apostasy Records. Heh, Clever"

D iscontented with herself and her situation, she finally went searching for answers. Aimlessly, she drove around town, hoping anything remotely identifying as such would reveal itself to her. Her cell
phone rang in her purse; she muttered "of course" under her breath.
She arrived at a stoplight, using the moment to answer. "Damn," she
said, noticing the caller.

"I thought we were going to spend the night together? I waited
all night for your call, nothing," Jack stated.

"Something came up, babe." She attempted to answer sweetly.

"More like someone," he mentioned. She went silent. "I called
your room, before calling Max. No answer."

"Tsk, sweets. We're going to have to talk about this later." She
saw a mysticism shop hidden among populist stores. "Jack, I really
have to go. We'll talk later, okay?"

"Don't bother," he said before abruptly hanging up.

"Shit," she groaned, throwing the phone back in her purse.
"Deconstructing the Howlite?" she questioned the name of the shop,
searching for a parking spot.

It is a vintage storefront, slightly Parisian in style. She peered through the windows, eyeing the owner behind the counter organizing merchandise. The store was neatly designed with low tables covered with different eccentricities, ranging from labeled herbs, leather journals, and various gemstones in bowls. Morrigan smiled slightly; she had forgotten for a time how much she missed it, shopping for tools, learning the craft. She opened the door where wind chimes greeted the enterer; it was instantly soothing as she crossed the threshold.

"Hi! Don't be shy, please immerse yourself in the magical goodies," the shop owner cheerfully greeted her.

"Hi," Morrigan stiffly returned. She walked through a moment, examining the masks and amulets on the walls. Again, she looked at the owner, who smiled, noticing her stare. She smiled back, trying to seem less suspicious, next putting her attention on two other shoppers present behind the columns, trying this time not to seem obvious. Eventually, both shoppers made their way to the register, quickly leaving after making their purchases.

Morrigan gradually moved toward the front, greatly eyeing a book on how to incorporate Psalms in candle magic. She picked it up, shifting through the pages, remembering how the book of Psalms and Proverbs were her favorites from the Bible, a work she hasn't read in years.

"Calming," she mentioned randomly.

"Excuse me?" the owner asked.

"The howlite gemstone. Calms among relieving stress and other properties." She recognized.

"Very good! You know your stones. Name's Rhiannon," she introduced herself, extending her hand.

"One of my favorite songs. I'm Morrigan." She accepted, returning.

"Ah, Irish roots? Perhaps, not coincidentally, my parents named me after it. I'm proud of them."

"I doubt it, my mum just really liked the name," Morrigan admitted. "Exudes strength, and . . . fate."

"But you know the origins. Impressive. Not a lot of people care about their names." She stared at her briefly, reading her. "You're a witch!" she announced suddenly. Morrigan initially was speechless.

"Aren't most people who come into your shop a witch or something?" she remarked bitingly.

"No. Some are lost souls in need of help, looking for answers, questioning their destiny. I sense you're in that motley bunch yourself."

"Uh . . . I'm no witch or wiccan. I used to be years ago, before that, Baptist, now I'm . . . nothing." She shrugged, lowly admitting.

"I don't think one can stop being a witch. If it's in you, it will always be there. And if you stray, it will find you again." Morrigan stood speechless. "You wanted to combine the two? Witchcraft and Christianity."

"Wishful thinking. I did years ago, but that's impossible."

"Impassable. Nothing is impossible." They shared a heartfelt laugh. "And don't say you're nothing. I can sense you still want to. Don't you?"

"Umm . . ." She could sense she was getting uncomfortable.

"Morrigan, despite what others will say. Everyone's path is different, that is positive and expected. Maybe, yours is meant to combine the two. In any event, that all depends on you. You're still a witch, luv," she finished.

"Why do you say that? I mean, it sounds like you speak from experience."

"My mother owned this shop, she taught me a lot. Yet, I still spent half of my life running from all of this." She tapped the side of her head. "Tell me something, Morrigan. What do you believe in?"

"Nothing. Not anymore," she answered regrettably. Rhiannon dropped her head in disappointment. "And that's what he counts on," she said, looking her directly in her eyes.

A vision of her nightmare flashed through her mind; she started breathing heavily. "Who?"

Her cell phone rang in a split second, distracting her from Rhiannon's statement.

"Hey, Timmy, what's up?" she answered without checking the ID. Her face scrunched up. "Timmy, calm down. I can barely understand you. What board meeting? What?" He screeched erratically from the other end.

"Okay, I'll be there soon." She hung up. "I, um, have to go. We'll continue this conversation?"

"I look forward to it," Rhiannon answered.

"Oh, I'd like to purchase this book." She went to hand it to her.

"Keep it, it's yours."

"How much? I can—"

"It's a gift. One witch to another." She winked at her. "Now go, that sounds important."

"Thanks. Thank you." She tipped the book to her before running out to Blue Thunder.

"All right, I'm here. Hell is going on?" she asked about the urgent call.

"I don't know! I know I just got a weird blocked call earlier today for us to be at this place, at a certain time. I think it's the label about the tour, having us sign with them. They won't let us in there," Max anxiously answered.

"What?" she questioned before an interruption.

"Morrigan, good to see you. We're in here." Gaston pointed in the direction of the conference room located in headquarters.

"Gaston. What is this all about?"

"What it's always been about. Come inside, they're waiting for you."

"Guys." She twitched her head for them to follow her.

"We don't need them," Gaston quickly mentioned.

"This is a label meeting with the bands, correct?" she asked.

"Yes and no, just Mystic," he swiftly answered.

"Right. Mystic. Which doesn't consist of only myself, so my brothers will be present," she sharply insisted.

"Well, aren't you noble?" he remarked. She giggled.

"That's the 'heart of glass' Gaston I know," she remarked, flipping him off in the process before entering. He frowned.

Sleekly elegant, yet intimate, the area was inviting. Bone-colored carpet throughout, the walls a combination of dark mahogany brown, glossed shelves, and pearl-colored flat surfaces. Matching the dark mahogany is the table, seated for eight, with four individuals, judging from their attire, high-level casual executives, already seated in their cushioned black leather seats. At the end sat a brunette woman who bore a striking resemblance to Chastity except she's older, presumably the CEO. Next to her left, an empty seat for Gaston, and sitting to her right, noticeably a gentleman with very relaxed energy; he's the only one wearing red Converse high tops with his slacks. He rested back in his chair, slightly hidden by the man sitting next to him. He's odd, while everyone else was sitting up straight with eagerness. Gaston made the necessary introductions before taking his seat while Mystic sat unanimously at the entrance end, with Morrigan in the middle, Max at her right, Tim at her left.

"Victoria, is it? Are you Chastity's mother? Pardon me, you look so much like her," Morrigan mentioned.

"Why, yes, I am. I'm also the chief financial officer of Apostasy Records." She took pride in that declaration.

"Interesting label name. It's nice to finally put a name to an entity," Morrigan mentioned.

"Yes, we do apologize for that. We're still fairly new and wanted to keep some aspects secure before going public," she answered.

"Acquire acts? Get your ducks in a row."

"Exactly!" Momentary stillness erupted. "Anyway, Chastity told me you asked her to join. Good thing, too, Mystic really needs another member to fill your sound."

Gaston slightly shook his head disagreeably with Max scoffing under his breath.

"So let's talk terms, I'd like to know what I'm agreeing to."

"Of course! We have a lawyer present to go over any other details you may not understand. And I will explain the overall contract, but I want you to know you all signing with us is strictly optional. Please, do not feel that it's a must to sign with Apostasy . . . now." She signaled to Gaston to hand out three contracts. Morrigan's fingers tapped slightly under the table on her thigh.

"Don't use two hands, and keep these on the table," Morrigan instructed her band, whispering, covering her mouth.

"What?" Timmy asked.

"Just do as I say, Tim," she insisted.

"Oh, and this sullen gentleman to my right is Rene," Victoria joked. "He's to oversee we do a proper job." They laughed.

"Hello, Rene," Morrigan said, while looking over the paperwork.

"Hello, Morrigan." His voice was slightly sinister in tone; her blood ran cold. His voice was unnerving but unfamiliar.

"Are you . . . French?" she asked cautiously, without taking her eyes away from the table.

"No, but I believe I was conceived there." With his voice slightly changing, the whole group chuckled.

They looked over the contracts, while Victoria went over certain details, when Morrigan rolled her eyes listening and reading a few egregious details. She raised a finger.

"Sorry to interrupt, I have a question. What happens when I lose my audience?"

"Why would you lose your audience?"

"Once they discover we're inauthentic. Corporate puppets who apparently needs a team of songwriters and studio musicians, they're going to leave us stranded. Sure, you have it nicely disguised in here on paragraph twenty though. Our material is—"

"Decent," Victoria interrupted. Gaston looked shocked, while Rene glared at her. She noticed, correcting herself.

"Wrong choice of words. Please, I wasn't trying to be insulting."

"I wasn't insulted," she insisted calmly.

"It's not a question of skill level or talent, you all are immensely talented. The audience takes to you, and through us you could reach an even larger landscape. It's just a matter of efficiency." Morrigan sat back in her chair, spun around, thinking there was no way she would spew her audience bullshit garbage.

"Humans—we have a tendency of wearing ourselves thin, exhausting ourselves. Honestly, our resources are meant to help you be your utmost self," she further explained. Morrigan and her bandmates looked at one another, their minds made up.

"I respect that," she said appreciatively. "So I must"—she reached for a pen—"respectfully decline," placing it on the contract, away from her.

"What?" Victoria asked.

"You did state it was optional. You made it a fact to mention twice," she reminded her.

"Surely did," Max confirmed. Victoria took a deep breath.

"Considering the time we wasted on you this last month of the tour. November is near completion, and Mystic hasn't fulfilled their dates and obligations," she began distressingly. Max and Tim slightly arose, when Morrigan touched their shoulders, easing them.

"My sincerest apologies, but you called this meeting ahead of time. We will gratefully play the remaining shows. However, we are not interested in a deal with your company at this present time," she replied very calmly.

"Fine, we will give you time to rethink your decision. Talk to her," she whispered to Gaston, which Morrigan overheard. She chortled, shaking her head dismissively as though he of all people could change her mind. Her fingers bent, tapping once more out of sight, as everyone stood to leave. Giving Max and Tim a visual cue, they left as well, leaving only Morrigan and Gaston.

The door closed behind her, as she sat waiting for his best pitch.

"You should seriously consider signing with them. Everything is at your disposal, you play their game, be their mouthpiece. It's a fair trade. Equals success for you!" He imparted. She got up, walking to the corner of the table, sitting on it.

"I'm going to try and communicate a thought to you. Musicians, writers, artists, we're an eccentric breed. We sacrifice our well-being, levels of sanity, our souls even, and as a woman, sometimes more for our art. To share ourselves fully, to constantly hit the pavement, hustle, and grind to keep the wheels moving, people informed, hoping to get the same reaction back. Hoping along the way someone gets it and appreciates it. I know you must've felt that way at one time. Doing it my way, sometimes as hard as that may be, keeps me honest. That's success in my opinion," she finished.

"You actually believe that, even now?"

"I tried appealing to your better nature. What was I thinking?" she admitted.

"Just sign, if not for you, at least for the band, for Jazz. In her memory! I promise you everything will work out." He grabbed the contract, moving closer to her, trying to force her to take it.

"No!" She pushed away the papers, as well as him. "No one can promise that! I'm not signing that contract, this is my choice. And guess what else? I don't want to be part of any label except my own!" she yelled.

"Plans are dependent on you." He stressed, moving in closer.

"Get someone else." She attempted getting off the table when he forcefully grabbed her.

"We can't!" he screamed, trying to bend her over. She fought. He threw her hard on the table, planting himself between her thighs, pinning her down.

"Fuck you, Gast!" she yelled angrily.

"It's more like the other way around." He ripped her jacket sleeve. "Even though, I've heard you're more into ladies lately." She began laughing hysterically.

"As always, you're late to the party, Gaston. So what are you going to do? Rape me, Gast. Violate me into agreeing? That I'd like to see!" She continued laughing, to which he slapped her.

"I was hoping I wouldn't have to," he answered.

"You want me?" she asked randomly.

"What?"

"This could be a pleasant experience. However, I need to know, do you want me and how bad?" she asked seductively, giving herself to his frame.

"Terribly always," he answered, hurriedly unfastening his pants. She grabbed his penis, stroking gently, kissing him, when suddenly he screamed out in agony.

"Oh, I'm sorry, am I handling you roughly?" She mocked, crushing his penis in her left hand. She grabbed his face, kissing him hard to silence him. Her teeth gripping on his tongue, she snapped her head back, spitting out her extraction. Punching him, she then proceeded to castrate him with one swift maneuver. He was no match for her; unable to defend himself, he bled profusely on her when she kicked him off onto the floor.

"Did you want this?" she asked sarcastically, referring to his dislocation in her newly formed claws.

"This is vital, isn't it?" She giggled insanely before it set aflame in her hand. She bent down beside him, his breath quick, his eyes wide staring into the abyss; she waved her hand over his face. Then, briefly the true Morrigan snapped back, realizing what she's done.

"Oh shit, Gast. I'm sorry," she said softly; seeing him dead, she closed his eyes. She stood now looking at her tattooed deformity, her claws extracted. "That's new," she remarked. It began speaking to her with fingers methodically bending; she understood, listening.

"You're right, he was. Not much of a loss," she responded.

"*Morrigan!* What's happening in there? *Open the door!*" yelled Max and Tim as they banged on the door. She noticed her appearance in one of the shelved wall mirrors. She's covered in his blood, dried on her lips and chin, her jeans soaked from her crotch to her knees. The tattoo spoke again.

"Go ahead," she agreed aloofly. Then, her hand waved over her face and lower body, cleaning her appearance. She walked to the door, opening to their continued banging.

"Morgue!" Tim exclaimed. "What's happening? We heard screaming." Gaston's lifeless corpse was invisible to Max and Tim from behind the door and table.

"Nothing, we should go," she answered unaffectedly, pushing past them, closing the doors behind her.

"But we heard," Max began, noticing her ripped jacket sleeve. "What happened to your jacket? Did he do something to you?" he said, concerned.

"Everything is fine," she said.

"We're talking to him!" he insisted. They pushed open the doors when the doors supernaturally slammed shut, barring them from entering.

"Maxie, Timmy, keep away from there," she warned. Each slowly turned around to face her; her tattooed arm turned up, with closed palm.

"Cookie M, what's going on? What's wrong in there?" he asked, pointing his thumb. She smiled, shrugging.

"Just drop it, time to go." She walked away. Speechless, they looked at each other, then Timmy reached for the door handle once more, when Max said, "Drop it. Come on." They followed her in silence out of the building to their cars.

"Timmy! Take my car. I'll ride with Morgue." He threw him his car keys.

"Get in. Follow me," she told them, starting the engine.

"So where we headed?" Max asked casually.

"My temporary place." She laughed, looking at him. "We're still obligated to perform, they're still obligated to house us."

"True." He paused. "What you and Gaston discuss?"

"Not going to quit, are you?" she asked.

"Nope," he answered.

"Okay, I'm saying this once, no more. He tried to convince me how better off we would be signing with them, I declined, of course, it got physical, so . . . I slit his throat," she said. He stared at her in complete shock. She erupted in laughter.

"Close your mouth, bro. I only kicked his ass, left him slumping in his chair." She grabbed his shoulder playfully. "His throat is intact." He still stared, mouth agape.

"Dude!" she exclaimed.

"I'm sorry." He straightened up.

"I can't believe you actually think I would kill him!" She greatly pretended, wholly aware of her act.

"I don't! I was just . . . astonished! Quite the joker," he remarked. "Can we have a chill evening, watch movies?"

"Sure, dude. Whatever you want," she answered distantly, thinking. "I also booked the attached room, you guys can stay in there, or you can stay with me, while Timmy sleeps next door, whatever."

"Cool," he said happily, chewing on gum.

They arrived at the hotel, exiting their vehicles; a familiar woman's voice called her name before they could enter.

"Mom?" Morrigan and Max called out when they saw Raven walking toward them.

"Oh, you remember who I am? I was unsure, since I barely hear from you! Finally, I was able to track you down," she remarked angrily. "Max, Tim. How are you two?"

"Mom, it's been a long day. We just want to relax," Morrigan answered.

"I don't remember asking you." Morrigan rolled her eyes. She reached into her jacket pocket, pulling out two key cards, passes them to Max.

"I'm in 575, I also got 573. Right next to each other. If you need anything, y' know the front desk knows you, so don't do anything I wouldn't do."

"I'm afraid of what that is," he joked.

"Dude."

"Sorry."

"We'll be up in a minute," she told him.

"Later," he said, walking inside with Timmy.

"See you boys later!" Raven mentioned before snapping back to Morrigan.

"What the fuck is your problem? I've been trying to reach you, others have been trying. I can only get in contact with Max. Libbey, bless his soul, is worried sick about you! Seems like you're avoiding us!" she argued.

"Ma, you just don't get it." She reacted calmly.

"Oh, I get it! You need to get your shit together!" Raven yelled.

"I know, I know that, Ma! The reason why I haven't been calling is because . . . I'm trying to protect you. Both of you," she admitted.

"Protect us from what? Your bullshit?" she exclaimed.

"Y' know what, Ma, just drop it!"

"You're fucking up! You almost get killed onstage, don't even have the common sense to tell me!"

"Don't you think I know that? Seriously, has it ever run across your fucking mind? No, you're too fucking busy criticizing me!" Morrigan erupted.

"What's happening to you?"

"Ma, you're not the only one to ask me that. And guess what? I don't have an answer for any of you."

"I knew this would be too much for you to handle," she mentioned.

"What are you going on about?" Morrigan asked.

"This tour." Morrigan scoffed, shaking her head.

"Ma, fame is not the reason for this, it's more serious than money, than limos, whatever else typical is rolling around in your head!"

"Then what the fuck is it?"

"I don't know," she admitted. "I honestly don't know."

"You don't know? Damn it, Morrigan, what do you know?"

"Can't tell you what I don't know. Urgh!" She groaned, falling limp against Blue Thunder.

"What's wrong? Morrigan? It's that damn tattoo, isn't it?" she said, helping her up. "The fake tattoo," she remarked.

"It *is* fake!" she snapped, fueling her arm more. "*Urgh!* It's nothing!" She clenched her teeth.

"Some nothing," she remarked. Morrigan gained her strength to stand.

"Ma, I got to go. Just go to the room. I'll talk to you later." Brushing her off, she walked away.

"Morrigan? Morrigan?" she called out to her daughter, to no reply.

She entered a nearby bar, some eyes following her as she settled in; she ordered.

"Whisky." Her fingertips steadily tapped the counter. "Shut up," she whispered. A guy smoothly sat beside her, as the bartender passed her, her drink. She drowned it, impressing the guy.

"Nice choice."

"Not interested. Another." She shot him down, ordering again. This same action repeated for nearly an hour.

"I love a woman that can handle her liquor." He flirted again, brushing her hair back; it incensed her. She clicked her tongue, holding an empty glass in her left hand.

"Careful, I tend to bite and disembowel when my demands aren't met. Can you handle that?" she asked, cracking the glass in her hand. It emitted a shrill sound, catching those in the immediate vicinity attention. She smiled crookedly, freaking him out; he quickly walked away, muttering "freak" under his breath.

"Sorry about your glass," she apologized to the bartender, passing it to him. "Hit me."

"Can I interest you?" He tried to suggest something less alcoholic.

"Just pour."

He proceeded. Her tattoo flashed hot again. "Can I have some cold water too, please?"

"Sure!" he answered happily.

Receiving it, she splashed her arm with it. "Thanks." She drank, her fingers tapping furiously. She strained, forcing it to cease.

Flashbacks of Gaston hit her; his murder continuously playing in her mind, along with the painful burning sensation, caused her to drop her drink.

"Damn it!" Slamming down her arm, she threw money on the counter, storming out. Checking her cell, there were four missed calls from Chastity. She dismissed them, attempting to make a call. *Blink, blink,* emitted randomly, signaling low battery; it turned off. She scoffed, shoving it in her back pocket.

She struggled down the street, sweating heavily; she wandered to a pay phone, dialing a number. No one answered. She tried another. A man answered.

"Hey, Libbey!" she greeted him excitably.

"Morgue? Hey, kiddo!"

"Yeah, I swear you spend more time in that club than you do at home."

He chuckled. "You're probably right. But the same could be said for you."

"Yeah," she admitted meekly.

"What's wrong?" he asked, sensing her tone.

"Nothing! I just wanted to hear your voice, is all."

"You sure that's all? You don't sound well, Morgue."

"Yeah, well, I miss you. Even though I saw you recently," she admitted.

"I've missed you too, kiddo. How's my other kid doing? And Tim? How's his leg?"

"Maxie's fine. He's not with me though. Timmy is great too, his leg will heal right up, with a minor scar," she explains, relieved.

"That's good! I'm glad, you need all your band in one piece and healthy." He paused. "Shit, did that sound insensitive?"

"Please, Libbey, it's the truth. Plus, you can say whatever the fuck you want." She finally managed to chuckle.

"Yes, comes with age. How are you and Jack?"

"Um, unfortunately, we're still the same indecisive losers."

"I didn't mention it before, but keep him. I got to admit, he's a good one, he's trying. But don't scare him away!" he jokingly warned to an eruption of laughter. She quieted down.

"Uh, are you busy tonight?"

"No. Morgue, what's wrong?" He listened.

"I lied. Something happened today. We didn't sign with them. I made a conscious decision not to! Something is wrong, what happened after," she rambled on.

"I'm sorry, Lib, I need to talk to you in person. I should've listened to you those months ago. I did something bad. I need to see you tonight." She struggled to speak, holding her arm.

"I'm so hot! I fucked up, Lib!" Out of breath she managed, on the verge of crying.

"Okay, can you get here soon?" he asked eagerly.

"Maybe in an hour, I'm not too far." She looked around, seeing if anyone was around her.

"I could meet you wherever," he responded.

"No! I'll be there."

"Well, take Max with you!"

"Yeah, I'll pick him up on the way."

"Good, you come here! We'll handle it, whatever it is." he assured her.

"I love you, Libbey," she told him.

"I love you too, Morgue. Okay? Just get here!" When Libbey hung up, the phone clicked signaling the dial tone, yet Morrigan heard faint crackling on the other end. Quickly, the crackling intensified until she felt heat to her ear, she moved the handset away from her face, transfixed on the earpiece until it sparked, exploding in her hand. Morrigan shielded her face, while running out of the phone booth. But when she examined the phone, everything was normal. The handset simply hung swaying off its hook. In a state of shock, she stumbled up the block before suddenly losing her balance, falling to her knees. She clutched her chest, sweating profusely as torturous heat erupted. She groaned, trying to catch her breath until the heat subsided, she gasped. "Oh no! Libbey!" she bolts back to the hotel room. Timmy opened to her frantically banging.

"We have to leave now!" she exclaimed, practically in a fever.

"Oh my god," Max remarked, as they pulled up to a smoking 69 Clam. Firefighters were still battling the blaze that engulfed the club. Libbey's car was still in the lot.

"Libbey . . . Libbey . . . Libbey!" She ran out the car toward the fire, freakishly calling his name in weird vocal intervals.

"Somebody get that girl out the way!" a fireman yelled.

Max grabbed her, pulling her back with Timmy and Raven's help.

"Oh, God! No!" she exclaimed. "This is serious, oh God, this is serious." She was breathing so hard; her lungs were being deprived of oxygen. She broke down, sobbing; she just kept repeating, "I did this . . . I did this." Everyone looked at her in shock and disbelief.

Eventually, they extinguished the fire, while the crowd that attracted to the sight looked on, quiet and gossiping.

There Morrigan and Max stood for what felt like the longest time, staring at the once burning inferno of what used to be their childhood hangout where they both bonded and cultivated their musical skills. The air was dry, deathly; smoke filled the air with what was left of the 69 Clam in shambles.

"There was someone inside, we won't be able to know for certain who it was until the dental records," the marshal informed them. "I'm sorry."

"It was Libbey." She strained to speak. The firefighter looked at her suspiciously.

"How soon will you know what caused it?" Raven asked.

"There must have been a leak. Remains of a shotgun were found too, if that was fired, it could have caused it.

"That gun was for protection." Max quietly answered.

"Well, we'll know more after some tests." the fireman explained "We'll be in touch."

Information was passed between them.

"What are we going to do?" Tim hesitantly asked.

"I don't know, Timmy, I don't know," Morrigan honestly admitted. "I don't know how to solve this. That's why I . . ." Morrigan peered among the spectators, where the older stranger was standing among them.

"I need to know what the hell is going on," Raven demanded.

"Son of a bitch!" Morrigan bolted to the crowd, but by time she arrived, he'd disappeared again.

"Shit!" she shouted.

"Morrigan, what the hell is going on?" Max took off behind her.

"I saw him!" she declared.

"Saw who?"

"The fucker that gave me this tattoo, this fucking curse! I fucking saw him! Right here! He killed him, Max! He fucking killed Libbey, man! It's all my fault . . . *Fuck*!" she bellowed upward. She stormed back to the group.

"Mhorr—"

"Mom! Not now! I'll explain it in the car. Get in!" she declared. She explained *almost* everything to everyone, from her nightmares, to that night at the Clam when a stranger *gifted* her, to present affairs. She held them up until they arrived back at the hotel.

"Well, do you all feel better?" she asked, looking at her mom directly. For once she was speechless, the vitality drained from her face. She struggled opening the door.

"I got you, Ms. Bloodchild," Tim said, helping her.

Morrigan didn't budge; hands still on the steering wheel, she gripped it tighter. Max, behind her, moved forward, tapping her shoulder.

"Cookie M? Sis?" he asked cautiously.

"What, Max?"

"Are you coming inside?"

"I'll be up in a minute."

"Libbey. I . . . I can't," he implausibly stammered.

"Max. Go up, I'll be there soon."

"I don't think you should be alone."

"I won't be. I'll be fine." She tried assuring him. He got out, leaning in the driver's side to hug her. She kept her eyes downward, vaguely acknowledging him. He kissed her forehead. She tapped his arm lovingly.

"I love you too, Maxie." He stepped back slowly; waiting until he was fully inside the building, she slammed Blue Thunder into reverse. It screeched as she drove to the back entrance. She went to take a swig from Jazz's flask.

"Fuck." It's empty. She entered the back door, taking the stairs to the fourth floor. Using a key card, she stumbled into a dimly lit room.

"I've been calling you," Chastity announced, sitting near the window; she stood.

"How did you get in here?" Morrigan asked rudely.

"This is my room," she corrected her.

"Oh," she said, noticing the decor. "Well, how did I get here?" She vacantly giggled.

"Are you all right?" She approached her slowly.

"Oh, I'm fine! Just peachy. You look good, Chas, were you waiting for me?" She grabbed her arm, pulling her closer; she kissed her aggressively. In response Chastity snatched away. Morrigan giggled.

"Are you drunk?" she asked, turning around the bed.

"Oh, I'm supremely sober." She lay on the bed, propping her arms behind her, her feet up.

"So what did you call for?"

"I wanted to know . . . how the meeting went," she admitted.

"So you called Max?"

"Well, yeah, I-I wanted to warn you. I tried calling you first."

"No. See, I checked your calls. They weren't until hours after the meeting. Plus, Max didn't know who called him, the number was blocked. Question is, why block it? Why lie? Unless, you didn't want someone else to know."

Chastity tried to exit the bedroom when Morrigan flicked her wrist, slamming the door shut.

"Where are you going, Chas? We're just talking."

Chastity began to flicker the lights on and off, shaking the furniture. Morrigan smiled, feeling the bed beneath her tremor, unimpressed, she remarked, "Ooh, spooky." She hopped off; closing her fist in an aerial motion changed the lights to red, stopping the tantrum. She approached her slyly.

"I don't want to fight you," Chastity stated mildly.

"Oh, you might want to," she responded, plucking at her. Chastity slammed back against the door, attempting to punch her. Morrigan slapped it away, aiming for her neck; she tightened her grip.

"I warned you if you lie to me, I would kill you," she repeated.

"Mor-Morrigan." She struggled, scratching at her wrists. She loosened her grip.

"Tsk, tsk, tsk." Her claws extended, with the point of her index nail tapping her chest. She scratched on two deep marks, which caused her chest tattoo to bleed. Chastity cried out.

"They skimped out on you, luv," she remarked, realizing her power over her. "In case you didn't realize where my sudden hostility stems from, but tonight I lost the only man I *ever* considered a father, my father."

"I didn't have anything to do with that, Morgue!" She tried explaining.

"Shh . . . Shh . . . I didn't say you did." She wiped away her tears. "However, I think you know who. In fact, I'm sure of it." She pointed at her, pacing.

"He's old, yet handsome, charming, silver eyes that flash gold, sneaky smirks here and there. I know it's not a lot to go on but in our little circle, you had to."

"I don't know his name," she interrupted. "I've only seen him in passing, after this." She motioned to her chest tattoo. "He's an elder."

Morrigan sat on the edge of the bed. Chastity knelt between her, continuing.

"My mom said it was time. Took me to S. The rest is history."

"S?"

"I know only an initial. I'm obedient, I don't ask questions. I'm sorry, Morrigan. I never thought it would go this far, that I would . . ."

"Would what?"

"Fall in love with you." She gazed upon her, kissing her. Morrigan coolly lay back, leaning on her elbows, letting her continue. Eventually, she participated, wrapping her right arm around her waist. Her left hand pointed, shaping a gun to her heart, slowly penetrating her skin.

"Do I look like I love you? How about I stop this pretty heart of yours? Make you like me." She heartlessly smirked, threatening her. "You know more." She clutched Chastity's chest.

"Ask and you shall receive!" she blurted out. "If you're willing, it'll tell you more."

"What? Who, S?"

"Our hosts." She felt along her arm. "You've heard it before. When we first met. Remember?"

"Warned me about you." Morrigan, realizing, rested.

"I bet. They're the Fallen," she whispered. Morrigan thought.

"Former angels?" Chastity nodded.

"Apostasy Records. Heh, clever. Thanks. Now get out of town. You're checking out tomorrow. I don't care where you go, but you can't stay here."

"But I'm a target. What I told you . . ."

"You only confirmed suspicions."

"And that's enough! I'm a liability," Chastity whined.

"How's that my problem? You knew the risks. I have a feeling you knew. If you were straight with me, maybe." Morrigan telekinetically opened the door, putting on her jacket.

"You're on your own." She left her alone in misery and fear.

CHAPTER TWENTY-FIVE

"I Thought It Was Time You Knew the Truth"

66 **W**e're coming closer, you two." Raven announced. The driver eased up near a recently dug plot, parking at the edge of a slightly secluded spot where numerous large trees decorated the pathway, pushing back headstones.

Several faded plaques partially buried in the earth ran along the trim of the road. To the far right, mausoleums watch over the deceased.

"Take your time," she advised, facing them before exiting. "Come on, Timmy."

Max looked at his sister while she nervously scrunched up her navy blue lace dress above her knees. He placed his hand on her lap, holding hers. She turned to face him.

"Are you ready?" he asked. A block more they would be visiting Maye's resting place, a thought that hadn't escaped Morrigan's tortured thoughts.

"No," she answered, looking out the window to see familiar faces with some new surrounding the open space to bid farewell to a fallen comrade.

"But I can't hide out in here either. I haven't been here since . . ."

"I know," he said. "Maybe, we can visit her after?"

"Yeah, maybe," she answered.

"Let's go, sissy." He fixed his glasses when they stepped onto the disturbed grass. Jack smiled at her from afar. She waved back, wearing a weak smile. They further approached.

"Jerry, Kirk. You guys made it," she greeted.

"Of course, grrl. Wouldn't miss it," Kirk responded. Jerry hugged her.

"Quite the turnout," Jerry acknowledged.

"Yeah, it's funny. I didn't realize how much of an impact Libbey had on the industry," she responded.

"He didn't really, um, speak about his, uh . . . He could be very modest," Max mentioned.

"Yeah, Lib was quite the force," Jerry fondly remarked.

"That's a cool necklace! A vial?" Kirk observed.

"Thanks! Some of Libbey's ashes filled it. I wanted something physical, weird, I know," she admitted.

"No, it makes sense," he responded. Max tapped her, pointing out Jack approaching.

"Hey, you two will be all right," Jerry said, giving them privacy.

"Why do we keep meeting like this?" Jack jokingly remarked.

"Cursed, I guess."

"Thank you for calling me," he said.

"Thank you for coming."

"Come here." He pulled her closer. "You're so beautiful. Don't cry. I'm sorry, is that pushy?"

"You're fine." She looked to the sky, then back to him. "Kiss me." He did, pulling her lips to his.

"We're about to begin," the priest told them, as Raven held the urn.

"Wait, Mom, let me."

"Are you sure?" she asked.

"Yeah, I can handle it, if Max?" She held her hand out to him.

"That's why I'm here!" he responded. She cracked open the top, dropping a guitar plectrum inside. Together they gently lowered it into the ground when the priest began his service.

"The Lord is close to the brokenhearted and saves those who are crushed in spirit."

Musical tributes were given from the group, including from Morrigan and Mizzy. Although, she broke down halfway through. Mizzy finished their song, while Jack helped her down, keeping his arm around her.

"See you back at the house?" he asked her as the service concluded.

"Yeah." They kissed again. He walked off to the side to speak with the other attendees.

"Cookie M."

"Hey, Morgue. I'm keeping that up in his honor!" Timmy expressed.

"Thanks. Listen, you two, I think we should end Mystic," she suddenly announced.

"What?" Max cried.

"Morgue, don't be ridiculous!" Timmy asserted.

"Listen to me! It's getting too deep. We don't really know what the fuck is going on! And until I find out, I can't take any more risks," she explained.

"Well, whatever the fuck it is might as well take us all now because I'm not leaving. I know damn well Max ain't either, so it's already decided. Majority rules. Mystic continues," Tim sternly declared.

"That's sweet, Timmy, I truly appreciate it," she began before Max's interruption.

"Timmy's right. As I said before, sis, we'll figure this out together," Max confirmed. "Trust it."

"Libbey said the same thing, last we spoke," she expressed.

"I understand what you're saying, sis, I truly do but if you're alone!" Max tried explaining.

She looked off into the distance of the mausoleums where the stranger appeared standing, beckoning her to come forward. He ducked between the tall structures.

"I'll be right back, Max. You guys stay here okay?" she told them sternly. "Don't follow me!"

"Whaa . . . what is it? Where are you going?" His eyes followed hers straight in the direction she's looking, but he didn't see anything or anyone. Something deep inside told him he should stay. So he did, waiting for her return.

"Morgue?" Timmy called out.

"Let's wait here," Max told him.

Morrigan ran furiously past the two rows to a section closed off by tall guarded chambers; then she saw him from behind the same figure. When she angrily turned him around, he looked much differently than before.

Now the stranger is much younger, dressed to the nines in black satin and burnt red silk. His suit was uniquely designed of patterns, almost telling of a story in ancient dialect.

"I made the right choice. You wear it well," he remarked, referring to her inked skin. She recognized the markings on his jacket matched her tattoo.

"You tricked me," Morrigan said angrily.

The stranger looked at her questionably, slyly defending himself.

"No, I didn't. I just saw sadness and a passion in you that couldn't be ignored."

His hand went to touch her face, but she snatched it away.

"Don't touch me!" she screamed. "You never even gave me a chance to answer, you just took me! Who are you?"

"Hmm." The stranger laughed curiously at something that Morrigan couldn't quite understand. He continued with his thought.

"You want to know something? I like you, Morrigan. You're different and interesting, more than any other human I've known before. For most of these things"—he plucked his finger to describe his disgust in humanity, as if they're flies—"it's always the same thing: greed, hatred, or pride . . . But not you . . . You don't care about any of that really."

"Hah!" she blurted almost by accident. All she can manage was a whispered chuckle then sighed with a sense of regret.

"You like me. Is that right? Then take this shit back! Why are you doing this to me?" she asked.

"Because I can!" the stranger responded.

"What do you want?" she yelled. Not that she suspected he would give her answers. She still hoped for something more. Something concrete.

"You'll find out soon enough." She glared at him, lips pursed.

"Come on! You didn't think you would get answers that easy, did you?" The stranger smiled crookedly. Then his silver eyes flashed red.

In that instance, up arose a long-forgotten memory in her mind; she saw those eyes before.

"Oh, God, I remember you, in a dream. It was you at the swings when I was a little girl," she spoke, remembering when the stranger first tried to tempt her.

"You tried to offer me candy of all things and said it'll be more where that came from if I was to come and sing for you now and always."

"I admit I wasn't very clever back then," the stranger spoke, confirming her memory.

"But I like to think I've improved since then, much like you because we're way past candy now, aren't we?" He clicked his tongue.

"I think you missed something though, I also mentioned my friends would love to hear you as well." He put his hand out toward her one more time, but she backed away, stumbling on a crumbled step. Her back hit the wall of a mausoleum hard.

"Morrigan, I sense you don't trust me . . . How about a token for your cooperation?" the stranger asked her.

"Who are you? Same as the club, because I know it's you. I shouldn't have to ask that again!" she proclaimed.

"Fair enough. My name is Seere, that's what you can pronounce in your tongue. What I am, you'll find out in time," he answered.

"I already know," she said.

"You are smart . . . Anyway, I'm going to go out of my way here and give you one person free," he told her.

"One person free?" she asked curiously.

"Yes, after all you're running low." He chuckled evilly. "This person I will not touch personally to harm."

"One person off limits, huh?" She tried to pry for more information.

"Sure, in a manner of speaking," he responded.

"No. We have to be clear on terms. This person is off-limits to you and your consorts in all ways, you will not touch this person, nor will you send someone to harm or kill this person. You will not even mess with this person's mind to try and make them hurt or kill themselves! This person is completely—" He interrupted her.

"All right! Okay! I got it, they're totally off-limits, separate from this. Damn, you're smarter than I thought," he finished.

"Thanks." She scoffed.

"Terms are defined." He sighed. "Okay, so who is it?"

"My mom," she answered honestly. His eyes briefly rolled.

"Fine, done! The deal is made," he confirmed.

"Yippee," she answered sarcastically. "How can I know?" She dropped to her knees, gasping as the newly formed deal immediately bonded on her tattooed sleeve, her link between earths and the unnatural.

Morrigan wised to the stranger's trickery; she realized nothing will come easy to her if she planned on breaking his deal. She spit out, gaining her strength, standing, physically shaken.

"One more question though. Why'd you kill Libbey?" she asked, knowing the answer, but still begging for an explanation.

"He was a distraction. You don't have time for distractions, our business concerns it," he answered heartlessly.

"You'll pay for this, Seere," she told him directly.

"Maybe."

"Morrigan, what's going on? Who is that?" yelled Max, running through the mausoleums toward her. Seere disappeared before he gained.

"You saw him too?" she asked.

"I saw an old man. Who is he? Where is he?" he answered.

"Let's get back to Ma's," she nervously told him.

Inevitable mourning overwhelmed the repast, dwindling them down to only six little rockers. Morrigan sat on the edge next to Jack and Jerry on her mom's shimmering purple couch, holding on to a decorative pillow, with one hand on a drink. Max sat in a chair somewhat next to her, loosening his tie, unbuttoning his shirt. She split her drink with him, passing it over. Mizzy and Kirk sat across from him on a matching love seat.

"What's going to happen to the Clam? I know it was his baby," Kirk asked.

"Yeah, did they figure out the cause of it?" Jerry asked, brushing his hair back.

"It's unknown," Morrigan answered somewhat vacantly, staring off, trapped in thought.

"We don't know, Libbey never discussed his business with us, not in depth," Max answered.

"He taught us how to run bar, order stock, basic important stuff like that. I guess I've always wanted it," she responded, realizing.

"He must've had insurance then?" Jerry asked. "Have you two even checked into that?" he said, realizing their clueless faces.

"No. We haven't," Morrigan answered. "We've done what everyone else usually does in a state of grief. Avoid it."

"I think what he's saying is, you need, should consider, finding a will or any of his important paperwork," Jack hesitantly suggested. "We understand, it's difficult."

"No, you don't!" Her arm heated subtly; everyone became quiet. "I'm sorry, babe. You do."

"It's okay," Jack responded.

"No, it's not. It was shitty of me. Especially, I hate comparing scar tissue, it's vulgar. I apologize. You all are trying to help." She looked to Max, who nodded in approval.

"We'll check it out," he responded. Glum expressions remained.

"You do have his key, right?" Max asked matter-of-factly.

"Yes, dear. I have his key on here, somewhere, ah, here it is!" she said, finding it on a busy jangle of keys.

"I know I haven't hung out here in recent months, but I will never part with this."

She opened Libbey's two-story apartment. It was perfectly fitting for the modern Renaissance man. Artistically designed, yet comfortably efficient. Downstairs stood a smaller-scale tattoo parlor.

Artwork of various movements decorated different sections of his home, from Postimpressionism in the living room area, to surrealism in the kitchen. Morrigan walked further in toward his Les Paul sitting in the corner; she picked it up, feeling its weight, strumming the strings. A light flutter of a tune emitted. She thought of the times they jammed together, when he first gave her guitar lessons, teaching her little theory tricks for remembrance.

Then, a flashback from the finger prick surprised her, paired with the flames from the explosion. She felt wheezy, quickly placing it back down, walking around. She knew she would miss him; she just didn't realize or appreciate how much.

"Did you ever . . . tell him what happened?" Max suddenly asked, flipping through a book.

"About what?" She eyed a vintage ashen chest; it turned up empty.

"You know, earlier with the apartment and stuff," he mentioned lowly.

"No. I never did. I couldn't. I don't regret not telling him either."

"Do you think?" Max started to ask.

"I know he most likely would've let me live here," she answered. He remained silent.

"Did he have a safe or anything similar that you remember he might've told us about?" she asked him.

"Not that I know of," he answered, looking around, checking shelves.

"He must've told us about a special place he put his important papers or something?" she mentioned, disappointed.

"I don't remember one, sis, I'm sorry."

She sighed, drawn to his coffee table covered in papers and a few scattered CDs. She sat to it, searching aimlessly, when she saw his sketches of their proposed indie label.

It read "Moonstruck Records" in large cosmically colored bold print. In the upper left-hand corner, he wrote a little note "M&M's label." Starry eyed, she was smiling.

"Max, come here." He walked closer. "Look," she said, showing him the sketches.

"Wow! His skills amaze me. He always believed in us. Even when we didn't. Shit, dudette," he pondered. Underneath the sketch she noticed a small key on a bracelet band.

"Max, see where this goes," she said, handing it to him.

"Okay." He hurriedly accepted. She continued searching on the table, unsure of what until her fingers singed on a photograph of the adult education building at its grand opening. It's a basic picture of its structure, nothing fancy or prominent, but she's intrigued.

"Check upstairs!" she yelled to him.

"Where?"

"His bedroom." She grabbed her keys, listening to his heavy boots until they suppressed; when he's completely upstairs, she left.

The sky was blackening as night spun her web over the city. Morrigan arrived at the two-story derelict building aging severely; its decrepitude was merely masked by the troublesome vines overtaking the structure.

"What am I looking for here?" she whispered as a wino passed through the alley. Her fingers contorted, answering her.

"Great." She cased around; noticing a shattered window she pointed her flashlight inside. No one was stirring, only quiet. Finishing the broken job, she climbed carefully inside. Within was worse; an unnerving silence swallowed her. She flashed her light around, noticing nothing unusual.

"Just the usual rot," she thought to herself. "Only a classroom," she muttered.

"Okay, I'm in. What am I looking for?" she impatiently asked. "What about my dreams?" she responded to twisted bends. She closed her eyes, centering herself in the middle of the room. Finally, when she was still in her thoughts she took a few steps forward, making a slight turn.

"Ma? Seere," she spoke, replaying the dream in her head.

"It was here, it happened right here. Wait." Her nightmare continued past the point of her waking up. "Oh no . . . No, I didn't. I couldn't!" she screamed aloud, clutching her head; it felt as though it was splitting open. She fell to her knees, the heat overpowering her.

"I did this. I accepted it. I agreed, I would sing. Oh, Lib," she subtly cried.

A cracking sound was heard behind her; she slowly turned around, standing. A chair screeched across the floor behind her on the opposite side; she flashed her light to see nothing. Then a desk slid toward her, almost knocking her over. She threw it.

"Seere? I know you're there, you bastard!" Silence.

"Come on, these are cheap tricks! I grew up with horror films." A loud crash was heard upstairs, directly above her.

Crreeeekk! She followed a crackling along the walls, circling the inside, until it met a window. *Smash!* Shards shot toward her; she blocked her face. The walls followed in pursuit as if someone punched them. She went to run when she was flown.

Slamming against the wall, she fell to the floor. Reaching for her pentacle around her neck, it's gone. She's thrown against the wall again.

"Fuck you, you shit!" she screamed lividly. An unseen force threw her again; she slid down. It dragged her, pulling down her jeans, ripping open her shirt.

"*No!*" she screamed gutturally. "Fuck off!" Wind blew in aggressively, deafening; the air suffocated her. Until hysterical laughter was heard in the distance. The winds calmed, but the laughter grew closer.

"I couldn't resist. You've grown into quite the fetching creature." Seere revealed himself, standing atop her. He reached to help her up; she slapped away his hand. He shrugged. Crawling from underneath him, she kicked him, straightening her clothes.

"That's not nice," he remarked.

"Go to hell." She insulted him.

"If we're lucky," he quipped.

"You did this shit! To get me here!" She figured.

"I thought it was time you knew the truth," he admitted smugly.

"It doesn't change anything. I was a child."

"Perhaps, but have you ever thought that you belong to this? I mean, you fit my"—he clicks his tongue—"so nicely. He really likes you." He winked. "Helps you occasionally, even when I tell him not to. Anyway, this could be the best situation for you. If you stop fighting me," he egotistically suggested.

"Did you kill Jazz?"

He sighed impatiently. "There you go! I'm giving you my best pitch and that's all you can think about, meaningless sentiment."

"Did you, Seere?"

"As much as I despise them, you must admire humans, they do most of the work for us. So back to my selling. You've been in this, practically since birth, just accept it."

"You don't really need me to sign to Apostasy." She's unwavering in speech.

"Of course not, I already own you. With what the guitar, the tat. Apostasy Records is earthly leverage."

"Correction, my ax isn't yours, you just poisoned it. And I never, honestly agreed to this. Not consciously."

"Still with that boring tune? Stop fighting and embrace it! I didn't realize you were going to be this stubborn." He winked playfully. "I like it."

She shrugged. "Then you should've spoken to my mom." She snickered. "You won't get me."

"We'll see about that." He glided a few inches, only to stop.

He raised his hand. "Does Max still drive without a seat belt?"

"No," she murmured. Seere smiled wickedly.

"Oh, he's so cute! He loves you dearly." He waved in a cutesy manner before vanishing.

"Please, *no!*" she screamed to no avail. Immediately, she tried calling him.

"Damn it! When I need him to answer!" She thought. "What?" Assisting her, this foreign entity tapped and contorted through her furiously, speaking softly only for her usage.

"This constant eye closing is going to get me killed eventually," she quipped to the fallen angel bonded sinisterly to her. Yet, she located Max, driving near her location. She ran out to her car.

Morrigan sped out, intending to meet him head-on, hopefully before Seere; maybe she could save him. She pulled into an alley, waiting for him; she heard his engine approaching although he was still distant. She eased out, trying to call him again, when she's fully visible sitting in the middle of the street. His car suddenly flipped twice, landing on its top; it screeched a few feet down the street. Feeling the impact, she ran toward the wreck; people exited their homes. She saw him injured, hanging from his seat belt; before any onlookers could get closer, she tore the door off its hinges, tossing it aside. She pulled him out. Unconscious and bloody, there's still a pulse as he rested in her arms.

"Someone call an ambulance! Fuck it, I'll call." She managed out her cell. Wiping the blood from his face, she gently rocked him. "I got you, bro. I got you."

"Chastity," an alluring voice called from the shadows; the lights flickered, dimming. It caused her to stop running. A fog consumed the train platform. Seere stepped out.

"Where are you travelling to tonight?"

"Nowhere," she answered meekly.

"Somewhere." With a wave of his hand, the bags she carried hit the walls.

"You failed us," he said, when faces vaguely appeared in the fog.

"I'm sorry!" she begged. Her mascara stained her face; her eyes widened.

"It doesn't make a difference now, however, that means there's no use for you anymore." He approached her, his body frame covering her face; she shivered as darkness conquered. Then it faded. The lights returned to normal to reveal an empty platform.

CHAPTER TWENTY-SIX

The Finale

M orrigan sat alone in a musky cold hospital room, with only his outer shell. It provided no comfort for her, only serving as a reminder that everyone close to her was at risk, a walking dead. So he just lay there exposed, hooked up to machines, unaware of his surroundings. She briefly contemplated taking Seere's deal; after all she had no way to fight him, no plan of action. Maybe if she did he'd set Max free, then she realized he would but not in the way begged for.

"Max, can you hear me? I did this to you, not directly, but it's still my fault. And I'm sorry. I know you're tired as hell of me saying this, but I'm going to fix this mess. I'm going to get you out of this coma," she stated, half choked with sobs. She laid her head on the bed. "I love you, Maxie." She yawned, feeling his callused hand from years of rocking. She drifted into a deep sleep.

Awakening in familiar surroundings, she's startled, lifting her head from a bar counter.

"Damn, Cookie M, even in your dreams?" he remarked smiling, referring to her drool-drenched left cheek. He slid her a dark-colored drink and napkin.

"I thought you would like it better here," he informed her.

"Max?" she asked. He only smiled.

"Maxie, is it really you?"

"Yeah, in the . . . well, spectral flesh," he answered.

"Wait . . . Then that . . . Wait, wait, wait! Are you? *No!*" She began crying hysterically.

"No! Sis, no! I'm not dead! Stop crying. Chill! I'm fine. Well, I'm still in a coma, but everything else is above board." He calmed her, coming from behind the counter ethereally to her amazement.

"How?"

"Seere couldn't kill me," he answered.

"So he'll try again," she said fearfully.

"You'll be ready next time," he said. "Plus, we do have protectors."

"You sound so confident," she remarked.

"I am . . . confident-ish. You're not very receptive to positive energy. I admit, it's a gamble."

"Dude!"

"What? You're not!"

"Whatever." She slumped down. "Is Libbey around?" she asked hopefully.

"Try praying. Maybe he'll show up," he responded.

"I'm not praying." She scoffed.

"See? There it is," he remarked, mocking her pout. She folded her arms angrily.

"He's not here, sis. Foolishly, I admit I thought by recreating the Clam he might, could show up, but I haven't seen him or Grandma. They have talked to me though."

"Really?" She brightened up.

"Yeah. I miss them too. Which brings me to this, Cookie M. You need to go back to Deconstructing the Howlite."

"How'd you?"

"What difference does it make? They told me. Anyway, I don't have much time, so I should make this quick. You need to get supplies," he informed her.

"What kind?"

"You'll know when you arrive, anything else Rhiannon can assist you, even that crafty tat of yours. Also, challenge him on mutual ground, you've been there, you know it. It's no stranger to either one of you. However, you can still trick him."

"How in the hell *can* I do that?"

"Finish your drink," he told her, pointing, which she did. He smirked.

"Also, it's time you tell Jack the truth."

"It's best he doesn't know," she said quickly.

"And how's that been working for you? You should trust him, you're going to need him." She sighed softly. "Time has come for me to leave you, well, for you to wake up," he stated.

"Okay, Jacob Marley," she teased him. "I don't think I can do this without you, Max," she fearfully admitted.

"You won't be. I'm always with you. Oh! I almost forgot, you'll find a surprise at Libbey's, same as I did. By the way, Jazz said, get a good night's sleep and lay off the liquor." He winked, laughing, before Raven woke her.

She gently shook her again. Morrigan arose, yawning.

"Go home, Ruby, I got this shift."

"Thanks, Ma. I'll be at Libbey's." She gathered her stuff, hugging her mother. She took one last look, almost as a safety measure, before leaving.

Exhaustion overwhelmed her when she entered his bedroom, everything still untouched from when he last slept there. She didn't have the strength to run her fingers along his earthly possessions; instead as soon as her head hit the pillow she peacefully conked out. This time with no nightmares to upset her, to send her screaming in a spine-shivering realization; no, this time the nightmare was reality. Not wakening until the next morning, she almost didn't notice a hefty envelope in her hand addressed to "M+M."

She examined the contents, realizing they were from Libbey, but unsure if he was the one to grace her with it. The contents read him leaving his apartment to her (which he owned), "bury some roots, Morgue," the 69 Clam to both her and Max "to do what they will," and an insurance policy for it, "just in case, to my only annoyingly cool kids." He noted in a letter dated two years ago.

She screamed happily, feeling somewhat relieved, before her tattoo warned her.

"Right." She placed the envelope over her heart in the inside of her coat before leaving.

"Back so soon! Good," Rhiannon happily greeted her when Morrigan dolefully entered, a personification of forlorn expressions.

"Damn, you look hellish! Like you've been through battle," Rhiannon remarked, initially unaware of the sharpness in her words.

"More like preparing for the war," Morrigan quipped, taking out the envelope. "I need to stamp a protection spell on this."

"Stamp? It's been a long time since someone mentioned that method. You remember how?"

"Yeah, I just need the tools."

"They're in the back. Follow me," she said before flipping the "CLOSED" sign on the shop window and locking the door. "I have a feeling you'll be here awhile," she told her. They walked back to the stock area that was filled with even more tools, except it also operated as an altar to create.

Rhiannon then gave Morrigan the necessary tools needed to complete a wax stamp.

"You got a spell in mind to say over it?" she asked. "Because if not, I have like-minded books."

"I'll wing it," Morrigan gruffly answered, taking to the tools easily as she had years before.

"What's attached itself to you?" she asked, watching her work.

"Funny you would mention that," she responded, melting then mixing the wax. "Because I need banishing tools." She closed her eyes, chanting, "*Et beatus dea Deus . . . praesidio.*" She proceeded to stamp the thick envelope with shimmering blue/lavender wax.

"You've come for supplies? I have a feeling you have many of them already."

"Your feelings." Morrigan chuckled. "Mine aren't potent enough. All I really need is crystals, gemstones, a particular chosen several." She took out a handwritten list, passing it to her. "Half need to be grinded though . . . to dust."

"What?" Rhiannon exclaimed.

"Doesn't have to be fine, slightly coarse will do."

"That's not an hour job," she painfully admitted.

"I have all night. And I'll greatly compensate you," she answered.

"I don't want, ah, it doesn't matter, let's get to work. Oh, that reminds me! Here." She placed a howlite necklace attached to a silver chain around her neck. "Could help with that troublesome entity."

Morrigan felt the cloudy white stone with gray veining, focusing on its strengths. "Thank you."

They worked all night, gathering quartz of differing colors for sufficient antidotal purposes. They listened to the roar of the tumbler and grinding of gemstones. It took them into the hours of early morning when their work was finally complete. They loaded Blue Thunder with the materials, four big black bags, eight-inch candles, a medium box, etc.

"Looks as though that's it. Thanks again for your help."

"Sure, you have everything?"

"I have everything I need."

"Need help with setup?" Rhiannon asked.

"I'll cast a generic circle and call it," Morrigan quipped before sitting in the driver's seat, hanging her left arm out the window. Rhiannon chuckled.

"You never answered my question. What's attached itself to you?"

"A repressed nightmare," Morrigan answered.

Rhiannon grabbed her wrist, pushing up her sleeves; she admired the ink. With her right hand, she empathically absorbed the torment, flashes of torture both past and present, paired with intense burning sensations all etched on her skin. It filled her when she quickly released her grip, stumbling back. Morrigan opened her door to help her.

"No! Don't touch me! I'm fine, I'm fine, it just takes a minute to adjust." She gained her normal breathing, standing properly. Morrigan closed her door, feeling damned.

"I'm sorry," she said lowly. She put the key in the ignition.

"Wet it," Rhiannon advised her, leaning in the window. "The powdered crystals, it'll spread easily and unsuspectedly."

"Hmm . . . Good idea. Thanks."

"Blessed be."

She thought on it a moment. "Blessed be." She drove off, watching Rhiannon wave in her rearview mirror. She smiled before stepping on the gas.

Eventually, she reached Libbey's place while simultaneously recognizing that damn friendly BMW parked out front. Jack sat on the front waiting for her; he smirked. In that one action it said, "You can't get rid of me that easily."

"What are you doing here, sweets?" she asked, approaching him with the box in her arms. Still fashioning a smug smirk, he leaned back. "Want to set that here?" he asked her. She dropped it on his lap. "Not quite what I meant, but all right," he remarked.

"What are you doing here?" she asked again.

"Looking for you, thinking where have I possibly overlooked? Then it dawned on me . . . Libbey's! You didn't know, but him and I got close over these three months. Anyway, I'm here because I wanted to give you this. My extra set." He held out a pair of keys, purposely placing them in her hand.

"I thought it best I stick around, for the both of us," he told her.

She didn't quite know what to make of it or whether to overthink it. Paired with what she had to uproot she was to a point of exhaustion. And she wanted to avoid it altogether, simply accepting his keys and walking past him. Yet, Max's words on making revelations stuck in her mind.

"You might not want to soon enough," she said suddenly.

"What do you mean?" he asked.

"Nothing. I mean, it's good you found me, I've been meaning to tell you something. First, I need to shower and change, it's been a long night. I'm going to visit Max shortly, want to wait and go with me?" she asked cautiously, hoping he'd decline.

"You couldn't deter me . . . if you tried," he responded directly in her face, winking before kissing her forehead.

"Romantic," she teased him, disappearing in the shower.

A strange nurse walked into Max's room just when Morrigan and Jack arrived. Morrigan approached Timmy coming from a snack vendor; it's currently his turn to watch over him.

"Hey, man."

"Hey, Morgue. Jack," he tiredly greeted them, chewing on Skittles.

"Timmy. How is he?" Jack concerned, asked.

"No improvement. Head trauma. Doctors said this could go either way."

"Timmy, who is that nurse? I've never seen her before," she asked, watching her around Max through the windows.

"Um . . ." He thought. "I think her name is Jane. Or something," he answered.

"Janice?" she corrected him.

"Yeah, I think that's it! She's assigned to him today, been in there frequently."

"Frequently?" She scoffed at the notion. That hospital is not known for efficiency.

"I'll take over from here, Timmy," she mentioned abruptly. Before he had a chance to respond, she was nearing the door.

"Hello, Janice," Morrigan politely addressed her, entering inside, then noticed Janice hide a needle inside her pocket.

"Hi. I'm only checking his vitals," she responded nervously.

"Okay."

She tapped his morphine drip, checked his oxygen. Morrigan was hesitant of her as she lingered.

"Well, how is he?" she asked suspiciously.

"He's showing good signs. Try not to worry," she suggested, attempting to leave quickly when Jack entered.

"That's a step in the right direction," Jack noted, attempting to uplift her. Her fingers lightly tapped as she seemingly dismissed it.

"You don't remember me, do you?" Morrigan suddenly asked. "Well, I mean, you wouldn't really after all it was almost a year ago."

"Your grandmother?" she correctly guessed.

"Well, great, but yeah. I'm surprised, you look so different." She alluded to her changed physical appearance.

"A lot can change in almost a year's time."

"That's true," Morrigan agreed.

"I'll check back later," she announced to the room, stepping out where Tim stood waiting.

"Hey, Maxie!" she announced in a shrill voice, her demeanor a false state of cheerful. "Look who's here to see you!" She referred to Jack, who stood beside her, looking at Max soundly still as though he was sleeping.

"Hey, Max, how's it hanging?" he asked jokingly. Morrigan snickered. She sighed deeply.

"I just want him to make it out," she regrettably mentioned.

"He has to," he told her.

She didn't acknowledge this. Eventually, she stammered, "Jack, what if . . . what if I told you?"

"Told me what?"

"That he's here because—" His phone rang, interrupting her.

"It's just the office." After checking, he ignored it. "What were you going to say, baby?"

She stuttered. "Nothing. Just rambling." Her smile faltered.

"You're scared. I don't have any answers. I wish I did but continue to talk to him. He's listening."

"Yeah." His phone rang again.

"Damn it! I'm sorry, babe."

"Just answer it, it's important," she told him.

"Not more than this, than you."

"It's your livelihood, your dream come true. I'll understand." She assured him. He stepped out of the room, answering. She relaxed in her chair, pushing her hair back, before rising to check out Max.

She looked over him, straightened his sheets and pillows; taking out the envelope, she placed it underneath his head gently. She wiped his forehead, kissing it. "I got you, Maxie," she whispered. Then she rubs her temples, on the verge of breaking. Jack walked back in. "Is he okay?"

He noticed her reaction. "Are you okay?"

"I'm fine." She sniffled, proceeded to blow her nose.

"I should stay," he said.

"Is it a new client?" she asked.

"Um, yeah. There's been some issues since they came on board, they want me for the final version approval. But they can."

"Go," she insisted.

"I don't want to leave you alone," he responded.

"You're not. My mum will be here shortly. And can you drop Timmy home? If it's not too much or he can just stay here."

"He's staying here, he told me in the hall," he answered.

"That's my bandmate." She smiled softly.

"Are you sure, babe? I can stay," he asked again.

"Go. I . . . I'll see you when you get back. We can go home together," she mentioned to assure him.

"Does that mean you accept?" he begged. "Ah, don't answer. I won't push it." He kissed her goodbye. "I'll be back as soon as I can." She nodded as he left. Timmy walked in shortly after.

"Dude, go get some real food," she told him, mocking his meal of chips, candy, and soda. "Not the best diet."

"I'm fine. This is fine," he responded tiredly, rubbing his eyes.

"Least get a bottle of water for good measure," she teased him. "Seriously, I can handle it. Get lost, nourish yourself, sleep! He would want you to, instead of staring at him like a creep."

"But it's all right for you?"

"No. But I promised him. I can do that, y' know?" She chuckled, standing. "I'll take care of him and you." She hugged him tightly.

"All right, luv, I'll get some real food." He grabbed his jacket, checking to make sure his wallet is inside. "I'll be back."

"Peace!" She saluted him before slinking back into her chair. She drifted off to sleep for what only could've been twenty minutes when a man's scream woke her. She jerked to see Janice again, this time her hand on his breathing tube.

"What the fuck are you doing?" Morrigan rose, angrily slapping her hand away.

"I am preparing for the final step," Janice began to answer coldly when Morrigan interrupted her.

"You're not pulling the plug on him," she stated sternly.

"I know this is hard for you to accept."

"You won't fucking touch him, unless I say so! Y' know what, bitch, get out!" Morrigan commanded.

"I'm sorry, Morrigan, but it's doctor's orders," she stated calmly.

Morrigan snickered, casually walking to the windows, closing the blinds, and locking the door.

"Doctor's orders," she repeated to herself. "Seere sent you," she said, cracking her left knuckles.

"He said you loved him, he was right," Janice admitted vaguely. "And he loves you too." She sassily mocked. "That's the connection, ain't it? Why he's not dead? Blood connection but no blood shared." It dawned on the nurse.

"You're boring me. And that's not a good thing to do. So tell me what did you do with Janice?"

"She didn't want to go along with the program, so we had to fire her!" She laughed ecstatically, as Morrigan's arm heated.

"Anyway, I have special business to attend." As Janice turned her attention back to Max, Morrigan bum-rushed her.

"You evil bitch!" She took the clipboard from the foot of the bed, bashing Janice's head with it. She went down hard with a loud crash. Her arm began to blister and burn, but she felt no pain as her claws extracted. She spied a thigh tattoo on the imposter, another contract.

Janice stood, telekinetically sending a few scalpels toward Morrigan, which she promptly sent into the wall. Angering her, Morrigan decided to capitalize on it, goading her into attacking her physically.

"Come on." She smirked, motioning her hands. She let Janice get one punch in which she barely reacted to, merely turning her head back forward, prior to wrapping her hands around her neck and head butting her, breaking her nose. Janice stumbled back when Morrigan kicked her in the stomach, sending her flying to the floor.

"Any more?" Morrigan screamed. She tried to rise again when Morrigan helped her up by her neck. She threw her in the closet. Kneeling, she relayed a message.

"You should've left. However, I want you to tell him that he'll be joining you soon." Then she thrust her hand in Janice's chest; the blood splattered on her face. Morrigan proceeded to crush her heart, setting it aflame.

Her head dropped lifelessly to the side when Morrigan's tattooed deformity spoke to her. She nodded, struggled upward, leaning on the side of the bed briefly to gather strength, then walked to the mirror to wash her face. Janice's mangled corpse reflected to Morrigan in the mirror. As she started to dry her face, the corpse spontaneously combusted, shocking her; she whipped around to witness the body burn to wither, until there was nothing left.

"Hey, Morgue! Open this door!" Timmy yelled, knocking hard. Still breathing heavily from the event, she telekinetically unlocked and opened it. He almost fell through, noticing something off in the atmosphere, yet nothing was physically amiss.

"What's happened? They said," he asked, startled.

"Never mind it. Did you eat?"

"Yeah, I brought you some too." He handed it to her slowly. She grabbed it, going quickly to Max, looking over his monitor; everything seemed fine, including his vitals. *Tap, tap*, her fingers bent; *tap, tap*, the fallen spoke.

"No, he's fine," she answered. "Tsk."

"Is he?" Timmy asked.

"Huh? Oh, no. Yes! I was just talking. Are you all right?" she asked him, dismissing its suggestions.

"Yeah," he answered softly. She groaned, rubbing her arm.

"Timmy." She grabbed him urgently. "Find a nurse, bring her up here to check on him."

"What about?"

"Just do it!" Her voice, raspy, growled. He nodded, running out.

"What do you mean, I can't save him?" she angrily questioned.

"How is he?" Chastity, pale as a sheet, asked from the doorway behind her, shortly after Timmy left.

"Better than you. Or me for that matter," whisking around, she answered, noticing Chastity's torn clothes and feeble appearance.

"I'm glad." She struggled to speak. "I know . . . I have no right to ask but can we go for a walk?"

Morrigan hesitated. "Fine." And she put on her jacket.

Chastity led her to an abandoned playground overtaken by weeds, a few blocks from the hospital. They sat on the secluded swing set, gently rocking; the sun caressed their faces through the windy bitter chill.

"How'd you escape?" Morrigan asked, exposing the tension.

"They can really come in handy sometimes, even my mother. What good that did," she answered, referring to their ink.

"Why did you bring me here, Chas?"

"Think of this as . . . a mercy killing," she answered.

"A what?" Her bootheels dug in the ground at her response.

"Listen, Morrigan. I don't have much time. As you know our tattoos are more than fallen hosts, they're links to extreme power, they're contracts with evil. And depending on the person that embraces it, they could do whatever they want, sometimes without trying. However, usually that person must serve a darker purpose. What I told you before is true, I was a good Catholic schoolgirl, although a spoiled one, who betrayed a lot of beliefs for this tat and my family. So you're right. I did know the risks," she told her, looking off into the distance.

"And I do love you, Morrigan. I betrayed them for you and I will do it again. But I do hate that your heart isn't with me, I only wish we had more time under better circumstances. He deserves you though," she finished with a whisper. After listening to her confession, she sighed softly for what was to come.

"What is Seere's endgame, Chas?" she asked.

"You know the saying, 'Even the devil has people in high places.'"

Morrigan closed her eyes in regret, shaking her head lowly.

"Thank you, Chas. I am sorry, but if it's any consolation, I guess I fell for you too. I did," she tearfully admitted, as tears fell from Chastity's eyes.

"You will rise above this. Sing to me please?"

"*Benedicite hoc puero, matris,*" she whispered a melodic spell, singing her already weary form to sleep. Then she rose to kiss her, draining her life force; her chest piece faded, then gradually so did she until only ashes remained that blew upward in the wind.

With freeing her energy, the action attacked Morrigan's body, more than any death before. It all incensed her arm, yet it didn't speak; it just continuously scalded, causing her immense pain as when she first received it. She gasped; unable to breathe, she hung on the rusty chains.

"Please stop, please," she begged gently, before further groaning. The swings swung back, loosening from her; she fell forward. Then she took three deep breaths, managed to her feet; she began to walk from out the playground, and continued somewhat aimlessly, struggling down a street, until she stopped. There stood a cathedral.

Morrigan cautiously entered the church, initially wanting to only rest on the steps; she stumbled upon a pew, still holding her arm to appease it. She slumped over in sweat, half beaten and choked with sobs. She stared at the altar.

"What's troubling you, child?" asked the priest, his voice, familiar, bellowing suddenly beside her.

"What isn't?" she sarcastically answered. He recognized her.

"Daughter Morrigan!" he exclaimed happily. She glared.

"Sorry, I'll keep it informal. You look terrible."

"Thanks, I know," she admitted.

"What brings you here? I didn't think I'd see you," he began to reminisce.

"What does it mean, is it true the Lord will never give you more than you can handle?"

"That's what the scriptures—"

"To hell with the scriptures! I'm asking you, Daniel! Because I didn't ask for this! Nor can I bear it any fucking longer!" She aggressively pulled down her jacket sleeve to show him her curse.

"Ugh! I'm sorry," she apologized, making a sign of the cross, an old habit returning.

"Where did you get this?" He touched it; she snatched away. His touch felt like acid.

"Don't touch it!" she yelled, covering it. "And it's more like who gave it to me?" She caught his reaction. "You know about this?" she asked.

"I've heard stories, read texts, recognized symbols," he fearfully admitted.

"What is it? Besides the obvious."

"A contract," he answered. "With hell."

She gasped, thinking back of Chastity. "Well, damn . . . You wouldn't by any chance know how I can get rid of it, do you?"

"No. But how else do you break a contract? I might, can ask around." He attempted to comfort her.

"I don't have that kind of time. Thanks anyway, Danny."

"I know you don't want to hear it, but the Lord will guide you, if you listen. Follow your path."

"Do you believe in magic, Daniel?" she randomly asked.

"The church will disagree, but yes, I do," he answered. "In magic and science!"

"Humor me, Danny. Can there be a combination of this with magic?" She toyed with her howlite stone.

"I think you know the answer to that. It's your path, remember? This is the time to worship Him in your own way, the way the divine is calling you to. You've always known what to do, you just never thought it was viable," he relayed. Someone entered for confession.

"Looks as though I'm needed. You must be strong. They believed in you, now it's your turn. Continue your potions, Morrigan." He winked.

"Do good works, Danny." They both chuckled. She arose, rubbing her eyes. And then like a red-hot poker or a torch, it started again, this time spreading throughout her body. She turned toward the altar to see nothing but darkness and heard faint crackling. She ran outside.

Simultaneously, when Jack arrived at his office, parking in his garage, unable to make it upstairs, a stranger approached him.

"So you're Jack, the boyfriend." Seere emerged from the shadows; an overhead light illuminated his face. "I can see the attraction."

"And you are?" Jack defensively asked, holding his posture.

"You don't know me, now is your opportunity though. I'm a childhood friend of our special Morrigan," he answered.

"You know my name, I don't know yours. How'd you know where I work?"

"My apologies. I feel I know so much about the people." He snickered. "In her life, sometimes I fail to properly introduce myself. The name is Seere."

"How do I fit into whatever this is?"

"Sharpshooter, much in common with her. Well, I deduce that you could assist me with this minor issue I'm having with her. I don't know if you've noticed, but Morrigan doesn't always realize when she needs help. Or is inclined to ask for it."

"True," Jack agreed.

"See? We're getting along famously! I digress, it's the issue with this record label business, see, I believe Mystic would be a perfect addition to my label. Plus, she deserves the spotlight. I was wondering, maybe you could give her a push? You and I both know the pitfalls associated with up-and-coming labels, and I understand her tenacious spirit, but I have everything she needs. It's better that way, then eventually I'll pass the reins over to her," he said.

"Really? She's never mentioned you, yet you would do all that for her?" Jack questioned suspiciously.

"I mean if she'd ever listen!" They shared a good laugh, while Jack continued to probe.

"What could you offer me, if I assist you in persuading Morrigan?"

"You think I'd go that low to get what I want? You're right! However, I can't very well give you her, she's a whole entity. But I could possibly give you a portion of the company, that way you'll still have partial control of her. After all, that's what you really want. Isn't it?" Seere suggested.

"You're selling something, but it ain't a label, that's why she wants no part of it. No one can control her, nor do I want to. I can't help you. Now get off my property."

Seere scoffed, shook his head in disappointment. "I guess some men can be trusted." He rapidly closed his fist; instantly Jack's blood ran cold, his body freezing, straining to receive oxygen, yet he was fully conscious of what Seere said next. "Unless you want to end up like Libbey or Max, I'm not picky on your demise, you will do what I ask. That's if you want to stay in her life. Think about it." He released his grip, as the lights flickered before settling. He disappeared. Gaining control over his body again, he got back in his car, rushing to the hospital.

"Morrigan?" Jack anxiously asked, busting into Max's room. "Raven, Timmy, where's Morrigan? I need to speak to her!"

"I don't know where she is. She was gone when I brought the nurse back," Timmy answered.

"Nurse?" Jack asked.

"Yeah, she insisted. He's fine though, his levels had spiked, but he's stable now."

"How long ago was this?"

"Maybe an hour ago," Timmy answered.

"What's happened, Jack?" Raven asked.

"I can't explain, I just have to find her." He rushed back out.

"She hasn't been answering her cell!" Raven yelled as the door slammed shut.

After checking Libbey's to find she wasn't there, he realized where she must be.

"Morrigan? Morgue? Please, say you're in here," he exclaimed upon entering the apartment. He heard the shower running, then her agonizing screams in the background.

"Morrigan?" He entered the bathroom; steam expelled as he opened the door, noticing the foggy mirror. He saw her in an extreme state of distress, semiclothed, wearing only jeans and a bra with water blasting on her.

"Stay away from me!" she yelled gutturally. He went to pull her out.

"Shit! You're burning!" he exclaimed, quickly backing away, only to reach toward her again. Yet, the water was ice-cold.

"Get out now!" she warned, grabbing his shirt roughly, attempting to remove him.

"I can't do that." He got in with her, trying to hold her.

"Please!" she begged. He ignored the heat, gently touching her until it subsided. She grabbed his neck, wanting to hurt him. Their eyes met, swarming their souls. Each exposing frightening vulnerability, of one she sinfully possessed and one that showed he failed in trying to protect her when he was unprepared. Yet, he did not falter; instead he remained available in physical and spiritual presence, then she pulled him closer, kissing him deeply. He soaked in the freezing water; however, it did nothing to sway them from consummating their next act.

"Not that much furniture?" She noticed after their bout of love-making. They lay in bed, wrapped in each other's arms.

"I just bought this place," he admitted. She remained silent. "To be close to you."

She exhaled deeply, rising.

"I've been trying to avoid this, but I owe you an explanation. This is . . . real." She proceeded to tell him the entire truth.

"I thought they were just nightmares, turns out they're memories. He's trying to break me, and if he can't, he's going to kill everyone I love until I do," she finished.

"I'll take the risks," he told her. Something in his delivery, his tone, tipped her off.

"He visited you?" she asked.

"When I got to the office. Threatened me. I went to find you after."

"Then he'll kill you."

"He can try."

"I can't lose you too, Jack."

"Hey now, you won't. We'll handle this together," he confidently promised.

"I need to sleep," she suddenly announced, lying back down, closed her eyes; deeply she breathed until the hours faded, holding on to his hand. It was still dark when she woke in the early morning hours, while Jack slept soundly beside her. She gently got out of bed, dressed, and was about to head out until she looked back at her guitar, leaning against the wall in the bedroom corner, almost as though it observed her too. She then took it in its case, and drove to the cemetery.

Airy clouds covered the sky with the night chilly but settled as she climbed over a crumbled brick wall. She walked in the middle of the street, hands in her pocket, scarf around her neck. There was a sense of foreboding trailing her with barren trees towering over, their thin branches stretched over a full moon, beautifully sinister.

She turned to see if anyone was behind her, yet there was nothing, no one stirring, only the sound of whistling winds and whispering souls, her nerves manifesting. She decided to hum, still following the trail, then she softly sang.

> ♪♫ *I'm just a little broken, always remind*
> *you more than your token . . .* ♪♫

Until she found herself facing Maye's grave. There she stood staring, silently begging for an answer, soon verbalizing her thoughts.

"Help me, please! I know what I need to do, but I don't know where to start. I hope Buttercup didn't disappoint you too much," she painfully expressed.

"Start from the beginning, Buttercup." Maye's voice rang clearly through. Then she remembered, a memory suppressed. Maye had taught her a spell, when she was a little girl, in the form of a song. It was to repel evil spirits. "Trust your magic," Maye urgently whispered, compelling Morrigan to make her leave.

During which she called Jack, now somewhat aware of her disappearing patterns, and asked him to meet her where it started.

Morrigan sat on a zodiac-printed blanket, hidden beneath it a medium-sized pentacle made from the crushed crystal powder, a cross amid it. Telekinetically, she lit the candles placed around, providing dimmed lighting. Her guitar in her lap, she began to play a mystical punk riff; it awoke the snake, breathing, when her blood droplets danced on the fret board. She began to sing.

> ♪♫ Comatose twins, we were squalor living,
> hideaways in our flatline cave.
> He was my . . . ♪♫

"Come out, come out, wherever you are . . . I know you're there, Seere." She acknowledged him, sensing his presence.

"There's been a change in you. One I can work with," he said, coming out of the shadows.

"Did you like the song?" she asked.

"Bit autobiographical for my taste, it's smashing!" He smugly chuckled.

"Good. I'm assuming you know why I called you here." She stood; taking out the flask she sipped from it. "I'm thinking it could be my first single with Apostasy Records."

"Does this mean you've finally come to your senses?" he asked in disbelief. "Perfect!" he exclaimed.

"Yeah, let's say you've finally convinced me. Although, you did have help. Come on out, babe!"

Jack stepped out, grabbing her guitar from her.

"You both listened. I'm impressed," Seere remarked.

"Yeah, so I'll sign now, in pen or blood, whichever you prefer. Or to make it easier on you, just put it on this, there's space somewhere." She examined her arm. He cleared his throat, seemingly bothered.

"When it comes to this form of confirmation it is still done traditionally," he responded, whipping up an old-fashioned scroll. He cleared his throat again.

"Bit tight in here." He acknowledged, eyeing the area.

"Something wrong, Seere? You don't look well. What am I talking about, can angels even get sick?" she asked jokingly.

"Not normally, unless." He searched more.

"Pen or blood?" she asked.

"What?" He looked at her.

"Pen or blood? You kept wanting me to sign, so are you going to give it to me?" She held out her hand to receive it.

"Blood is fine. Why stop with a winning formula?" He started to hand it to her, with the tip of the scroll teasing the edge of the pentacle; he suddenly stopped, pulling back. His expression changed; he knowingly nodded, turning around. Morrigan and Jack exchanged glances.

"Spare the switch, and spoil the witch," he quipped, laughing hysterically. Her tattoo spoke to her, bending rapidly.

"Oh shit," she remarked nervously.

Seere tucked the contract in his coat, then formed a dagger in his hand. Jack, assuming it was meant for Morrigan, ran to protect her when instead Seere aimed it at him.

"No!" She realized, initially trying to misdirect it, but her powers failed. Then she physically blocked it in enough time. Her blood splattered on Jack, as the spear punctured her heart from the back. She let out a guttural scream before falling into Jack's arms.

"Oh, you're not that powerful, darling!" Seere remarked at her futile attempt to stop it telekinetically. "I only gave you what could stop lower levels. Nice try though," he explained.

As she lay dying she spoke to Jack in shallow breaths, gurgling on her own blood.

"I guess this would be a perfect moment for cliché talks of love, huh?" She sighed. "Tell my mom I tried and that I love her . . ."

"Please, baby, don't speak," he pleaded desperately.

"Tell her! And please watch over Max. Promise me," she finished tiredly.

"Please, babe, I know. I will, I will, Morrigan," he promised her sadly. "This isn't . . ."

"Such lovely sentiment," Seere said unaffectionately as he watched them caress each other one last time. Hearing his sarcastic remark, they glanced at him angrily.

"Go fuck yourself, Seere," she murmured. "Now take it out!" she commanded Jack. Still bleeding profusely, he cautiously pulled out the spear. That removal hurt all the greater than when it first entered. She gasped, trying to muster enough breath.

"I do love you, Morrigan," he told her.

"I know." She chuckled. Afterward he kissed her, tasting her blood in his mouth, mingling with his saliva. She felt solid in his arms as they both held on to each other for dear life. Morrigan was hurting and desperately wanted to let go. She reached up to him, pulling on his body with little strength.

"Morrigan, baby?" he asked, looking at her confusingly. She kissed his cheek and went to whisper something in his ear, but before she could part her lips, she expired. He instantly felt the energy leave her; he only held tighter and sobbed.

"Such a waste," spoke Seere with such conviction in his voice. He walked over to them with his long black coat swishing with every step he took. He stared for a moment admiring his bloody work, trying to kiss her lips. Jack pushed him away. It caught him off guard.

"Don't touch her! You have no right to touch her!" Jack screamed furiously at Seere.

"You really do love her, well, did, don't you? That's rare." He scoffed.

"She could have been so special in the ranks, if she would have just given me what I wanted," Seere said, reminiscing their time together.

"She never made a deal with you!" Jack said angrily. "You cheated, you evil bastard!"

"That's true, she was a reluctant participant, but a participant nonetheless and thank you," Seere responded. "Well, I guess she won't need this anymore."

He then grabbed her tattooed arm along with the fallen angel that possessed it and took it all back. Thus, breaking the deal.

"Damn, I had such high hopes for you." He turned around, walking away in his version of mourning.

"That didn't quite go the way I planned," Morrigan suddenly spoke, arising from the dead.

"But I'll take it." She cracked her neck.

"Clever little witch, damn." He turned around in shock before realizing she was only healing. "But you're powerless now," he smugly declared.

"Au contraire, now I can banish you." She kicked a gemstone in place that offset where he stood. Jack fixated another stone; they began the spell.

"That's cute!" he remarked before realizing the spell was working, as he stood in her circle.

"You ingrate!" he exclaimed, angrily trapped. Suddenly, dust particles in the walls from crushed gemstones broke away, consuming him.

"I forgot to tell you, even we're entitled to forget. With the spilling of Gaston's blood and Chastity's last kiss, you officially sealed our deal. I will forever be a part of you!"

Then an outline of the accursed tattoo reappeared. He took her guitar into the circle with him. "Parting gift." He nodded.

"Morrigan, let it go!" Jack warned.

She willed the dagger in her hand, running into the circle.

"Morrigan, no!"

"I love you, Jack! Now finish the damn spell, I'll handle him."

"That's my girl," Seere quipped when she entered the circle.

"One good turn deserves another," she said jumping atop him, continuing the spell in Latin, as the building rumbled.

"You can't," Seere begged, weakening as he aged.

"This place has been blessed, see, we hid that from you. Isn't it beautiful? Take this to your friends." She lunged the dagger in his heart, twisting it in.

"You said you'll be with me forever? So be it, but this ax is mine." She snatched it, running out the circle.

"No!" His screams faded when he disintegrated. The circle then closed, his dagger disappeared, and the inlay inkling on her fret board returned to normal.

"Is it over?" Jack asked, approaching. She made a fist with her left hand, feeling a heat dissipate.

"Let's get to Max."

They rushed, arriving at the hospital, to see doctors trying to revive him.

"Morrigan, he . . ." Raven, rattled, tried to speak when a doctor exited, his head low.

"I'm sorry," he said.

"I need to see him! Now!" she demanded.

"Alone!" They hurriedly cleared everyone out as she entered. "Jack, I need you."

"Maxie, we have too much left to do. Our band, our label. You're always with me, so come back." She brushed back his hair.

"Yeah, she finally said she loves me. You have to witness that." Jack mentioned.

"That's right, revel in it. Come on, Maxie." She bent over, whispering in his ear. "It can't only be for death." She placed her left hand on him, humming softly, then kissed his lips; softly she breathed into his mouth. Still he's flatlined.

Until he gasped, his vitals coming through strong.

"Fucking A," she and Jack mutually exclaimed, as she grabbed his face in her palms.

"I knew she loves you, dude." He managed to speak, grabbing her arm, examining it.

The outline is now vivid with fewer markings although the snake is still present with only its coloring returned.

"I guess so. It's good to be back," he said. She untucked the envelope from beneath his pillow, tapping his chest with it.

"I finished that song by the way," she told him, as Jack called the doctors back in.

"Can't wait to play it. I bet it's a hit." He sighed in relief. "Love you, sis." She winked, as she and Jack exit, wrapped in each other's embrace.

"You finally told me you love me," he mentioned. She playfully rolled her eyes.

"I do," she admitted.

"Took you dying to finally admit it, but beggars can't be choosers," he quipped.

"Shh, kiss me." It's passionate and raw. She rested her head on his chest.

"Think you can take on a new client, an up-and-coming label? The owner is possibly possessed, but she can handle anything," she happily asked.

"The name?"

"Moonstruck Records!"

"Needs work." He played along. "Sure you want to mix business with pleasure again?"

"If you can handle it, sweets." She dared him.

"I can handle anything!" Jack remarked cheekily, as the snake slithered along her arm.

The End

About the Author

L e' Vian Dae is currently a second-year MA film and media arts
student at American University. As an author of dark poetry
and short stories, she can be seen published in anthologies *A Lovely
Darkness: Poetry with Heart* and *Subliminal Messages: A Collection of
Poetry, Prose, and Quotes*. Shortly after graduating high school at seventeen, she attended DeVry University where she earned cum laude
while overcoming hardships.

An aficionado of all things creepy, magical, and spine-tingling,
she is also a horror filmmaker and actress. Inspired by her mother's
passion for the arts, and thankful for the sacrifices she has made, Le'

Vian aspires to always speak for the underdog, whether it is through her stories and films of self-aware, persevering anti-heroines in a hypocritical society or punk blues music as Venus Axe and the Flytraps.

Le' Vian is in progress of writing her first feature-length screenplay, based on her debut novel, *Just A Little Broken*. She currently resides in Oxon Hill, Maryland, working closely with her strong-willed, grounded mom.

CPSIA information can be obtained
at www.ICGtesting.com
Printed in the USA
LVHW111450040320
648982LV00008B/147

8-29-20
MEYER

4/21/21